THEATRICKS

Eleanor Gwyn-Jones

OMNIFIC PUBLISHING
LOS ANGELES

Omnific Publishing
1901 Avenue of the Stars, 2nd floor
Los Angeles, CA 90067
www.omnificpublishing.com

First Omnific eBook edition, December 2013
First Omnific trade paperback edition, December 2013

The characters and events in this book are fictitious.
Any similarity to real persons, living or dead,
is coincidental and not intended by the author.

Library of Congress Cataloguing-in-Publication Data

Gwyn-Jones, Eleanor.
   Theatricks / Eleanor Gwyn-Jones – 1st ed.
   ISBN: 978-1-623420-74-1
   1. Contemporary Romance — Fiction. 2. England — Fiction.
   3. Theater — Fiction. 4. Acting — Fiction. I. Title

10 9 8 7 6 5 4 3 2 1

Cover Design by Micha Stone and Amy Brokaw
Interior Book Design by Coreen Montagna

Printed in the United States of America

For Joe Mik,
With so much love.

Chapter 1

He flicks open the lid of the small velvet box with an endearing schoolboy fumble. And there it is, gleaming like the spires of Oz, the whole of Emerald City encapsulated in three carats that wink at me from one brilliant crystallized compound.

"Well?"

The small word, filled with hope, balloons within my ears. I scrape my eyes from the glistening green gem to the earnest face looking up into mine. I glance around self-consciously — one hundred pairs of eyes heavy on me — diners suspended with forked mouthfuls hovering, jaws open and waiting. And the noise seems to disappear almost instantly: all the clattering of cutlery on crockery, chair legs dragging on wood, ice cubes jiggling against glass, is sucked up into a silent vortex, a swirling tornado orbiting our table. The room revolves too, spinning on its axis. I think I am about to be sick.

I know that acid churning; I should be well used to it: the routine rebellion of my body, the gastric mutiny before setting foot on stage, enduring those torturous moments when I realize, "Shit! I've forgotten my lines!"

I look to the audience of diners now, panic simmering in my stomach.

And he's waiting.

Shouldn't I reply with something momentous, poetic, Shakespearian perhaps? Shouldn't I regurgitate something other than my rosemary encrusted lamb chops and pomme puree? Something that I can tell our children, and our children's children? Something witty I can put on Facebook?

It's not as if I haven't rehearsed this moment: the knight on bended knee, pledging his love for all to see, proffering a great sparkler that will be the envy of all of one's colleagues and childhood rivals which, now betrothed, one will flaunt with unnecessary hand-waving and finger-flashing, all with one's now ambidextrous left.

This fairy tale is exactly how I imagined it. Maybe lacking slightly in backdrop, as we huddle into our narrow table, the bustle of the busy restaurant brushing uncomfortably close and—okay, it's not the beach tiki bar on some white-sand, sun-kissed, tropical paradise, where we stretch out bronzed limbs and sip piña coladas whilst watching the pink sun sink into the Caribbean Sea. It's London. It's raining. What's new?

But all the same. This is the man I imagined my life with: the only man who ever challenged me to be a kinder person, to be more savvy in business, to be a more confident lover, because he already was. He could, and would, do anything he set his mind to, and if that isn't an aphrodisiac, I don't know what is.

People would look up when Cole entered the room—not to admire his handsome features, but because here was a man born to nothing, who had scaled far higher than anyone ever predicted, and had done so with integrity. What a pleasant change from the backstabbing business of the theatrical underworld, where the whole premise—as much as I will defend it to the death—is to pretend; where every actor silently screams, "Look at me! Look at me! Love me!" Cole is already assured. People do look. People do love him. He doesn't have to ask for it. Except now.

It's meant to be, isn't it? After all, Cole is one of the few people who had actually pronounced my name right, without the challenges Mother's unconventional choice usually invokes.

"And I'm Enna."

"Enna? That's unusual. I've never met an Enna before," he said.

"I doubt you ever will again either. When Mum was pregnant, she fell in love with the name 'Jenna,' but then my aunt gave birth and beat her to it. So, here I am. Enna, not Jenna."

He smiled. "I like that. Enna."

And I liked the way it sounded, steeped silkily in his deep American accent, heavy on the "na."

"Enna," he said, rolling the syllables over his tongue again, like a comfortable slipper he was trying on for size.

"Of course, it can be a bit of a pain in the arse," I blathered, filling in the silence of new acquaintance, "especially when people call me 'Enema.'" It was quintessential verbal diarrhea—each word, unbelievably, flowing from my lips without a thought of consultation with my brain. "I mean, who likes to be compared to colonic irrigation?"

He looked at me again, long tumbleweed moments filling the space between us. Then he erupted into laughter, a loud guffaw, an unselfconscious blast of "Ha!" He laughed so hard he bent over, enjoying the full lung-filling roll of it.

I remember trying to hold on to the giggle, desperate to escape, so I smacked his beefy bicep instead and told him that it really wasn't funny.

"Don't you see?" he said between hoots. "You're the butt of a joke!"

"What did he say?" I hear shouted from the revolving dining room in deafened tones.

"Beryl! Shush! He just asked her to marry him."

"Oh! I love a good proposal!" The unabashed voice comes out of nowhere and crashes into my thoughts, hurtling through my reverie to take a spin around my brain.

Fear gurgles from deep within. *The stomach has more nerve endings than the spinal column,* I recall, clutching my unadorned hands to my stomach. This is it! This is the first life change in the series: fiancé…wife…mother…grandmother. Oh God, now I feel really ill.

"What did she say? Cyril? What was her answer?"

"Sssssh!" Cyril and our audience whip their rubber necks around to reply.

I'd like a brain, a heart, courage, a nice pair of ruby slippers, and then I'd like to go home, please, I think as I smile at the room through my teeth.

Twenty-eight isn't too young, is it? I mean, I don't have to get barefoot and pregnant straightaway, do I? I can be a wife *and* a theater director. It's not the end; it's the beginning!

He repositions, his kneecap grating on the wooden floor. The proffered box in his hand trembles slightly. It is odd to see him, the Superman of Scranton, on his knees.

"Okay!" I hear my voice saying. Hardly a sonnet, but it is all Cole needs to hear.

A wave of delight passes over his face, and he rises to my side, clamping the stone to my finger.

The dining room erupts with noise as the diners applaud and charge their glasses, as champagne corks are fired and vows are renewed across the ivory linen. The room stops revolving, and instead it is me who is circling, spinning around and around in his generous arms.

"Sweetie, you've made me so happy. So happy!"

I am the victim of a champagne conspiracy, I think as I pry open my swollen lids to the morning. I don't even like champagne, but those diddy little flutes are so deceptive; two toasts and the glass is empty, only for my joyous fiancé to top it off again. No wonder it is called cham-pain.

I lie still, my head too heavy to lift, as I remember the night before the champagne fug. I lift the strange appendage into my line of hazy vision and examine the new addition. Sunlight streams through the gaps between window and curtain and bounces blindingly off my many-faceted finger. The emerald casts a virescent glow over my once flesh-colored hand, and I wonder if the ring has cut off my circulation and my hand is, in fact, exhibiting the first signs of gangrene. I waggle my fingers to check—phew!—I'd hate to choose between the ring and digital amputation.

I wave to the ceiling, imagining the Grace Kelly style dress, the tiara, the veil, the balcony scene with the rapturous crowd filling the Mall, clamoring for him to "Kiss her! Kiss her!" The light dances off my show-stopping ring, projecting a mesmeric laser show. Emeralds have to be luckier than sapphires.

"Mrs. Krupski."

"Mrs. Enna Krupski."

"Mrs. Cole Krupski."

"Mr. and Mrs. Cole Krupski."

It sounds so odd to my British ears. After twenty-eight years, can I really wear any other surname but Petersen? Peter-sen, straightforward, no nonsense, originally from Peterson, meaning Peter's son. Krup-ski. Kru-pski. K-rupski. What does that even mean?

This will take some getting used to. I write my name in the air, trying to imagine my signature, perfecting the loop from the P to the S. I waft each style through the air and suppress an embarrassed giggle — really, I am far too old to be practicing my joined-up hand-writing — but my schoolgirl jittery titters aren't quiet enough not to wake the mound beside me: my fiancé.

After a delicious morning romp, a Sunday roast pub lunch in Richmond, nestled by the fireside, I drive him to Heathrow airport to wave him off. These weeks together always end too soon.

My hands have taken on a new life and are doing a lot of waving. I am conducting an invisible orchestra. Really! I can hear my music when I walk through the familiar and dreaded airport zones that will rob me of my boyfriend — my *fiancé* — once more. The soundtrack to Cole's departure, Rachmaninov's stirring symphony, swells to its passionate climax as I prepare myself for the ritual parting at the security gates of terminal four.

"So you do like it then?" he asks for what must be the twentieth time.

"Yes, Cole. It's perfect." I admire my left hand again and think that, with all this waving, I shall have to invest in a manicure.

"Not exactly perfect. It's 'eye perfect.' Emeralds are hard to find completely flawless. But the flaw is pretty deep in the stone, so you can't really notice."

"I don't care. I love it," I say, polishing my jewel with proprietary protectiveness.

"This is the last time we'll have to do this," he says, shouldering his suitcase strap and burying me in his bear embrace.

"Ah huh," I say, muffled by a mouthful of blue lamb's wool.

"And then we'll be together all the time."

"Ah huh," I reply, removing the fluff from my mouth.

I watch him shuffle his way along passport security, through the machines that go *ping,* and he turns, smiling, checking for the one hundredth time that I am still here.

"I love you," he mouths as he takes his last look.

Cole the Impressive Businessman kicks into action. He hires an immigration attorney and reads the entire, bizarre, intricately complicated US Immigration Website, quoting chunks to me down the telephone line. This isn't the newly affianced telephonic planning I had in mind. It is all so boring: the endless stream of forms to be filled and questions to be answered, each a variation on the same mind-numbing one before. It wasn't like this in *Green Card* when Gérard Depardieu married what's-her-face with the hair.

For the first time in our year of Ashtead to Scranton commute—or as Lucy calls it, "funding Richard Branson's pension"—I am looking forward less to the sound of the telephone bleating after a long day at the theater. The immigration paperwork is a bore; it's making Cole a bore. I know it's not his fault, of course, but he is easier to blame than the US Ambassador.

I wouldn't usually class myself as a frowner, but my forehead aches after every transatlantic discussion. This "contract" is rather more complicated than I had thought. My lightly freckled flesh gathers up like a Roman blind at the mere mention of evidence of this, signed statement of that. What?

Why can't we just be together for an extended period of time? Why can't we country swap between productions? Why must it be so rushed, ninety days from US arrival to getting married? It takes longer to compost.

Has my brain taken an unapproved leave of absence? Have the impulses failed to make the connection between "marry me" and uproot your life, move three thousand miles west, and leave your family, friends, theater, career…?

But it's me; I did this. I said yes. Well, "okay" at any rate, and I do want to be with Cole, but the declaration of US dependence seems so…weird. I mean, I have always liked America—I love it—but that doesn't remove or displace the fact that I am English. True blue, crap at sport, English.

I'm being stupid. One of us has to make a move; it should be me. That is the logical business decision. After all, there are theaters in Scranton, aren't there? Yes, of course, there must be. Besides, Cole had only just been made VP of Scranton Aggregate Inc. after fifteen years with the company, and I wouldn't let him sacrifice that, even if he wanted to. Which he doesn't. End of.

Scranton will be just marvelous: all that space, the clean air, affordable living, tax-free clothes shopping, ice-cream parlors, drive-ins, bars that don't close before midnight, peanut butter with everything, sports teams that win, sunshine, snow, dreams…and Cole.

I won't have to worry about the congestion charge, bleeding out more for petrol than any other civilized country seems to pay, ordering steak that will probably cost my entire week's food budget, remembering to take an umbrella everywhere I go.

The weeks grabbed between productions to spend together have always been so glamorous, fun, and surprising, as if I were living somebody else's life, someone from the *Dallas* or *Dynasty* of my childhood.

That luxurious suite overlooking Central Park, with a fireplace in the bedroom and a cascade of exotic fruit so shiny I thought they were plastic; the Italian restaurant with the five stars, where the waiter stood by my chair during my entire long and chatty trip to the loo, just so he could replace the thick, ivory damask serviette in my lap when I, eventually, returned — I could have died; the front row center tickets to see *Curtains*, with David Hyde Pierce, because he knew I had loved him in *Frasier*.

After the show, with rosy-cheeked smiles, he took me to the worn corner booth at the late-night diner on the corner of Somewhere and Mafia. We huddled to keep warm out of the snow and ate maple-syrup-soaked buttermilk pancakes at two o'clock in the morning, mopping every last slick of the syrupy sweetness from the plate. After we lingered so long that even the waitress was yawning, he braved the cold and hailed a cab. I sat, watching for his command through the steamy diner window, and thought then that this was a man I could share my life with. The man I *wanted* to share everything with, not just pancakes. We bundled into the back of the springless, seated, bright yellow jalopy, and drove through the Christmas-lit city, watching the twinkling picture-postcard of towers, spires, and window displays. I felt like a little girl in the Magic Kingdom.

"Merry Christmas," he drawled, his hot syrupy breath warming the bare patch of skin behind my ear, radiating currents to make my numbed fingertips tingle. He moved my hair aside and slid a glistening Ceylon sapphire pendant around my neck.

Even the memory makes me grin from ear to ear. It's not the glamor though. Even stripped bare, without Michelin-star restaurants and absurdly generous jewelry gifts, we just work. The back of my eyelids picture his hands on me as I relive flashes of our hunting trip to his friend's cabin in the woods of Montrose. I replay the frames as he turned to me on the quad, in the middle of the woods, cut the engine, stripped me down, and pounded himself into me like a rutting buck at full moon.

What am I thinking? How can long, thankless workdays and weary, lonely nights, wearing embarrassing slippers, drinking a bottle of wine, and eating strange cheese, even compare? *Enna, they don't.*

It is just — my grin reels in — there's so much to say goodbye to. Not just Mum and Dad, Leo, Lucy, the theater, but all the little seemingly insignificant Lego pieces that make up England: all the faces and places that aren't familiar enough to guarantee a slot on the annual visiting schedule. Friends whose weddings I will inevitably never attend, whose children I will only ever see in silent form on Facebook or photocopied onto the Christmas round-robin letter: "It's been a busy old year! Timothy was again top of his class, excelling in Maths, Chemistry, and Latin, and he was made captain of the cricket team! He wants to study law, and we're hoping for Oxbridge entrance. Here's a picture of Timmy blowing out his candles at his tenth b'day this year!"

I will miss summer fetes with scones, fresh strawberry jam and clotted cream; singing with gusto at Christmas carol concerts and scoffing warm mince pies topped with a dollop of brandy butter; enjoying the patriotic pomp and heart-swelling pride of "The National Anthem," "Rule Brittania," and "Jerusalem"; watching Six Nations Rugby matches from the nook in the Salisbury Tavern; the Epsom Derby; Henley Regatta; school reunions, hen parties, shopping in M&S; all the normal events that allow welcome collision with old friends, boyfriends, teachers, neighbors, rugby drinking buddies.

No "Oh my God, it's been ages! You look great!"

No rapidly exchanged gossip in the bakery aisle:

"Didn't you hear? She's pregnant again!"

"Again?"

"Again. She's like a rabbit!"

"Don't they have television?"

Defining moments in the nation's future history, freak hurricanes, or England actually winning the World Cup, I'll never be there for, will never be able to join in that patriotic union of mourning or celebration, the camaraderie of a small isle.

I'll miss hearing about things like the death of a minor celebrity, not considered important enough to make the international headlines. The news will trickle across months later, forgotten, on the back of a newspaper cutting Mum will send about osteoporosis prevention or how to make the perfect risotto. This non-American event will scream again of my separation, my divorce from my homeland, and all the people, places, crises, catastrophes, and much cherished Britishisms. I won't be there for them. They won't be there for me.

Lord! What about the wedding? The great aunties in their eighties would never make the trip. It'll be one of those sad ceremonies with everyone sitting on the right of the church, and who'd sit behind me on the left? It's depressing. I'd have no friends to throw me a surprise hen party with ridiculous inflatable penises or drunken karaoke; I'd have no friends.

But, in Pennsylvania, I will have Cole. My rock, or brick, or whatever the expression is.

I twist the gleaming green jewel around my promised finger. It slips off quite easily. Ha! Maybe my fingers are losing weight with worry. Maybe nervous tapping and twitching as Cole explains another form works like finger aerobics. Or more likely, I'm just cold or gratifyingly low-sodiumed.

I slide it off completely and place it on the mantelpiece. It glows. It reminds me of kryptonite.

Chapter 2

"Hey, sweetie," he cheers down the line. "The final ten faxed pages should be coming over to you now. Are you at your desk? Can you get them? Ten. Count them. Make sure they're all there. I've filled in my pages. All routine questions."

This is all so exhausting. He's exhausting: his coaching through file filling and check writing, his endless enthusiasm. It's difficult for me to swallow, literally. There's not just a lump in my throat; it's a goiter. The more he plans, the more I agree to, and the bigger it gets. Am I the Pinocchio of throats?

"So have they come through?"

I spin around to check the noisily regurgitating fax machine spewing paper out onto the floor. "Uh huh…I've got them. When do they need to be completed?" The warm handset slips from its nook between my shoulder and ear. I re-clamp it, my craning neck feeling the strain.

"Well, I told the attorney that you would express them so that they arrive by the end of the week." Transported thousands of miles across vast oceans, beamed up to satellites, routed through miles of telephone lines, I can hear him smile.

I try to clear my throat. "The end of the week? Jesus Christ, Cole! The new show goes up in two weeks! I can't let everyone down. I've got a million things to do. And it's not just the documents which are, I have to tell you, a complete bloody hemorrhoid nightmare, but I haven't had a chance to tell anyone yet! Not Mum, not Dad. I can't just rush this. 'Hello, Mum, guess what happened to me today. Yes! I'm moving to America to get married. Cheerio! Ooh…ah…little thing, awkward really, but I may not see you very much, and there is every likelihood that you will miss the formative years of your grandchild/grandchildren, but if it's not too much trouble, would you quickly knock me out a creative essay on the virtues of my fiancé and what a great couple you think we make? That would be lovely! Oh, and if you could hurry up about it, that'd be smashing because I need to send it yesterday!'"

I pause for a much-needed breath.

The chipper voice on the end of the line is silent.

"Cole?"

I can hear his smile slacken.

"Cole?"

His disappointment travels three thousand miles just as loudly as his excitement had.

"Oh, sweetheart, I'm just really tired. I'm tired and hungry, and I just want this whole thing to be over."

"I'm busy too, Enna, but I'm making time."

"Yes, I know." And I know, too, that if he knew how much time I was dwelling on these answers, he'd tell me I was "wasting dollar time on a penny task." But how do I fill these ambiguous questions; get my head around how I will uproot myself, my house, my career; cast, direct, and produce a show; run a theater, a staff of volunteers; and not feel overwhelmed by it all?

I scrape my hands through my hair, releasing the tight ponytail ring. "I know it has to be done. It's just so intrusive. And why in Hades does it have to be so complicated? Aren't I a great candidate? Doesn't America want me?"

"America wants you! I want you! This is procedure. It's nothing personal, and you'd be pissed if they didn't check. Besides, it gives you an opportunity to list all the reasons why you are great and why I love you."

"Well, that rather forces my hand with Mum and Dad."

"You have to tell them sometime, and you know that they'll be pleased for us," he ventures encouragingly.

"I'll do what I can. I can include Mum and Dad's affidavits later."

"Do it tonight, pickle." I can hear his wide, generous grin return to the line. "They need the papers by Friday, so send it by FedEx or UPS, but make sure it gets there. Send it out on Wednesday."

"That's tomorrow!"

"You can do it. You can do anything you set your mind to."

Yeah, if it weren't already set to one hundred and one other things.

"Okay, okay! I'll get on with it now."

"Good job, pickle. I'm proud of you."

His eternal American enthusiasm, his "good job, high five" mentality, is so charming, he makes me smile in spite of my frustration. He bids me good night, and I hang up to tackle this Herculean task.

I stare at the blank forms: pages and pages of more questions, each with its requisite heavy-typed black box for me to commit my answer within. It's like learning organic chemistry all over again, and I didn't enjoy that the first time.

How can I prove so much in one little box? Surely leaving home, family, friends, and theater to be with Cole was proof enough? Now I must rip my heart out and squeeze it into the confines of an inadequate box for the edification of Immigration Services?

The door swings open, bringing in a gush of air from the foyer, and my mother.

"Hi!" She stands in the doorway in her favorite scarlet woolen coat, her hourglass frame bolstered with bulging shopping bags juggled under arms and hooked around every finger. "I don't want to disturb."

"Ma! You are not disturbing me. Let me help you. Lord, you're like a pack mule."

"A Sherpa!"

Her fingers are red and white from where the plastic bags have bitten into her flesh, but she doesn't seem to notice. Unloaded, she perches on the desk and flings off her coat, blanketing the immigration documents to reveal an even brighter layer of fuchsia pink. "I just dropped in to see if you wanted to come for dinner tonight. Lindsay's got a hen night party, so Leo's all alone, and you know he never can survive a night of having to actually entertain himself. Dad invited him over and he's making a spag bol."

I hear Cole's voice echo, *Do it tonight, pickle.*

Mum's expectant smile shines down at me.

"Dinner. Yes. Yes, that would be nice."

"Oh, but you love Dad's spaghetti! I thought I'd get a better reception than that. But if you're too busy…" she adds sing-songily, crossing her arms.

I'm missing my cue to smile as a good daughter should, but I can't. My face doesn't feel like my own, but some Botox disaster. The network of tissue and threads of muscle and sinew connect tightly in a mask of inexpression.

She must notice my unusual reticence. Dad always said about the Petersen women, "If talking were an Olympic event, Kay and Enna would be on the winning team."

"What's the matter? Is there something wrong?"

Wrong? What's wrong is that this should be the happiest, most exciting time of my life, and instead I am frantic with worry. *I'm worried about filing forms, leaving you and Dad, leaving the theater, my home, my life; stepping into the unknown and finding it's not what it is meant to be; and I have* the *most amazing three-point-two carat cushion-cut "eye perfect" emerald, set with two flawless baguette diamonds, but I can't even wear it because you don't know, and my fingers have been nervous they've lost weight!* I stream it all mentally but keep my jaw locked.

"Oh, Mum!" I sigh instead.

She fixes me with her look of gentle inquiry.

"It's all just so complicated. I feel as if I'm being pulled in so many different directions. I feel like I'm playing an exhausting tug-of-war, and I'm the rope. I don't know what to do. I've reached my Enna-lastic limit."

"You worry too much. So there must be lots to do for the new show, but you'll get it done. You always do." She puts her arm around me, framing me, but her misdirected sympathy only makes me feel all the more traitorous. How can I leave my mum? I can feel my nostrils sting as tears begin to seep into my eyes.

If only Cole were here instead of a faceless voice on the end of the telephone. If only he weren't the excited, expectant voice who rushes home from work early to catch me five hours in the future, who grasps the phone as he walks through the door, loosening his tie as he dials the long foreign number. At least if he were miserable,

I wouldn't feel like such a bitch all the time. And when I do hold my tongue, when I pretend everything is cherry-topped and chocolate-sprinkled, I end up replacing the receiver and resenting him for his perpetual optimism. *"But I'm going to miss so much,"* I've said.

"Yeah, but you'll have everything you need here, sweetie," he replied softly into the receiver, through wires, up to satellites and into my ear, like it's the simplest transition in the world.

"Come on, darling. What is it?" Mum asks again.

I look into my lap, trying to focus on the weave of the herring-bone tweed, but—quite inconveniently—my vision blurs through a haze of tears. My cheeks crack their mold, and then her fuchsia arms are around me, holding me, shielding me tightly within her maternal cloak. I burrow for her warmth and safety. How will I replace this? Not with letters, emails or phone calls. There we sit for minutes, without saying a word. But I have to speak.

"Do it now, pickle," he said.

I sit up straighter and wipe the glistening trails from my cheeks and nostrils. The kaleidoscope circles of her greeny-blue irises con-tract, and the dark pools of her pupils expand, as if she is reading my tears—each another traitorous signal of my defection.

"Oh, darling," she whispers. "He's proposed, hasn't he?" The question is so quickly and simply put, saving me from elaborate tongue-tied explanations, requiring a simple yes or no.

I lower my swollen lids and nod slowly, I can't trust my voice.

"Well that's fantastic news!" She beams, as she braces my shoulders and looks at me, before gathering me in again for another squeeze.

"But…but…aren't you upset?" I stutter.

"Why in the world would I be?"

"Because, well, because you want me near."

"Bugger that, darling! I want you to be happy."

My face crumples inwardly like a failed soufflé, all the hot air whisked up inside suddenly imploding, and a reprise of strangulated sobs rise up. "I—" sniff "—am—" snot "—happy!" I mewl, col-lapsing in a soggy heap.

"That's it, darling!" she rallies, rubbing my arm, as if it hides some secret inflation device to pump me back up again. "And Pennsylvania isn't so far away. I mean, you could have married a tribesman from the Masai Mara. You know, the ones you read about with the fifteen-inch penises, and then think what your father would say!"

"Mum!"

"It was in my *Woman's Weekly*. You should read it. Very different culture."

"You don't think Dad will be angry, do you?"

"Angry? Cole's not a politician, or unemployed, or an actor, or French. He'll be thrilled! Come on. Cheer up." She produces a used handkerchief and places it in my hand. "Now, how can I help?"

"Mum —" I sniff loudly " —you just have."

We spend the next hour in the office going through my immigration application and attendant forms. They are tricky; it is easy to miss one of the many boxes or forget to write "N/A" as instructed, rather than a simple no in answer to all the excruciatingly obvious questions: "Is it your intention to enter the United States to sell illegal narcotics/commit an act of terrorism/become a bigamist?" *Hmm, well now that you mention it...*

After many cups of tea and more than a few of Mum's spirit-rallying mottos — "two heads are better than one" and "many hands make light work" — we complete the forms with surprising word economy.

My shoulders straighten under their lessened load, and my throat feels less obstructed. Immigrant petition for fiancée on behalf of alien, Ms. Enna Petersen, supported by American citizen, Mr. C. Krupski, thoroughly dissected, analyzed, annotated, and financially supported. Dates of travel, daily itinerary, lists of witnesses, and accompanying photographs; see exhibits A to R. There! My relationship laid bare for the eagle eyes of Uncle Sam. "America Wants You!" the top-hatted and tailed, goatee-bearded cartoon exclaims. *Yeah, just not very bloody much.*

"It's like an interrogation by the Inquisition!" Mum says as she takes another slurp of tanned tea. "They won't call and ask me things, will they? I'm sure I won't be able to remember. You know me. Can I plead early onset Alzheimer's?" She laughs quietly at her own joke and then takes another sip. "How long until you leave?"

My stomach knots. "I don't know," I admit, reality rushing in, lead lining my lungs. "The embassy operates by its own rules, but if they process quickly, I could get my visa days after my embassy interview."

Another pause. I can see Mum working hard to fight the silence; her lips twitch with unvoiced thoughts. We squeeze hands to fill the space that is empty with words, but full of so much else, an invisible umbilical cord plugging us in to the Petersen frequency.

She smiles, a decisive lip-fastening smile, as if she has come to a conclusion. "I'm glad. He's good for you."

At eight forty-five p.m., I finally call it a day. After two hours of trying to teach the volunteer lighting technicians the subtleties of fade, I am ready for a drink and a lobotomy.

By the time I arrive at Mum and Dad's, the back door is already fogged up with inviting steam, and the air, though cool, is thick with the Italian aroma of roasted garlic, onions, and peppers, along with familiar, hearty family food smells. It is, to me, the best smell in the world, this scent of home.

Dad turns to greet me with his usual cheer. "Chickadee!" He is standing by the stove, stirring his famous culinary masterpiece, his apron splattered artistically—the Jackson Pollock of tomato sauce.

"Smells great, Dad," I say, sucking up the fragrant air.

"Grab a glass and get your gnashers round this. It's quite a good Sangiovese."

I join him at the stove, armed with our glasses, and take over the stirring. "I'll stir this. You can do the mushrooms," I say, reclaiming my old role.

He chops intermittently as he relights his cigar and turns up the volume of the jazz pianist tinkling in the background. He slices through the plump brown gills of the mushrooms with gastronomic flair, flicking his knife through the air in time to the bluesy beat. "Isn't this good?"

"The wine or the music?"

"Both."

"Yup, they are," I agree, surveying the scene and enjoying the silent synchrony of our symbiosis.

He looks up and catches me staring, smiling a big bemused smile. "What?"

"Oh, nothing." *But I'll miss this,* I'm thinking.

Mum peers around the door, a beam plastered over her face. "Oh, hello, darling! Didn't hear you come in. So…?"

"As subtle as a chainsaw, Ma." I laugh, tending to the sauce.

"What?" asks Dad again, undeterred by my conscientious stirring. He empties the load of chopped mushrooms into the sauce and retrieves the spoon from my hand. "Come on, what's going on?"

I never could lie to my dad. "Well…" A lungful of oregano wafts up my nose, another scent to remember. "Look at this!" I say, gathering up my long sleeve and uncovering the glowing gem on my fourth finger. "Cole asked me to marry him."

"Aaaaa!"

And I am enveloped.

"Well, it took you long enough to tell me! Cole asked for my blessing when he was here last. I've known for weeks!"

"Dad!" I don't know whether to hit him or hug him back. "You could have told me!"

Mum joins the family scrum just as Leo arrives at the door.

"What's all this? Did someone die?"

Oh, I will miss this.

<h1 style="text-align:center">Chapter 3</h1>

The enthusiastic American attorney tells us, "It's a crap shoot." Strange expression to English ears, as if the embassy officials are about to let fly with steaming mounds of shit catapulted in our direction. "It really depends on how busy the embassy is as to how quickly they will process the paperwork. If it's a slow week in the Middle East, Mexico or Eastern Europe, you might be lucky."

I don't know when the crap was shot, but it landed *splat!* on my doormat only a week later. The heavy, white-enveloped edict demanded I attend the embassy interview and have a medical, not with my own doctor, but with their approved embassy physician. The bill for the services was also included. Oh, deep joy. And, double crap, the interview and medical coincided neatly with opening night. Ta da! *Splat! Splat!*

I force myself to bed at a reasonable hour. I set my alarm clock and my mobile phone, checking and rechecking that I have entered a.m. not p.m., "wake" not "off." I toss and turn like a rotisserie chicken, pecking at my pillow as I think of some other unthought-of question. What if they ask me if he's ever broken a bone? Failed an exam? Had wisdom teeth?

My unsleeping mind mines all the many and varied things I don't know about Cole, about America. And the scene suddenly clears through the blood vessels on the back of my eyelids.

I'm waiting before a door, about to twist the handle. I touch the metal with only my fingertips—the lightest of touches—and on contact the door flies away from my hand, swings open, and the back draft sweeps me in like an invisible tidal wave.

The heavy door slams. A metallic slide, like the sound of a knife being sharpened, resounds behind me. I turn quickly to see the bolt being drawn across the door, and then the top bolt, and then the bottom. But no one is there. Panic grips me, a hammering in my stomach, a dry palate that no amount of anxious swallowing will cure. I turn in circles, checking the area—isn't that what Dad taught me—never leaving my back unprotected, turning to the wall, the door, the wall, the desk, the wall, the door, the wall, the desk, the wall…

"Sit. Down."

My skin almost lifts off my bones at the sound of this resonant, uncompromising growl.

"Who's there?" I falter weakly.

"Sit—" clack "—down." Clack…clack…clack. Out of the darkness behind the imposing desk, the stamping of a walking cane pronounces itself. Orchestrating with a hefty thwack is an imposing man, perhaps seven feet tall, dressed in long blue and white striped trousers, top hat and tails. He uses the cane not as an elderly gentleman would, but with a cold, detached, military authority.

He stops before me, lifting his cane high off the ground. For a second, my eyes widen and I flinch. He's going to hit me! I look into his gimlet eyes, disbelieving, and I back up slowly toward the door, trying to calculate how I can conceivably withdraw three bolts and escape before being cudgeled. But, advancing still, he lowers the cane and jabs it into my stomach. I'm more shocked than hurt as automatically my body folds in the middle. Suddenly there is a fumble of hands and a scurry of flesh and fists, and I don't feel thumps; I just hear them: mine glancing but not connecting, almost whistling in air, and his solid, buffeting strikes, heel of palm and flank of stick. It's quick and confusing, and the tussle forces me back into a chair.

The blows stop and I open my wild eyes, like a poor heifer in one of those mad cow disease documentaries who sees the bolt about to mallet their skull into their brain.

"I said, sit down." Gimlet Eyes looms above me and forces the hard bone handle up under my jaw. He straightens, lifting my chin and inspecting my face. "Petersen, Enna. White. Five foot nine. One degree, four A-Levels, ten GCSEs. Achievements? Nothing. Merits? None. Current employment…failing!" He snorts with relish.

"So, tell me…" He lowers his face to mine again. His hypnotic eyes tunnel into my brain, scouring it for lies, searching for my worth, sucking information out through my pupils. "What, exactly, would you offer America? Why should we want you?"

His long goat's face lengthens as his mouth opens, and I think he just might dislocate his jaw and consume me. I can't move. I can see his teeth and I can hear my heart pound in my ears, but I can't fight and I can't run.

With his free hand, he throws off his top hat, switches the cane into his left, and trails the cold, hard handle down my neck and into the notch of my throat. I can hardly breathe, and all I can think is that I want to go home.

I try to inhale, to say something, but all I can voice is a sticky wheezing sound. What would I say anyway? Would I beg for clemency, for asylum? Or would I whisper out my defenses?

"Oh come, come. Don't you think I already know? I know your failures. You were never as good as you pretended to be. You are decidedly average. You call yourself an actress? A director? Well, what good is that? You are worthless."

I can feel the tears trickle down my cheeks, unable to swallow, barely able to breathe and desperate to find something, anything of any worth, but what have I done? What have I accomplished?

When I was nine, I sponsored a child in Africa. I earned the Duke of Edinburgh Award and only got lost twice on my expedition. At university, I was president of the Drama Society. When my neighbor broke her leg, I volunteered to walk her ferret. I recycled—when I had the time. I wrote handwritten letters. I didn't step on or salt slugs, merely hurled them in another direction. I am a hard worker, a decent, grounded, all right sort of person. I'm a good egg!

"I can't hear you!" he booms, twirling the cane from its fleshy harbor and thwacking it down on either side of me, on the armrests. I am trapped in the machinery of some manic metronomic gauntlet.

He roars with laughter, thudding the cane. "Tick, tock, tick, tock."

"NO!" I pry open a wakeful eyelid. He has gone, and the memory of the dream vanishes like lightning. I lie in the dark cave-like bedroom and listen to the metronome beat of the second hand marching me through the dawn.

The train into Waterloo takes less than forty sobering minutes. The crisp morning awakens my senses, and I stride along, marveling at my own human exhaust.

I arrive at the Grosvenor Street Clinic twenty minutes early for my appointment. The large black door, furnished with an intimidating brass handle and knocker, is unyielding. It is cold. What I'd give for a hot chocolate with swirly cream!

"Well, hive bin waiting fur tree monts and fie-nally the date comms. Well, I'od planned t' be livin' dere by naoow." I hear a jovial ginger chap address the group of multi-colored faces congregating near the clinic.

"It's a farce, the whole thing," agreed the tall Asian man standing next to Leprechaun. "My girlfriend has had to quit her job as an elementary school teacher to become a sales rep. Just so she can prove she can support me on the affidavit. It's ridiculous."

What's this? My ears strain, and my eyes bulge. Can it be that I am not alone? Are there stowaways in my transatlantic boat?

My index fingers start to take on their first signs of frostbite, the arterial constriction plain to see in my two-tone flesh. I mustn't think of that. I must concentrate, think of answers to unasked questions.

As the minutes crawl by, the queue of men and women, all ages, all races, snakes further down the street. Leprechaun, Tall Asian, and other background faces, faces undistinguishable in a line up, compare stories, laugh, and clap their hands to keep warm, as I sit frozen from the top step of the cold stone stoop. The individuals all so normal looking—you wouldn't think that they too have fiancés who have swept them off their little, sensible Clarks-soled feet and rescued them from a life of gray, bundling them up into a world of Disney colors and limitless fantasies.

At eight fifteen a.m., finally, I hear the bolt being drawn and, hurrah, warmth! At the end of this lavish reception room, a woman sits in state behind a leather-topped bureau. I advance toward her, proffering my papers.

"I'm Enna Petersen. I have an eight o'clock appointment."

The lady tilts her immaculate face toward me. "Yes, you are all eight o'clockers. If you would like to fill in this form, return it to me, and wait in the drawing room for your name to be called." The drawing room. Not waiting room.

I return my form to her and "withdraw" to the seat nearest the grand fireplace, watching the room fill and feeling my fingers defrost.

The others chat away happily, comparing their transatlantic entanglements. I listen with my head buried in my book, my disappointment mounting. I had thought that the story of Cole and Enna had been so unique, so romantic, but hearing, amongst the hubbub, similar histories makes ours, all of a sudden, less special.

"What are you reading?" I hear, as a stranger takes up the chair beside me.

Can I ignore him?

"Your book? What are you reading?"

I keep my eyes trained on the print. I could pretend I'm deaf… or French. *Pardon, monsieur, je n'aime pas…Merde!* I'm going to have to acknowledge him, aren't I? Really, it's a stupid question though. The book cover is less than ten inches from his nose, and the title is written in block capitals. I'll have to go for mock surprise, the *Oh, sorry. What, me?* line.

I tear my eyes from the page, the moue mouth ready to form the O, when I see him for the first time.

Chapter 4

I catch his eyes: dark, warm pools of melted, lustrous Bournville chocolate that twinkle at me. I can barely distinguish where the inky pupils stop and the swirly irises start. I freeze like I've been shot, the O paused on my lips, and in the same moment, I can feel the blood pour into my frozen fingertips, like the floodgates have been released.

I have never really paid much attention to eyes before. Yet these eyes, these pools of inviting molten chocolate, are mesmerizing, and I want to look away, but I can't. Warmth flushes across my face.

"I'm Will."

"Sorry," I blather, embarrassed by my silence, "I'm just…rather absorbed in smuggling drugs off the coast of Spain at the moment. Oh hell! I mean, not really!" I exclaim with anxious looks to the oblivious interviewees. "I probably shouldn't say that when waiting for my immigration interview, should I? It's the book, you see. Not me. I don't smuggle drugs."

"Don't worry. If they cart you off in chains, I'll explain." He smiles.

"Thank you," I say, unable to continue holding his gaze or meet his smile, but he carries on regardless.

"Good choice though. Arturo Perez-Reverte, not an obvious choice, but what a storyteller."

"You've read him?" This has to be a line. How many men do I know who read anything more challenging than *Nuts* magazine—well, at least back at university. How many men do I actually know full stop? Not including my techies or the gay retinue at the theater. *Okay, Enna, you need to get out more.*

"You are surprised. Actually, I've read two of his. His writing keeps me guessing; I like that. I like to be surprised. So many books are just formula."

"You're right. I don't have enough fingers to count how many times I seem to have read different versions of *Pride and Prejudice*! Some with werewolves, with zombies, contemporary, set in America, set in an Austenland. It's all the same."

"Well, people want the fairy tale. They want a heroine, like Lizzie, with whom they can empathize."

With whom? With whom? My Mum would love this chap!

I goggle at this man in disbelief, my eyes wide with every sign of a severe thyroid problem. A man who actually reads and then—holy Pulitzer, Batman—wants to talk about it?

I did buy Cole a book once. It was my favorite. I had such high hopes he would devour it, but on my next trip to visit, there it was, propped up on the bookshelf, its red bow still neatly tied around it, a monument to our differences.

"Enna Petersen," a nasal voice resounds over the intercom.

"That's me," I admit, collecting my things. "Wish me luck. It was nice meeting you…"

"Will."

"Yes. Sorry. It was nice meeting you, Will."

"You too, Enna."

I am shown to a waiting room—not a "drawing room" this time, but a sterile, whitewash-walled box of a room decorated with a large map of America. I put my bags down and survey my new surroundings. I wonder if they will ask me questions about the States. *Exactly how many are there again?* And what if they ask me to name them all?

"Ey-nah?" a large Asian nurse demands as she whisks back the curtain to reveal her cupboard-sized work room. I take an inventory: one cabinet, one chair, and one table covered by rows of empty vials. Those glass leeches quietly hum with anticipation as the sturdy nurse pounds the floorboards and sends seismic tremors through the table legs and across the open mouths of the blood-craving containers. Three vials stand already full, the thick coagulated fluid coating the sides of the tube like molasses.

"In here," she orders, "and roll up sleeve."

I busy Self, peeling back my layers when, bam! She throws the needle into my arm with the nonchalance of a drunken darts player.

"Ho, small vein," she marvels. "Squeeze. You must squeeze like this —" she demonstrates, clenching her fist " — or we have no blood and have to do it all again." She chuckles.

Oh goody. I squeeze my fist and pump blood into the syringe for all I'm worth.

Finally satisfied with the load she has leeched, she pushes me out back into the cold waiting room. And there I wait. And wait.

I try opening my book and picking up where I had left off, but my mind can't concentrate. Words swim before my eyes.

An hour or more passes. Why is this taking so long?

I try to count the states of America but keep losing track around Idaho as I look up and see another patient given the human pin-cushion treatment by the Beast of Beijing and then taken through to the next part of the assessment. The procession of multi-colored waiting room faces — Tall Asian, woman with the loud voice in the drawing room, Will— are all escorted past me, but I am left waiting. Did I get the Advance Directly to Jail card? Do not pass go! Do not collect two hundred pounds? I seem to have the monopoly on the waiting room.

Have I been forgotten? Did the snotty receptionist read my thoughts, know that I wanted to be quick and so is torturing me with this endless waiting? Or…wait a minute…I was second to have my blood tested and then, other people bypassed while I, whose blood still seems to be being tested, am left waiting.

Oh. My. God.

"Sarah Hobbs," shouts the needle-happy nurse.

The startled Sarah looks up from her recently taken chair and turns from the demanding scowl to me.

"Oh no, I don't think it is me next. This lady has been waiting longer. It must be her turn?"

"No. I know my job. She—" the militant nurse points in my direction "—has to wait."

"Oh. Sorry," mouths Sarah with a look of genuine sympathy.

Thoughts explode like fireworks across my hemispheres: first, little sparklers, which set off gently fizzing traffic lights, which ignite great dangerous rockets firing over the innocent plains of my brain, bursting with a big bang and a shower of consequences.

I'm…diseased.

Oh God, oh God, why did I let Christian, acting friend/male model talk me into a "fun" night away from university? Why, oh why, had I got so very drunk and not insisted on a condom? I must have been thick. *You stupid, stupid girl! Why didn't you think?* And, God! Hadn't he just returned from that modeling campaign in Thailand?

Well, that's it, isn't it?

Oh please, God, no. I promise, if you make everything okay, I'll never drink again, not even a spritzer or a sherry at Christmas. Just please make it okay.

Oh, Christ…and Cole! What if I've given some deadly disease to Cole? And—oh God—not just Cole, but the others in between! I'm some filthy virus-spreading vector, responsible for the infection of ex-lovers, and their partners, and their partners' future partners, and so on and so on, and it's all *my* fault!

I scrabble in my handbag for the trusty bottle of aspirin, something to take the ache away, to dull the thud of the executioner's drum roll. I know it's in here somewhere. A handful of lint, mat of hair, my wallet, my phone, my lip balm…

"Ey-nah. You come." Ms. Congeniality herself, Nurse Sing, stands above me, hands firmly placed on her substantial hips. She escorts me to the next room, barely even looking at me—she must be so disgusted—and she holds up a curtain, indicating one of the eight changing cubicles. "This, you put on," she says, producing a paper robe from some magical cubicle stash.

The cubicles are deathly silent. Am I the only one here? Of course… the diseased are probably quarantined from the other, healthy, sober, condom-using folk.

Once closeted behind my severely drawn curtain, I bend to see any other feet in the adjoining slots. All have been and gone, it seems, even Sarah Hobbs.

I noiselessly undress, shivering as I jump from foot to foot on the cold, tiled floor. Should I leave my knickers on? Yes? No? She didn't say. Bugger. Maybe the doctor will need to do a cervical smear, and here I am with a thong embroidered with little yellow duckies, each with a little speech balloon proclaiming, "I'm quackers!" Or maybe, the doctor won't do an exam but see that I've taken them off and then think I'm a real hussy.

They go down. They come up. Down. *Shit, Enna, make a fucking decision. It's too cold to fanny around getting your knickers in a twist.* And I'm so angry. Angry at my own stupidity. I'm angry that I have put Cole's future, my future, other unknown futures, in jeopardy. Fogged with fury, I yank the knickers back up but can't get much higher than my knees. Oh shit. They *are* twisted, a canary-yellow figure of eight. Balancing on one leg, I extract my foot from the lingerie vice at half mast, turn the flimsy cotton the right way, and hop as I dip my toes through with a wobble and a—*Holy crap! I'm going down!* I reach for something to grab hold of—a fold of curtain—and I can hear the material tear slightly from its curtain pole. But the panel steadies me just in time, and I recover my balance before really making an entrance. Oh Lord, as if I don't have enough worries. *"Yes, doctor, she's potentially riddled with a bevy of contagious sexual diseases and was found with her knickers around her knees. She's quackers!"*

I pull them up decisively. *Oh! Duck it!*

"Enna Petersen? Are you ready yet?" an unamused male voice calls.

"Coming," I call, hustling out of the cubicle and smiling feebly for a bit of reassurance.

He doesn't return the smile or greeting. Oh God. He knows, doesn't he? He has seen that I have AIDS or something, and he is full of loathing for my stupidity. "Come this way."

I'm doomed.

"Right. I have to X-ray you. Press your chest up against this and keep still until I come back into the room."

I stand ramrod straight, almost forgetting to breathe. The X-ray whirrs and flashes. The plate against my chest is cold. I want to cry. I will not cry. I will be strong.

When the machine shuts off, the nurse re-enters and escorts me wordlessly to the next room. I recall that bloody mad cow disease documentary again. This is what a cow must experience, being cattle-prodded up the ramp into the abattoir, before the blinding bright lights startle and disguise the path of the metal bolt hammering down through the shattered bone into the soft brain. This present dread seems familiar.

I blink through the brightness. There is a suited man in his thirties sitting on the other side of a large mahogany desk. He shuffles his papers in a newsreader fashion and looks up at me, smiling.

"Hello, Enna."

"Hello," I reply nervously, waiting for the bad news, or the hidden camera, or some kind of unforeseen.

"Take a seat. I'm just going to ask a few questions before examining you. All your injections up to date? Your Hepatitis? Rubella?" The doctor rattles off the list of vaccinations, ticking the boxes as I hand him my records.

"Well, that all looks good. Pop up on the trolley for me."

I lie rigid on the paper sheeting.

"Okay. I'm going to give you a breast exam first. Do you conduct breast exams yourself?" he enquires while adeptly pressing around my chest.

"Well, my fiancé does quite regularly." *Good Lord, what am I saying?*

"It is important that you check yourself," he says sternly. "Your heart and blood pressure seem fine. Have you had a smear recently?"

"Hmm." I nod. "The nurse said I had a healthy pink cervix." *Jesus, Mary and Joseph, what* am *I saying?*

"Well, good. It is all good. Make sure you collect your chest X-ray on your way out and present these sealed documents to your immigration officer at the embassy." He moves back around his desk, and I sit up on the bed, still waiting to hear my blood test results.

"Get dressed now."

"Oh, I—"

"Is there something else?"

"Well, yes, isn't there? I mean, I thought…I was waiting for the blood test results for so long that I thought there might have been a problem."

"No. No problem. I just like to see my patients alphabetically. Helps me keep the paperwork in order. That's all. Good day."

I scurry back to my cubicle coop and practically rip my paper dress off. I haven't got AIDS. I am healthy. I have a lovely pink cervix after all! Oh, thank God. And I vow I will never, ever fall prey to drunken, uncondomed romps again. Ever.

I stride down Grosvenor Street, X-ray under arm, and on my mission to the embassy. It is quite an imposing sight. The high-sided edifice, like an Egyptian pyramid in granite, is surrounded with fortress-like defenses: impenetrable, spiked metal fencing ready to kebab even the most acrobatic intruder; armed police officers with rifles, ready to make human Swiss cheese; police officers with German shepherds stationed at each corner of the perimeter, snarling for a taste of terrorist. This isn't London; it's bloody Guantanamo Bay. I swallow hard and walk on, stepping into the confines of the metal maze.

The fence leads me around the first three sides of the building. I can see the granite top; I just can't get to it. There is no break in the wire, no conveniently appointed signs, just enormous dogs and rifles and burly men who look as if they would sooner shoot me than answer a polite question. I hustle on and search for a way out of this rat trap.

Finally, the fencing opens out, exposing one side of the building, lined with people, hundreds of people, waiting for admittance. My heart sinks and shoulders sag. I didn't expect this. If I have to wait at the back of this line, I will never make it in time for curtain up. I am cold, I am tired, I am hungry, and I was supposed to have an eight a.m. appointment! Bastards!

"Enna!" Will muffles through his soft gray scarf. I can't see his mouth, just those eyes. They are bright and shiny, and sparkle in the cold, overcast light. "Thought you'd be long gone. What happened?"

"Dr. Pheelish only just saw me, and now I've got to stand in this! I missed my eight a.m. appointment hours ago, and now they probably won't even see me. I've got First Night tonight, and I'm never going to make it in time. And, even if I do get inside Colditz here, they will mark my records late and probably deduct points for not being punctual!" I steamroller without pause for breath.

"Take it easy. It's okay," he says as he offers an arm. "Come on!" He folds my stiff, awkward arm through his and escorts me past the long line of shivering people draped in multi-colored fabrics, bundled up in blankets and black headscarves.

"Oh, I can't jump queue, Will. That's not fair!"

"It's okay. You have an appointment. All these other people don't. That is why we can present ourselves straightaway."

I look at him to take in this new information. I suppose I really should start reading things better. It's not that I intend to be slapdash, but where, oh where, do I find the extra time to fit all these things in?

"You'll get wherever you need to be in no time, you'll see!"

I present my papers at the first security hut and am directed up the ramp, around another small wire fence maze, and into the United States embassy.

The embassy is rather like an overgrown post office. Rows and rows of bolted-down plastic chairs fill the length of the room. The left side of the room is illuminated by floor to ceiling windows tinted blue and casting a gloom on the natural light. On the right side of the room stand twelve or so booths manned by bored looking officials. Bright fluorescent strip lights hum overhead, and hanging down from the ceiling are blue TV screens filled with numbers.

The portly guard on the door instructs us to take a ticket. It seems quite bizarre, taking the tongue-like ticket from the mouth of the machine just as I would at the deli queue in Sainsbury's.

"Number two?"

"Yes, I'll have a couple of slices of the honey roast ham, a pot of those black olives, half a pound of goat's cheese, oh, and a visa, please."

"Number two hundred forty-seven," the loudspeaker relays as the number flashes up on the blue screen under cubicle twelve. I look at my ticket: 512. Oh, good grief. I collapse heavily into a vacant chair in the front row, stretching my tired, cold legs out in front of me.

"An eight a.m. appointment will only get you so far. Wake me up when it's time, will you?" Will says, slumping down next to me, his face disappearing into his nest of scarf.

I observe the diverse cross-section of people hunkered into their plastic seats, some eyeing the screen, some the back of their eyelids. There is little talk now, and the mood is somber. I watch the parade of passing numbers that will lead to mine.

Five hundred eight flashes up on the screen. 508? Have I fallen asleep and not noticed the several hundred desperate would-be immigrants bypass me? Ah-ha! There are two queues: one calling numbers in the two hundreds—maybe for those who didn't have an appointment—and one calling the five hundreders. 508. Only four to go. Hoorah!

Will shuffles in his seat. "How about I get you a coffee?"

"Oh." Coffee. Yes, I would like coffee. What's the protocol on accepting coffee from strangers? My brain tries to process quickly.

"It's only a coffee. It's not a date." He chuckles.

Yes, silly me. Coffee. No harm, just coffee.

"That'd be nice. Thank you." I fumble in my bag for some change, but he looks amused and tells me to keep it for next time.

The blue screen blinks overhead as we sip our frothy coffees, marooned on an island of plastic chairs amidst a sea of tired eyes.

Will is, I am unsurprised to learn, an English graduate from Warwick University. He stayed on for his Masters and from his research had written an interactive one-man production, touring to theaters and festivals across the country. It was at the Edinburgh Festival that he had met Melissa, an American theater student. They had met exchanging flyers for their respective shows on the Royal Mile, had found a rubbish bin to dispose of said flyers, and spent the afternoon huddled out of the rain in a little bagel and coffee shop on the square.

"And that was that. Mel's eager to perform over here now, and I want to take *The Shakespearian Rap* there, so it makes sense."

"You make it sound *so* romantic!"

"Oh no, I don't mean it like that. It's just, having to justify our relationship for the visa, having to diarize every single thing, has rather taken the romance out of it for me. Mel's great. I don't think I could ever find someone that could be a better partner in life."

"She must be very lovely." And I believe it for a millisecond, before emerald green envy tinges my imaginings. I bet she is young and blond, a cheerleader with inflatable boobs, perma-tan, and almost too-white teeth, who says, "Okay?" in a high-pitched squeak at the end of every sentence.

Okay, so maybe I'm a teeny weeny bit jealous.

She is probably young and annoyingly perky though. All the résumés sent recently begging for theater jobs seem to be from such young actresses—some born in the late nineties! The nineties! How did this happen? Surely they must still be fetuses? Can they even read? When did this happen, this miraculous time shift, where time has flown and suddenly I'm not cast as the young ingénue anymore; I'm the hapless housewife?

"So, how did you meet your fiancé?" he asks, his eyes still sparkling in a very distracting and inconsiderate fashion.

I take a long sip of my hot, silky latte, thinking of the lines I usually spew when people ask this question, but the words don't come as fluidly as usual. "Funnily enough, our stories are pretty similar. We were both on holiday in Florida. Met, got talking, and didn't stop."

He sits, waiting for more, framing questions with his thick, dark eyebrows.

"It was difficult with my job, especially now that I am going to be leaving. Because of the non-existent budget, I run the theater single-handedly, so I'm responsible for everything. I can't teach someone all that, and no one seems to fit the bill as my replacement anyway. The board of directors is considering someone who is completely incapable — someone's nephew, Hugo Somethingorother, fresh out of RADA and ready to take on the world!

"It breaks my heart, you know, because the theater has been my second home, and to see it crumble before my eyes is…well, it's difficult."

"Couldn't you work with the board to find a suitable replacement?"

"Are you interested? Believe me, I've tried. At this stage, I think the only way Hugo would not be appointed director was if I was suddenly to stay on, but that's not going to happen. After this interview, I shall be three thousand miles away and Ashtead will have to solve its own problems."

"Ashtead! You didn't say it was Ashtead! As in Ashtead, Surrey? My God. I performed there with *The Bard's Ballad* in two thousand and two, just after I graduated. It was one of my first professional gigs, before I re-wrote the show!"

"Wait! I remember that show! Oh my God, that's crazy!"

"Did you see it?"

"Well, no. That was the summer I was away, work-shadowing for the Southwold and Aldeburgh Summer Repertory season. I recall the publicity though. I was an incredibly devout, maybe teetering on 'nerdy,' theater-goer!" I take a sip, amazed by the coincidence. "Wow! What are the chances of that?"

"It's a small world, especially in theater circles. I remember Ashtead. The showers didn't work very well and the carpet had slug trails on it —"

"Oh, I ripped those out as soon as I took over! That is just…crazy though, isn't it? That you and me would have shared that history, and now here we are today, doing the same thing! So very bizarre. What do you do now then? Do you live in London?"

"I wish. I am a traveling troubadour. I go where the work is. You?"

"I have a house in Ashtead. It's small but convenient. The theater is only a few roads away. I can walk there in the summertime. Actually, it used to be the digs for the theater, back in the day. On Skinners Lane."

"No! You're having me on!"

"Don't tell me you've been in my house, too!"

"Five hundred twelve. Five hundred twelve," the almost inaudible voice mumbles through the loudspeaker. Despite watching the numbers and sitting, waiting for over an hour and a half, I feel caught out.

"Number five hundred twelve, come on down!" Will exclaims.

I try to. I put one leg in front of the other, but the rush of pins and needles prickling my foot make walking rather awkward. My weight settles unsteadily, and I stumble, dropping all of my carefully sorted paperwork.

"Oh God!" I drop to my knees, trying to retrieve the cascade of paperwork.

"Five hundred twelve. Five hundred twelve," the robotic voice repeats again impatiently. Will dives to the floor to help me collect the forms.

"Oh shit, oh shit, oh shit."

"Five hundred twelve. Five hundred twelve to cubicle three."

"Oh shit, now it's all out of order."

"Keep calm. Take a big breath. It's nothing you can't deal with. Here——" he hands the last fugitive page to me, his warm fingers brushing softly over mine "—you can sort these out as you get up there. You'll be fine. Good luck, Enna Petersen."

I half run to the cubicle, shuffling my papers into some semblance of order. The embassy officer eyes me impatiently as he continues stamping the documents already in front of him.

I re-organize my pages and take a deep breath—just as Will said. Just as Will said? Oh! I didn't say goodbye.

I look back to the waiting area, but the seat next to mine, where the stranger with the soft gray scarf and the molten eyes had been sitting, is empty.

Chapter 5

I present the documents: my passport, birth certificate, checks (plural, for the many differing visa-processing services), applications, medical report, X-ray, affidavits, photographs for evidence, photograph for visa, et cetera, et cetera.

"I think that is everything." I present the expensive load of paper through the slot in the Plexiglas screen. The officer flicks through the documents like a bored croupier before telling me to take seat in another row of chairs.

What? Wait? Again? Perhaps this is the embassy trial of endurance: he who has the best bladder and sits it out, wins the visa!

After another achingly paralyzed period of time, I am summoned to another non-confidential row of cubicles. This officer, also shielded by Plexiglas, eyes me suspiciously.

"State your name."

"Enna Katherine Petersen."

"State the name of your fiancé?"

"Cole James Krupski."

"Where did you meet?"

"We were both on holiday. Oh…er…I mean, vacation. We were both on vacation in Florida."

"And what do you do?" he sneers.

"I'm a director and actress. I run Ashtead Theater and—"

"Yes, yes." He stares through me, and without removing his beady eyes from mine, he lifts his hand and stamps the documents. *Thump, thump*. Take that, Exile. "Leave your passport here. Your visa will be sent to you. Be sure to complete the delivery package and pay at the front desk. You may go."

That's it? Two minutes of paper flicking and obvious small talk questions? *Don't you want to know what his college major was, or what his boss is called, or that he uses an electric toothbrush?*

"Miss?"

"Wha—"

"I said you may go. Please don't hold up the line."

Twenty minutes later, the train pulls away from the platform at Waterloo. Finally, I can close my heavy lids and let the folds of frown relax. I'd done it. We'd done it. I now had carte blanche to throw up my hands and dive into the unknown.

For the first time ever, I'm not keeping to the neatly manicured path of school, university, bit parts, theater tours, lead roles, directing. I am changing course, and after all the months of planning, of immigration-gestation, of labor and "It's a visa!"—a tangible, undeniable, real thing.

I glimpse out of the window to the passing blur of the station. Flashes of matchstick men and women all dressed in shades of black line the platform of Clapham Junction. Amidst the swath of black there is a neck enshrouded in gray. My head whips around to catch a second look, but the train is too fast for my tired eyes. Could that have been Will? *Oh, Enna, don't be silly.*

And anyway, I'm not looking. I'm not interested, because I am a very happily visa'd woman with the most gorgeous, kind, and considerate fiancé, ever. But what are the chances? What a funny quirk of fate to meet someone on such a similar path. Birds of a feather, I suppose. There are only so many theaters. And yet, I wonder if I had not toured Europe, if I had stayed in Ashtead that summer of 2002, if we would have met then. I linger over this as the train lulls me back home.

There's time enough for a quick change, a cup of tea and a slightly stale chocolate HobNob biscuit, before the First Night. Thank goodness I keep a little black dress at the theater for rushed occasions such as this. *Why, Enna, you could almost be organized!*

The board had chosen *King Lear* to be the season finale. It would not have been my pick—certainly not to be my directorial swan song in England. What a rip-roaring laugh-a-minute choice that was, but what do I know?

As I stand amidst the dower crowd, thoroughly depressed by the horror of First Night reality, I take every glass of champagne offered; I am celebrating, after all. The board lingers in the foyer, passing gilded compliments. I smile a champagne-fueled smile and endure it until Mum can, at last, drive me home.

She drops me off, watches me step over the threshold, and tootles off in her little VW Bug. I can't remember feeling this tired, and it's a serious workout to even summon the energy to clean my teeth and wash my face. At last, I dive into the cozy confines of my bed, wiggling wildly to warm up the cold sheets. I turn to the bedside table, feeling for the familiar buttons of the alarm clock and uncover instead the telephone, its red message light flashing like an emergency beacon. *Oh, go away.*

I turn over, wrapping my duvet further around me, swaddling my arms in like an Egyptian mummy.

I open one eye and turn to the machine. It's winking frantically, a silent machine form of Tourette's. I shut both eyes tight. I am going to sleep. Thirty seconds…a minute…

"Oh, bugger it!" I sit up and press play.

"You have—" the machine pauses "—four new messages. First message, left today at one twenty-nine p.m. *Beeeeep.*"

I wait with my eyes closed, but the line goes dead. *Uh!*

"Second message, left today at three oh one p.m. *Beeeeep.*"

"Hi, sweetie, just me calling to see how the interview went."

Eyelids snap open like unleashed roller blinds.

"I guess you must still be there. Hope they are not giving you a hard time. Err. Okay. Call me when you get back. Love you, pickle."

Shit.

"Third message, left today at six ten p.m. *Beeeeep.*"

"Pickle, it's me. Just remembered you have your First Night tonight. So, err, break a leg, or whatever they say. Hope the embassy went well. Call me."

Double shit.

"Fourth message, left today at eleven fifty-nine p.m. *Beeeeep*."

"Pickle…? Did the embassy abduct you? I'm at home. Call me."

Shit, shit, and thrice times shit. Cole. How could I forget my fiancé? I shuck the rest of the duvet and resignedly dial the foreign number.

"Hi, sweetie!" exclaims the transported voice, with no hint of re-crimination.

"Hi. Look, I'm really tired. I've had a really long day. I've just got your messages and everything is fine."

"You got the visa?"

I can picture him, suspended in animation, poised, holding his breath, waiting on my answer.

"Yup."

"That's great! Really great! I'm so proud of you."

"And the First Night went really well, so it has been a long day."

"I was thinking of you, hoping those jackasses wouldn't show you up."

"Yeah, well they did okay. Look, I'm really done in. I'll call you tomorrow."

"But you haven't told me anything about the embassy yet. Did they ask you tough questions?"

"No. It was fine. Talk tomorrow?"

I hold the receiver out to replace it and hear a faint, "Okay, sweetie, you get some sleep, I—"

The morning comes all too soon, and I am hurled into consciousness by the ungodly bleat of the alarm clock. I turn on the bath taps, squeeze in the last of the relaxing bubble bath, and fumble through the medicine box for a restorative aspirin. I sink into the steaming waters, my disembodied head floating above the clouds of foam. I lie back to rest my pounding head, my pulsing eyes, my sluggish brain.

The telephone hails loudly. *Urgh! Stop the noise and let me be!* I slide deeper in the water and hold my breath. One, two, three—it's so quiet and so warm, and peaceful—twelve, thirteen. I burst through the bubbles and take a breath. The telephone has stopped ringing.

After a short soak, my head feels restored, my retinas re-attached and I'm altogether more human. I wrap my towel around me, fix another around my sopping hair, twisting the blue towel into a Marge Simpson topsy turban, and I wait for the water tornado to drain. The water gurgles down the pipes, but I can faintly hear the telephone again. Now who would be phoning on the morning after a First Night? Why wouldn't they ring my mobile? Unless it's Cole phoning for our landline-to-landline deal. But he wouldn't phone this early; he's five hours behind.

When silence is restored, I exit the bathroom and switch the light on to better investigate my wardrobe. Almost immediately, the phone starts ringing for the third time.

What the what? I hitch my towel with one arm, balance the falling turban and finally snatch the receiver.

"Yes?"

"Have you seen the *Ashtead Chronicle* this morning?" asks the caller with the unusually familiar voice—hate it, hate it when people assume I know who they are. *World, take note: I am not Mystic Meg.*

"I'm sorry?" I retort, searching through the remembered catalog of voices in my brain, hopeful for a match.

"You're the toast of the town! Okay, so your cast is 'second rate,' but Richard Kane, Arts Editor, raves, 'Enna Petersen shows touches of directorial genius. Lear fumbles for his sanity, running across stage as if he doesn't know which way to turn—" The voice-recognition Rolodex stops flipping.

"Will?" I ask, surprise bursting through my armor. I sink down to the corner of my bed.

"Yes, Clouseau it's me! I'm outside in the rain with the paper. In. The. Rain!"

"Outside? Here? Outside my house? Here? Right now?" I look around blindly, expecting him to leap out of the wardrobe like Kato or something—Surprise!—and I re-hitch my fugitive towels. "Look, sorry, it's just...I've just got out of the bath."

"I don't want to impose, but it's monsoon season out here."

Little kicks hammer away inside my stomach. "But I'm not dressed!"

"Perhaps you could let me in before I drown, and I'll stay in the kitchen while you get ready. I'll make you a cuppa!"

"Oh. Sure. Sorry. I'm just…surprised." I freefall through thought to the last time a man caught me unprepared: I was innocently expecting a chocolate bombe, not an emerald ring. "You should have called."

"I tried! You didn't answer."

"Oh." He's right there, I suppose. "But…" *I mean, this is weird, isn't it?* "How did you get my number?"

"It was on Facebook, under the contact info. Sorry. It was meant to be a surprise. Presumptuous of me." He sounds disappointed, and I wonder why I am programmed to be so cynical and defensive. Why can't I just be nice and welcoming? "I just, well, I saw the article this morning, and I knew you were only twenty minutes away, so I thought I would bring you a celebratory pastry from the bakery."

"Oh."

"I mean, work isn't exactly thick on the ground, and waiting for the next gig can get boring, so I thought…"

"What?" And I don't ask to be coquettish; I just really want to know. I mean, why would a man, albeit a very nice one, with whom I have a great deal in common, but who is affianced, come a-calling?

My question seems to flummox him for a few long seconds, and when he replies, he seems almost awkward, very unlike the smooth, erudite man I met yesterday. "That…I thought…we could chat."

"Chat?" A smile cracks and spreads across my face.

"Or drown. Which is looking the more likely of the two, given the current inclement conditions."

"Hmmm…you know, I was taught never to answer the door to strangers, especially if they offer you sweeties!"

"Oh, bam! Relegated to stranger status. Ouch. You're tough. Well, I will take my cakes and leave then."

My smile snaps back. "Let's not be too hasty. I'm coming down." I give my towel a final yank to secure it and hurry downstairs. A strange reaction for someone who wanted a quiet morning with no intrusion, but I really don't want him to go. And I know, too, that I shouldn't give a shit if he stays or goes, but I'll think about that later.

I slow down for the last stair and walk to the door with as much grace as I can muster. All traces of champagne bubbles on my brain have fizzed out of my head, and I am revitalized again.

I open the door a crack and see Will hunched over the newspaper he is protecting from the rain.

"Hi!" he says, dripping on the doormat and shaking his head like a wet dog.

"You're wet!"

"So are you!" he says, eyeing my towel and turban as if they are invisible.

I'm sure I must be blushing. "The kettle's on the side, tea bags and mugs in the cupboard above, milk in the fridge, water in the tap," I call over my shoulder, hurrying to make it upstairs before my towels abandon me.

A quick wardrobe inspection does not inspire me. *Come on!* I think as I stand before the crammed hanging space. *What are you waiting for? Frigging Narnia?*

I have one arm in the sleeve of my coral wrap-around when reality strikes. What am I doing? I have a stranger downstairs, probably rifling through the drawers for jewelry, credit cards, money… *"Yes, officer, I did let a stranger in and left him unattended, but I couldn't decide what to wear!"* I tiptoe to the top of the stairs and listen for telltale burglarly sounds. Nothing. A cupboard closing, a chink of china, but nothing incriminating.

I jettison the dress and opt for a cozy, cream angora V-neck sweater and my tweedy, herringbone brown trousers. With a quick brush, a squirt of perfume, and a wave of mascara, I'm done in record time.

I descend the stairs with far more elegance than I had going up them. "Will?"

There he is in the lounge, crouched by the fish tank, peering through the slight fuzz of green glass to locate the aquatic resident. "Magnificent!" he says, turning toward me.

"Oh." That was unexpected. "Well, you look nice too." I glance at my reflection in the aquarium glass and try not to smile ridiculously.

"No, no, I mean the fish. Lionfish, isn't it?"

Oh. Uh. Awkward. Smile and move on.

"Yes, that's right. He's Sergeant Bob Whipple."

"What?"

"Sergeant Bob Whipple. That's his name. Bob Whipple. I like the sound of it."

He looks from Bob to me. Oh God, he thinks I'm deranged.

"And the 'Sergeant' bit?"

"Oh, call it an army brat's fancy. Besides, Bob's a militant little bastard so it suits him. He's eaten every poor little clown fish I've introduced into the tank. He looks slow and graceful, but he lies in wait and swallows them whole."

"Unusual." He crosses to the sofa, and I see now that he has tidied the coffee table. The scripts, set designs, photocopies of immigration applications that usually litter the coffee table, each with their attendant tea ring — my official stamp — have been neatly sorted into stacks. *Ground, open sesame!*

He has found plates and laid the cakes out on them on the cleaned table.

"Nice place."

"I share it with my brother, but he is away a lot. He stays at his girlfriend's," I say, perching on the sofa. I look around the room, suddenly noticing for the first time the balls of fluff nesting under the TV cabinet and the film of dust coating the screen. "All this mess is his. My brother's. He really is such a slob." I'm lying, of course. "Actually, I'm boycotting the housework until Leo does it."

"I like a place to look lived in. It tells me far more about you than you imagine."

"Oh?" I dread to think.

"You should see your face! Don't worry, I'm not some Freud wannabe, but I think a lived-in house shows you have more to live for than being a domestic goddess. And believe me, that's not a bad thing."

"Is Melissa a domestic goddess?" I ask without knowing where the question came from. I really don't want to know about Melissa, so why am I throwing her in here?

He shifts forward, looks surprised, and then he steeples his strong hands, lacing his fingers together as he pauses for a moment to think. His index fingers lean against the dark valley between his nostrils and full lips.

"Melissa enjoys that type of thing. She likes a lot of coordination, Giada recipes, Martha Stewart crafts…and those decorative cushions. Bloody cushions. Pillows, she call them. Pillows! I've explained that pillows you sleep on and cushions decorate the sofa, but to her, they are all 'pillows.' Jesus, you should see what she has done to my bed. I have to mount a full-scale expedition over cushion mountain to actually find somewhere to sleep at night."

We share the laugh.

"Cushions don't excite you?" I ask with a tilt of the head.

"Honestly, that sort of thing is nice, but it takes too much time. I'd rather be performing, or writing or reading. Don't tell me you think differently."

I can feel my smile grow. *It's a fair cop, Guv.* "I prioritize. I have to. Ashtead won't run itself, and there is so much to be done there. It needs far more than the touch of a domestic goddess. In truth, the theater needs those people from *Extreme Makeover*!"

"So in saving the future of theater—" he nudges me jovially "—you can't have much time for friends and family. Do you get to see them much?"

"I see them when I can. Okay, probably not often enough. Lucy—she's my best friend—works abroad a lot. It's ideal, really. If she lived here, she'd be sick to death with me always postponing. Mum and Dad pop in when they haven't seen me for a while, to check that I haven't starved or been eaten by feral badgers."

Another nudge. "What about other friends?"

"It's hard to find time for everyone and everything." I shrug, disowning my friendlessness.

"Except for work and wine, right?"

I smile and half laugh with him, but something about that strikes me as very sad. This is getting altogether too deep and introspective.

"Best check on the kettle. Water should be boiling by now." I rise and so does he.

"Enna, this is going to sound odd, but don't you think sometimes fate puts you in the path of people for a reason? I mean, like some kismet thing. I haven't been able to stop thinking about how weird it is that we are both on the same course: performers, linked with Ashtead, and now both on a transatlantic track. I think we were supposed to meet, perhaps to help each other get through this immigration thing. I don't know."

"Well, it is nice to know there is someone who understands what a pain in the arse it is!"

"Here, here to that! Jesus, the money! Can you believe how expensive it is?"

"I know! It is a racket, isn't it? Seriously put me off the whole business!" I volley back lightheartedly.

He seems to catch my comment and hold it for a while. He furrows his brow and tilts his head toward me. "You know, Enna, I really hope you don't think me out of line, but why *are* you going?"

The laughter and the smiles cease. *You know why I'm going.*

"What do you mean?" The water bubbling up the sides of the kettle rumbles faintly. *Why did you have to go and ruin a perfectly nice chat?*

"I mean why, when you obviously love Ashtead, would you give it up? I'm not sure I would, in your position."

"Well, you're not me, are you?" I say, a little rankled, my cheeks burning.

"No. Sorry, I didn't mean to hit a nerve."

I can hear the water boiling fast now.

"It's just, you've hardly said a word about your fiancé. Is the visa thing really more for work?"

Bam! The bullet surfs through flesh, muscle, cartilage, surging through to the core, searing tissue, and sending impulses racing to my very fingertips; his question nails me. And I know my mum taught me better than this, I know he is practically a stranger and should be treated with kindness, but this really, *really* irks me.

"How dare you. How very bloody dare you. I'm giving up everything to be with Cole. My theater, my house, family, friends, well, friend. If you think I am doing it for an easy pass into the States, to start from scratch as a theater no one, well, you don't know me at all." I look him in the eye and march from the room.

I take a deep breath to recover my composure. Oh shit! He didn't really deserve that, did he? After all, what had he actually said that was so insulting? That I don't go around wearing an "I heart Cole" badge? And now I've jumped off the deep end, and he thinks I'm a nutcase with only one friend and, apparently, no cleaner.

I pour the water and watch the tea leaves waltz.

In some wild minute of fantasy, it occurs to me that he is looking for proof—Will is an undercover embassy agent for the Department of Homeland Security, charged with the task of weeding out the fraudulent fiancées! That's how he found me. I am being surveilled and investigated—that's why he's asking me these questions! I knew the embassy was vigilant, but this?

Chapter 6

The minute elapses and the fantasy fades. I can't imagine the embassy wasting man power on me. I'm hardly Mata Hari.

"Enna, look—" he rounds the doorway "—I really didn't mean to offend you. And you're right."

I am?

"I shouldn't assume that just because we are emigrating actors that we think the same. I don't know you at all, really. I suppose I just feel as if I do."

The steam rises in my face. I feel embarrassed and childish and, adding to the glow of what now must be strawberry cheeks, oddly flattered.

"Come on," he says, "let's start over. Have some tea, a bite of cake, and I'll read you the review."

"Okay. Sounds good. I'm sorry. This visa thing has me all on edge. I'm not usually this bonkers, honestly." And we both smile and accept the last few minutes of awkwardness over a cup of tea. How very English we are.

It is, I'll admit, so lovely to chat to someone interested in everything. I mean, it's completely harmless—we are both thoroughly, blissfully in love with other people—but it is still…exciting. And it's not that I'm a narcissist or self-obsessed — am I? — only, it's rather nice to have someone actually ask questions, someone who actually listens to the answers, who doesn't cut off my sentences because I'm too loud or rambling. This man actually looks at me while he's listening.

And he *is* listening to me. My brain buzzes as the cogs turn, trying to find intelligent responses to his unpredictable topics. He enthuses about his theater tours, politics, Darwin and evolution, theories of humans evolving from aquatic apes, of meteors causing mass extinction, and as I sit, nursing my cup of tea, I tingle.

Granddad would have liked this man. Wait. What did I think? Did I really just think that? *Enna, seriously, you are not some fickle fifteen-year-old! You are a committed, visa-toting, emerald-gilded fiancée with responsibilities.*

"I'll phone in the week," he calls, making a run for his car.

I stand at the door, waving him off, the curtain of rain falling fast in big fat drops that explode on the pavement and make the puddles dance with ripples.

My eager waving ceases, my smile retracts, and I re-lock the door. He's gone. I'm deflated. *Jesus, Enna! No more of that. You can't. I won't let you do this. He is just an actor. You are bound to have things in common with him. Stop making more of it than it is.*

I must pack! Yes, pack I must. I run upstairs to start the dreaded process — one I had been putting off. Now that the visa has been approved, I have no excuse not to. None.

I may not be able to find Narnia, but I can sure as hell find refuge in my closet. I heave two cases, fit to burst, downstairs and leave them in the hall. Maybe there they will inspire some bravery to seize new opportunities; then, I can shake this cowardice or guilt or doubt, or whatever it is, whatever is inching over me.

The tea things stare at me from the cleaned coffee table: the plates smeared with luscious trails of vermillion jam, daubs of melted éclair chocolate, glistening crystals of sugar, the cups with the dregs of stone cold tea.

"I'm going! You can't stop me," I tell the crockery. "So you might as well wipe that smug smile off your plate!" And with great over-efficiency and much clattering, I stack tea things. China chinks against china. The teaspoon hits the sink with a reverberating ring. The washing-up liquid plodges out of the bottle. I open the tap wider to force the gush of water faster and louder, but the soundtrack to domesticity cannot drown out the internal monologue Self is desperate to have.

Stop thinking! Just stop! He's just a man. An actor. You've met plenty of those before. Naturally, we have a lot in common. That's to be expected. And, okay, I am mature enough to admit that there may be a little frisson of something, if we were not attached to others. But we are. That is that. It doesn't mean I can't like him as a person. I turn off the tap, seize the tea towel, and rub the plates so thoroughly the pattern might come off.

Jesus, Enna! This is not a Disney film. The candlestick and the teapot do not talk, and however much you rub them, no magic genie will appear! I am going mad.

I grab the telephone and hope that a human voice will reaffirm my hold on sanity.

"So, what are you telling me? You met some bloke yesterday and now you've got cold feet?"

"Frostbite. Don't sugarcoat it. You do think I'm being—"

"An arse. Yes."

Good old Lucy. Nothing like a good verbal slap to get one's head out of one's—

"Arsehole. I love you, but that's what you're being."

"Uh." My chest sinks back into its place. The mirror above the telephone table captures my deflation.

"Enna, isn't it convenient timing to suddenly meet a potential someone?"

"Bloody inconvenient, if you ask me."

"Going to America is a big step. You're bound to be nervous. Look, maybe you should step back. What do I know?"

"So what? What are you saying? I *should* step back?" the reflection in the mirror asks, desperately poised for the verdict.

Excruciatingly long pause.

"Enna, here's what I think: you met this man yesterday, who you might well be very suited to, but, hello! He is engaged to another woman, and he is moving to be with her! What the fuck? Get a grip."

Oh. I had forgotten that. *How could you forget that?*

"And, what's more, I think this whole process has made you forget how much you adore Cole. Reminder: You do. It's a big thing to commit to one person, and you're so friggin' indecisive that you are always going to wonder if you are making the right decision."

"Or whether there is someone better just waiting around the corner," the lips in the glass say quietly.

"What? I didn't hear that," she says brusquely, as though she is finished and has other things to be getting on with — a lunch date, an article deadline.

"Nothing. Look, better go. Thanks for the therapy. Speak soon."

She doesn't challenge the staccato parting, and I replace the receiver thoughtfully.

If anyone knew me better than Mum and Dad, it was Lucy. For well-balanced, unbiased, informed opinion, ask Lu. After all, we have been friends for over twenty years and I know her! I know about her first snog, first fumble, first hangover, first legover. I know that she cried during *Titanic* but will never admit it. I know that during our fourteenth summer, she pretended to have her period every week to get out of swimming class. I know about the flirtation with her editor. I know she snores. I know this. She knows I know this, and she knows similar secrets about me. It's an unspoken blackmail, but it's okay because I also love her.

It was my first day at St. Catherine's when we met. Lucy had already been there for two years and knew everyone and everything. She was undoubtedly the prettiest girl in the year, with her luminous pink Alice band crowning her blond hair, her perfect white teeth and her golden tan. She was a catalog child, even in a hideous gingham shirt, bottle green tunic, and beige socks. I was new, pale and gawky, and didn't know anyone.

Miss Calgate, the sports mistress, used our first lesson to check through our gym kits, checking off that every item on the school list was present, labeled, and initialed. I didn't impress her with my lack of organization, but all was there in some form or another: pleated sports skirt and tracksuit — hand-me-downs from our neighbor — sports shirt, an interesting shade of chewing gum from many washings; acrylic, scratchy, green athletic pants — from the school secondhand shop; and my prized possession — the one thing Mum had bought me new — the Dunlop-green flash trainers.

Lined up against the Reeboks, the Addidas, and the Nike Air, my trainers made of canvas did look different, but I was still proud of them; they were new!

Shona Harris was kitted in far better labels. Not that I knew that at eight years old, but I believed what she told me. She smirked at my footwear and, when Miss Calgate was out of sight, threw one of my green and white canvas shoes up above the eight-foot lockers. I remember I felt my cheeks burn with rage and embarrassment, and my eyes prick with tears. I jumped futilely to retrieve the missile, listening to the sound of Shona Harris's hissing laugh.

I made clownish remarks all the while — that actually I enjoyed jumping or somesuch twaddle — determined not to give Shona the satisfaction of knowing that I was upset, and eventually she grew bored of my pathetic kangarooing and left the locker room.

Lucy walked in to find me red-faced and thoroughly miserable. "What happened to you?"

"Shona threw my trainer up there, and they're new, and I can't reach it." I tried really hard not to cry — I didn't want to be labeled on the first day as the class crybaby.

"Where?"

"Up there."

"Oh. Okay." And Lucy took the red and black secondhand hockey stick in my locker and effortlessly hooked my trainer on its cashew-nut end. "Here you go."

"Thanks!" I managed a smile, so relieved to be reunited with my shoe and that someone had helped me.

"And don't worry about Shona. She does that kind of thing to any girl who is prettier than her."

I remember feeling so unbelievably, inexhaustibly thrilled that this beauty would say something so nice. She must think that I am pretty!

"And besides, she's a complete turd sandwich, and you don't want to be friends with her anyway; you want to be friends with me."

"Okay," I said, even more thrilled that, not only had she called me pretty and suggested I be her friend, but she'd just said "turd sandwich"!

Through the rapidly passing years of different universities, different adventures, different professions, we always came back, and it was as if we had seen each other yesterday.

Now working for *Foreigner's Friend*, Lu traveled around the globe, writing, fulfilling her dreams. And here I am…fulfilling mine.

Sort of.

I look into the mirror above the telephone table and smooth out the creases puckering on my brow. *Relax. Lu's right, this doesn't mean anything. Will's taken. I'm taken. Get a grip.*

The theater is already abuzz with nervous energy. The volunteers are getting the tea, coffee, and ice creams ready, like so many mother hens; I've stocked the shoe-string bar and folded the programs. I can hear the usual premature hen-flapping as I work in the office, trying to concentrate on the involved PRS forms. I calculate the royalties for using just a snippet of the *Neighbours* theme tune in last season's production of *Romeo and Juliet*. Oh, the large price tag for such a short-lived burst of modern musical irony.

I have yet to write the press release for the paper, notes to the cast, and on and on. Just writing the to-do list makes me feel exhausted, but the purpose, the adrenaline of creating something, keeping the theater alive, is energizing too. Life without work would be unthinkable.

My mobile sings operatically from my pocket. The long number takes up the entire screen. It must be Cole. It must be important for him to call the mobile, not the landline—I know he gets stung by international calls—and paranoia strikes: maybe he's intercepted some traitorous telepathy. Maybe he knows that I ate cakes and drank tea with someone who cannot be pigeonholed into the family and friends slots. *That's ridiculous! I'm ridiculous! I haven't done or said anything wrong!* Yet my stomach churns.

"Hello?"

"Little pickle! How are you?"

"Good." I shuffle the papers on my desk, more for sound illustration than for news reader efficiency. "Busy here with the show, but the newspaper review was generous."

"You are a directorial genius!" Will's words echo around in my head.

"And now I'm about to give notes to the cast before tonight's show."

"So the show went well then? You didn't tell me anything."

"Yes, sorry, just, you know…busy, and I was absolutely exhausted last night."

"I understand, sweetie. When you live here, you can relax and sleep all day if you want to! I can't wait for you to arrive. I looked at flights, and Newark is looking cheapest, then Philly."

My stomach — ever the first responder — flips, twists, and triple salchows. *Enna, get a grip, get-a-grip, getagrip!*

"Don't worry about the cost anyway. Just pick whatever is easiest for you."

Easy? What a fucking joke. Nothing about this easy. *Enna, you knew this was coming.*

"Sweetie?"

"Sorry, yes. What?"

"Dates. When are you coming?"

"Er…not sure yet."

"Well, do it soon, right?"

The auditorium fills with noise as the audience bustles in, recognizes familiar faces, and hullooh's over the rows in loud, robust theatrical voices. We've kept the traditions — I insisted on that — and, at eight o'clock, the crackling record spins, silencing the rambunctious crowd.

"God save our gracious Queen…"

I have it on CD and minidisc, of course, but there is something authentically Ashtead about the record player. I only wish it had been an ornate gramophone. I whisper the words under my breath as I type away in the office, *"Long to reign over us, God save our Queen!"* And I work on waiting for the hubbub to start up again at curtain call, the audience sweeping through the aisles and out on the street, just like the tide.

I love my theater, from the worn, red-velvet flip-back seats to the faded, draped velvet curtains. I remember when I was eight years old, Mum taking Leo and me to the theater to see our first play, *My Giddy Aunt.* The whole week leading up to the performance, I was on pins.

Dressed in my favorite lilac dress and matching Clarks sandals, we walked to the theater. The outside was strung with fairy lights, and people stood politely sipping glasses of wine, their programs in hand, waiting for the clock to chime. My eyes were agog; there was so much to see! I recall being mesmerized by all the ladies who looked so glamorous, their rouged faces and red-tipped nails, little fingers raised, wafting and twinkling through the air as though conducting their own orchestrated speech.

When the clock chimed eight o'clock, the drum roll rattled, and the crackling record spun into action. Everyone around me stood up and held their heads high as the anthem resounded. Mum sang in her operatic voice. Leo glowed nectarine red, looking away to disown his obvious parentage, and so I took the cue and sang as loudly as possible, just to embarrass him more. *"Send her victorious, happy and glorious."*

The curtains opened and the play began. I can't remember the plot, only being completely inspired. The actresses all so beautiful, even the ugly ones. The actors so manly, even in knitted cardigans.

When the curtain fell, I applauded so hard and so long that my red-hot palms ached. I was wide-eyed, high on the luster of the greasepaint, the suspense of the storyline, the slick of sweat and real, live action. I was hooked.

Anxious to prolong the spell, I begged Mum to let me wait at the stage door and get a deeper glimpse into this new, magical world.

I stood in the dark passage, my insides knotted, hopping from one foot to the other, waiting for someone to let me in. Agonizingly, the door was not closed firmly on its latch, but left leaning against its doorjamb, buffeted by the occasional breeze. I knew these scenes were not for my eyes, but I couldn't help myself. I spied through the crack. Bodies and flesh and uncovered limbs bathed in bright light. The wind blew and the door swung open just for a second, just long enough to step back into the shadows and see the whole golden animated scene. The reflections of just a neck and chin, an arm and a shoulder, a lip and nose, bronzed body parts, amputated by the angle of the light bulb-topped mirrors. The voices were loud, heckles back and forth, as if witnessing an ad hoc pantomime.

"And Alec forgot the line about the salt and pepper!"

"Oh, no, I didn't!"

"Oh, yes, you did!"

I saw tissues thick with tan foundation, fisted into sullied snowballs and tossed limply to the floor. The caked makeup, the graying moustache, the curly blond wig, the sun-blush fishnet stockings, all peeled off—the show within a show witnessed illicitly by an eight-year-old voyeur.

Fast footfalls click-clacked on the cement, and suddenly Mum's intense stare zoomed into focus. "Come on, darling! How long does it take to ask for an autograph?"

With my pen and program in one hand and white-knuckle nerves in the other, I knocked on the stage door and was invited backstage. The actors stopped mid-peel and turned their attentions to the gangly, freckle-faced girl beaming with excitement and waving a pen in their direction. They asked who I was, what I thought of the play, would I be coming next week.

Would I be coming next week? Try for the next twenty years!

But a lot had changed in the intervening years between audience member and theater director: the season had gotten shorter, the ticket prices higher, the red velvet duller. Now, the sad striations of pale pink in the pleats of the curtains revealed how old and tattered Ashtead had become.

Age is cruel, I think, making my way from the now empty auditorium to the equally vacant bar. I put my four pounds fifty in the till and pour myself a large glass of Chateau Crap.

Maybe Cole was right. I ought to forget it. There was only so much one person could do with a limited budget. Shaky sets, moldy costumes, and incompetent actors — this was not the topflight theater I was trained for. Hell, it wasn't even middle.

"You can't fight the tide," he had told me.

I was so eager to prove everyone wrong, that DVDs or an endless menu of televisual treats were no match for live theater! It didn't matter that at home, one could fart and scratch and press pause to visit the loo; one could order in and cheaply enjoy a delicious and entertaining evening; one could get front row seating and see every minute flaw in high definition. Surely that convenience could not compete with Thea-ate-tor?

But audiences *have* dwindled, costs *have* skyrocketed, and there's not a thing I can do about it. I am not Moses. I swirl the cool glass in my palm. I've failed.

"Drinking alone?"

"Wha—?" I turn so quickly I practically fall off my stool.

"Sorry, didn't mean to startle you," he says walking toward me, straightening his amused grin. I ought to strangle Maureen for not locking the foyer door.

Here he is again. Will. Swathed in his scarf of gray.

$$Chapter\ 7$$

"**W**hat are you doing here?" I ask incredulously. *Stop being delighted. Stop being delighted!*

"I came to see your play," he announces casually, taking up the stool next to me.

Huh. Okay, that's reasonable. Surprising, but reasonable. Why wouldn't an actor come to a theater to see a play after all?

"And, for the record, the *Chronicle* reporter was correct. The director is a genius!"

Fast follow up and flattery — *is this okay?*

"Thanks for coming, but I think we both know that is too generous."

"I don't think so. The audience should feel uncomfortable. The whole point of Lear," he says, filling the small bar with his Shakespearian tones, "is to show how, through arrogance and greed, man can go from seemingly having it all, to having nothing. It is through his suffering that he is redeemed and discovers what is truly important. And even though he has this epiphany, he still loses."

"Nice explanation, Lord Olivier," I say, quickly taking another sip, "but I want people to enjoy themselves, not go home and gouge out their—" Hand! His hand is on my hand; I can feel it—the warm drumstick of his thumb! I glance down, but he continues, oblivious to the shockwaves rippling up my goose-pimpled arm.

"People know what they are in for when they book the tickets."

I hate that my mutinous skin responds in this way. Red alert messages pulse from my brain, but I can't pull my hand away. Oh God, am I enjoying this innocently erotic touch? I can even feel the hunk of emerald sandwiched between my hand and his, reminding me, warning him.

"They aren't expecting perky *Mary Poppins*. A good play makes the audience feel." He squeezes my hand casually under his and swivels on the barstool to face me.

Breathe. *He's an actor. He is just being friendly.*

"When I left the auditorium this evening, everyone was talking about it. One lady was in tears, saying she ought to call her estranged daughter. That's a reaction. You're not going to stop the world, but you can pause it for a brief moment and allow people to reflect. That is what you want as a director." Will leans forward — Oh Christ! — and I sit back. He takes a glass from the hanging rack. "May I?"

"Sure."

He pours the bottle and takes a sip from the glass. I'm relieved to be wrong — that he's placing his lips to the glass and not me, to have been saved from the embarrassment of having to tell him, in no uncertain terms, that I am an engaged lady.

"I have a guest book," he continues. "I ask the audience to write their own review. I can find out what worked and what didn't, and it has helped me evolve the show. Perform, adapt, evolve. Take Shakespeare: most everyday people on the street would hear the verse and be completely put off. But, if you can translate it in a language people understand, then they can appreciate the story, the meaning behind it. Your *King Lear* was visionary. You could have played it safely, traditionally, but you took chances."

His enthusiasm lights up his face. The chocolate of his eyes burns amber; it's bewitching.

I must think of something to say. "So, with your show, you're really just paraphrasing Shakespeare. You're a plagiarist!"

He laughs, taking another sip of wine. "That's harsh! But fair. I like to think I'm spreading Shakespeare to ears and brains that wouldn't usually be interested. That is why I've toured to so many schools."

"I wish we could appeal to ears and brains in Ashtead. This time next week, the house will almost be empty. I don't have the money or the time to keep this afloat. Within two years, there'll be twelve-story luxury apartments standing here, and there is nothing I can do to stop it."

The wine fridge starts to hum.

"There might be something we can do. Leave it with me. Got to catch the last train. Best be off." He drains his glass, gets to his feet and disappears as stealthily as he had entered.

Thoughts fire like harpoons across my brain. "Something we can *do*." What *something?* What *we?* We only met yesterday and now *we* can *do* something? I swirl the golden liquid, swooshing it up the sides of the glass. *He's just being nice. He's an artist; naturally he wants to help.*

The liquid whirlpool subsides. I never invited him. In fact, I didn't invite him to my home either. Or give him my address. Did I mention where I lived? But he stayed there, of course, when the house was digs for the visiting actors. That was it! No big mystery.

I swirl the wine in the other direction. Oh God, why does he have to be so interesting and exciting? I don't need any interest or excitement. I need rock solid Cole. Perhaps I'm tired and emotional — there, that's it. I am missing Cole and that is why a handhold is suddenly making me weak-kneed. Nothing more.

Anyway, even if he did want to help, I must not rely on the kindness of strangers. I must look to myself. And maybe there is something I can do before I leave for America, something to buoy up the ship. I'll find some way to leave with a few of my ambitions still afloat, one last hurrah! I'll phone Cole. Yes, tomorrow, when I have thought it through rationally, I will telephone my fiancé and discuss business! He's a great business brain. He can be interesting and exciting too.

Even at six a.m. his time, his voice chirps out of its morning fog when he hears it is me.

"Pickle!" I can hear him shaving, the slick slice of the razor glancing close by the ear piece.

"I'll phone back, just wanted to bounce ideas and see if they travel."

"No need. So what if I show up at work with odd socks or my dick hanging out of my pants. We have to save your theater!"

As little as he knows of theater, Cole is receptive to my business ideas. *See, Enna, he's very supportive!* Of course, I'm not quite convinced of whether he's indulging me because he thinks my ideas make great business sense, or just because he loves me, but I'll take the encouragement either way! I pour my runaway stream of thoughts into his ear, and he manages to find positive aspects about everything, suggesting that grants and loans would be the normal business route; although charity fundraisers and auctions—a fun addition to build awareness—would raise funds too. Sound, sensible, reliable advice.

Loans, though. Eek! The very thought of using money that is not technically mine has always sat uncomfortably with me. It may not be as business-like, but a ritzy glitzy, celebrity fundraiser seems a fun and far more appealing idea.

Perhaps I can mastermind some fantastic event, calling on celebrities to support live, local theater. I will be the Bob Geldof, Sting, or Bono of the theatrical world, calling on the public to take a stand. Forget your convenience takeaways, your DVDs, iPods, computers, and gyms, people! Come to the theater and help feed a starving population of actors and actresses. Save this endangered habitat!

I could ask celebrities to donate their help: answer telephones, perform skits, sing songs. Dame Judy! Emma Thompson! Kate Winslet! I would send out press releases and invite the media, perhaps a royal or two—they like the arts—or maybe Victoria Beckham or Fergie. Fergie will come to anything if there's a finger sandwich. Donations will come flooding in; the public would pay large sums for tickets to this black-tie gala event. The evening would be a sellout success! The profile of the theater would rise. The queen would hear of my efforts striving to save my beloved pile of bricks, preserving its history forevermore, and would knight me, Dame Enna Petersen! Sound trumpets!

Or perhaps, we could do a combination of the two? Theatre-Aid and an eensy teensy loan? That would be an excellent budget for the theater to work with. I will not have been a failure and would have secured a large chunk of cash for the theater's future. It's a better position than right now; that is for certain.

The telephone rings, and my knighthood vanishes in front of my eyes.

"Hi. Will here." It's Will. Will here. Will, here? I look around the office, half expecting him to suddenly leap from the stationery cupboard or the corridor. "About last night, I've been thinking and I've had an idea."

"Where are you?" I ask, fumbling across the desk for my open handbag, grappling for a lip-gloss, a hairbrush, a mint.

"Actually, I'm just round the corner."

Thank God, I think, slouching back in my chair.

"And I was wondering if you had a moment or two for me to stop in?"

I *knew* it! This man pops up more often than a toaster. "I've been working on ideas myself, but I'm getting a bit stir-crazy. How about I meet you in the Starbucks on High Street in five minutes?"

"Enna! C'mon, support the little man. Not the faceless machine! Ever been to the little coffee house by the pond, just down from the rec?"

I suppress a laugh. Lord, it's been years since I have even thought of the rec—the recreational area, the park. Scene of grazed knees and one bloody lip; where I had got drunk as a teenager and made a complete arse of myself; where I had been chased by girls who wanted to punch me for something or other. Lower Ashtead, a part I had forgotten existed, really. Huh. I hadn't been there in over a decade.

"Sure. I know it. I can meet you there."

Will sits in the corner on the comfy sofa seats. BeaNtific is more homey than the generic beige High Street chain. There are family photos on the back wall, and the whole place has a distinctly home-made air. Baked cookies of irregular shapes line the counter like fat, little jellyfish. The chalk board boasts today's specials: roasted veggie panini, curried parsnip soup, lime chocolate cheesecake. I should come to Lower Ashtead more often.

He springs up as I approach. His dark stubble has grown thick overnight, giving him a swarthy, intense look.

"Ahoy there!" I drop my handbag to the floor and myself to the seat. His eyes travel upward, slowly taking in the brown boots, skimming my stockings, over the curves of my fluted teal skirt, the swells of the chocolate brown cowl neck, resting at my face. He's looking—unabashedly looking—and I don't know how I feel about this. I mean, he shouldn't be looking *that* long. Should he? Although, this *is* a rather lovely outfit, and hell, just because I'm engaged doesn't mean other people can't look at me.

Okay, I admit it; I rather like his approval.

"Hi! Glad you could make it."

"It's good to get out of the office."

"Great. Good. Well, I've been giving this a lot of thought since last night. Our conversation gave me a great deal to think about. And however inconvenient the timing for both of us, I think I've just got to come out and say it."

Little drums beat rapid fire.

"There's no denying we have an awful lot in common—"

Accompanied by trumpets and flutes and the whole string section.

"You and your theater have struck a chord in me, and now I am really torn—"

My internal soundtrack swells to a jubilant crescendo.

"But, I've decided. I'm going to postpone the move to perform my show at your theater."

My hands drop into my lap. The string section scratches to a halt. "Perform your show?" The words are difficult for me to swallow; the goiter is back. Why is it so impossible for me to say what I think?

Because you can't. Because it hurts people. Smile sweetly and suck it up, babycakes.

"Hmm…that's a thought," I manage to say.

"I could perform at Ashtead for a month or two, inviting all the schools in the Surrey area and surrounding counties."

I sit speechless.

"Well? What do you think?"

What do I think? I don't know what to think. It's unexpected. It's not Bob Geldof. Or Bono. "But we haven't the money to pay you."

"Come on, Enna! You need to establish a niche. It's staring you in the face. I'm staring you in the face. Me. I've got no tours lined up for a while; you need something fresh that will sell at the theater. It's kismet! What with the money you'll make from *The Shakespearian Rap,* you can afford to employ a small company. Then you can really put that directorial genius to good use." He perches on the edge of the sofa, grasping my hands in his.

"But the board? They are traditionalists."

"Then it's our job to open their eyes. Anyway, they booked me for one show back in two thousand and two. The show is much better now. I'm so much better. What are you waiting for? Do you want your theater to be knocked down, or do you want to save it?"

I'm thinking. I'm thinking it sounds ideal. It sounds great. It sounds like a future.

"Come on! It's a challenge," he says, still gripping my hands, "and together, we can be unstoppable!" His words strengthen my resolve. We *could* do this. This really *could* work.

An excited smile plays on my lips, before I recall, "But, Will, I'm due to leave at the end of the month. I can't commit any more time than the next two weeks."

"Well, don't go."

A laugh escapes before I realize he's not joking. "Don't be silly. I can't not go."

"Why?" The question hangs between us.

"Well…because I'm going. Because I got my visa. Because I promised."

"But you don't have to." His eyes flood mine. "It is *your* choice. Don't go. Stay." He grabs my hand tighter, holding it aloft like a microphone between us, waiting to pick up the next anticipated line.

I see his lips move, the notes of words floating through the air to my awaiting ears. They seep deep, vibrating into my bones: the anvil, the hammer, the tiny stirrup, and into the cochlea, beating the cilia, generating an electro-chemical signal which tunnels into my brain. I think my head might explode — the frequency too dangerous for my brain to compute. These words, this blasphemous idea, goes against my programming and my promises. I'm hard-wired to be dutiful, but to Cole or to the theater?

"You make it sound so easy. But it's not, Will. I want to help the theater as much as I can before I go, but I can't stay. You know that."

"Because you love him?"

"Yes," I say without hesitation, and it's true. I do love him. And, yes, it's true I can't explain away this chocolate-coated chemistry, this theatrical connection, but shit! Cole and I have made plans! I've spent hours dangling from a transatlantic telephone line, listening to the man who loves me more than anything, listening about the life that awaits me — the exciting *Dynasty* life. But why is my stomach in spasm? Why does Will sitting inches from me make me feel like a Catholic before confession? I haven't done anything wrong.

He lets my hand free-fall and stands abruptly. "God! I'm offering you a chance to help you achieve something…your dream, and you're leaving?" He takes a stride, pauses, and turns back. "You say you love him. Maybe you do, but I see you, Enna. I *see* you, and I don't think he could make you happy."

I look into the intense stare blazing down on me and blink incredulously. Is this happening? Is this *really* happening? I rise slowly, stalling to breathe and not let my temper get the better of me. "Well. That's just great. Super. I'm so pleased you shared. Thing is, Will, you don't really know anything about me. Christ! We've known each other for how long? Forty-eight hours? And you have the gall to judge and make assumptions about me? Well you can keep it, because I don't need your charity, and I sure as hell don't need you playing Oprah with my love life."

His nostrils flare. "Oh, for God's sake, it's not charity. I'm trying to do you a favor."

"I can manage on my own, thank you."

"Sure you can! You're doing a great job."

I flinch at his sarcasm, but grit my teeth. "Why are you doing this?"

He shakes his head.

I can't read him. "Why are you here? Why do you care?"

He sucks the air through his teeth and lets out a sigh. "Why do you think, Enna?"

"Oh, don't give me riddle bullshit! Answer me!"

He shoulders his backpack but says nothing.

"You think I want to abandon my theater?"

"Well, you're not trying very hard to save it."

"Bullshit, bullshit, bullshit! I'm doing everything I can; I have done everything I can for the last five years, and I'm tired. I will give my theater a fighting chance, but I can't put my life on hold. I have to go."

"Go then."

"I will."

His eyes flame and he shakes his head. "Fine. If that's your decision, so be it." And he exits BeaNtific.

Silent suspended seconds pass as I stand, disbelieving, before slowly the other noises creep in and I become aware of mugs of steaming lattes and café mochas frozen in mid-air, their drinkers poised, watching me. Haven't I acted in this scene before? When another man asked me to change my plotline in front of an audience of eager faces?

The milk frother whirrs and gurgles into action, and our audience resumes their muffin nibbling, reading, and crosswords.

Chapter 8

I march back to the theater, charging from one emotional extreme to the next. First anger, then indignation, then confusion, then sorrow.

I look at the photograph of Cole on my desk. Happiness beams from his face. His big, bear-like arms wrap completely around me, like some man-made papoose. And I'm smiling. Really smiling, not a wide-eyed shot for the camera, but a joyful, goofy, toothy smile. Yes, this is the man, different from me, but who makes me laugh and laugh.

He had been floating in my pool. Well, not mine per se, but out of season, I was the only one who used it, so therefore, it was mine. I heard the noise first and looked over the balcony to see the great chunk of a man splashing about, not even swimming but frolicking in *my* pool. I grabbed my towel, book, and cocktail and ran down the stairs to defend my territory.

I took up surveillance from the sun lounger, pretending to read whilst keeping one shaded eye on the intruder in the waters. He loped from the pool, shaking himself off like a Saint Bernard dog, before plunging into the Jacuzzi opposite. He did have an amazing stature; that, I suppose, I would allow him.

"Hey! You French Canadian?"

I peered at the voice over the tops of my glasses and down my English nose. "Excuse me?"

"French Canadian?" he shouted louder over the bubbles of the Jacuzzi, as if all French Canadians must be deaf. Then he did this bizarre chicken flap with his arms as if to illustrate, but his flap slapped the waters and splashed my face with hot, chlorinated water.

My hand leapt to my wet face, knocking off my sunglasses, releasing my book which crashed into my cocktail, smashing the glass and juice over the thick, cream, library-borrowed pages. I was devastated by this domino rally of disaster.

He must have seen the look of wild horror in my eyes as he flew out of the spa to my side. "Sorry. No, I mean, *merci*," he stuttered as he mopped the sodden pages with his own towel. He blotted each wet page with such care and attention. "It might be a bit sticky for a while, but it should be okay," he said, miming actions to accompany his lines. He had this beatific smile.

And I suddenly looked at myself. *What a complete arse,* I thought, stifling a laugh. But he saw and he started to laugh, so I laughed more. In fact, we both laughed more, and we laughed so hard that I lost my balance. In the milliseconds of teetering, fingers splayed, trying to catch the air, I caught him instead and pulled him with me. There we were, on the paving around the pool, sticky with orange juice, attracting the insect life of Florida and laughing like teenagers. He stretched for his camera nestling in his belongings on the neighboring lounger, flicked a dial, and wrapped his arms around me, waiting for the green light to flash.

"I'm Cole."

"Well, Cole, I hate to tell you, but that was a library book."

"You're English!"

"And I'm Enna."

As the sun beat down on our backs, we sat side by side, dangling our legs in the pool. We talked about everything: places, people, experiences, The Beatles. We didn't feel the red sunburn spreading across our backs.

When Dad arrived poolside, eager to hurry me up for our last evening of drinks with our friends, I was sorry to leave and keen to stall him.

"Dad, this is Cole."

"Hi, Cole," replied my father. "Nice to meet you. We are off to meet friends at the bar around the corner. You should meet us for a drink later, if you like."

"I'd like to, but I offered to take my parents to the casino—you know how it is, but maybe I can swing by."

I couldn't help but feel disappointed. As I showered, perfumed, plucked, and preened, in the hope that he would change his plans, I replayed the poolside conversation, analyzing every nuance.

"Do you like The Beatles, or no?"

Or no!

"That towel's yours. This one's my-in."

My-in! His accent was so charming.

I paced my way to the bar with excited expectation, humming.

"Hey, chickadee, you look nice. What are you drinking?"

I loved evenings out with Dad's friends. There was always some outrageous anecdote being told, but that night, it was difficult to concentrate and keep my eyes from watching the door.

John was holding court at the bar. "So I told him, and I spoke slow, 'cause these French waiters have a problem with English, 'I want the seafood bisque.' Whaddya know, he brings a steak! 'Waiter, I didn't order this,' I says to him, and he replies, '*Oui*, it is so. You say, *I want zee fat beef steak.*'"

I prodded my daiquiri, gnawed my straw, and watched the quarters of the seemingly endless football game on the screen above the bar tick by. He wasn't coming, after all.

The animated coach on the screen called another time out.

Oh, dear God, shoot me!

"Hey. Sorry I'm late." His loud voice boomed heartily from the doorway.

"Not at all," replied Dad, before I could get a word in. "I'll do the introductions."

What did we talk about? I can't even remember. I just know it was non-stop. It was very easy. The football played on the TV overhead, and Cole explained the rules to me, which, of course, I vaguely knew, but pretended not to. Cole insisted on "catching up" and buying Dad shots of Jack Daniels.

After five steins of beer, several shots of Jack, and no dinner, Dad was starting to droop. The plan had been to eat after happy hour, but Cole had unexpectedly extended the happiness. When the game finally ended, I suggested taking Dad back to the apartment. So we walked under the bright night's sky, Dad rabbiting on as Cole and I walked silently on either side of him.

"That's Orion's belt? See? And that's Cassiopeia."

I chivvied Dad into bed and bid him goodnight, closing his door and neatly tripping across to the balcony where Cole was waiting.

I don't think either of us knew what to say or wanted to spoil the moment, so we just stood looking out over the bay. My stomach flipped with anticipation. The view was mesmerizing, the windows of light shimmering in the water below. He held out his hand and took mine in his. His hand was so big and warm; it covered mine like a mitten. It was dark on the balcony, but my eyes had adjusted and I could see Cole's chiseled face as I looked up at him. He must have felt my eyes on him, as he slowly turned, pulling my right arm gently, like an unrehearsed and slightly tentative dance move. He reeled me in, and I remember thinking that I fit so neatly into his warm body, with his strong arms enveloping me and my head nestling in the nook of his shoulder.

I was wrapped safely in his arms, watching the lights as another flicked off for the night. It felt like we had being standing for hours before he pulled backward, lifted my chin, and kissed me. Not an ardent, fumbling, rampant kiss, but a slow, lingering, passionate kiss, *A Brief Encounter*, 1940s black and white film kind of kiss. And some first kisses can be so anti-climactic, full of slurps and clashed teeth and god-awful "dear Lord what did you eat?" breath, but this was uniquely easy and unhurried. I could taste the faint whisper of whiskey, and it warmed me. How different, I thought, were the over-eager boys in their twenties from this self-assured, dexterous man in his thirties.

We clung on to the night, half-dreading the unstoppable morning, huddled together on the reclining sun lounger. The curve of my spine fit perfectly in the arch of his warm body, almost like two human monograms, a C curved around an E. With the shrill chorus of the cicadas in full serenade, accompanied by the palm leaves rustling like tinny maracas, we watched the balmy Floridian night disappear before our eyes.

I woke to the sounds of the waters breaking to see an ungainly brown pelican flapping upward to catch an air current, a telltale fishtail still frantically flapping between the lips of the bird's bulging beak. The poor plastic lounger creaked, and I could feel that Cole had woken too. I turned to study his sleepy face squinting into the light. He blinked a couple of times as if taking a second to recognize me before his handsome features creased into a smile.

"Hello," he greeted me, rubbing his sleep-fogged eyes.

"Hello," I replied, replacing my head on his chest and wishing that time could stop. I closed my eyes, determined to remember everything of this brief encounter: the sound of the palms, the waters, Cole's breathing, the unfamiliar squelch coming from beneath me…

"Cole?"

"Uh huh?"

"Cole. Is that…is that your stomach?"

And he looked so unbelievably sheepish and embarrassed—I could have just thrown my arms around him. "That noisy, huh? Well, I am pretty hungry. You think we can sneak out for breakfast? I know a great place…"

And there, on the last day of my holiday, without ever expecting it, we had found each other.

During the eight hour flight home, I didn't watch the movies or go to sleep, but replayed the conversations and remembered the feel of him. As the plane descended through the clouds and rattled and bumped its way along the landing strip, a fugitive tear escaped and ran down my cheek. *If only things were different, I might have been happy with him,* I thought.

Three hours later, back in my sardine-tin house, on my third cup of tea and second load of laundry, the doorbell rang. I answered the door and gasped. A huge bouquet of flowers decapitated the body standing in front of me.

"Ms. Petersen?" the voice from behind the flowers asked.

"Err. What? Yes. I mean, yes, that's me!"

"These are for you."

I took the bouquet carefully in both hands, scared to touch it—like holding a newborn baby.

The delivery man's head appeared from behind the blooms, and he smiled a toothy, yellow grin at me. "Someone must be in love with you!" He chuckled and hobbled back to his van.

The bouquet was sensational! Not a thin, limp, cellophane-wrapped bunch of carnations, but a big, fat, fragrant bouquet, bursting with stargazer lilies, ivory roses, fuchsia orchids, gerberas, twisted willow—a cinematic bouquet that nobody usually receives in real life. And they were for me! I gently propped the flowers up in the kitchen sink and removed the envelope. I slipped my index finger under the flap and lifted the card.

Who knows what the future will bring, but I hope mine includes you.

I said it back to myself, mimicking his accent, "I hope my-in includes you," and gave myself a hug.

This was a man who left me in no doubt that he wanted me. He wanted me!

How could I even contemplate turning my back on him?

And yet, can I cheat the theater out of this chance? Can't I please Cole and the theater? That's a compromise. A sensible, business solution.

Kamikaze words swell in the goiter of the unsaid.

"Cole, it's Enna."

"Pickle!" He sounds so delighted, so surprised.

"I have a business proposition for you." Yes, keep it business; he'll understand that. "I have received an offer of help for a theater project which may really help the Ashtead's chance of survival."

"U-huh."

I steamroller on. "Well, the point is, I need to stay on longer here to make it a success."

"I see." He's putting on his poker voice. "What kinda time frame are we looking at here?"

"Umm, indefinitely?"

Stony silence.

"I mean, I don't know, to get the production up and running… three months?"

"You've got to be kidding me!" The disappointment in his voice is palpable.

Oh God, it's so exhausting to be this disappointing, and I immediately want to take those words back. Erase and rewind! Erase and rewind.

"Enna, I really don't want that. You know I want you here more than anything."

"I'm sorry, Cole."

"No. No, sorry doesn't cut it. You gotta shit or get off the pot. You know I support you, but Ashtead is crumbling. It's a money pit. It's an energy pit. How much time and effort are you going to invest before you realize that?"

He's right, but this could be the chance Ashtead needs. Am I just going to give up without trying?

"I wasn't going to tell you this until you got here—I wanted it to be a surprise—but I got you an interview at the Scranton Playhouse. Turns out, they're looking for a new artistic director. I made some calls and you're a shoe-in. Scranton Playhouse, pickle! It's a great opportunity, a great future. It's a new theater with a main house and a studio, and you could really put your stamp on things. Imagine being there at the beginning of things; you could have such an impact here."

Oh shit.

Two different men in two different countries offering two different fantastic opportunities. I should feel like the luckiest girl in the world. I feel sick.

"Oh."

Cole, who is usually fairly reticent about all things theatrical, suddenly seems to know more than I gave him credit for.

"A three-hundred-seater playhouse with resident professional company. They do open casting calls in New York, too, when the production calls for it. The studio has a mixture of new and experimental theater. You'd be salaried, have benefits, good vacation time… it's a really great position, Enna. They are looking to hire by month's end. I told them you'd be here before that."

"But, what if I don't get the job?"

"Sweetie, believe me. Inside tip, you are by far the best qualified."

"Can I think about it?" Even my own indecision annoys me, but I have run out of excuses and need to make a decision, not an automated weak-willed "okay." I must be sure of what is the right thing to do. I must give a "yes" and I must give a "no."

"I want an answer by tomorrow."

But I'll settle for a tomorrow.

I chew on the plastic pen until the ink starts to leak, and I hurl the missile across the office in frustration. Oh God, I hate decisions. It's like having to choose between your children. How do you do that? *No more of that, Enna. You have made your choice, remember?*

But what if a new route has appeared? Can't I "recalculate?"

I reach for the phone again, this time dialing a different long, foreign number.

"Hi, where are you?"

"Hawaii. And it is very, very early."

"Shit."

"What?" I can hear the sleep coating her words and can picture her lying on her back with the phone sandwiched between her head and the pillow.

"Lu, Will has come up with this brilliant plan to save the theater, so I decided to stay here, at least for a bit, then I phoned Cole and he told me he has secured this ah-mazing job as the director at Scranton Playhouse and—Holy two buses at once Batman—I don't know what to do."

"Huh!"

"Yeah. So…what do you think?"

I hear some readjusting, settling of pillows, whispering.

"Oh crap, you're not alone, are you?"

"You're not the only one with buses, you know! Don't worry—" More rustling "—Gabe has shuttled off to find me some breakfast."

"Gabe?"

"He's with the whale watching tour. We were talking about humpbacks and got quite into it."

"I see." Our feline smiles meet somewhere on the line.

"Okay, so cut the crap. What's the problem again?"

"Cole and Scranton Playhouse job or rescuing Ashtead Theatre with Will? Got to pick one."

"Humph! Do both."

"Can't. Cole is now or never. Will is a limited offer."

"Can't Will do it without you? I mean, can't he run Ashtead for you? Then you'd have that saved, and you wouldn't feel so bad about leaving it without a savior. Or is the real issue that it's not just Ashtead you would be staying for; it's him?"

The office spins a complete revolution around me and stops. I rise to my feet. That's it! "No, Lu! We're just friends, but, you know what, I think I could do it! I think it'd work. If I can get Will back onside and line him up with Ashtead, I can still fulfill my promises. Brilliant! Of course! Thank you! Thank you!"

"Good, now bugger off and let me sleep. Humpback tutorials are exhausting."

Will! Oh my God, yes! Will could help Ashtead and save it! I could still fly to the States and become the new artistic director of Scranton Playhouse! It's perfect! Perfect! It makes complete logical sense. It's not giving up on Ashtead; it is ensuring it into the care for someone more able to help. I am doing what is right, what is for the best even.

After several meetings between the board and Will, they agree to take his production on and give it a try. My replacement, Hugo, is not so keen. He wanted to rule the roost and is disgruntled to have his first directorial decision taken away from him.

"It's for the good of the theater," I tell him.

Will seems sulky about the whole deal too. I thought he'd be thrilled to get the chance of performing his show and earning some extra cash for his transatlantic move, but if he is grateful, he does not show it.

With bags packed and visa clutched, I say a tearful goodbye to the theater. I had hoped Will would show up to say goodbye at least, but no, he has been notably absent since our work negotiations, or maybe I have been so wrapped up in the move and it has all happened at such a pace, that I haven't noticed.

Mum and Dad escort me across the threshold. I press my palm to the glass revolving door and transmit an apology. I try not to think of the alternatives now, try not to look back like Orpheus, but keeping my thoughts in step with my actions seems impossible. *Keep focused and committed*, I school myself. It is sensible; it is logical. A good business and a good life decision.

A blurred whirlwind, a tornado of activity, surrounds me when I arrive in the funny old land of PA. No wicked witch ex-girlfriends or future mother-in-law await to jeer, but everyone is utterly lovely to me. I do get the distinct feeling that Cole has primed people to keep me busy: his sister offering to take me out whenever she needs to "run to the store"; the neighbor who asks me if I would walk his dog; the friend's girlfriend who thinks it vitally important we start looking for wedding dresses immediately!

It's all very sweet, I know everyone is trying to welcome me, but really, I would prefer to grow accustomed to it by myself. Make my own mistakes. Drive on the wrong side of the road without someone beside me in the passenger seat stifling a laugh, saying with glee, "I knew you were going to do that."

Cole himself is very solicitous. He rushes home from work at lunchtime, just to check that I'm still there. He says he can't believe his luck. He races through the door, loosening his tie, and there he finds me, folding laundry or Windexing windows or trying to cook something English just to prove we have something to offer in the way of world cuisine.

Whilst waiting for something to happen, I take on this role of domestic wife: the laundry is still creased in spite of much ironing and many burn injuries, courtesy of the upright steamer thingy; windows are ever streaky; my cakes refuse to rise—there's no self-rising flour in America, it seems—and after my first week of "interesting" dinners, Cole does suggest eating out, a lot; but we do have fantastic sex! Hoorah!

He has set up the interview with the playhouse, and he couldn't do more to make me feel welcome, except perhaps doing nothing.

The Playhouse is impressive: a shiny, sponge-seated auditorium and a high proscenium stage—and that's just the main stage. Cole has, in fact, shortchanged the venue in terms of facilities. It is an arts haven, with a gallery in the foyer, other studios for pottery, stained glass window making, writers' groups, radio players, a sewing circle, scattered around the vast Artistic Empire. Also, a small, everything locally grown and handmade café with an indoor water feature in the foyer. As theater complexes go, I have stumbled upon a treasure chest of possibilities.

The theater has a mailing list of over two thousand, is paid grants by the county, and has regular houses that would make Will weep.

I meet the outgoing A.D. who is retiring post-renovation, and he takes me on a tour. "I am so excited your fiancé recommended you. We didn't know how the theater would fare left at the hands of some of the applicants we have interviewed, but I can see that Cole's right; you would be perfect for the job."

After the official handshake, he sets me loose to wander around the building and get to know the theater myself. I walk into the auditorium and inhale. It doesn't have the familiar rubbery smell of Ashtead, but a new air. I walk up the steps of the rake to the back row and imagine heads in front, bobbing to see the action. The space-age lighting rig hangs down impressively; the scenery is hung from fly bars. The stage is just the right size, clean and bare, and I can't help myself! I run back down the steps three at a time and leap across the stage, cartwheel, and cancan in celebration.

"Weeeee!" I squeal to myself as I cartwheel from stage right to stage left and back again.

The theater is currently dark, but I am asked to submit my ideas for the season — *my* ideas, not having to be approved by a board, or ask permission, or forgiveness, but I get to choose and produce my own uncensored selections. I finally have free-rein to make artistic decisions in a spectacular space with a supportive theater-going audience!

As I sit in the pool of light focused on the stage, my legs hanging over the edge, I dream up my choice season, shamelessly including my favorite classic dramas, some comedies, a thriller, maybe an experimental piece we create and workshop here, heck, even a musical — why not; we have the room.

Of course, it will take a while to sign contracts, et cetera, but it is a relief to have found my niche in Scranton so effortlessly. It makes me almost believe that perhaps these things are predestined: that I was supposed to meet Will; the powers that be had determined he would take over at Ashtead, and I would get the chance to run a beautiful, modern, funded theater.

To think I had been worried about fitting in, that I would be such an alien! Hell, it's delightful to be different. People listen to me, are respectful to me, and strange as it may seem, I rather enjoy this teeniest weeniest bit of celebrity.

"Oh my God, just listen to that accent! I could eat it up. You could read me the phone book." Not just at the theater, but at the stores, the gas station, restaurants, and diners.

"Are you from…England?"

My motherland is held in such high regard by others, and it is so very flattering, even if it does make me feel far from home.

I learn to put on my Scrantonese just to shop quickly. I can say "heyna," "my-in," "trash," and "what-ter," but it's not really me.

I wonder if our children will speak in some weird Anglo-American hybrid. *"Can I please just get a ride already? Thank you very much, Mummy."* I will have to preserve their Englishness and insist they learn not to forget the poor neglected letter U.

After one week, I have folded and refolded the entire contents of the airing cupboard and laundry. I have washed the windows inside and out—I'm sure the glass must be thinner. I have learned that lamb chops, duck breasts, and okra are very hard to find at the local Price Chopper, and I have discovered that morning television is crap this side of the Atlantic, too, only there are more channels of it.

Cole sweetly says my cooking is "nice," but still the suggestion of dining out does not diminish. I have tried to channel my inner Nigella Lawson, Delia Smith, and Jamie Oliver, but I don't really have the patience for it. If a recipe says it takes twenty minutes, it takes me an hour and still tastes *al dente*. My mind races with all the other things I should be doing to get on with the theater: invoicing, purchasing, researching, directing. In the time it takes to learn the intricacies of how to prepare and cook a beef Wellington, I could have written a script. And yet, here I am, taking on this role and trying my damndest to tackle the most complicated of English dishes. A task made no easier by having to translate ounces and grams into cups. Seriously, what kind of measuring unit is "cups?" Cups can vary in size, after all, so it's not uniform at all. Cole's Mickey Mouse cup is far bigger than his World's Greatest Boss mug. I mean, it wasn't my fault I made enough pancake batter to feed the Israelites. Who needs loaves and fish? Just cook with cups.

It may not be my natural talent, but at least the industry of cooking and cleaning is better than waiting for the telephone to ring and the playhouse to tell me that they are ready for me to start.

I'm wearing my Union Jack plastic apron—a joke leaving gift from Leo—along with a pair of frilly, yellow rubber gloves. I am measuring out the flour—not British plain flour, but American all-purpose—when he comes up behind me, circling his arms around my waist. It makes me jump, and I spill the spoonful all over the side.

"Oh, Will!" I cry without thinking, shrugging off the surprise embrace.

Cole's arms recoil.

I freeze, deer in headlights. "You stop that! Oh, *will* you stop sneaking up on me!"

Oh! Oh! Oh! I can't believe I said that! Why did I say that? Did he notice? Am I flushing? I know I am. Maybe he didn't catch it. I must keep my head down and concentrate on the all-purpose, like on stage when I fluff a line; just crash on with confidence! He'll never know!

"Who's Will?" he asks, planting a kiss behind my ear.

Shit!

"What?"

"You said Will. You tried to cover it up, but you did just call me Will. Is he the actor guy?" he asks, rubbing a glowing green apple on his chest before biting into the skin. He says it with such nonchalance; I am ludicrously miffed.

"Oh, did I?" I turn from the counter to face him, feigning as much sanguine as my acting skills can manage. "I must have been thinking about Ashtead, wondering how it is doing without me."

He takes another big bite. "Have you heard from them yet?"

"No, I haven't," I reply, and I'm not lying. I've been sitting on my hands, going cold turkey. Why else would I be laundress, window cleaner, and kitchen monkey?

"You ought to talk, pickle. Satisfy your curiosity. Then you wouldn't stand here, staring into space, pretending to cook, thinking of other guys."

"I wasn't thinking of other—"

"Uh, uh, uh." He stops my words, laughing, tossing the apple on the side and gathering me in his arms. His chest seems a vast expanse, there, lying taut beneath the thick lilac shirt with the navy and white polka dot tie. He kisses my lips, erasing the words I've been waiting to say.

Our one week in America anniversary cake—Nigella's chocolate fudge cake measured in grams and ounces—is put on hold for an hour. Instead of playing Suzy Homemaker, I give Cole my whole-hearted attention. He slowly peels every item of clothing from me, a strange, mid-afternoon kitchen striptease. Lord, I hope no one pops around for a cup of sugar, or coffee or all-purpose. My clothes, discarded one by one, puddle at my feet, but I'm not cold; his hands are warm and radiate heat and energy and love all over me. He scoops me up in his arms and charges up the stairs, two at a time.

By week two, I know how to use the washing machine without shrinking Cole's clothes or turning his Jockey shorts pink. I can work the DVR, set the house alarm without it going off immediately, and I can find my way from Scranton to Clarks Summit and to Wilkes-Barre. I already have a favorite lunch place, know the name of the librarian, and I have found something I can cook that Cole really likes! Okay, so fajitas aren't exactly the tribute to British cooking that I wanted his taste buds to fall in love with, but…

Life is good. I can't find a word of complaint. Who wouldn't want these weeks of cohabiting bliss? A gorgeous, funny man sweeping me off my feet, telling me that I "don't need to be all domestic. We'll have a cleaner come in." Is my cleaning that terrible? Truth is, I would bite his hand off to have a cleaner, but I know I would feel so embarrassed; I would have to clean before the cleaner came! Maybe when I start as the A.D. at the playhouse, then we can cast someone in this role.

Scranton Playhouse still hasn't called, and I am starting to climb the walls. The novelty of domesticity is wearing thin, and I need to feel spotlight on my skin. Perhaps there is a specific stage light vitamin D that actors and directors require?

I have been good—I've been so good—and I haven't pestered the new regime at Ashtead either, although this has been pure bloody torture! I haven't even sent a casual email. Ashtead is not mine—my-in—after all, but I've earned a reward, haven't I? Maybe just a little text? A howdy, partner!

I reach for my mobile and sit for ten minutes, typing and deleting before I settle on:

> So, what's Hugo like?

I send it and immediately have to leave the house and walk around the block, just so I don't feel as though I'm waiting for a response.

And there it is, awaiting my return.

> Come back!

I smile and shake my head. Huh! I'm being missed! Goody. Is that wrong? Ah well.

> You should see this theater. I'll have to get you in for a tour when you live stateside. So how is it working out with Hugo?

I am about to find some industry so that I am doing something, not just waiting for texts, but his response is almost instantaneous.

Won't be living there. Melissa and I finished. Done.
Hugo is big arse. Can't stand him.

What? Wait! My legs disappear beneath me, and I have to sit on the kitchen floor. My thumbs act independently.

Am sorry. What happened—on both counts?
Why Hugo arse?

I hear a car slam, and Cole comes in the back door before I have time to press send.

"Pickle! Whaddya doing on the floor?"

"Nothing. I think…I…dropped an earring." I wave my hands across the floor. Why am I lying?

"Oh." He drops his briefcase and kneels to feel the tiles. He straightens and looks at me. "But, sweetie, you have both earrings on."

The wind rushes out of me. "Yes, I know. It's the back bit. Think I dropped…ah! Here it is!" I palm a pretend metal butterfly and quickly fix it to the back of my earlobe.

"That's lucky!"

"Yes."

He takes my hand and lifts me to my feet. So kind, so chivalrous! He kisses me and goes upstairs to change out of his suit.

I listen for his footfalls climbing the stairs, ascending further away, and when I judge he reaches the top, I pounce on the mobile and press send. I feel like a naughty teenager, but it's harmless enough. Cole was the one who said I ought to satisfy my curiosity after all. Why is it over with Melissa? Why is Hugo an arse? I am aching to know—and in that order.

Cole gallops back down the stairs.

I switch the phone to vibrate and stuff it in my back pocket. "So, what are we doing tonight? We have the shepherd's pie leftovers from yesterday."

"No!"

"It wasn't that bad."

"No. I mean, well, we've been invited to Richie's house for game night. He's getting pizza, some beers. He thought it would be a fun way to welcome you to Scranton."

Game night. This has disaster written all over it. Talk about how to alienate new friends! I shall have to bite my tongue, not get overexcited, and most importantly, not get drunk and obnoxiously competitive.

Cole's gang is there, welcoming faces I have met on previous trips. All keep telling me how changed Cole is, how in love he is, how they are so pleased I am here. I don't know whether to feel bursting with happiness or imploding with the weight of expectation. "We've never seen him so happy!" Do they realize what a pressure that is?

Doug says that since this is the first time they have ever had everyone in a couple at the same time, we should play couple's teams. Personal pride dictates that I must be fabulous and sparkle with intelligence; my country and my fiancé depend on it. I know Cole will be good at this—the American history, the sport, the science and nature—but this is a real chance to show him and his friends that I am more than Cole's "theater geek."

"Sweetie, it's just a game. Don't worry." He must sense my competitive hackles rising. "But if you could handle the arts questions, that'd be great. I'm about as good at those as you are at cooking."

I whack him on the arm.

"See," Shelly says, "It's like they have been married five years already!"

Everyone laughs. I laugh.

He hasn't messaged back. It'll be past midnight in England. Maybe he's gone to bed already? How late would it be, five hours in the future?

"Enna? What do you think?"

"What? Sorry. What?"

"Your guess? How many years does the US Army require its ready-to-eat sandwiches to remain ready to eat? Timer's on."

"Oh…it'd depend what's in them, I suppose," I say noncommittally.

"Come on…you're running out of time."

"We'll go for five." Cole smiles at me indulgently.

"And the answer is…three. Wah wah wahhhh," Doug replies with glee as the other competitors "urgh" and "errr."

The questions go around the table, and I get a few correct, though most—annoyingly—on other people's turns. And it's not that I want to sound as if I have sour grapes or anything, but they are different from British questions—I'm sure we don't have Arts and Entertainment question cards about Ren and Stimpy or Gwen Stefani—but I have a beer, a few slices of greasy, hot pizza, and I try to forget about the device burning in my back pocket.

We are a great team together, prompting each other's brains to find the right answer, and we are tied in the lead with five wedges, when my mobile vibrates vigorously. I try to ignore it, but in the close fit of my jeans, it is a pocket riot.

Doug looks up from asking Shelly and Ryan their question. "It's too late to phone a friend for help, Enna! Okay, where was I…"

Cole leans over to me. I can smell the hops and barley on his breath. His smile is wide. "Sweetie, your ass is still ringing. Aren't you gonna get that?"

It would look strange not to, I conclude, though I don't really want to share the message, whatever it is or whomever it is from, with the now tipsy trivia teams.

I nod and reach for the mobile. I can always glimpse the message and stow it away safely, stashing the teleported treasure of words for my eyes to feast on later. My fingers reach around the mobile and draw it up the denim, but my finger is caught, the claws of the emerald hitched on the stitching. I tug firmly, breaking the thread with a satisfying snap, and almost send my ring flying off my finger, but I drop the phone and keep the ring balanced on the tip of my fourth digit.

"You gotta be careful, Enna," I recall him saying, *"Emeralds are fragile."*

Cole bends to pick up the phone, break dancing on the floor, screen side up with inbox listings illuminated. He pauses with the phone in his hand. The blood rushes from my head. He looks from the cell to me. Can he see my pale panic? Can he see my heart beating through my chest? Shit. Surely he must hear it? The room goes silent, and in my ears, the racing *lub-dub, lub-dub* beats in stereo surround sound. It's not just Cole who is looking at me either, but now I can feel that play has stopped, all banter has ceased, and all eyes are on me. He looks back at the phone, and he wipes the screen.

"That was close. Thought it was cracked for a minute. Here you are, sweetie."

Chapter 9

For the first time since my arrival, I feel thoroughly homesick. Cole cuddles up to me and falls asleep with his large arms pinning me to the mattress. I stare into the face of the brilliant alarm clock and imagine the scenes that have taken place without me, three thousand miles away, of the classically trained RADA young blood wanting to prove the worth of his expensive education versus the contemporary original with national seasons under his belt.

It appears the board, in spite of Hugo's family connections, sided with Will, and Hugo felt the insult deeply. Hugo stormed out. That was two days ago, and he hasn't yet reappeared. The theater is in chaos, trying to find out what the prognosis is, but it seems no one has a clue. From the hurriedly exchanged texts whilst in the bathroom — "I think I have stomach cramps. Probably too much pizza" — Will is treading water too.

So, what r u doing there?

Am hiding out in the bathroom, texting u. Why r u up so late?

Can't sleep. 2 much 2 do. Double now Hugo bailed.
Wish your beautiful face was here.

Come on!

It's good then? All u wanted?

And it was funny, farcical really, like a scene in a comedy: the heroine sitting on the furry loo seat cover in a land far, far away where anything was possible, surrounded by love and fun and pizza, hearing the tinkling of laughter in the background, and here she is desperate, desperate for another string of syllables to magically transport into her palm. Is this all she wanted?

'Course. Having a great time. Can't wait to start work though.

It's true; this inactivity is seriously undermining my self-worth. I will have to start working soon. If I don't, I'll start scrapbooking or basket weaving or — good grief — playing Farmville or Candy Crush or whatever awful time-leeching game is on Facebook next. I will call the playhouse tomorrow and find out exactly when I can move into my new office, when I can peep my nose into the files.

Lucky you.

Thanks! And Melissa? R u okay?

I'm fine. I'd be better if you were here though.

Incorrigible! Good night!

x

I sleep with my hands across my chest, and I dream of home.

"I'm taking you away for the weekend," Cole announces to his reflection in the bathroom mirror, eyeing my slow progress as I sit on the vanity and shave his face.

"Ooh! Where are we going?"

"I was thinking you might enjoy a trip to New York. I know you've been down, waiting to hearing from the theater, and I know I don't have much here to keep you occupied."

"Don't be silly. I have lots to do here."

"You're bored, Enna. I can see it. And it makes me feel bad that I've taken you away from your home, so I just really want us to have a fun weekend. Will you let me do that for you? Top shelf everything. We can walk in Central Park, take in a show, have dinner somewhere fancy, or maybe order lots of room service." He juggles me from hand to hand — a dangerous game when I am the one with the razor.

"Don't! I'll cut you! Seriously! You're such a child."

So we decide that this weekend will be a happy weekend getaway. Friends and family have been rallying like cruise directors, and in the weeks I have now been here, Cole and I have spent very little time without friends or family "popping by." I'm thinking of taking up naked vacuuming just to really embarrass the uninviteds and make them think twice before coming over without calling first.

New York is freezing in the winter, a cross-street cold that not only numbs the fingers and toes, but burns the ears and locks the jaw. Still, we wear gloves and earmuffs, and I'm stuffed into my jacket like a loaded potato. The city should smell of exhaust and fetid subway air, but I am surprised to note the signature scent of NYC is the delicious, hot, sidewalk-roasted cashews, peanuts, and pecans. The Nuts 4 Nuts food carts waft their sweet scent on most of the major streets, and eventually, I relent and beg Cole to buy me a scoopful. He presents the twisted paper cone full of glistening caramelized cashews like a posy, and we share them as we walk along the streets, arm in arm, waddling close like penguins for extra heat.

This is my playground now. How strange. How different from the haphazard city planning of London, the less restauranted, more retailed motherland.

On neutral territory, strolling around the street markets along Hell's Kitchen, I can, for the first time, see how I play into this new scene: A.D. position at the playhouse; handsome, warm, generous husband who adores and supports me; friends who come over for movie and game nights; two kids to shuttle from sports practice to theater rehearsal and back again; a dog with an eccentric English name; weekend getaways to New York, Philadelphia, Lancaster, and Niagara Falls. I know this is a fabulous, safe, steady, attainable future, and I'll never want for anything.

But—must there always be a but—as happy as I am, there is this pit, an acidic, ulcerous pit deep in the pit of my stomach. Whenever I feel the vibrations of my mobile in my handbag or back pocket or whirring across the table, the pit simmers like a volcano.

Give my regards to Broadway, he sent to me in the car.

"You're like a teenager!" Cole had said as I pounced on the message and thumb-tapped a signal back. "Seriously, do you think this weekend could be about us and not with your head halfway to England?"

It could, but…this is my lifeline, my umbilical cord to the motherland. I switch the phone to quiet vibrate and am, for some unknown reason, suddenly afflicted with a particularly over-enthusiastic bladder and have to visit a Starbucks loo every few hours.

He books dinner at Patsy's—an Italian midtown restaurant with painted walls, bright lights, and solicitous waiters—a great excuse to wear my newest royal blue dress with slashed sleeves and ruched sides. He leans across the bread basket and tells me I look more beautiful every day, and I bask in the glow of his gaze. Loosely holding hands across the table, I really try to give him my full attention. I really try to ignore the mobile—or cell, I should probably call it now—jitter-bugging silently across the table. The handhold gets a wee bit tighter.

We talk about the menu options, the décor, the waiter, and there it sits throughout, daring me, on the middle of the table, in between the table advertisement for Patsy's sauce and the dish of olives.

"Pickle, we've got to start talking about the wedding."

"A huh?" I say through a mouthful of bread.

"We're already over thirty days into the fiancé visa. We have to make the arrangements, the marriage license, all of that soon."

The mobile whirrs again and does its impressive table break dancing.

"What exactly do we need to do?" I so want to answer it. Would that seem disinterested in this important conversation?

"I need your birth certificate, stuff like that. Then we get the marriage license, and then pick a judge and a date."

My stomach growls. "Oh."

"Pickle, I did tell you."

"I don't remember."

"Well, you were busy with packing and getting Ashtead together. Don't worry. It's all pretty standard stuff. We'll have another wedding afterward, if you like. Maybe we should have it in Ashtead, so all your friends and family can see how beautiful you look."

Marriage license, yes, sounds a little familiar.

"And we have a time deadline for this?"

He sounds mildly exasperated. "Pickle! You know this! We have ninety days, well, fifty-one days and counting, now."

Bugger.

Am I waiting for some sign from the hand of God? Some *deus ex machina* to float down from the dead hang above my stage? Some greater power to say, "Yes, Enna, you are one hundred percent correct to choose this lovely life of career opportunities and infinite love here in the US?"

Cole withdraws to the restroom, smiling, and gives me instructions to order for him.

I wait a full ten seconds before snatching up the undetonated text message.

> Finally, word from Hugo 2day—prima donna.
> He isn't coming back. Feels artistic integrity being questioned.

I click on the next message.

> Board r considering closing.
> Not going to outlay costs if no "true artistic direction."

My stomach howls again. Ashtead close?

"Sweetie, you've gone pale. Are you feeling all right?" he says, returning to our little couple's table.

I look into the loving face of Cole, hazelnut whirls filled with concern, and I wonder if acid can actually erode your guts, your spleen, your backbone. Why does doing something courageous suddenly feel so cowardly?

"It's nothing," I reply, shaking it off, but the remainder of the evening passes in a blur. The capered and anchovied puttanesca seems tasteless, and the full-bodied Cabernet seems like water. It doesn't touch the sides as I gulp glass after glass.

When we return to the beautiful, chic hotel room, with crisp white sheets, I don't even notice the Manhattan skyline view but bolt for the toilet and am phenomenally sick.

Cole gently knocks on the door, desperate to help: to hold my hair, to rub my back, to go to the pharmacy, something. Although I don't know what I want, I do know that I don't want to be touched. I need aspirin, Alka-Seltzer, Pepto Bismol, and some space.

The weather forecast on Channel 7 predicts torrential rain for the day, and since neither of us have raincoats or umbrellas, and I feel like I've been hung, drawn, and quartered, we decide to drive back to PA and enjoy an afternoon relaxing by the fire. Cole will watch his beloved Eagles play, and I will read and move as little as possible.

"Pickle, what's wrong?"

"Sweetie, what's wrong?"

"Sweetie-pickle, what's wrong?"

"Pick, what's wrong?"

The entire ninety-minute journey is littered with differently branded "what's wrongs?" I know he means well, but if he asks me one more time, I swear I will hurl Self from the car somewhere along I-80. Ashtead can't close. I won't let it close. Surely I can coach Will through things? As soon as I get back to PA, I will telephone and outline a plan for him to work with the board. I can fix this.

And the thoughts spark around my circuitry, excited to be thinking about the next steps for the theater again rather than how to make the potato on the shepherd's pie crunchy.

Cole takes in the bags, and I collect the mail. Hoorah! Finally one for me, complete with theater stamp! My start date from the playhouse!

As excitedly as my fragile-state fingers can work, I seize the letter in hand and hobble to the calendar. *I'll have to mark my wedding on there too*, I think with a large, glottal swallow. Oh, why I am scared? I've already committed myself. I thought it was men who were supposed to get commitment shy?

I uncap the pink felt-tipped pen to circle my start date and then I scan the letter.

> Dear Ms. Petersen,
>
> It was a pleasure interviewing you for the position of artistic director at The Scranton Playhouse. Unfortunately, during our vetting process, we have found that we will not be able to contract you. We were not aware that you do not yet have a Social Security Number, and the time that it would take for you to go through the proper channels would be too long for Scranton Playhouse to wait.
>
> I am sorry that this formality is causing such an insurmountable roadblock. You were my number one choice as my successor.
>
> Yours etc.

I am lampooned, poleaxed, KO'd. *What?* Why didn't the attorney tell me? Or did the attorney tell me and I wasn't listening? Panic grabs me and holds me in its straitjacket, and my mind races. But…I thought England and America were friends! I'm going to be married here in fifty or so days; doesn't that count for anything? And then how long will it take? I could be jobless, purposeless for what, three months? Four? Five? Six? More? Oh *What…the…what?*

The paper flutters to the floor.

I want to go home.

"What is it, pickle? Are you feeling okay?"

"I can't work. They won't let me work. I can't take the job," I say, shell-shocked, floundering, insensible.

He slips his arms around me. "Oh, pickle, I'm sorry. I know you really wanted that. But there'll be others."

He keeps me upright, and his words take a moment to filter through.

"Really?" I extract my wet face from his shirt and look at him, waiting for the truth. "Really? There'll be others? Other theaters in need of artistic directors, ones that have studios and funding and an inside water feature? I don't think so, Cole! How am I supposed to work when I can't…work? What do they expect me to do? Learn a language? Take up cross-stitch? Plant…I don't know…plant fucking cabbage?"

"Pickle, don't be upset—"

"Upset? Cole, I'm…I'm…I don't even know what I am. I can't believe I didn't know about this. Did you know about this?"

"Well, I thought it might take a while." He flushes pillar-box red. "But I didn't know th—"

"I don't believe it! You knew!"

"I thought there could be some chance—"

"But you let me get carried away with the idea anyway? Unbelievable!"

"Sweetie, you were sent all the information I was," he says in his frustratingly reasonable tone. "Enjoy it. Take a break. So what if you can't work for a year. You can—"

"*For a year? A year?* What?" And the acid erupts and flows through my veins. All hint of my former, fragile self transforms to raging Boudicca. I charge upstairs, grabbing my suitcases from the closet and hurling them on the bed. I hear his footfalls thump up behind mine.

"Sweetie, what are you doing?" He grabs my elbow and twists me around.

"What does it look like I'm doing, Cole?"

"Don't be like that."

"Huh. Unbelievable! You don't expect me to be angry? Cole! This is my job. This is me. This is what I live for, and you lied! You've taken me away from somewhere I could have been of some help. More fool me for turning my back so readily. More fool me for believing you." Tears catch in my throat. "I…I can't stay here."

All the hours taken to carefully pack my cases on the journey out are reduced to seconds as I throw in the contents of the wardrobe and drawers.

"Enna. Enna! Don't be stupid."

"You think I'm overreacting? Have you any idea, any, what that theater means to me?"

He looks forlornly at the cases but says nothing.

"You could have been honest with me, Cole. You could have just waited that little bit longer for me to get everything set up for the move, to get Ashtead established. Then I would have been over here like a shot. But instead you got me that interview and pumped up my expectations, knowing all the while that I could never be artistic director. Knowing that I would be captive for a year."

"Enna, you're being over-dramatic."

"Yeah? Sorry. Goes with the territory, I'm afraid." I zip up the suitcases and lug them to the floor. Even in anger, he tries to help me with the cases, but I will not let him lift them. I do it on my own.

"Pickle, now you're being unreasonable."

"Oh yes, God! Give me the powers of reason!" And I stomp downstairs three times heavier than I had ascended them.

"Would you stop being a drama queen for just two fucking seconds!" his voice booms from the top of the stairs.

I have never heard him speak this way, and I pause, cases in hand.

"You seriously think I would lie to you? I worked my guts out to get you here. I've pulled every fucking string to get you that job. And you sat back and did nothing! You expect everything and yet you do nothing! You had all the paperwork I had. I know because I fucking sent it to you! But you couldn't be bothered."

The vertical creases between his eyebrows seem so dark that he looks like he is wearing some tribal war paint. I want to get out of here. I need to leave. I heave the cases to the door.

"You're just a little princess, and when things don't work out just the way you want, you run. You bail!"

"I'll call you later. I can't speak to you right now."

"You're unbelievable. You selfish little—"

I don't hear the rest. I slam the car door and twist the radio volume to sonic boom.

Chapter 10

I don't go to Shelly's, or Jen's, or any of Cole's friends, because I realize they are exactly that — *his* friends. A fresh batch of tears streams down my face. They wouldn't understand. They only see his generosity and love for me and think that's enough. But it's not enough; I need something for me, something that I can do and be good at. I don't just want to be his appendage, his cling-on. I wanted to be his partner.

I drive out to the highway and enjoy the rip of the accelerator. How dare he! How bloody dare he! Selling me on false promises and then sweeping the whole thing under the carpet like it's nothing! Doesn't he understand? It's not just a job. It's validation. It's self-worth. What the fuck else am I going to do around here, where I don't know anyone and no one knows me?

The familiar tones of the English DJ, brought to me through the wonders of satellite, register through my loud thought cloud. It is a comfort to hear something from home. Home!

I am almost surprised when I arrive at Philadelphia International Airport. I leave the car in long-term parking, making a note of the location so I can email Cole where to find it.

Flight BA0068 leaves Philadelphia at 22:05 hours. I have a window seat, a headache, and for the first time since university, I have reached the limit on my credit card.

I don't want to speak to anyone. I don't call Mum and Dad yet, or Lucy or Leo, or Will. I will make my own way. I hoist the suitcases into the taxi, and I heave them out again when I get to the house. I still have my keys and my little car in the garage, as yet unsold. Providence.

Leo is not at home, and I collapse over the threshold, spent. And now, I cry.

And cry. And cry some more, until I resemble a large peeled tomato, the nerves, veins, and arteries close to the surface and exposed. I switch my body to autopilot and go through the necessaries: a call to Christine Monk on the board, and she is thrilled to hear I am back.

"Oh, I knew you would be back. I just had a feeling! And I'm always right about my feelings, darling. And of course, don't you even think of reapplying! You must come back to us. You must!"

Then, a text to Cole in spite of the international expense.

Am safe, back at home. Sorry if you were worried.
I am sorry I can't just be there and not do anything.
The theater is me. It's in my DNA.

I chicken out the minute I send it, and I shut off my phone so I can't read his reply, at least not for a while. I know he'll be disappointed, and I can't cope with his hurt in addition to my own. I'm emotionally exhausted. His angry words, as he stood on the stairs, replay over and over. Did he send me those papers? Could I have known about not working? Could I have saved everyone time, money, and heartache?

But he is the one who encouraged me. He set up the interview at the Playhouse, knowing all along that I couldn't take the position! So it *was* his fault. I could have read about the work issues; I could not have. But it wouldn't change the fact that he knew and he didn't tell me. Well, I don't need a modern space station of a theater; Ashtead has a history, and it needs to be preserved.

I think of texting Will, but to what end? I'm a mess. I need a little time to get myself together, to become more solid that the human blancmange I currently resemble. But, Cole! Oh God!

I must work. Isn't that why I'm here? Partly. And when I save the theater, then I'll figure out what I'm going to do.

I make arrangements with Christine Monk for the new artistic director — me — to start, effective immediately. The office is almost the ordered chaos I had left it in and holds no actual presence of Hugo whatsoever. The files spilling open, posters rolled up on every surface, disposable coffee cups undisposed of. Even the answer machine is messy with so many recorded messages.

Listlessly, I press play and listen to the slew of messages: Quotes from companies I contacted ages ago about repairs. Lucy heard something from Mum. Am I back? If so, call Mum who's had a call from Cole. Am I back? If so, call a reporter from *The Chronicle* who is interested in running a piece. Cole asking the theater if I have been in contact; Cole again, asking if I do happen to get in contact, could he be notified.

My stomach lurches at the sound of his voice, and I am consumed with sadness and then anger, then back to sadness—a masochistic loop. How could he have not told me?

I sit at my old desk, my fingers easily finding the impressions in the worn wood, reading it like Braille. I wiggle the mouse, and the screen comes to life. Another message, right at the top of my inbox.

> From: Cole Krupski
>
> Subject: none
>
> I can't believe you have flown back. I hope this is a joke, Enna. Do you realize what you've done? If you are in England, if you have flown out of the country, you can't come back on that visa. You've wasted it, thrown it away.
>
> I don't even know what to say to you right now. I'm so mad at you. I can't believe you would be this unreasonable over a stupid job! I thought you wanted to be with me. Were you just coming for the job? I'm so confused. I'm so hurt.
>
> Do you even know, do you have the slightest freaking idea how much it cost to get you here? How much I paid the attorney? Do you? And then you go and pull this shit. You are unbelievable. Un-freakin-believable! And selfish and self-obsessed, and you know what? I don't think I'd want you back right now even if you came crawling on your knees.
>
> Keep the ring. Or sell it for your precious theater. That's fitting. Get married to your theater. May it bring you happiness. Whatever.

The sound and space and color are sucked out of the room. All that remains is the screen and my realization. What was it that the customs officer said at Heathrow? Something about the visa, how to use it again, but he was vague and I just…oh, I just assumed he was commenting that I had one; not that it would be annulled, negated, terminated. I wasn't really focusing. I just wanted to get back home.

My vision floods with the haze of built up tears, and they fall like lemmings to the computer keyboard beneath. I can't breathe. I snatch noisy breaths between loud, snotty sobs. What have I done? Have I ruined my chances? But he lied to me. It was his fault. I am the one who should be cross, not this pathetic, weepy mess! So why can't I dam this flow? Why can't I return to America? Surely, surely, I could explain if I wanted to? And as I imagine never waking up next to his beloved body again, never feeling his arms around me, never smelling him — *Oh God!* — living without that intoxicating Hermès cologne that is the essence of him, I cry uncontrollably. For hours. I don't know where it all comes from. Are tears leeched by some invisible suction, from cell to eye to spew down one's face? What have I done? What have I done? What have I done? Oh, God, what have I done?

The office door swings open and a wide-eyed, head-bobbing Maureen, theater volunteer-cum-martyr, scurries to my side like some demented ferret.

"Oh! You're back! And you're crying! I thought I heard crying! There, there," she coos, clamping me to her bosom. "What's wrong? You can tell Auntie Mo. Is it that big American lug of yours?"

"He's not mine anymore." I sniffle.

She produces a hankie. "Blow! Well, don't you worry about it, lovie! He didn't deserve you anyway. Fancy him insisting you uproot, leave us all here!"

I sit still while Maureen revolves around me. She's enjoying this, flapping and puffing and feeling important. She dusts with extra care this morning, talking to herself, telling the bookshelf all the many reasons why she never thought I should be with an American anyway. "Too far! Far too far! You can't even get a bus there!"

I don't respond to the email. Or rather, I try to, but I can barely see through my tears, and every hazy sentence I tap out seems pointless. I can't say sorry and accept culpability. I want my theater too, and clearly he will never understand that. How could I expect him to? He's a businessman. What does he know about the arts? How can he even comprehend passion; he works with aggregate! I delete my attempts to explain, letter by letter. I'm just lost, devastated, battered, bruised, incensed, frightened, and I am sorry—for hurting him now, for hurting me too, but not for following my passion.

But I can't lose sight of the fact that Cole told me to my face that that job was as good as mine.

I suck in a deep, cleansing breath.

"If everything else around you goes to shit, focus on those things that you can change." Mum had always been one for rallying mottos. I hold fast to this one and swipe my face with the back of my hand. Well, I can't change that now. I can't think about what could have been. I have to concentrate on the things I can control, like Ashtead! Yes, that'll be a good distraction, and then I'll work the rest out.

I pick up the telephone and dial the number repeated on the answer machine.

"Mr. Howard. Yes, it's Enna Petersen, Artist Director of Ashtead Theatre. About that interview…"

A week and many Kleenex, a little tin of Vaseline—to balm the raw skin from lip to nostril—several stern talks with myself, long repetitive choruses of fortifying anthems, a frivolous purchase of new, red, patent stilettos later, and I'm feeling a lot less…hopeless.

I actually manage a beaming smile when I glimpse the front page of Sunday's paper, complete with a rather pleasing picture of myself, pre-Rudolph redness.

The journalist makes my vague ideas of shows for children sound far more advanced than their actual embryonic state, but as Mum would say, "Where there's a will, there's a way!" Ironically, the Will who made a way is about the only person in England who hasn't phoned this week.

In another parallel universe, I'd grab the telephone and call Cole.

"Guess what?" I would say, unable to contain my excitement.

"Pickle! What?"

"My article is front page news!"

"That's wonderful. I'm really proud of you," he would say.

I shake the scene away. It's been a week without word. It's hard to stop dwelling. How can I not? No, I must not be sad; I must be angry. It's so much easier to be angry.

In the interests of keeping myself busy and avoiding asthma brought on by cretaceous dust, I don a pair of yellow rubber gloves, grab a duster, and hit play on my iPod. I high kick with delight—it's my Britney! I wipe and wiggle, polish and gyrate, lunge and squat with every pass of the vacuum. By track eleven, I have abandoned the vacuum, but for an occasional microphone, and leap around the room—a spastic frog, gamboling gazelle, swivel-headed meerkat all rolled into one. The sweat rolls satisfyingly down my face as I choreograph another fast-paced routine, singing at the top of my voice. Hmm. Another irony: Britney being therapeutic—ha!

I hit replay and I'm onto my second, now slick, routine of my favorite Britney tune, "Toxic."

Crouch and squat, and sway, 2-3-4. I sing loudly, crooning wantonly to the vacuum, shimmying around it, snapping my head up sharply to the beat. The bass thuds and I slide into the splits—I haven't been down here for a while—on to my back, and I scissor my legs in the air, in the manner of some Britney, Madonna, *Flashdance*, *Showgirls* hybrid. There's no way to gracefully get to my feet, so I propel back in a botched backward roll, laughing as I flop to the side, lying uncomfortably on a pair of shoes. Hard shoes. Hard shoes…with feet in them. I scream and jump up, tracing the shoes, the feet, the legs, to the face. Britney purrs on, and I rush to the stereo to switch her off with an unceremonious click.

"You scared me!" I shout, incandescent with embarrassed fury.

"I'm sorry. I did ring the bell and the house phone, but I guess you didn't hear." He doesn't look the least bit sorry. He looks positively delighted.

My initial fright dissipates, and I stand facing him, foolish and exposed. I can just imagine what I must look like: red face, sweaty hair, a manic pole dancer with bright yellow rubber gloves. And, of course, there *he* stands, looking gorgeous and smooth and annoyingly unruffled, making absolutely no attempt *not* to look at me and my translucent white, sweat-soaked T-shirt and threadbare yoga shorts. This is not the Kate Middleton-Windsor elegance I strive for.

"I was just doing…cleaning-robics. It's very popular," I say with all the dignity I can muster. "I'm not in the mood for taking social calls, so if you don't mind, I really am very busy." I grab the vacuum cord and wind it up with great importance.

"Oh, I can see, but I…well, I saw the piece in the paper and figured you were back. The article did mention a Shakespearian rap show for kids…"

"Yes. I'm trying a new direction for Ashtead."

He takes two strides toward me and pulls the cable out of my hands. "I see. Well, if you need anything, I happen to be very close, personal friends with this brilliant, underrated, under-used Shakespearian hip-hop artist. I could put in a good word for you."

"You're incorrigible!"

"You're an enigma." He smiles at me, deep into me. "You came back so quickly. I was surprised. I thought that…"

I can feel a lump rising in my throat. "Will, I really don't want to talk about this. Yes, I'm back. I had an interview, but now we do need to put the publicity to good use."

"'Course, but is this just a fly-by stop gap for you, or are you staying?"

I turn to look in his face, his expression no longer self-satisfied but sincere.

"Are you still together? With him?"

Why does he care? What does it matter? "Not that it is any business of yours, but no. I am not."

His eyes soften, and he offers me a sympathetic smile. "Well, let's save this theater then!"

And as much as it feels like my skin is burning, that I'm disfigured and will never stop feeling this entire body ache, I am relieved, and I smile. It feels so odd to be smiling in this strange state of mourning.

$$Chapter\ 11$$

He promises to be brief so I can shower and get back to my Sunday, but our "quick minute" lasts over sixty.

Sunday night I spend alone, and for the first time in a week, I can contemplate actually eating more than a handful of nuts or a lump of cheese. I actually have an appetite. The week of non-stop crying has had very little to offer in the way of nutritional substance. *Wine is not a major food group, Enna!* I decide I will use my new domestic skills and bake a lasagna. I enjoy the distraction of shopping, the industry of creating the sauces and layering them together, the bolognese, the lasagna sheets, the roux, the bolognese, the pasta sheets, the roux, mozzarella, parmesan. It smells so good. I cut myself one small square and marvel at the strings of melted cheese as I pull the portion out of the casserole dish. Maybe I am not a domestic failure after all. Maybe I could have done it, had I really wanted to. I eat the square, and another, and another.

Monday, a fresh start. Today I will think like a man. I will compartmentalize, and I shall not cry. Not one tear. Not a drop! I turn into the corridor leading to my office to hear papers shuffling. Will's here already. And I thought I was the early bird.

"Morning!" I say, sweeping the office with one look. The filing cabinet is open, and Will flicks casually through my folders. "Making yourself at home, I see?"

"Hi!" he mumbles distractedly, focused on the paperwork in his hand.

"What have you got there?"

"Oh, nothing. Just familiarizing myself," he replies, snapping the file shut and giving me his full attention.

"Nothing will come of nothing. Speak again," I say, feeling smugly Shakespearian and intelligent.

He gets the *King Lear* reference and smiles. "How are you this morning? You look tired. I bet you could use some coffee."

"Yes. That would be very nice, thanks. Milk, no sugar, please, then we can get down to brass tacks."

"I made notes last night." He hands me my coffee and flaps some note cards. "We need to define our area and send out great publicity to those schools within that sphere. It doesn't have to be Disney-glossy. The kids aren't booking the show; Teachers are. I've already done some sketches."

His designs are detailed, and I have to admit, I am thoroughly impressed. They look polished. They look attention-grabbing. They look…expensive.

"They're great, Will, really great. But you have to understand, we are working with no budget here. We can't possibly afford anything like that. *I* can't possibly afford anything like that."

"This is business. Pure and simple. You shouldn't be touching your own money. You should be getting a small business loan."

Business, pure and simple. Yes, I suppose it makes sense. I've just always had this dread of credit, like it's a bad word or disease or something. I've always been the saver. Even when Dad offered to match my savings so that I could get the bike I really wanted, I turned him down. I wanted to prove I could do it without help — stupid, misguided thinking that was! By the time I made it on my own, the price had increased by another twenty pounds, and BMXs were no longer cool anyway; horses were, and Dad said there was no way in hell I could have one of those!

But, if a business loan is what it takes, then I'll do it! Or at least, I'll think about doing it.

We spend a good two hours solidly brainstorming and devise a strategy and a division of efforts. I'm to start on publicity. I draft and redraft until I come up with a rather pleasing cover letter to the schools. Will puts his skills to work on the promotional material. Before we know it, it is almost two p.m. and we have worked through an Equity-enforced lunch break.

"I see, you're a slave driver!" he says, standing in front of my desk, patting his expensive-looking watch.

Men and their need for lunch! I send him off to forage for himself whilst I continue to plow on, locked into the secure marsupial pouch of chair and desk.

I glance up at the clock, the regimented black numerals standing to attention, marking my time. A quick email break, then. I deserve it!

And the senders are…I seize, freeze, and forget to breathe. There is one from Cole.

> I've thought long and hard about this. I'm nearly 40, Enna, and I don't want to wait until sometime never when you finally decide you are ready to leave your precious theater.
>
> I'm not the bad guy in all this. Did I know it might be tough to get a green card and get to work quickly? Sure, but I guess I thought everything would work out, that maybe the theater would sponsor you or something, and that you would be committed enough to stick around. I never wanted to trap you; I just wanted to love you. That should have been liberating, right? But one hurdle and you go running the other way.
>
> And I still cannot get over how you just threw it all away. How could you do that? All that time and money, and you can just leave? Did I ever really matter at all to you, or was I just an amusing intermission in the Enna Show?
>
> I would have put you first, you know. I never would have held you back. I need to move on now. ~C.

The screen flashes again as another stealth email lands. Another from him.

> But if you ever need me, just call.

Just to know he has been sitting at his office desk, as I am sitting at mine, thinking of me, writing to me, is enough to fill my eyes with fresh tears. To fill up with hope, then anger, guilt, disappointment, hope, anger, guilt, disappointment, repeat.

He's moving on. Fine. I accept that. I am the one who walked away. So why does my stomach feel like it's imploding?

I'm hungry. No, that's not it. *Look, just concentrate on the theater and worry about the other stuff later. I have my house, my theater, my family—*

I can hear Will charging up the stairs, the sound of his eager feet beating down the corridor, chasing my reverie away.

He appears through the door, his smile reaching me first. "This is going to be really great, you know. Really great. You'll see."

The Education and Outreach—we decide to give it an important sounding name—is an ingenious scheme. He explains to the letter that it's a numbers game. With a five-hundred-seater venue, we can accommodate several school groups for each matinee. Multiply that by fifteen pounds per ticket, and that is seven thousand, five hundred pounds per performance. Some nights we could even do evening performances. That's fifteen thousand pounds per day.

"Holy calculation, Batman! Who even needs a loan when you are banking sums like that!" I just cannot believe it could be this easy. There has to be a catch. But fifteen thousand pounds a day!

Think of the all the renovation I could do! The re-roofing, the re-upholstering, the re-carpeting, plastering, paving—the theater will have a new lease on life! I feel giddy. Finally, I will have the means to make Ashtead the foremost producing house in the whole of Surrey. We will snatch it from the jaws of the property developers eagerly licking their collective chops to knock it down.

"We will need a couple of thousand to get started with the publicity, but that'll be a drop in the ocean, really," Will advises.

"Thousands?" I'm sure I must blanch, but it's business; I know this. "Well, if we are going to do this, let's do it well. I suppose I could get a business loan. With the projected figures, how could they say no?"

"You're right. A standard business loan definitely sounds the sensible way to go."

"Well, let's go to the bank today and get the wheels turning."

"Great idea."

My idea! I'm a galvanized businesswoman with a great idea and business plan, and I'm really, really going to save my theater!

"I'm proud of you, pickle!" I imagine Cole saying.

The bank manager, Mr. Digby, a very affable man with a solid handshake—good sign—welcomes us into his office with a cheery, jolly butcher kind of laugh. Will and I give an overview of our plan for the theater and our predicted box office takings. Will's projections and eloquence are impressive.

Mr. Digby, "Call me Neil," listens attentively, hiding his reddening poker face behind steepled fingers. "It certainly sounds like a solid business plan. I'd need to see something on paper, of course."

"Of course," Will and I chime in unison.

"I hardly need to say that seventy-five thousand pounds per week income is a profitable return. But that is, of course, best case scenario. How much would you need to get the ball rolling?" He leans in further, his impressive stomach seemingly cut in two by the desk—like a magic act, the girl sawn in half. *Here he is, folks! The incredible bisected bank manager!*

"Fifty thousand," I hear Will say coolly, and I buck back to reality.

"I thought fifteen would be enough?" I ask with surprise, searching his face for signs of monetary Tourette's. "You think we really need that much?"

He places his hand over mine and squeezes my fingers gently. "Well, you did say if we are going to do this, we should do it well, and we ought to leave ourselves some room for maneuvering."

"I don't know."

"Enna, we stand to take in a box office of seventy-five thousand per week. That doesn't include merchandise and the take at the bar."

"Your figures are certainly impressive," Digby cheers on. "Better too much than too little, I always say." And, judging by the size of his blossoming belly, this is indeed a mantra Digby lives by. "I'll need some paperwork from you. Fairly tedious forms to fill, but all straightforward."

Will turns in his chair to face me as Digby shuffles through the filing cabinet, searching for the relevant documents.

"Look, I don't want you to feel I'm treading on your toes. If you think fifty is too much…"

"No, I just didn't expect it. That's all."

"If it makes you uncomfortable though?"

"It's fine."

"Here we are!" exclaims Digby, seizing the papers. "Shall we begin? Now, you are applying as co-signatories, yes?"

Lord, how official, I hadn't thought of this. "Oh, er, yes—"

"No. I'm just the hired—"

"Will, it was your—" I turn to face him. He counters to face me, both of us flushing.

"Whatever you'd like—"

Our words collide, our responses so perfectly, awkwardly timed.

"Yes, co-signatories," I say, half laughing with relief. Yes, it feels so much safer having someone to share this responsibility with.

I swirl my cursive across the page and pass the silver, blue-tipped baton to Will. *Here I am, Ashtead, making a difference. We are making a difference.*

Will works tirelessly with the designers, providing sketches and copy for the print. I watch from my desk as the JPEG documents ping-pong back and forth across the superhighway. He edits this, tweaks that, and is so persnickety that he borders on the anal. He says he will only be satisfied when he is sure I would be satisfied. I have no decent answer to that.

"So, do you want to see it?"

I look up from the glare of the computer spreadsheet to see Will leaning back, commanding the wobbly desk chair with no hint of wobble.

"What?" I mumble, as my mind drags itself back from the brink of Excel formula hell.

"The image. They've emailed me the final draft."

"Oh!" I slip from my desk confines, and I catch the back of Will's revolving chair. "Show me."

He looks up and nods before clicking the mouse. "Here it is!"

It is perfect! Not too primary color, not too text-based and stuffy, not too cartoony, but just right. Will's image is bound to interest students and teachers. The classic Shakespeare bust with bald head, moustache and big puffy ruff has been made cool with a pair of shades. Around this iconic image, smaller drawings circle the head like juggling balls. The first inset reveals Bottom, complete with donkey head, and Titania in corset and garters, draping herself around him.

"Won't the teachers think it a bit too…too…sexy?"

"I hope that's *exactly* what they'll think! Aren't most English teachers closet nymphomaniacs? At my school, I learned more biology studying Chaucer than I ever did in science."

The second inset shows a rosy-cheeked, cartoonish Sir Toby Belch and his stooge, Andrew Aguecheek espying the yellow-stockinged, cross-gartered, po-faced Malvolio. The image makes me laugh out loud.

The third miniature illustrates Macbeth with dripping dagger in hand, being schooled by Lady M. The final juggling ball shows a handsome Hamlet pretending he is mad to a poor, confused Ophelia.

"You have to have Hamlet," Will says. "The archetypal hero torn by which direction he must choose, who he should trust. It's classic. Plus it has poison, sex, insanity, and sword fights. Kids love it."

It is a feast of a picture. I can feel my eyes bulge with excitement. It's real. It's really happening, Ashtead is shoved a foot further back from the precipice.

"Thank you," I whisper, eyes still fixed on the screen. Will rises to stand beside me, and we stare at the screen in silence, a contented, familiar silence. We approve the design, place the order, and schedule the print run. On Friday, we will be the proud parents of ten thousand posters and flyers.

"What the fuck, Warren?" The sounds from the office on Friday morning are not harmonious. "You promised today, and I scheduled today."

I sidle in the door and see Will at his desk, standing up with his taut back to me.

"No, it's not good enough. Look, Warren, my deadline is today. Today was in the contract, and today it will be. I don't care if you have to mince your precious little arse down to Office World and run off ten thousand copies at your own expense, but I will have my copies."

I stand speechless as Will fumes. I have never seen him this… fierce. He starts and turns, flicks up his head in a frustrated "hello" and whips back around quickly. It occurs to me even the most seemingly easygoing people can turn. And I remember happy-go-lucky Cole, inflamed, enraged, standing at the bottom of the stairs as I lugged my bags out of the door. Maybe you never really know someone.

"Yes, you do that. If I haven't received delivery by twelve noon, I will be telephoning the head office, and I doubt Mr. Karides will be impressed to hear of your staggering incompetence." Will replaces the receiver, takes a moment, and turns toward me.

"Remind me to never piss you off," I say, taking the restocking form and retreating to a safe distance—the bar.

After an hour or so hunched in the claustrophobic confines, counting bottles of Schweppes, I hear the door latch click and hurried footfalls. I bob up to see Will running toward me, waving his arms above his head victoriously.

"They're here. They've arrived!" he whoops, grabbing my hand and pulling me along as fast as my uncooperative unathleticism will allow.

We pause in front of the brown paper packages. I cross my fingers, take a deep breath, and we fall to our knees, ripping the paper off in our impatient frenzy. With sheets of brown wrapping paper cast aside, we stand back and eye the finished hard copy. It's even better now than it looked on screen.

I turn to congratulate Will, but he is at his desk, with the telephone receiver balanced between his ear and shoulder.

"Warren? This is Will…from Ashtead…Yes, I know…they are here…I just wanted to apologize for this morning. I was quite out of line and shouldn't have taken my frustration out on you…No, no, I should not have spoken so rudely. Thanks again. The posters look fantastic. I appreciate it."

I am amazed. "That was nice of you."

"Yeah, well…I was an arse, but I didn't want to let you down. I've been doing a lot of that lately."

"No, you haven't. Look at everything we've achieved so far!"

"I do, Enna. I don't mean to, but when Melissa and I split up, she said that was her main problem with the relationship, that I always let her down. I was more committed to myself and my projects than ours, the team's. I don't want to do the same with you." And he says it as plainly as if he we're ordering a pizza.

What? Wait! Does he mean he wants a relationship with me? And, if so, how do I react to that? I'm his boss, his professional employer. Nothing else. Move along, thoughts. Move along!

"Well, if you ever need to talk, you can certainly ask for my opinion." *There! Well done, Enna! Friendly, yet still professional.*

The response from the poster mail-out is phenomenal. More schools call daily, desperate to book. I'm even getting calls from schools I have not sent information to. The teacher grapevine seems to spread with a speed and distance I never expected. Will continues preparing for the fast approaching performances with seasoned nonchalance.

I decide to give the foyer a facelift. It'll only take a weekend. How hard can it be? So, I set to work, wheeling my roller. Two hours—and half a pint of sweat in—I realize this is not my greatest business decision.

"Can I say I told you so yet?" he calls, pushing through the revolving doors.

"Bugger off," I mutter, loading the ever-thirsty roller.

"Told you so."

I don't really mean to hit him—just hurl a missile in his general direction—but a clot of creamy emulsion catapults from my paint drip towel and lands, Goliath style, right between his eyes. Surprise, surprise!

"You got me!" He sounds amazed. Actually, *I'm* amazed. I've never hit a target in my life. "Right, Petersen, now you're going to get it!" He shrugs off his jacket and charges toward me.

"No!" I shriek, ducking between the ladder's legs, dodging and feinting either side of the frame. I make a run for it, nimbly leaping over the precarious open paint can and recently refilled roller tray. "Careful!" I yell. "Watch the paint pot. And the ladder. This is not a playground! Will! Will!"

"That's not going to get in my way!" he shouts, on the rampage. He shoves the ladder out of his way, and I see it totter, but I carry on running, fighting the burn in my thighs.

Don't look back, I think, but I can hear his thunderous stride coming closer and closer and then his arms are around me in one quick swoop, and I can't move forward. He collects me up, rotates me round, and unimpeded by my legs beating frantically like egg whisks in mid-air, he cushions my back and cradles me in his arms as we thud to the floor. The bracing sound of the ladder clatters to the ground in perfect synchrony. It is startlingly loud and shocks our childish giggles into silence. We are a collective heap, a tangle of exhausted limbs.

I look at him.

He stares at me.

The loud silence is punctuated by our exchange of heavy breaths.

His face is freckled by flecks of cocoa-bean-colored emulsion. Close up, his eyes look like chocolate saucers as they stare into mine.

I can feel the pulse of my lips, the tightening of my chest, and all I can hear is the breath drowning my thoughts: *What are you doing, Enna? What are you doing?*

He gently reclaims his arms from the small of my back and draws his hands up. I close my eyes and can feel his hot palm cup my face. He hovers nearer, so close I can feel the warmth of his breath, his thumb grazing my lip.

I feel the air suddenly suck back. I open one eye and see that Will has jumped to his feet and is towering above me.

Chapter 12

"Sorry. Flashback to old rugby days. I didn't hurt you, did I?" He extends a hand to help me up.

I don't know what to say. "I'm fine," I lie, my pride rising to the surface and armor plating me. I'm trying to process: was that just my imagination, or was he really going to kiss me? Because it seemed to me like that is where it was going. And, in spite of my schooling myself to be professional, plus the fact that my little pulmonary pump is currently in internal intensive care, I'm not sure I would have stopped him.

The silence of thought is awkward.

"Well, I only popped in to say goodnight. See you on Monday."

And out he swoops.

I sit on the floor, growing cold in my painter's garb. We're friends. No, we are professionals. I am the boss and he is the employee. Besides, it's ridiculous to even think that a recently un-affianced man and an even more recently un-affianced woman — who, for the record, still can't quite believe that she'll never wake up next to her unfiancé again — would really be getting it on in the public, tiled floor of the foyer.

Ridiculous.

Next morning I rally bright and early, keen with purpose. I won't think about Will today, or Cole. There is a more useful man I need by my side: my dad.

"Sure thing, chickadee!" he says without hesitation. "I'll come straightaway."

With a thermos of tea in one hand and a couple of brushes in the other, Dad comes to the rescue. It is a relief to spend time with him, working side-by-side. He passes me the angled brush, and we start touching up the lines around the sockets and skirting boards. I paint delicately, keeping the light switch plate unsullied. Dad dips his brush into the tray, re-loading it and daubing the creamy emulsion along the coving line.

"I'm glad you called," he says, concentrating on smoothing a run of paint. "I received an email from Cole." *Kapow.*

My brush slips from my grip and swipes the switch with a blush of paint. "Oh, shit, shit, shit," I gasp frustratedly, as I hurdle the tray and grab the towel where it lies discarded from the night before. I try to wipe the fixing clean. *Out, damned spot. Out, I say!*

"He just wanted to know how you were. Your mother didn't think I should tell you, but I thought you'd want to know."

The paint has smeared the green and black porcelain facing. As much as I rub with the caked towel, the paint gums up the cracks.

"Anyway, your mother says it's obvious he still loves you. I don't know about that. Perhaps that's why he emailed. To keep in touch."

What, will these hands ne'er be clean? No more of that.

"Oh, bugger, this switch. I ruined it. Ruined it. Dad, would you just..." I throw the useless towel down petulantly. I don't mean to sound so angry, but if I don't, I know I'll cry.

"It's not ruined. It's fine. It's fixable. You can make it right. You can make everything right if you want to," he says, retrieving the towel and working the paint off.

"I don't know. I just don't know what to feel or do. It's as if every choice I make is a test. And I don't know if I'm making the right choices, and if I'm passing or failing."

"What are you talking about? You're doing a sterling job!"

"Choices, Dad. There are always choices. How can you do everything and please everyone?"

"Well, you can't, chickadee," he says, pouring the stewed tea from the thermos. "You have to live your life the best you can, doing what is best for you and least harmful for others. Look after number one. Sounds selfish, doesn't it? But if you're on the battlefield and you get injured, then who can you help? Now, if you keep your wits and check your area, you can help others when they need you. Tea?"

I slurp from the thimble-sized cup.

"I'm not on the battlefield though, Dad."

"Just do your best."

During one of her talk shows — which I never normally watch — Oprah said that every day you should make a list of "reasons to be cheerful." I curl up after a long day of painting — everything hurts — and with my duvet swathed around me, try to make my mental list:

1) The foyer is painted. A-ha! I did it.

2) My dad is great.

3) Schools are booking the show.

Reasons to be mortified:

1) Cole wrote to my parents. (Signifying what exactly? Big head fuck.)

2) Will, who unceremoniously didn't kiss me, has not telephoned/emailed/popped up to surprise living shit out of me. (Huge head fuck.)

3) Am mortified because I thought he was going to kiss me.

4) Am mortified because I would have let him.

5) Am mortified because does that mean I don't love Cole?

6) And I'm pissed off that Will makes me forget and makes me smile — doesn't he realize I am supposed to be upset about Cole?

7) Am concerned about this so-called professional relationship. How many bosses are chased and tackled by their employees? Not very bloody many, I should think.

There! Seven reasons to be thoroughly miserable.

Another Monday, and I find the perfect antidote to back-to-work-itus, my secret weapon, my confidence booster, my mental DD cup: the designer, chocolate brown and beige leopard print wraparound dress that I snapped up at the Joseph end of season sale. It was a complete steal and is now quite the loveliest thing in my wardrobe.

I sashay into the freshly-painted foyer, but it's not the cocoa bean, color 304, that catches my eye, but lots of William Shakespeares in shades. The foyer is festooned with flyers, posters, even black and white photos of Will and an old headshot of me from the early two thousand and something—intense stare, right hand to temple, splayed fingers clawing through curly tresses.

"Oh, good Lord!" I exclaim, horrified to see this exhumed photograph.

"What do you think?" He appears from out of nowhere—why am I surprised?—and I stumble on my chocolate wedges, tottering across the foyer like a hairy, inebriated crab. Bugger, bugger, bugger.

I look up at the voice through a veil of hair, brushing the strands from my lip-glossed lips with as much dignity as I can muster.

Will leans against the wall at the top of the staircase. His cool blue jeans, his midnight blue shirt untucked and open at the collar, his dark hair tousled—even when he doesn't move, he has swagger.

"Will!" I exhale with exasperation. "You've got to learn to cough, or knock, or something."

"Sorry. I was waiting for you. I wanted you to be surprised."

"Surprised and horrified. Please take the photo down. And please, please, would you start to wear a bell!"

As the day of the premiere inches closer, I seem to be caught up more and more with the trivialities: teachers concerned about content, fire safety, insurance, parking, student handouts, and where and when their students will eat their packed lunches. God forbid they miss out on a packet of crisps!

The telephonic babble leaves my eyes to wander the office, often alighting on the triangular back toiling away as he to's and fro's from office to stage. Less often, it alights on the photograph of me wrapped in Cole, now relegated to the shelf.

I've broken the habit, I think. I've been working, smiling, laughing without him.

Perhaps in an alternate universe, I am living with them all, all the Could Have Beens that I thought at one stage or another I could not live without: Cole, Jeremy, Tom, Giles, and, in the future, maybe even Will. I like that. Perhaps I am the alpha female and have my own happy harem in the theater, or perhaps I'm not missing out on any potential futures after all. That somewhere, somehow, Enna is finding a life for herself in Scranton with Cole, being a domestic goddess in Islington with Jeremy, serving her country and her captain in the Royal Logistics Corps, training dolphins with her childhood sweetheart, as well as saving her theater. Maybe I'm not missing out at all; I'm just doing it somewhere else.

Over the PA system, I can hear Will rehearsing on the stage, learning where the floorboards squeak and creak and where he must leap. His voice crests and falls with a hypnotic rhythm. He paints pictures with his words, his inflection, his subtle intonation. I swivel in my chair while he transports me to the enchanted forest, where Titania slinks across the stage, the rasp of her comely voice purring in step with the sway of her rounded hips. All this he weaves from the music of his voice — a magic flute, a Pied Piper.

For the first time in a long time, the office looks shipshape: empty in-trays, groaning out-trays, a thick pile of checks standing proud in the letter rack, sheeny surfaces excavated from the paper landslide. We are nearly there, a week until curtain up, and the transformation from knackers yard to cash cow will be complete. Sure, I'd love Ashtead anyway, from the underground passages to the dead hang above the stage, but the satisfaction of making it a prospering business is so exciting. To have something that you love and believe in, and suddenly have others love it too — that's it. That is why I did this.

Now I have this opportunity to share this magical place and prove that perhaps the strange theater lady who was supposed to move to America, but who didn't, isn't so misguided after all.

The irony is, the person who would really appreciate Ashtead's meteoric rise is Cole. If he could see it now, then he would understand that this is what I needed to achieve for Ashtead and for myself.

"There you are! Still attached to your desk, I see. I don't think you've moved all day." Will charges into the office, a ball of energy bouncing off the walls.

I smile back as I try to stifle a yawn.

"Well, I've got a surprise for you." He pulls an envelope from his back pocket. "Ta da!"

"What's this?"

"Open it and see."

I suppose I am expecting another school check, accidentally addressed to Will or something, but it's a gift certificate to…

"Elisium, Spa for Health and Wellness. It's for you," he announces in his Hamlet voice.

I examine the voucher, a question on my lips and a pucker on my brow. "It's not my birthday."

"I know. I just thought you might like it, that's all. I wanted to say thanks for taking a chance on me with the show, and you've been working non-stop, so…"

"Well, that is really thoughtful of you. Thank you." And I mean it. I am really touched. Another yawn rolls up my throat, and I don't hide it as well this time.

"You're exhausted. Why don't you go for an afternoon massage, or something? I can man the fort here. Treat yourself."

It's not such a bad idea. Yes, I can go for an hour or two. And my brain will probably be far more productive afterward. Cole always said that even the best business minds take breaks.

"You know what, I think I will."

I have never been to Elisium before — I've never been to any kind of spa actually — and am really quite excited at the prospect. I give Mum a quick call, offering to share my certificate, and although she refuses to let me "waste the gift on her," she happily agrees to come along for the fun "and maybe a wax."

Now, although I am a novice, in my mind I am a spa professional. I can mix with the upper crust, the ladies who lunch, who order a chilled bottle of Chardonnay and smoked salmon salad. The kind of ladies who languish for two hours, waving forked rocket leaves in the air; harried garçons dancing upon them, snapped to attention by perfectly manicured, red-tipped nails flashing in the sun. An exfoliated, moisturized, painted and coiffed breed who speak particularly loudly as they reiterate their specific dietary instructions.

"And, that's San Pellegrino. Not Evian. With slices of lemon." And with a flick of their talons, they dismiss said water boy and continue their conversation about their latest trip to Monaco/charity event with Prince Andrew/possible adoption of unfortunate orphan from Somalia, "because, darling, Iman is from Somalia, and they truly are a beautiful race. Exquisite bone structure."

Such is my over-imaginative impression of spa types, and I am interested to meet this sisterhood of women who actually do very little and think even less.

Or so I believe, but the wind is rather taken out of my sails as I enter the waiting room to find it filled with, well, normal people. Normal people wearing beige.

I don't recognize any of the four women waiting but smile generally around the room whilst I make my progress to the seated receptionist who, with her red tunic and shining earpiece, looks every inch the efficient *Star Trek* Uhura.

"Hi, I'm Enna Petersen. I'm booked for a two o'clock."

"Have you ever experienced Elisium before?" she asks, steepling her hands together, showing off the most amazing two-inch talons, intricately decorated with black, red, and white varnish.

"No. I'm an Elisium virgin!"

"Right," she mutters, fixing me with a withering look. "You need to fill out these, then bring them back to me."

I take the forms thrust toward me and leave her with a broad beam, but she doesn't crack. Ah well, if she is too busy to be friendly, then sod her. I am having a good day. I am a successful theater director wearing beautiful three-and-a-half-inch scarlet stilettos, and I can do anything!

I fill in my disclaimer, skimming over the multitudinous clauses, signing my rights away in the event of a tragic spa accident. Seriously, what are they envisaging when they write these things?

"KAMIKAZE JACUZZI SHOCKER — Local theater director boils in temperature-defective whirlpool bath at local spa!"

"OILY MASSAGE LEAVES A DEADLY MESSAGE — Calamity as slicked local theater director slips on massage oil, cracking open head and rupturing marvelous, undervalued brain!"

"FOOT FUNGI FIASCO — Local theater director has feet amputated after violent reaction to salon nail varnish!"

"Hello, darling! Sorry I'm late. There was a sale at Monsoon!" She bustles in with her big handbag bursting at the seams and falls gratefully into the chair beside me. "What have you got there?"

"I'm agreeing to any number of spectacular salon deaths."

"What?" She clutches her handbag protectively with a look of mock shock horror.

"No, not really. You have to complete this 'In the event of…I will not sue you' form."

"Well…" She chuckles into her hand. "You didn't book a…*dye* job, did you?"

Chapter 13

A tall, goateed, white-uniformed man approaches me. "Miss Petersen?" he whispers, laced with a thick, rolling R. "Come wiz me."

I follow his rapidly disappearing frame through the maze of ornate arches decorated with plastic ivy and purple grapes. My meerkat neck is on a swivel as we pass various dimly lit rooms, each swathed with a different colored chiffon scarf. I hear none of the expected whale music or panpipes, but instead the trickling of water which, I discover, springs from an impressive water fountain, where clear water streams between the mouths of overflowing Grecian urns. Lucky I don't work here. I would constantly need to pee.

"Zee fountain of youth, health, and wellness!" he announces. "Please, you take a coin and make wish." He passes me a rustic terracotta pot filled with small silver coins. Slightly bemused by this unimagined rite of passage, I half-smile and take one of the proffered pennies. He retreats and turns his back to me. The coin is no bigger than a five pence piece, deeply engraved with the tarnished picture of an urn. I flip the coin over in my hand as I try to decide on a meaningful wish—when in Rome.

The reverse of the coin shows a single letter, an E. E for Enna! I clasp the coin with wonder, awed by the bizarre coincidence that

I should choose a coin with *my* letter on it. My spirits soar! How funny fate is.

Another wave of thought.

Oh!

Spirits plummet, E is for Elisium, E-diot! And yet, ridiculous as it is, as much as I know you make your own luck and everything else is just coincidence, maybe, just maybe, it will be lucky for me.

I feel the cold metallic sliver cut into my palm as I squeeze my fist tight. With almost religious conviction, I close my eyes and concentrate on wishing. I expect a wish list of fantasies to swim in front of my eyes: visions of the theater packed with patrons applauding another ground-breaking performance; me looking on like the proud parent, my hand held, feeling so small in someone else's, a clutch of beautiful, intelligent children around me. But the red-black blur persists, and instead of seeing my inspiration, I hear my own voice resounding quite without thought.

"I just want to be happy," it says. I throw my penny and watch it descend.

We pass the fountain, and my goateed leader draws back a final sheer curtain to reveal "Zee Temple of Elisium. Vel-com. Take a seat," he says in his unplaceable European tones. He indicates one of the velvet-upholstered thrones surrounding a mosaic-topped table laden with exotic fruit and jugs of flavored waters. He watches as I self-consciously sit in state and await the unknown. "Zis is your first time, no?"

"Yes." Shit, what gave me away?

"Well, just relax and enjoy zee experience."

What's with all this "experience" nonsense? Surely going to a spa for a massage can hardly be described as — gasp! Hold breath — experience. An "experience" is trekking through the Himalayas with a llama; the rollercoaster of performing nonstop for three weeks at the Edinburgh Festival; traveling to Andalucia on a university field trip, meeting a handsome local called Juan and being taken on his moped at breakneck speed along the coast roads, clinging to his taut bronzed body, before he stops, sweeps you into his muscular arms, carries you to a deserted star-lit beach and makes love to you five times before the sun comes up. That is an *experience*.

He stares at me inquiringly. He is very intense looking, with his pale skin, hair pulled into a ponytail, emphasizing his dark strong brow and deep set eyes.

Russian perhaps, I think. *Like Rasputin.*

"I am Xavier. I will be giving you your experience today."

I try not to giggle childishly.

"First, I will give you some cucumber water to hydrate yourself. You can make zis yourself at home. It is very good for yourself. After, you take zis robe and slippies and take off your clothes in changing room. Zee lockers are for your own use. When you are ready, you take yourself shrough zat door zeyare, take off robe, lie on bed, and I will see you have good time."

"Okay. Thanks." I choke, trying not to spit my cucumber water and hydrate Xavier too. I take the robe and "slippies" and emerge "myself" from the changing room a few minutes later, ready for my "experience."

I peer through the dim mood lighting and take in my new environs. Candles flicker in their sconces, creating an ever-changing light show on the pale walls and filling the air with a hint of jasmine. This room is accented with aqua sheers draped around the door frame and the shower cubicle in the corner. The massage bed is the focal point, with strategically positioned towels at chest and bum level, and beneath them what appears to be plastic sheeting. *That's weird.* Is Rasputin about to wrap me up like a bloody sandwich?

As instructed, I disrobe quickly, hoping my curiosity has not taken up too much time, and Xavier does not walk in and catch me in full pale, slightly chilly, glory. I flick off the flip-flops, fling my robe, and hop up to the high bed as elegantly as nudity allows.

I kneel on my weird, sticky bedding, all the while eyeing the door handle, ready to hit the mat should Xavier enter and find me still positioning. I shuffle my knees down the bed to lie face down, but the sheeting clings so well that it sticks me. I do half a press-up and assess the damage. The plastic beneath my boobs has been shuffled south. Where my legs used to be covered in flesh, they are now securely bound like two frozen chicken fillets in individually plastic-wrapped portions.

"Shit. Shit. Shit," I curse under my breath, and I lift my torso and struggle to pull the cling. It's like I'm a human in a full body condom. With a few heaves, I pull the plastic back into place, covering the bed, and just as I settle again, fitting my relieved little face into the doughnut head rest, I see the aqua towels which should be draped over my buttocks, mocking me from the floor. "Shit!" I must have knocked them off.

I reach for the nearest towel, but my fingertips just graze the corner, unable to gain purchase. I stretch. I shuffle on my pallet, inching closer, but am still unable to grab it. "Urgh!" I rock from side to side, trying to gain momentum and reach the bloody towel, but the plastic sticks fast to every inch of skin it touches. I'm starting to sweat. He'll be back in any minute.

I eye the door knob. I eye the towel. *I'm so close. One more rock. I'm there. I've got it. I've got it. It's between my fingertips…*"Wooooooo." I flop to the floor, my slippery mermaid tail following with a dramatically loud, wet fish thud. "Shit."

"CLINGFILM CALAMITY—Local theater director found on massage room floor smothered by own sweaty clingfilm!"

I push myself up from the floor, but my wrapped legs are so tightly bound, I can't bend them and get to my feet. I shuffle, trying to peel sticky limbs from their wrapping.

"Hillow? Knock knock. Is everythink okay in zeyare?"

Shit, shit, too late.

"Umm, well," I call lamely, "not really."

Yeah, right, I'm a real spa professional! What Xavier must think, God only knows, but fortunately, his steely Russian expression does not change. He pries me from my sheath, ignores my abashed nakedness, and busies himself with rolling out a new sheet and fresh towels while I cower in the corner, brandishing the offending aqua article.

"It can get sticky, no? Now I turn my back. You get on, and I will cover you up."

My mortification is short-lived, as Xavier sweeps it away with every brush of his strong hands on my taut muscles. He switches on the whale music—I knew there'd be whale music!—and tells me in his hushed thick accent what oils and lotions he is using. His company is soothing, not obtrusive. Thank God. He is happy to concentrate on his work and I can…*wait for it…brace yourself, Enna…relax.*

"You are tense. You 'ave many knots here. You have lots of stress, I sink. I work that out for you. Zis is the Sumatra cocoa bean and vanilla exfoliating scrub. Zis is the soothing cocoa lotion. You will smell of zee milky chocolate."

I am standing on a wooden jetty. I have the rope in my hand. I push off, leap across the water, and jump on the sailboat, casting myself adrift on waves of vanilla and chocolate. The sun beats warmly on my skin. I hear the whales as they fluke up through the lapping oceans of milky chocolate, showering me with chocolatey spray as they dive deep below.

The hour passes all too swiftly. He whispers thickly in my ear, "Is time to shower now."

I stretch like a sultry cat basking in the sun. I feel energized yet heavy, as if I really *have* had the Andalucian beach "experience."

I watch Xavier as he turns the shower faucet and adjusts the temperature. "Zare, it is warm for you. I go and you shower, zen after you lie down again, and I finish you off." He frees the aqua sheer curtain from the tieback and lets it fall between the shower and the room. "For your privacy," he assures me. *Horse, stable, bolted* springs to mind, now that he is acquainted with every inch of my exfoliated skin.

The water pours down on me from the enormous showerhead, washing away every last grain of cocoa bean. I close my eyes and feel the surge of the water pouring overhead, luxuriating in the powerful flow. I run my hands down my body. I feel like the surface of a ripe nectarine, all those peachy hair follicles and dull epidermis rubbed away to reveal a smooth, glossy skin — a new me — albeit a little bruised. The dead skin is sloughed away, and I watch the soap and grains swirl in their watery tornado down the plug hole.

How strange and unexpected life is. A month ago, I was about to jump ship from my ailing theater into the arms of my lovely fiancé. Now I have a thriving theater, great prospects, and flawless, silky smooth skin. A fair exchange? I turn the tap and watch the final gulp glug down the metal gullet. I flick the beads of water off and reach for the towel. Am I happy? Am I? Happy?

Of course I am! I am a V successful, smooth-skinned artistic director with vast, indefinable potential. *Yes, Oprah, I do have reasons to be cheerful!*

I settle back down on the raised bed, this time keeping a firm grip on the fresh, white towels. Xavier re-enters and slathers me in wondrous hypnotic aromas. His hands do the work of ten, working in the chocolate cream blended with a hint of fragrant coconut. I smell good enough to eat, silky to the touch and, less fortunately, as horny as an alley cat.

"You look great. Really. You should take time off more often." Will eyes my reinvention appreciatively. If I weren't such a professional artistic director, I would swear his eyes were flirting with me.

"Well, thank you. I feel positively rejuvenated. What'd I miss?"

"Nothing, really. The line was quiet, so I started a spreadsheet of the accounts. I couldn't find one, so I created one."

"Oh, yeah, I hadn't got around to it yet. Great. I have always got by doing the accounts myself, but it is a time leech and energy vampire. Thanks."

"No problem." He winks appreciatively. "Oh, er…Maureen was in to clean. She's completely barking."

"Oh God, she wasn't in the office pestering you, was she?" I sink to sit beside Will on the desk top.

"Actually, yes. I guess she came in while I was on the phone, working some stuff out with the accounts, and she starts to go off on a rant, 'What do you think you are doing? Those are Enna's classified files. You put those away, you good for nothing!'" Will bobs his head and heaves his imaginary Maureen-boobs skyward.

I start to giggle. His impersonation is priceless. "That's it! You got it! Brilliant. Really brilliant!" I say between chuckles.

Will stops bobbing, and laughing, and smiling, and there, he just fixes me with that look of his. My laughter evaporates, and out of the silence, he lifts his hand slowly to my face. "It's good to see you smile," he says, though I'm sure I'm not smiling anymore. I am sure my face is dead serious, nervous even as my bottom lip trembles under his close attention. His thumb moves lightly across my lip and then he shifts toward me, and his lips are there, between mine, soft and warm, moving in concert, first slowly and then hungrily, taking my breath away.

"I…can't," I murmur, pulling away from him, casting my eyes at the floor. But, his lips are there again, searing my skin, at my neck, my earlobe, behind my ear, his warm breath igniting the touchpapers throughout my body. *Oh God, Oh God, Oh God. This is happening.* "This is…wrong. We shouldn't." *This isn't Cole. What am I doing?* "This is…completely un…professional."

His hands cup my face, caress my cheek. His fingers run through my hair and move down my shoulders to my waist. My eyes are tight shut. *I'm not doing this. This isn't me.* And yet, his lips meet mine again and we're kissing, and—

"The door!" I yelp, suddenly, mindlessly complicit.

Will slips from the desk to stand in front of me. Without taking his lips from me, he kicks the door shut. He pushes the desk chair toward the door, and I watch it roll into place, exactly under the handle of the door.

I am barricaded in. Just me and Will.

"Enna Petersen, I have been waiting months to do this." He nuzzles into my neck, and I almost lose the power to hold myself upright. But then I don't have to, for he does the most amazing thing.

With his large hands under my arms, on either side of my ribcage, he lifts me ever so slowly off the desk, high into the air, above his head, his arms at full stretch. The muscles in his forearms throb, and I see the blue veins rise to the surface of his skin. He holds me, the whole of me, in his powerful hands and in the grip of his stare. Our eyes are locked, an arm-stretch away, and the sheer power and desire are overwhelming. I want him; I know I do. I didn't know it for certain before, but right here, at this moment, I know I can't wait any longer.

"Will, I…" I begin to try to find the words, but he reels me back in, his tractor beam eyes undressing me with every incoming inch.

"No talking," he whispers, stopping my mouth with his.

And I can't help myself. My mind is possessed by my body, and it knows what to do. My legs wrap around his waist and pull him closer. His head jerks back, his ardent stare feeding off one last look, before some cue is fired and *clash*, our lips meet again in a fast and furious mesh of flesh and teeth, clothes and cuffs, fighting against fabric, buttons flying, limbs flailing. I'm breathing hard now, inhaling his sweet, raw sweat, like a catalyst awakening every sense, every cell and fiber, and I'm charged and live like an open socket, latent with electricity. We collapse to the floor, writhing in rhythm, my smooth, sweaty skin clapping his.

For the second time in one day, I am lying on the floor without my clothes on.

Chapter 14

I lie on the green carpet of my office, senses sobering, and I feel every bump, bruise, and carpet burn of the day. My limbs feel like I have been thrown at a wall. I survey the strewn clothes, the knocked over cups, the scattered papers; the office looks as if a tornado has hit. I gather my clothes and my wits. *No munchkins or wicked witches from any point of the compass. Just me,* I think, as I slip on my heels. I catch sight of my blissfully battered form in the mirror on the back of the door, and I can't help but grin girlishly at the reflection.

I make a vague attempt at a cleanup, righting the mugs, the chairs, the obvious, but am keen to avoid potentially awkward post-coital moments, so I hurry with the necessaries. I write a hasty line on a pink Post-it, stick it to the door to greet the showering Will, and slink out of the office.

A productive afternoon's work.
See you tomorrow.

I want to write more, of course. That I'm still tingling with the touch of him. That I can't believe it. That I wish I could lie in his arms. But lessons in love — or rather, detentions in disappointment — have taught me better than that. To be lusty is one thing; to be lusty and lovey dovey, quite another.

I make it to the revolving doors opening out onto the streets. I take a breath, place my sunglasses on, and brace myself for the cool sunshine.

"Done for the day?" The needling tones halt my stride and draw me back. The wicked witch descends from the west wing fire exit.

"Maureen! What are you still doing here?"

She stands there with her usual ineffective prop — her duster — dressed in her usual domestic disguise — her tabard and turban. I suppose it is quite appropriate, really. She *acts* a good volunteer cleaner, even if a review would find her abilities distinctly lacking.

"Who, me?" she bobbles.

No, Bette Davis. Of course you, you infuriating bag!

"Oh, I wanted to get those new curtains up in the dressing room. You know, before the big off!"

"Oh good." I nod back. Oh God, it's contagious. I'm nodding.

"I'm looking forward to seeing how you've made-over the office."

"The office?"

"All that banging and bashing! Sounded like the sky was falling in! His highness looked quite red in the face after all that humping around. I caught him in the green room taking his clothes off. He was about to have a shower!"

Oh lummy! Does she know? Did she hear?

"So I said to him, 'What a racket!' and he said to me that you had decided on a change around up there and shifted the furniture. You should know better than to tire yourself out, young lady. It's all right for him huffing and puffing and humping objects all over the shop, but such a small thing like you could hurt yourself."

I bite my swollen bottom lip, feel the little bumps on my chin where his stubble rubbed me raw, and I keep my smile to myself. "I'm stronger than I look, Maureen," I say as I replace my shades and head off into the late afternoon sunshine.

Home. It's a relief to step inside and shrug off the roles of the day: director, business woman, daughter, spa-goer, sex vixen.

The door closes quietly behind me, and as it clicks into the latch, I realize something has changed. I look to the wooden staircase, the bare kitchen through the glass door, the wilting plant on the radiator shelf. With keys in hand, I stand frozen, suspended in animation as I try to detect the change.

Then I see it: it's Cole chasing me up the stairs; it's Cole's cooking fogging up the glass of the kitchen door; it's the begonia that flagged us down with its bright red petals as we walked, arm in arm, past the florist. Cole insisted we stop and buy it.

I look at the limp leaves, the decaying brown petals scattered over the shelf, and remember its former glory. With my back to the door, my knees crumble, and I slide to the floor. Cole! What have I done?

The ghosts of Cole in the house rally around me, a tribal council demanding answers. Have I irretrievably, indelibly, undeniably moved on? Forgotten about him? Turned my back on him? Forever? Has my allegiance so quickly changed, mocking what was my almost-marriage?

But I was the one who left. He said he'd moved on, so was it so very wrong?

No.

So why do I feel as if someone is dying all over again?

I close my eyes to block the memories, but the homey images of Cole disrupted by the realized fantasies of Will are branded on my eyelids.

In the depths of the black swirl, there is a rustle, a rattle, a thud and a jarring pressure on my spine. *Oh, not a migraine. Please not the start of a migraine!* My ears, full of mental recrimination, open and awake other senses. Another thud to my kidneys. My eyes deglaze.

"Enna? Enna are you in there? It's me. What the bloody hell are you doing? Enna, are you all right?" I hear an elevating urgency in his tone which loosens my tongue.

"I'm fine, fine," I say, grasping the words, as present as a sleepwalker, aware just enough to make some sounds and crawl out of the way.

Leo pushes the door open and rushes in.

"Must have dozed off."

"By the door?" he questions skeptically.

"I was *really* tired."

"Well, you look like shit." Ah! Brotherly love! "Anyway, I came to tell you my news…Lins and I are officially moving in together!"

"But you practically live there anyway."

"Well, now it's official."

"Oh, good for you."

"Ah! You'll miss me!"

"Like a cold sore." I get to my feet and give him my best sisterly withering stare.

"Funny. Anyway, I'm celebrating, and since this is my last night of freedom, and I can't find anyone better, how do you fancy going for a curry?"

I stagger past him into the kitchen and blindly fill the kettle with water.

"Are you sure you're okay?"

"It's nothing. Seriously, congratulations. At least one of the Petersens can live happily ever after."

"Oh shit. Sorry. Insensitive, just a little? Well, Enna, I know it was messy and all, but you have to move on. It's been, what, a month since you got back? It's time to get back in the saddle. You'll start to get wrinkly and saggy soon, so chop, chop!" Leo thinks he is a comedy genius.

I have yet to disillusion him. One truth at a time. Here goes. "I have been chop chopping! That's the problem."

"Ew!" He reels backward like I have just unwrapped a truly obnoxious cheese.

"What am I doing? I should have a fucking degree in self-sabotage!"

"This is about Cole, isn't it? Are you having regrets?" Leo dispenses with his jokes and looks at me seriously. He braces my shoulders and looks me straight in the eye.

"No. Yes. I don't know," I reply, shrugging out of his inquiry. "That's the whole bloody problem. Life is a series of choices. I've made my choice; I accept that. I'm not a teenager…it's just…difficult. It's awful to think that there is someone out there who hurts, and you're the reason. I can't bear to think of him doing the things, going to the places we were supposed to go to together, alone, weeping into his whiskey. It's torture to think of what could have been. And I'm going in a different direction, but I can't help questioning if it is the right one. But today I took a giant leap down that other path, and it was like crossing the Rubicon. I can never go back now. And these fucking tears! Leo, why won't they stop?"

He hands me a rectangle of scratchy kitchen paper. "I hear what you're saying. Choices…difficult. But, you know, you shouldn't bottle these things up." He looks very earnestly at me. "I heard that on *Oprah*."

A healing laugh surges through me. "How about that curry? I'm starving."

Unlike most towns in England, constantly growing up and out, sprawling into every available patch of green, Ashtead has retained its tight-knit community, centered around the one main High Street and the little kidney-bean land mass of industry floating a mile away of Lower Ashtead with the railway station, the rec, the pond, the cafés.

The post office sells sepia prints of Ashtead High Street, circa 1910. Over a century later, it is almost the same. The brick buildings have kept their modest two or three stories, their character, and their history. The shops are individual: the butcher, the baker, the gift shop, the post office, the two banks closed for lunch, and early on Wednesday, the frequently sprouting building societies, the Indian, the new Italian, the Starbucks, and the pub, which has just, according to Mum, "gone gastro," so now offers more than just steak and kidney pudding and fish and chips.

The street committee flies their flags for St. George's Day. They tend to the hanging baskets which line the street in the summer, flourishing with red geraniums and dangling purple lobelia. In the winter, with much provincial pomp and circumstance, the village is adorned with fairy lights and glowing-nosed Rudolphs. Ashtead is a bastion of conservative values, which make *The Shakespearian Rap* somewhat of a risk. But I am doing a lot of living dangerously these days, it seems.

The Star of India has inhabited its aloof spot at the end of High Street ever since I can remember. The blue and gold sign changed about ten years ago to the current black and gold sign illuminated with neon pink lettering.

I feel a certain nostalgia toward this eatery. Back in its non-neon days, Leo and I would plead to go with Dad and collect the takeaway treat. We would race into the restaurant, heave open the set of heavy double doors, where the unintelligible yet cheery waiter would pat our heads and hand us an After Eight chocolate mint from the box on the counter.

I remember, too, the late nights, when Dad had some formal meeting or other at the officers' mess, and fuelled with a few whiskies, he would call Mum to pick him up. Dutifully, she would carry us from our beds, dressed in our pajamas, swathed in our duvets and, like a contortionist, place us in the back of the little green Renault 5, all without disturbing our slumber. She would drive through the night, hunched close to the steering wheel, peering into the darkness, her babies sleeping in the back. She never dared leave us at home on these night missions.

Rolling up to the mess entrance, she would cut the engine and wait for Dad as we slept soundly on. Oh, for a mobile phone in the eighties! When eventually Dad would appear, he would waste no time in waking us, tickling any foot which had strayed out of its cozy duvet hidey hole, and singing rude songs, much to Mum's silent, white-lipped fury. Leo and I regarded these nights as great adventures. None of our friends were marauding at midnight.

Dad would exclaim that he "needed sustenance. A vindaloo would do!" And there we would stop, in the middle of the night, at The Star of India, the little Renault loaded with its precious cargo: a merry dad, a furious mother, and two wide-eyed children, faces pressed to the glass, watching for Dad to get back into the car with his treasure, a brown paper-bagged curry for him and two After Eight mints.

Leo and I heave open those same heavy double doors and are hit by a wall of aromatic spices and comforting, warm, nutty smells. The bow-tied waiter rushes to greet us at the door. With smiles and nods, he welcomes us and indicates a table. I nip in and take up the velvet upholstered banquette seat so I can look out into the restaurant.

The inside has changed even less than its exterior. The long rectangular room, banked on each side with tables, has a warm chintzy feel: its furniture covered in pink velour; its swirly patterned red carpet—a mistake not just kept to the floor but extended up the walls also; its thick, pink linen tablecloths and napkins and matching pink carnations, a single stem in the molded white vase at the center of every table. The same strains of the sitar are played, and I have to sit on my hands to resist the urge to twist my wrists in the air and peck my head in time to the music. It is comforting to sit in this cove, in this restaurant that is full of such funny, familiar memories. Perhaps that is why I like it so much; it is like my lovely, faded theater.

Neither of us even has to look at the menu.

Leo spends the evening talking about Lindsay. It is nice to be distracted, and I half listen to him as I scoop up chunks of the rich, creamy korma in the pocket of the chewy naan bread and ladle it into my mouth. I savor the exotic flavors, the doughiness of the bread, the nuttiness of the pilau rice, rolling around in my mouth.

"And so that's it for me. Moving in is like a pre-engagement. The women of the world will have to get over it! So, tell me about this new bloke. Spare me the graphics, though. I'm eating."

I look up from my loaded forkful. "It's complicated." I lay the utensil down, wipe the grease from my fingers, and let my conscience out. "He's the guy who is helping with the relaunch."

"The Shakespeare bloke?"

"Yup."

"Wow. Well, nothing like shitting where you eat."

"Choice analogy. Thanks for that."

Leo smiles through a, fortunately closed, mouthful of vindaloo. My thirty-three-year-old brother, going on thirteen.

"I don't see what you are so worried about. You're single. I presume he is too. Cole was off the table a long time before Shakespeare was on the…what? The desk?"

I will tell him one of these days that he is not funny.

"You ended it when you chose the theater."

"No, I didn't! Cole lied to me first! He said there would be a job and then there wasn't. That's why I left."

"You sound like a twelve-year-old! Seriously, Enna, why would you let the job dictate where you should be? People are what matters, not places, not things. You can't blame Cole for not getting you that job. And if he did get a job for you, you wouldn't want it anyway, would you?"

"No, but you don't understand! It's the fact he knew. He knew I couldn't work there, but he wanted to keep me there anyway! He tried to trap me, Leo! That's not the way to make me stay. And now there is this peachy situation with Will — oh God! — and I thought the one thing I could rely on was myself, and now look what I've done!"

"Jesus, Miss Melodrama! What difference does it make, really? Maybe it was just a one-off, and he'll want to forget the whole sordid, little escapade?"

"Any dessert? Ice cream?" The little waiter appears at my elbow, snatching up our plates and bowls with practiced ease.

"Oh, no, thank you. I'm stuffed."

"Literally." Leo smirks, and I give him a swift kick under the table. The waiter nods genially and takes the messy pile of plates and cutlery to the kitchen.

"Who says he wants to forget it?" I demand. "And it wasn't sordid. Actually, for your information, it was pretty bloody special."

"Okay, whoa! No graphics. But to recap, and do tell me if I am getting this wrong, you're single. You're moving on. You've met someone you obviously have a lot in common with. You slept with him. It was, quote unquote, 'pretty special,' and the problem is…what exactly?"

"Well…well…"

My brother may have a point. *Really?*

The little waiter appears again, sliding the leather-jacketed bill to the center of the table.

Leo slaps his hand down on it. "Enna, listen. There is no problem. You are making a drama out of nothing. If you do have a relationship with this guy, great. Woo!" He gives a Jolson jazz hands wave, and it's hard to keep a straight face. "If it's just a one night thing, it may be a bit awkward, but you're both adults. It needn't be a problem."

When did my brother—who used to wear jeans with the crotch down to his knees and talk of nothing but skateboards—start to speak sense?

My mobile vibrates across the table. I glance at the illuminated screen and see his name. Will.

"Answer it, then," Leo prompts.

I open the phone, breath deep. "Good evening. Enna speaking."

"It's Will."

"You escaped from Maureen's clutches then?"

"Not a moment too soon. Look, I think we need to talk." *Here it comes, Enna, incoming, brace yourself: he had fun but now…yada yada yada and cheery pip and too-da-loo! I knew it. This is exactly what I thought would happen. Now it will be awkward and embarrassing, and the theater will suffer.* "Are you at home?"

"No, actually," I reply coolly. "I'm out having dinner." I can play the game. I don't want to, but I have my pride. Funny that this strong, professional voice can make itself heard over the inner voice, the voice clamoring in my ears for some sign of post-coital approval.

"Alone?"

I look up at Leo, and he diplomatically withdraws his chair and leaves the table.

"No." I remember just six hours ago, his naked body glistening and gliding into mine, the weight and force of him. "Leo is here. And you?"

"Desperate to see you!"

What? Wait a second. I had not predicted that.

"I haven't stopped thinking about you, wanting to touch you."

Oh, thank God.

I feel like a complete child. Here I am, a young professional in control and accomplishing great things, and yet, the merest sign of affection, and I'm bouncing from the ceiling like a Pepsi'd child at a birthday party. Seriously, the cancan is going on in my brain.

Perhaps my transatlantic navigation was a scenic misturn. Perhaps it was all in the plan — the predestined pathway — that I would return here and have both theater career and a man. Perhaps it is necessary that I feel hurt and guilt about moving on from Cole, because it validates what was: we did love each other, but now we must run our separate courses in pursuit of happiness.

Permission to get over it? Permission granted.

Chapter 15

I click my phone shut. A childish grin spreads like a fault line.

"You do realize how ridiculous you are?" Leo says, returning to the table. "You moo about guilt and betrayal and choices, then the next minute he calls and your face lights up like Chernobyl!"

"He's coming here for dessert."

"Oh, give me a break!" Leo laughs smugly. "Here's twenty quid for the bill. I won't stay. If I have to listen to poetry, I might vomit in my mouth. Another time."

As I sit and wait, wishing I hadn't gorged quite as much korma—that beached-whale feeling is never all that conducive to nights of naked abandon—it dawns on me that I am breaking all the dating rules. Not only have I mixed business with pleasure, I have done it without ever going on a date. I'm worse than a first-date shag. I am a no-date shag. Even worse, I am a no-date shag with curry breath!

The little waiter is polishing glasses at the bar. I grab him by the sleeve and plead, "Where's my After Eight?"

"Pardon?"

"You know," I say with a chuckle, trying not to sound insane, "After Eight, the mint. You know, for curry breath?"

He looks at me as if I am really, quite, quite mad. "After Eight? Oh, yes, After Eight. We stopped After Eight. So expensive now."

He continues to polish the glasses, and I resolve to keep Will at arm's length.

"You look gorgeous," Will says from the door, the other diners briefly raising their stares. He shucks his jacket and tosses it to the banquette. "Can I come and sit over there with you?"

Oh. I clamp my lips together and smile, trying not to breathe out. He moves around and dives in for a kiss, receiving a rather sad, tight-lipped offering.

"Something wrong?"

I shake my head and shrug my shoulders, turning to the side to inhale a quick snatch of air.

"You're all red-faced. Are you drunk?"

"I am certainly not drunk! Just in need of a mint."

"Oh, why didn't you say so? Here." He taps some mints into my palm and a few into his mouth. "I hope I'm not too offensive. I ate a pesto sauce this evening that was so garlicky I could probably put young children or animals to sleep."

I take a gulp of air and am relieved to resume breathing.

"Ashtead's improving. Better restaurants mean more people, and that means more theater-goers. You know it's worth getting the restaurateurs on side. If they promote us, we can promote them. Offer a pre or post—"

First-date shag?

"—dinner theater package. All it takes is a few subtle marketing tricks, and we could see a nice return."

He's talking to me as if nothing has changed. As if the fact that we spent the afternoon in a naked tangle has not completely ruined our employer-employee relationship. This…is…nice. Yes, this is very nice.

"I know the owner. I'll speak to him. Maybe suggest mentioning the restaurant in the program."

The other diners pay their bills and go. The waiters and kitchen staff trail home, carrying their brown paper bags of leftovers. Only Mr. Virani is left watching late night football on the TV in the takeaway pick-up counter. He tells us how much he loves Manchester United.

"We ought to have a rule: no shop talk," I suggest after discussing every merchandising opportunity under the sun.

"What would you like to talk about?" His arm is around me now, his fingertips tracing patterns over my shoulder.

"I don't know. You. I don't know anything about you."

"There's not much to know. Went to Warwick…toured pretty much ever since."

"You love it though, don't you?"

"I like dancing to the beat of my own drum, going wherever, whenever. There are times when a weekly paycheck would be nice rather than hand to mouth, but that's the nature of the business."

"Touring is tough on relationships though, isn't it? It was hard for me and Cole, and we weren't even dealing with nomadic existence."

"Melissa and I had our ups and downs, but it's only a problem if you make it an issue."

"So where's home?"

"Everywhere. Anywhere. I want to see it and do it all. Experience everything available. Trouble is, that can often be expensive, which is why I have to make the most of my bookings. I've often thought of performing on the cruise ships, travel and show. I haven't made it yet, but someday. The thing with Melissa really opened my eyes. We have one chance to do things with our lives, so you have to strangle as much out of every single opportunity as possible. But you have to do it on your own terms, be selective, not hitch your cart to any passing wagon."

I turn, hinged to him at the shoulder, like the turning page of an open book.

"Oh, you're offended. Don't be. I didn't mean you hitched your cart. You unhitched. That's far harder. I think you were amazingly brave to choose the…what do they call it? The path less trod? And to take this on and have the guts to see it through…well, that makes you pretty exceptional."

And just as I am trying to process his silver-tongued words, his lips are on mine, and I don't care if he thinks I've rehitched my cart or not. I care even less if I have curry breath.

Manchester scores a goal, and Mr. Virani cheers from somewhere, but we don't even look up. Our lips are locked and content to be so. I could happily drown in his kisses.

He drives me home, his care and attention trained on me alone and not the road, surely breaking every traffic code. The front tire scrapes noisily along the curb as he pulls up to my house.

I half expect he will charge for the door and throw me down on the nearest available surface, but he withdraws to his half of the car and cuts the engine.

In the dark, with only the streetlight shining overhead, his eyes take on a new intensity, less molten chocolate pools, but flaming orange orbs of fire, daring me to move. He is truly intoxicating.

"I said, what time tomorrow?" Will shakes my shoulder gently, his face furrowed with concern.

"What?" My vision snaps back into clarity, amber darkens to brown.

"Time? Tomorrow?"

"Sorry…I think I just zoned out for a minute. What did they put in my drink? Ketamine?"

"What? Are you sure you are okay?"

"I'm fine. Sorry. Fine. Sometimes I get these headaches…migraines, really, and they often affect my eyes. I should probably go." I reach for the front door handle. "I'll see you tomorrow at eight a.m."

"If you're sure you are okay. Look, if you're not feeling well tomorrow, don't kill yourself. I can handle it. There's lots I can do, and I don't mind. Really. Don't be a martyr."

I nod and concentrate on getting myself to the door. I scratch the key in the direction of the lock, dragging the tip over the surface until the metal trips over the tailor-made grooves. Contact. I turn back, waving, and hear the sound of the engine and see the blur of the car as it roars away.

My head does not throb yet, but if the hazy vision is followed by its usual headful of fun, it is only a matter of time. Migraines are not unfamiliar. At university, they were a regular event — my system completely shutting down, on strike. So I know the signs. The pattern is well-established: first, my vision blurs; then my speech dries up; my brain is squeezed into a meat mincer; and — the glorious, technicolored finale — I vomit with velocity and volume. *The Exorcist* girl had nothing on me. I am surprised to feel the first signs now, however. My blood sugar should be in seventh korma heaven.

"Was. Was. Was," I say out loud to the dark, empty house, testing the migraine signs. My worst attack, years ago now, stole my "was." I just about managed the letters but could not string them together. It was the most frustrating loss of words — a brief glimpse into the future loss of one's faculties.

I drop my keys on the radiator shelf amidst the fallen begonia petals and stagger through to the kitchen to fill a glass with water. I down the contents with thirsty swallows before crawling blindly, eyes closed, up to my bedroom. I feel the starched cotton of the bed's valance and reach up to the mattress to pull myself up, but I can't find the energy. My limbs are too heavy. After several lame attempts, I feel the plump duvet deflate between my fingertips. I ball the material in my fist and heave. Slowly, and with brain-rupturing effort, the duvet swoops to the floor.

Chapter 16

"Wake up, you lazy git! WAKE UP!" Leo, in a haze of daylight brightness, stands above me.

My irises recalibrate.

"I said, WAKE UP!"

"What time is it?"

"Half two. You are *really* late."

I bolt upright, rattling my brain from its dormant status. Oh God. I'm late.

"Relax. It's okay. Lover boy called the house line. You really must have been out of it. Anyway, he's covering, no problem. He says, 'Take your time.' So, heavy night?"

"No. I only had two beers. I don't know. Maybe I ate something dodgy."

"I don't even want to know why the hell you're on the floor again. Is this turning into some weird habit for you?"

"I think I was having one of my migraines, but different," I say, still trying to process how I did get here. "And now I feel like my head might fall off and my stomach burst through my belly button."

"I get that. It's called 'excessive living.' Take two Aspro Clear, and you'll be fine." He pats me on the head to conclude his diagnosis. My ears ring with each unbuffered thud. "Cup of coffee?"

I hobble downstairs and sink into the sofa once more. I feel like a little old lady, withered, bent, and fragile.

"You really do look like shit," Leo says with glee as he places the steaming cup on the coffee table, picks my legs up from the sofa, and drops them to the ground. "Drink this. I'll run you a bath, make you some toast and then you'll feel as good as new."

Upstairs at the theater, my desk is clear, my in-tray empty. Even the bundle of checks is sorted. Will has ably dealt with the business of the day. Good thing, too, as my head feels like it belongs to someone else—a rugby forward perhaps?

For lack of anything else to do, I count up the checks on my little calculator, just to make me feel better. Oh! And the total does! I have never seen such zeros amass on the digital screen. There is so much I could do to improve the theater, to ensure its survival.

I can see it! The warm glow of the new sumptuous red velvet upholstery and curtains, walls re-plastered and professionally painted—covering the cracks and my hack job, updated and more efficient heating, a new lighting rig, a new reinforced stage, a roof that doesn't let the rain in. I spin in the desk chair, picturing it all. And, hello, money to pay for the running costs, the PRS, the rights and royalties, fire insurance, public liability insurance. We'll have insurance up the ying-yang. We could afford radio mentions and advertisements in *The Chronicle*. I'll organize workshops and drama classes, and the theater will be full of happy faces.

"How are you feeling?" Will's mellifluous voice hums with concern as he rushes in the office. I can hear the vibrations pitter-patter across my skin. He must have been rehearsing, as he is dressed in his Shakespearian, flouncy white shirt, his smooth chest enticingly exposed between the fabric tie-fastenings. My head feels lighter already.

"Better for some sleep. Thanks for taking the helm."

"Anytime, m'lady."

I catch his words like a thrown bouquet.

"I was just counting today's batch of checks. It's taking off, isn't it? Are we in profit yet?"

"Well, off the top of my head, from advanced ticket sales, we have more than covered the loan."

"That's brilliant!" I exclaim. *Really, this should be celebrated with a kiss!*

"Once we get reviewed, of course, you're bound to get even more bookings. But we have to have a game plan. You have to be one step ahead."

Or perhaps an illicit office obscenity?

"Bookings are going well now, but eventually the well of school children will run dry. What else can you offer?"

Some horizontal desk work?

"More productions for school groups and adults, or do you want to change things up a bit a go for a different target audience?" He paces as he rhapsodizes, his face etched with focus.

I focus on imagining him naked. More specifically, coated in whipped cream and chocolate fudge sauce.

"I've got it!" he exclaims, slapping the desk with zeal and knocking the cherry off my chocolate sundae fantasy. "We have already agreed that the school audience is a good market to tap into, right? Well, let's shift the age group. Instead of offering Shakespeare to the secondary schools, let's offer a classic like *Treasure Island* for younger school groups during the week and family audiences on a Saturday matinee."

"*Treasure Island*? Yes, the pirate thing is always popular. Kids, teens, adults—everyone loves a good swashbuckler. Maybe in the evenings, we could produce a smaller adult play, perhaps a period piece. Maybe, oh yes, maybe *Gaslight*. It's a brilliant thriller."

"I don't know it."

"Okay, brief synopsis: Manningham, who seems the most devoted husband, tries to make his beautiful, young wife think she is mad, all because he wants her inheritance. If it is done well, it is packed with suspense."

"And you'd have a small cast?"

"Why not? I mean, that's the direction I want the theater to go in. I know it would be taking even more on, but we could play the leads. I've always wanted to play Bella. You could play Manningham. If, of course, that doesn't constitute 'hitching wagons'?" The question pitches higher than I intend.

Will turns on his heel, abandoning his pacing pendulum to face me. The lines bracketing the space between his brows fold inward.

It's a good idea, I'm sure. I know my theater and I know what will sell, but it's not just business he would be contracted to, is it? Is that why I am suggesting it, because I want to keep him here? Oh God. Am I doing what Cole did to maintain my interest? No, it's different; I know the job exists. Will's look of consternation doesn't budge.

"It's not a terrible idea," I say to fill in the sound. "And you wouldn't have to stay here forever. We could take it on tour when the theater goes dark during the summer. We'd still have creative opportunities. We could have complete freedom. We'd—"

"Okay. Sounds like fun," he says, as simple as that. "I mean, one step at a time. Let's get the *Rap* out of the way first. I don't want to sign a contract yet or anything, but that's not because I don't want to hitch the wagon. It's because…well, let's just see what kind of season we can come up with."

He leans over the desk and plants a kiss on my forehead. "Now, stop worrying. No wonder you get all those headaches."

"I'm fine. I'm excited! It's there for the taking, isn't it? We can establish a reputation for producing quality educational children's theater and dramatic adult evening shows, and there will be a long future for Ashtead."

"You really care about this place, don't you?"

"It's my home."

He shakes his head ruefully.

"What? Did that sound cheesy?"

"No, just…sad. Home isn't a brick building. You take it with you. It's where you connect and feel comfortable. It is part of you, in your blood, your marrow, your sweat, and your bones. You don't need this…the trappings." He turns through a revolution, taking in the office. "Because you've got this—" he taps his temple "—and this—" he holds his hand out for mine and places it on my chest "—and this." He puts my hand on my stomach.

"I have a home in my stomach?"

"You have guts, Enna. You have brains, passion, and guts. You take that with you, and you can have a home wherever you are. Don't forget that."

I want to burst into *"If I only had a brain…a heart…the nerve,"* from *The Wizard of Oz*, but he has this funny look on his face, sorrowful and brooding, and I realize he is being quite serious. This is not the time for a fun musical interlude. Instead, as I dissect his poetic words, I wonder if he'd told me this months ago, would it have made a difference? Would I have been looking for something else in America? Would I have felt at home? I suppose I'll never know.

The theater is alive with First Night anticipation. Even the crystals on the chandeliers seem to tinkle with excitement. The board and public are coming. It's the Gala Preview with reception, which will be followed by a week of evening performances before the schools descend for matinees too. We are sold out and have capped the wait-list.

I can see the changes everywhere I turn: the orderly office, the well-stocked bar, the busy box office, the photo displays in the foyer — all signs of a thriving, professional theater. The financial burden has evaporated into the luminescence.

The Herald and the *Advertiser* have confirmed their Press tickets, which await them at the box office window within conspicuous large white envelopes — a trick I picked up to keep tabs on the tickets and know, without asking, if they had been collected.

The Stage reviewers have not returned my calls or emails offering comp tickets, but I have not lost hope, enclosing their comps in a pink envelope. A good review in *The Stage* would make real waves in the artistic community.

I have organized the troops: Mum is on box office detail; Maureen and Rita on usher duty; theater stalwarts, Barbara and Sidney, will man the bar; and Colin and Malcolm, fresh from their sound and lighting debut in *King Lear*, are in charge of the techie booth. Oh, dear Lord, so much to go wrong!

I rush to the office to collect the inserts for our next production, *Pirates of Treasure Island.* I can't help but admire the colorful print work, a collaboration between the artistic director and the education and outreach liaison. The *piece de resistance* is the gleam from Long John Silver's golden tooth — my suggestion — a metallic special in addition to the usual five-color printing process. The gold cost a lot extra, but as Will said, we don't actually have to pay until the first month of performances is deposited. Then, we can have one big payday! Hoorah! And I was right; the golden tooth did make the poster. If we can hook the audience with the first show, then they will return for the next.

I shift the weighty pile of inserts to my left arm and the winking answer-phone light catches my eye. I check my watch. The house opens in fifty minutes; I have time. I press play and rest on the desk, waiting for the message to beep into action.

"You have one new message and three old messages. First new message…*Beeeeep.*"

"*Enna, it's Cole.*"

Oh.

"*I know we haven't spoken in a while, but your dad told me that this was your big night, so…I wanted to say good luck. No. Break a leg! I hope it goes well for you.*"

I flinch and arrest in aural shock. The top program inserts flutter to the floor.

"Wake up sleepy head!" Maureen peers around the doorframe. "Look at you. Here you are, the whole of Ashtead downstairs, and you're daydreaming!" She smiles toothily.

I sigh, move to delete the message, and bend to pick up the fallen flyers in one smooth progression.

"So, how do I look?" Maureen hawdles in. It's her own characteristic walk—a cross between a hobble and a dawdle style of geriatric catwalking. It's not exactly New York Fashion Week.

"Samaritans' finest?" I smile, eyeing the eighties putty-pink, pussybow collar with ruffles and ecru elasticated waist trousers.

"How did you know?" she asks with wonder.

"I know all, Maureen!" It is the only place she shops, after all.

"Oh. So, this is the next one, is it?" she asks, bobbing her head in the direction of the gold-toothed flyer.

"Yes, Maureen."

"And, er, is *he* going to be in it?"

"Who he?"

"His highness! Is *he* going to be staying around?"

"I get the distinct impression, Maureen, that you don't like him." I like this man more and more.

"Humph!" she snorts. "Well, it's not for me to say, is it?" she says, thrusting her disapproving chin into her wattles of skin around her turkey neck.

"Will has done wonders for this theater, Maureen. I don't ask that you should like him, but at least give him credit. He is an asset to Ashtead, and I would not be here today if he had not stepped in to help me."

"Yes, well, he's a wonder, I'm sure. I just…I just hate to see you get hurt. I told you about my Fred. Now, if I'd known before—"

"Maureen! It's First Night! I really don't have time right now, okay?"

Her boggle eyes grow even wider.

"Sorry, I'm nervous. I didn't mean to snap. Here, these flyers are to go in every program. Got it?" I place the bundle in her hands and hustle her through the door, ignoring her clucking.

Now, where was I? I came in here to collect the flyers, and—uh! The answer-phone message from Cole. "I can't think about that now!" I say to the answer machine. "I have a theater to save!" I grasp the hanger on the back of the door and change into my opening night outfit.

Five minutes before the house is set to open, I descend the stairs from the office to the reception.

Mum looks up from the box office and whistles. "Very pretty, sweetheart!"

I take a spin, revealing the tuxedo from all angles—the elegant black satin trousers and the cream shirt front, haltering around the neck with a black bow tie and tying around the waist, leaving the back between bare. I take another spin in the chandelier's spotlight, enjoying Mum's approval.

"I'm going to open the doors. Are you ready?"

"Break a leg!"

"Thanks, Mum," I say, moving toward the revolving glass door, but on impulse, I run back to counter front, reach over and give her a hug. "I'm nervous."

"Don't ask me why, but I am too." She gives me another encouraging squeeze and pats me on my way to unlock the revolving doors.

I see it as I saw it then twenty years ago—the revolving doors, the magic portal. Through it I look out and survey the crowds milling, admiring the traditional façade: the brickwork rigged with fairy lights, strings of little white lights wrapped around the black lettering, THE ASHTEAD THEATRE; a wooden sandwich board straddling the pavement, silently hulloing Ashtead's passing public.

TONIGHT: THE SHAKESPEARIAN RAP!

I unlock the door, and the throng bustles in. I wonder if there's a young girl fizzing with excitement, determined to take the glass revolving capsule all by herself?

Standing under the chandelier, I welcome the familiar faces and listen to the hubbub, the growing chink of glasses and the rustle of paper spirals being torn from Cornetto ice cream sheaths. The crowd shifts, and all of a sudden, I see the little girl I have been looking for. She is smiling nervously, standing still, the noisy swarm of activity swirling around her. I lift my left hand to wave, exactly as she lifts her right. The door revolves again, and she vanishes.

I weave through the bubbling crowd, a fixed lipsticky grin stuck to my gums. Many faces turn to talk. "Enna! Enna!"

I nod. I wave. I raise eyebrows, exchange shoulder shrugs, and point to my watch like an enthusiastic French mime artist. I sidle exaggeratedly past wine-toting members of the board, city council dignitaries, and nod at trench coat wearers. At a guess, these would be Mr. Herald and Mr. Advertiser. Why do journalists always wear beige trench coats? There seem to be only three types of people who wear beige trench coats: journalists, flashers, and Columbo. Do they think it awards them some kind of anonymity? Newsflash: it doesn't.

Dad stands aloof in the corner, wearing the burgundy and navy of his guard's tie, a glass of red gleaming in his hand. He lifts his glass to me and smiles. I wonder what he makes of all of this. *"All you lovies, air-kissing and talking incessantly with nothing better to do than to make things up!"* Good old Dad. This is probably his idea of torture. I give him a wave and pass stealthily to the back of the lobby and through the door with the "Private" plaque.

The passage snakes underground around the auditorium and surfaces backstage into many tributaries: one corridor to backstage left, another circles further to backstage right, one to the green room, and another to the dressing room. The passage is narrow—a claustrophobic nightmare—but my legs whisk me along. I lay a steadying hand to the cold, dank passages. The institutional green peels from its plaster and crumbles beneath my palm.

I hear singing from the dressing room, a low roll, rumbling on. I pause in the corridor and listen, the notes and lyrics not registering at first, but it comes together like the answer to a equation. *I've got it!* He's singing "Ol' Man River" from *Showboat*.

His reverberating, resonant bass makes the skin on my bare arms pucker and the long fair hairs stand to attention. I close my eyes and see the old steamer churning its way down the Mississippi. I roll my head around the open doorjamb, and Will looks up from tying his shoes.

"Just warming up."

"Don't stop! If music be the food of love, play on, give me surfeit…"

He straightens up and with a sheepish look, he starts singing again, but new words this time.

> *"I'll only sing out,*
> *If you will join me,*
> *'Cause I'm 'bout to go on stage*
> *And I feel wobbly.*
> *So just keep singing,*
> *Just join in singing with me now."*

I could be twelve years old, standing by the wall at the Downsend Boys' School disco. I shake my head in mute decline, but he takes my hand and pulls me into the dressing room, swinging the door closed. He gathers me in his arms. I feel the trail of his fingertips on my bare back, and a small, unbidden whimper escapes from somewhere deep in the pit of my stomach. We two-step in a circle, in the middle of the bare-bulbed brightness of the dressing room, and he sings softly into my ear.

> *"You and me, we don't sleep, always toil*
> *Tryin' to get this theater out o' turmoil*
> *Sell that show, better make back the dough,*
> *Or the bank's gonna make us feel woe"*

Charged by the touch of his electric fingers, I gather my courage and join in an octave higher, humming harmonies to his made-up lyrics.

Transported into his magical backstage world, I forget myself, the old paper-thin walls, the audience sitting just feet away behind the safety curtain. The notes rise in my throat, and I feel so…free. I have never been with a man who gets and enjoys what I do, who agrees with my principles and passions as much as this man. I can't imagine I would ever be standing backstage, singing with Cole.

Cole? You have to think of him even now? Jesus! Don't spoil it.

Will lifts me up in front of him, high above him, his forearms fully extended, and I feel so strong, so supported. Tornados may blow, tsunamis may devastate, but this is a different kind of natural, powerful energy.

"Enna!" Malcolm calls, frantically charging into the dressing room, breaking the spell. A panting and red-faced Colin follows hard at his heels. I am unceremoniously and inelegantly dropped to my feet.

"Yes? What is it?"

"It's just that…" the twosome fluster.

"Yes?"

"We can hear you," Malcolm hisses in an over-exaggerated stage whisper.

"We can all hear you," Colin blurts out.

"The mic pack." He points to the little black device, lying innocently on the dressing table, its green light winking at me. "It's on, and it is working *very* well."

<h1 style="text-align:center">Chapter 17</h1>

"**O**h sh—" I gasp, catching my runaway tongue. I dive to the treacherous microphone pack and flick the switch. "You control the volume in the booth. Why didn't you fade it out?"

"Well, yeeeees. Funny thing, really. We didn't know what it was at first. I get waxy buildup, and my hearing isn't as sharp as it used to be. Anyway, so there we were in the booth, weren't we, Colin?"

"Yes, and there you were down here, singing away…"

"And then we noticed that heads were turning, and people were getting all excitable, weren't they, Colin?"

"Oh yes, and then we heard Mrs. Monk saying that it was one of her favorites from *Showboat*."

"But we knew it wasn't the pre-show music, because, well, I sat on the CD you gave us and broke it."

"Then Malcolm got it! He said, 'That's Miss Petersen and young William,' and it was!"

Will and I stand in stunned silence.

"Why didn't you mute the microphone from the board?"

Colin looks to Malcolm. Malcolm looks to Colin. They both look at me and shrug.

"Never mind."

"Oh, don't look so sad, miss. Mrs. Monk and the other board members seemed to like the song."

"A real crowd-pleaser," Colin adds.

"They thought you sang it very prettily indeed."

I plunge into the chair. My mind races to the white and pink envelopes in the box office, and I pray that they have not been collected.

"COMIC CATERWAULING!—Ashtead Theatre director, Enna Petersen, held an unprecedented backstage warm up act, much to the bemusement of the conservative crowd!"

Malcolm and Colin return to their booth with much bustle. Will and I remain silent, waiting for the turbulence to subside.

"Well, we are nothing if not pioneering. How many productions do you know that begin with a backstage duet?"

"I can't believe it. Really, I can't," I repeat incredulously, sinking back into the arms of the green velour, feeling like a complete prat. "I wanted this evening to go so perfectly, and now we look like a bunch of clowns. The sooner we can make some money and employ trained techies, the happier I'll be."

Will tosses aside his base sponge and crouches in front of me.

"Hey!" he says, shaking my knee. "Hey! Enna, would you stop taking every little hiccup so personally. These things happen; people understand that. You can't be responsible for everything. I actually think it is pretty funny."

"You would. It's not your reputation on the line."

He knows I'm upset and lets it go, but I'm sorry for saying it. He is as much of a part of this theater now as I am.

"Enna, worse things happen at sea. They could have heard far more scandalous things." He leans in, grips my thighs, pulls me to the edge of the chair and into his firm torso. "Miss Petersen, on this auspicious occasion of the inaugural evening of entertainment at Ashtead Theatre, I wish to say how very lovely you look and how most ardently I would like to fuck your brains out."

"Oh, you say the sweetest things!"

"I mean it." He fixes me with his intense stare, and I feel a single bead of sweat run down my spine. His eyes remain locked onto mine as his hands writhe with octopus dexterity. They drum up and down the smooth satin of my trousers, rippling up the inner thigh and fluttering over my crotch, lightly at first, and then he presses harder and harder, the tips of his fingers drumming over me, feeling every contour of me through the fabric.

His stare remains fixed, daring me not to succumb, his fingertips working feverishly, and I try to hold out. I don't want to lose to control, not tonight, not now. I bite into my thickly lipsticked lower lip. I dig my nails into the armrest of the green velour and try to anchor myself for support, but he hits the spot and sends a seismic wave coursing through my body, shooting from my tingling clitoris, firing impulses, rocketing up neurons. Whoosh! They explode like synchronized fireworks in their floral finale, dendrites blossoming like a diaspora of dandelion clocks. And another wave crests and explodes, another, another. I arch my back, lifting off the seat, every muscle tensed and pulsing, and I catch my breath. My eyes water as the sensation beats me. Unable to fight anymore — not wanting to fight anymore — I break his stare and fall back into the chair, drowning in ecstasy.

"There." He gets up from his knees with a satisfied spring. "They could have heard that, and then you'd have something to worry about."

"You're a smug git," I say as I pull him close and hold him so tightly that I can feel the muscles slide over his back as he holds on to me.

"It's going to be great, you know. Trust me, it is," he whispers into my hair.

"I know."

He breaks away to finish his stage makeup. I check my *dishabille* in the mirror. So far, this evening is not turning into the elegant, sophisticated event I had planned. I run my fingers through my ruffled hair, and paranoia strikes. I turn slowly to Will and pounce on the microphone. The green light is not on. The switch is turned to off. I breathe more easily again as Will chuckles at my neurosis.

"You really are a control freak."

"And you're an arse."

"I know, but you love me."

"Hmm."

"You do. Admit it!"

I bite my smile into a straight line, but he is satisfied.

"You better go and silence the savages." He brings his hot lips close. They hover over mine as he whispers, "Knock 'em dead."

"Ladies and gentlemen…" I hang a suspensory pause, waiting for the wave of recognition to filter to the back of the auditorium and for the bobbing sea of faces to settle. A multitude of unrecognizable, glossy faces turn toward me. All I see are glistening eyes, glinting glasses, glossy gums and bright smiles. *Remember this moment, Enna. This is a successful theater.*

"I am so proud to welcome you here to Ashtead Theater. Marrying the old with the new is what we are about tonight. Not only has this art deco theater had new life breathed into it, but the production you are about to see is an original classic, Shakespeare updated with reverence, passion, and wit. The talented man responsible for this huge feat is Mr. William Angler.

"There are many people I ought to thank, but tonight I want to extend my gratitude to just one person, Will. I met Will Angler when this theater was at its very lowest. There was no money for renovations, no budget for quality productions or publicity, let alone trained actors. Will helped me turn that around, and with his great ingenuity, Ashtead Theater is on the road to recovery. We are even planning our next season with our very own adaptation of *Pirates of Treasure Island* for school groups, and evening performances of Patrick Marber's Victorian thriller, *Gaslight.* I look forward to seeing you all there. I owe all of this to Will, so Will, thank you. And now, please turn your mobile phones off, don't take flash photographs, and please enjoy *The Shakespearian Rap.*"

The applause from the warm audience gathers in my ears, and I smile into the light. The clapping continues loudly for several seconds, fading just in time for me to hear the loud cries of the lady in paisley print sitting in A8.

"I thought it was *Showboat*!"

I can't relax. I can hardly breathe as I wait for the verdict — will the thumbs go up or down? I sit rigid in my seat at the back of the theater, the still sea of heads in front of me focused on the stage. The silence is painful. There is a woman somewhere near the front, coughing. Somewhere in the vicinity of row R, I can hear cellophane wrappers noisily discarded. I can feel the worn pile of the velvet sticking against my back, the stubble of upholsterer's horsehair pricking my flesh.

Will comes out dressed as William Shakespeare: doublet and hose, beard and bald pate, a feather quill in his hand. He recites his introduction, weaving his lyrical lullaby over the music. It is not obvious at first that he is rapping, the rhythm and the meter seeming so like poetry. The audience listens intently.

The lights change, and the beat kicks in and reenters as Bottom with a donkey's head, waxing his lyrics to the hip-hop beat. Heads turn to consult in hushed whispers. I hear a seat flap up, and I turn. A man with a trench coat folded over his arm slinks past his knobbly-kneed neighbors on row F and makes his way to the exit.

Oh God! A trench coat! Oh God! He hates it. I look around, scanning the audience. Their stunned silence deafens me. It's too radical. They are too conservative. They want to lynch me. They want to string me up by my chic halter neck dress shirt frontage and feed me to the snarling trench coats.

Will effortlessly jumps from Bottom to the temptress Titania, jettisoning his donkey head for a wanton posture and come hither voice. He fills the stage like a balloon let loose. "What Angel wakes me from my flowery bed? It can't be my husband; he hasn't got a big head."

I cringe at the suggestive double entendre, slipping lower in my back row seat. I await the horrified stares between the members of the board, but instead I hear the hearty guffaw of Christine Monk. It rings though the silence like a church bell. Then, to my amazement, another laugh peals, and another, setting off a round rolling rally of mirth, until the whole audience is swaying back and forth in their seats, their laughter filling my ears.

"Darling! Darling!" Brandishing her glass, the contents perilously sluicing up the sides, Christine Monk nudges through the crowded bar, using her impressive armory of elbows and boobs. "Darling! It was fabulous. Better than fabulous. Wherever did you find him?"

"It's a long story," I begin.

"Well, get to the good bits. Have you bonked him yet?"

The surprise makes me breathe and swallow at the same time, and my ill-timed sip of red wine is directed down the wrong pipe. It burns up and down my trachea as I choke, trying to reroute it from my lungs.

"Oh, don't worry. I shan't tell your mother," she is saying, oblivious to my surreptitious drowning. She nonchalantly pummels my bare back with one bejeweled hand and takes another hearty swig from the glass in her other. "If you haven't though, you should. Ripe for the picking, I'd say!" And then she sails off into the crowd, crepey cleavage first.

"You all right, love?" Dad asks as I swallow up the last of the diverted drink. "Have a sip of this, chickadee."

"No thanks, Dad. Whiskey isn't quite the cure I'm after."

"'Course it is. Whiskey is the cure for everything. Though not with oysters. Did I ever tell you about my friend who had this nasty—"

"Yes, Dad, many times. Oysters, whiskey, bad combination. Now, stop trying to hijack the conversation and tell me honestly, what did you think?"

"Yes, good," he replies regimentally.

"Well, that's insightful. Really, I'd like to know what you genuinely think." Using his arm like a boat's tiller, I steer him away from the distracting crowd and through to the quieter foyer.

"I think you're very talented and that you have pulled this evening off beautifully."

"But..."

"But, well, it's not my cup of tea. Shakespeare is one thing, but rap? Whatever made you want to use that crap?"

"You're showing your age, Dad. The rhyme of the rap and the rhyme of the poetry complement each other. It's perfect! Think of rap as poetry to a beat. Didn't you laugh? Come on, you had to have laughed."

"I suppose. The bit with the yellow socks was pretty funny. And I did understand it, which is more that I can say about Shakespeare, but rap music? Couldn't you have used The Rolling Stones?"

"Tell you what, Dad, when Will has a free minute, I'll get him to rewrite *Macbeth* to 'Paint it Black.' How's that suit you?"

"Sweetheart, I've seen it once. Please don't make me come here again." He gives me a well-meaning squeeze. Poor Dad! He willingly goes on expeditions with a fifty-pound backpack clamped to his back, running through wind and rain, camping under a soggy canvas, eating army rations that look like dog food, and *this* he finds a test of his endurance! "There's your mother. I better cut her off before she starts talking to someone she knows. Then I'll be here till Christmas."

He ducks to kiss me on the forehead and makes a clean break to ambush Mum and escape without enemy interception. Mum resigns herself to capture. With a slight shrug, she turns to wave, blows me a kiss, and is shepherded home to base.

Will emerges, red-faced from the shower, and reaches my side after much nodding and palm-pressing.

"Will, this is Reverend Shelby. He's been on the board since nineteen sixty-six. *Isn't that right, Reverend?*" I relay loudly for the bemused octogenarian.

"Ah! Young man." He catches hold of Will's arm and inspects him through his less cloudy eye. "You make a good ass! Ha!" His thick, phlegmy chortle reverberates around the bar. His shoulders shake and hunch over as he enjoys his own joke, his sibilant hisses becoming louder hoots.

Other patrons join in the joke until the reverend starts to wheeze and cough, grappling for the handkerchief in his pocket.

Will looks to me, awkward and ineffective.

"Let me help," I say, bringing a chair for him and waiting for the hacking to pass. Seems to be an evening of choking.

He holds the handkerchief to his mouth and breathes heavily. The reverend looks up at me apologetically. His lips are a shade of mauve against the translucent white of dentures. "I'm fine, fine." He waves his balled handkerchief in his shaky fist. "I seem to be an attention hog, my dear. I'm sorry. These lungs! Does anyone know of a new pair going cheap?"

The bar titters again nervously.

"Well, dear, you have quite a menagerie, don't you?" he whispers, summoning another breath to continue. "You have an ass *and* a hog! You're like Noah, and this is your ark!"

My ark! I like it, I think as I wave off the last well-wishing straggler and switch off the foyer lights. With my coat hastily shrugged over my shoulders, I push the revolving doors and turn through one hundred and eighty degrees.

I expect some come-down, a perceptible drop, a return to the real world, but tonight the stage world and real world seem to merge. Gloss meets matte. Warm meets cold. Pretense meets reality. Art meets nature. It is all one wonderful, magical kingdom: the moths dancing around the street lamps; the horse-chestnuts standing straight, tall and almost bare on sentry on either side of the theater; the milk-white moon, full and clear in the night sky, a perfect orbit of yolk over-easy, its domed surface pitted and craterous; the marquee, unlit yet still luminous, with more winged creatures that have survived the cold so far buzzing in attendance.

"I love you."

I barely register the meaning of the words. Tonight, I too, am in love with everything. But then I feel arms encircle me from behind, smell that new familiar scent of Will, and I sink into the soft folds of his jacket.

"Where did you come from?" I throw over my shoulder.

"Nowhere. Just waiting for someone as lovely as you."

Wrapped in his arms, I stare out into the night. I want to gush, to tell him everything: how they *ooh-ed* and *ah-ed*, what they said, when they laughed, that I love him too, that it was meant to be, what great parents we'd make, that I would be miserable without him…

Instead, I turn to face his stubble-covered jaw, his welcoming lips, his molten eyes, and I say, "We did it!"

I climb out of the bath and reach for the towel. I hear the front door latch snatch into the groove and bipedal stampede up the stairs—Will returning from his early morning forage.

I towel myself dry, listening for him. It's still so new and yet it feels so familiar and easy. I like the sound of him in my home. I like sharing my pillow with him, lying face to face in the dark and whispering remembered observations of the evening. I like him popping out to get fresh milk and bread and other promised goodies.

The top stair creaks as Will releases his weight from it, and then I hear the hurried knock.

"I'll be out in a minute. Put the kettle on. I'm gasping."

"Enna! I got them! *The Advertiser* and *The Herald*."

"Never mind!" Suddenly, I'm not so thirsty anymore. The verdict has arrived. I hitch the towel around me and propel toward the door, tripping on the bath mat, slipping on the tiled floor and wrenching the door open with accidental momentum.

"What? They went to print that quickly? Oh God! Oh God! What do they say?" I cry, betoweled and bedraggled, wet hair dripping on my feet.

"I haven't read it yet. I wanted to wait for you."

I dive for the top copy and run down the stairs to the coffee table, casting the accumulated crap onto the floor and laying the sacred publication out flat.

"Okay, sit next to me and don't speak."

I turn the pages one at a time, scanning for the words I recognize. There! *Ashtead Theatre Rap Rhapsody.*

"Oh, I can't look," I exclaim, jittery with adrenaline. "You read it." I shift the page over to him. "No, I'll read it." I reconsider, pulling it back toward me. "Oh God, and look at the photo! Okay? Ready? Here goes…"

Will's head is already bowed, engrossed in the three-column article. I can feel my heart pounding in my chest. The pulse beats in my ears and the tips of my fingers.

"Unique approach," I repeat out loud. "Simple style in a complicated format succeeds in entertaining without dumbing down."

No dumbing; that's good.

"Contagious energy and enthusiasm." I beam. "The frenetic activity and constant changing of characters does, at times, leave the audience needing a breather."

That's okay. It's okay!

"Masterful reworking is a tour de force." Tour de force, that's more like it. "'Artistic Director' — oh this is me — 'Enna Petersen, shows great foresight and bravery with this no doubt controversial programming and, with the passion and talent Ashtead presented last night, she is sure to succeed.' Bloody brilliant! It's good, isn't it?" I ask for reassurance.

"Good?" His eyes sparkle with delight as he laughs a cheer. He throws his arms around my bare shoulders, and we jubilantly jump around the living room, my towel hanging on precariously. FA Cup winning team locker room celebrations could never have been this giddy.

"Next!" I say when we have calmed down enough to summon sense and breath. I scramble for *The Advertiser,* spreading its pages across the table. I lick my thumb and turn the pages, ready to read what great praise Mr. Advertiser is to heap upon us. "Arts section? Arts section? Page twenty-one. Here we go."

The bold headline screams from the page.

Ashtead's Amateur Night

I look at Will, his face reflecting my own horror.

"What?" he cries in disbelief, swiping the page from the paper and turning away from me. I don't want to see it, and yet I do; I have to.

"Will, let me see." I peer over his shoulder, but he stands and paces toward the window.

"Listen to this: 'William Shakespeare would surely have turned in his grave had he listened to the latest embodiment of his most popular works, *The Shakespearian Rap*, at Ashtead's newly renovated theater. The work is, at best, a comic rap regurgitation. Whilst it may have some value to introduce the Bard's work to those whose IQs match their shoe size, the oft used expletives, and gratuitous use of double entendre, reduce the performance to a base and puerile level.

"'Those who enjoyed the adult puppet musical, *Avenue Q*, might find the translation and performance similarly amusing, though I found little to recommend it. With a mass of props, useful to those dire stand-up impressionists popular in the nineteen eighties, the translator and performer, Will Angler, runs around the stage in various guises and switches character so often I felt I was watching the outpourings of a schizophrenic. His performance did show moments of skill, but the production in general, with the mundane hip-hop beat, minimal set and basic lighting, reduces *The Shakespearian Rap* to Shakespearian Crap.'"

"Stop!" I cry, covering my ears. "I can't listen to this."

"Unbelievable," Will mutters, continuing to read, continuing to darken in red-faced exasperation. "Who is this arsehole? Hang on, there's a bit about you here. You want to know?"

"Oh God!" I jump up on the sofa, clinging to my towel.

"You said you didn't want to listen."

"Yes, but I do now! What does he say?"

"'Ashtead Theatre's young director, Enna Petersen, shows enthusiasm but naïveté. She has great plans for Ashtead's sole surviving playhouse, and for that I must applaud her, but her experimental programming is too radical to entice and sustain an audience in this conservative diocese. Ashtead Theater produces passable amateur work, but for a professional production, you are better off traveling to Richmond."

"I think I need a second," I say, stumbling down from the sofa and slumping onto the floor. The rug and sofa and all comforting security have been literally swept out from under my feet.

Chapter 18

I stare at the chipped *Purple Passion* nail varnish on my toes. How could he be so blind? How could he be so deaf? Didn't he hear the laughter? How will this affect ticket sales? Doesn't *The Advertiser* have the largest circulation in the region?

Will giggles unfathomably, and I look up from my own well of disapproval. How could he possibly find anything about this even remotely amusing? His creeping titters boil into full rolling laughs, unrepentant, unabandoned laughs! He is transformed, defiantly holding the offending page aloft and ripping the paper to shreds, paragraph by paragraph, sentence by sentence, syllable by syllable, until the pieces of paper-snow fill the air and land meaninglessly at my feet. He is worryingly changeable.

"That doesn't make it go away, you know, Will."

"No, no, no, Enna, this is great. Positively, abso-fucking-lute-ly great!"

"Are you on drugs? There was nothing in that bullshit article to recommend us to anyone! Ugh! It makes me physically sick. Do you understand how damaging this is going to be for our sales?"

"What did he say? That it would only appeal to people with, and I quote, 'IQs like their shoe size,' right? Well, how many upstand-ing people last night said they thoroughly enjoyed it? They will be up in arms about this. Let's feed off it! We can whip this up into a media storm."

My heart—which I thought had long since flatlined—suddenly seems to pump again. The metronome beat thumps in my ears as I imagine the possibilities:

"PEOPLE RALLY TO ASHTEAD'S DEFENCE!"

"OUTRAGE IN ASHTEAD AS CRITIC SNUBS LOCAL IQ!"

"But, won't it look like sour grapes? Shouldn't we just accept his opinions? I don't want to drag this on. The least said, the soonest mended, right?" It's official: I am becoming my mother.

"Don't be naïve. It's business, Enna. You have to get ruthless. Kill or be killed. Survival of the fittest!"

Jesus, stop with the "naïve!"

"Come on, we're not discussing evolution now. We're talking about Ashtead."

"Exactly, and we have to use every piece of armory in our arsenal to survive. Are you going to fight, or just lie down and roll over?"

He's right. And that's what businessmen would do, wouldn't they? That's what Cole would do.

"Christine Monk!" I exclaim, remembering our crepey-cleavage benefactor. "She has pull, she knows everyone, and I bet she'll be furious when she reads this. How about I start with her?"

Within a few hours, the troops have been rallied, strongly worded letters composed, press releases written, Facebook campaigns created, outraged tweets tweeted and—Bonanza!—a time confirmed to speak on the local radio station.

"I think it is a disgrace. An absolute disgrace," Christine lamented down the telephone. "I am very good friends with Piers Johnson, the editor. Do you know him? Of course you don't. Well, he and Jeffery play golf together. Why don't I use my wiles on Jeffery and see what I can do. You've never seen me wily, dear, but I can be. You can count on that."

The office telephone rings continually: calls from concerned teachers threatening to cancel, asking for full refunds; calls from the concerned parents not wanting their cherubs to be "exposed" to such vulgarity, et cetera.

After a demoralizing day of trying to excuse and appease, I find the idea of being able to defend the theater on the air waves—without interruption—an exciting, vindicating prospect.

The receptionist sits behind the front desk, an immovable boulder. She shows about as much enthusiasm for being the welcoming face and voice of Lightning FM as I do for a rectal exam. As I begin introductions, I am halted by her raised finger.

"Lightning FM, this is Tina," she announces disinterestedly into her headset. "Putting you through." The prohibiting finger descends, and I realize that this is my cue to speak.

"Hello, Tina." I smile but elicit only an arm folding and an eyebrow lift. "Enna Petersen from Ashtead Theatre. This is Will Angler. We are here for a six p.m. interview with DJ Manic Mike."

She casts her overly-mascaraed lashes up and down before raising her finger into the air again. "Two people are here for you," she says sulkily into the headset. "Oh fine!" she replies to the unheard instruction. With much huffing and puffing, the reluctant receptionist pulls the chair back from her desk, grinding its legs over the tiles. She rises with a sigh and trudges around the desk. "Come on then."

The maze of corridors leads off left and right, each plastered from floor to ceiling with glossy, signed photographs of D-list celebrities. Tina turns another corner, and disorientating as these visions of tooth-whitened, perma-tanned, minor celebs are, we manage to keep up.

She stops in front of a large window, through which we see DJ Mike sitting at a sound desk bright with lights. Tina turns in her square-toed kitten heels and heads back down the corridor, her bottom jiggling with every stomp.

DJ Mike is a Surrey institution, surfing the Lightning FM airwaves for over twenty years. It is *the* local show to be on. Hoorah to Christine Monk for wangling it!

Mike swivels around from his chair and waves to us through the glass. His own whitened smile and twinkling eyes are dazzling. He removes his headphones and beckons us to enter.

"Hey! Hi! Hi! Will and Enna, right?"

I nod exaggeratedly, unsure whether to speak or mime.

"You can talk. I put on a continuous three, so we have about nine minutes. Take a seat."

Will pulls out the stool opposite Mike for me and takes the one next to it for himself.

"You haven't done this before, have you?"

"I have," Will says, jumping in. "Enna is pure theater."

"Don't worry. I'll be gentle." Mike laughs his familiar, hearty laugh, and I have to admit, I feel a little star-struck. "No, really. It's easy. Just try not to talk at the same time. I hate to sound like a schoolteacher, but sometimes it helps to raise your hand if you want to say something. Then you won't talk on top of one another."

Sounds easy enough.

"Ready?" Will whispers, turning to me and giving my knee a comforting squeeze.

I nod briskly. *I'm ready! I am evolving.* I feel the surge of adrenaline as I place the headset on. *I'm plugging into this radio frequency, baby!*

"And we're back with two guests from Ashtead Theatre in the studio this evening. We have Enna Petersen, theater director, and William Angler, actor and playwright. Welcome."

"Hello."

"Hi!" we say at the same time, forgetting to raise our hands.

"Now, I understand Ashtead's fallen on hard times of late. Tell me about that."

I launch my hand in the air, and Will nods encouragingly. "That's right, Mike, but that is not unusual for many of the theaters across the nation. There's lots of competition: DVDs, on-demand recorders, computer games, Internet surfing, email. It means that finding an audience has become more difficult. And if the people don't come, Ashtead suffers."

"Because you're reliant on the public's pound to keep open?"

"That sounds mercenary, but yes. We have a fabulous building with a glittering history, and if we want to keep it alive, we need support. That's why we have worked so hard to produce a quality show like *The Shakespearian Rap*."

"But, I understand, there has been some controversy."

"Well, the arts editor for *The Advertiser*, Henry Rudge, wrote an unfair and unwarranted critique, suggesting that our patrons had low intellect."

"The problem is," Will swoops in to say, "Mr. Rudge's opinion—which was not shared by the rest of the audience or Chester Irving, who saw the same performance and gave it five stars in *The Herald*—will influence the public and, ultimately, could stop them from coming to see the production and supporting our theater."

"Mr. Rudge does compare your adaptation to *Avenue Q*. Personally, I loved that! But can one man's opinion really affect the survival of Ashtead Theater?"

"Absolutely! I do want to say, Mike, that we put ourselves up there. We aren't here this evening, talking on your program—which I really like, by the way—to call for critics to be censored. However, critics are in a position of authority. People read and respect their opinions, and trouncing a production without any appreciation of what the directors and performers are trying to do can be lethal for a theater."

"Don't you think any of his criticisms were valid?"

Will waves his hand in front of my face and leans into the bulbous mic. "Frankly, no. Our show does not set out to act out some of Shakespeare's greatest plays in the traditional form. Anyone who can read the title should appreciate that. However, in the rap form, using modern words but keeping a rhythm, much like the traditional verse, I can act out the stories without the language becoming a barrier between me and the audience."

"It really brings out the humor," I slip in. "The show is very funny."

"I keep true to Shakespeare's intentions: the comic scenes in *Midsummer's Night's Dream* are funny; the dark, dramatic scenes in *Macbeth* are dark and dramatic; I just retold these great stories to music in rap rhyme."

"Would you be able to give us an example?" Mike asks.

"Go on, Will," I encourage, sitting up straighter. This *is* going well.

"Okay, I'll give you a taster, but first, let me set the scene…"

Will rhapsodizes about the star-crossed lovers, Pyramus and Thisbe, and performs their skit in the show—one of my favorites. Radio people start to cluster on the other side of the glass screen, looking into the studio. Even the soundproofing cannot block out their laughter.

Will and I smile with satisfaction. We squeeze hands, our palms pressed together. We watch as the switchboard lights up with callers.

"Will, that was great! What I have to explain to you, listeners, is that Will performed that without a script, without the background music, all on his own, those voices were all him. I wish you could have seen his facial expressions; he really brought the characters to life."

"What's that, Producer Mandy? Oh, of course! You can go online to listen again and see for yourself with the webcam. I see the switchboard is on fire — not literally, folks — so we'll play a little Maroon 5 before we chat some more with Will and Enna from Ashtead Theater."

Mike removes his headset, pushes off, away from the desk, and rolls around on his wheely-chair toward Will. "Let me shake your hand. That was fantastic! The ladies must love you."

Mousey Mandy, hiding behind two long, dark curtains of hair, slips into the studio and hands Mike sheets of paper.

"Mandy, my love!" he hails, extending his protective arm to secure her. "Don't run away. What have you got for us?" Mike points to the bundle of pages Mandy clutches in her small paws.

"They are just some of the responses so far. Some offers for funding, requests for tickets — people really like it. The calls are pouring in. Tina says the phone system might crash."

"Reaction. That's good, good. Well, do you guys mind hanging around? Maybe we can take some calls on the air. Would you mind?"

I raise my hand with lightning speed. "Not a bit!"

"And, that was Maroon 5 with 'This Love.' Well, 'This Love' may have 'taken its toll' on you, but our guests Enna Petersen and Will Angler from Ashtead Theater certainly haven't. We heard Will perform some of his *Shakespearian Rap* earlier, and the reaction has been astounding. Mr. Melvin, a headmaster at Ottways School for boys, asks if he can hire you to come in to his school to inspire his GCSE classes.

"Angela Earp from Epsom says, and I quote, 'This is exactly the sort of entertainment we should be encouraging, not criticizing. Mr. Rudge should be made to write a formal apology to be printed in the paper.' By the sound of things, most of you listening agree and think Mr. Rudge should apologize."

"Thanks for your support," I chime in. "At the end of the performance, we value what our audience thinks, so it's truly encouraging to hear your positive feedback."

"And, talking of positive feedback, I believe we have Charlotte from Hammersmith on the line. Hello, Charlotte?"

"Hi, Mike!" I hear echoing in my Minnie Mouse-esque headset.

"What's your question or comment for Will and Enna?"

"I was wondering how Will made it up. Was it on the spur of the moment, or is it something that took a long time?"

"Over to you, Will."

"Good question, Charlotte. Well, I'm writing raps or poems, or however you like to think about them, all the time. Walking down the street, an idea will occur to me, and I start linking words in my head. If the idea works, I commit it to paper, edit it, put a beat to it. That's how it evolves. Anyone can do it. You don't need money or a qualification. You just need to like words. I like to think of myself as a wordsmith."

"And where did the idea to translate Shakespeare into a rap come from?" Mike interjects, steering the conversation back on track.

"Shakespeare wrote these plays to be performed, not read. You have to read it aloud to 'get it' and allow the intricacies of the poetry and rhyme come out. So, a friend who teaches fourteen-year-olds asked if I would come into his class as a guest and talk about Shakespeare since they were 'bored' by it. Well, Shakespeare, read with expression, could never be boring. The stories are too well-constructed. I visited her class and realized it was the language that was preventing them from enjoying the stories. I stood in front of thirty or forty unimpressed kids slumping in their chairs, picked up a copy of *Romeo and Juliet* and, instead of reading the words printed on the page, I just started rapping. Within minutes, they were laughing and clapping and sitting up straight in their chairs. One kid came up from the back of the classroom and said that I was a phony, and he bet I had rehearsed that, so he challenged me to a battle."

"A battle?"

"Sorry, Mike. A battle is when two or more rappers throw down raps and rhymes, usually insults, that each one has to top. These can either be whole verses or one line insults."

"Can you 'throw down' a rap off the top of your head now?"

"Sure," Will answers, unfazed.

I swallow. Oh crap.

"Charlotte, are you still on the line?"

"Yes, I'm here, Mike."

"Would you like to suggest a topic for Will to rhyme about?"

"Oh. Let me think. Oh…this is hard."

"It can be anything, any topic, or word or phrase."

"At the moment, I'm sitting in my car in Chiswick, trying to listen to you over this awful rain."

"That's perfect. Rain. Car. Chiswick. I can use that."

"All right then. Well, we have to take a quick break for the news at six thirty p.m., and we'll come back to Will and his improvised rap afterward."

Will has closed his eyes and is holding the bridge of his nose with his fingertips. I look around and see that the corridor is a circus of people jostling against the glass. People at the back are hoisted in the air on shoulders just to get a look in.

"We're ready," Mike announces to us, and he replaces his headset and plays a jingle.

Will opens his eyes, composed and confident.

"Welcome back to *Manic Mike's Drive Time*. Before the news, you will recall that our caller, Charlotte, challenged Will Angler, the controversial *Shakespearian Rap* artist from Ashtead Theater, to recite a poem in rap. He has had about three minutes to get his thoughts together. Ready? Let's see what he's got."

Will clears his throat.

> *"Waiting in my tin can*
> *With the guns resounding.*
> *Firing atoms of hydrogen and oxygen*
> *Create such a pounding.*
> *These innocent elements*
> *Tap a thunderous drum roll,*
> *Or starter's pistols 'bang' on impact*
> *As crash and course, they flow.*
> *Like creatures with a vital pulse*
> *They beat their spermy tails,*
> *Tracing their predestined path*
> *Into Mother Earth's entrails.*
> *The core beneath is thirsty*

And sucks the life source up.
A long-neglect woman
Whose clock has not yet struck.
And foresee the surprised delight
When in Spring it is discovered,
A shoot, a sprout, a living creature,
The fruit of elemental lovers."

I look at Will, at Mike, back at the faces in the window, before the sound of applause erupts outside the studio, the eager faces whooping and cheering. Will breaks into a smile.

"That was the talented Mr. William Angler, currently performing his interpretation of Shakespeare's works called *The Shakespeare Rap* at Ashtead Theater. Thanks for coming in, guys. And for details on *The Shakespearian Rap*, click on the link on our website…"

We try to slip quietly from the building, excitement bubbling through our silence.

Tina looks up miserably as we pass, staring daggers as she repeats to the next caller, "Lightning FM, this is Tina. I'll put you through. Lightning FM, this is Tina. I'll put you through. Lightning FM, this is Tina. I'll put you through. Lightning FM, this is Tina, Tina, Tina…"

Out of the air conditioned studio, the evening is unusually warm, and for the first time this evening, my perpetual goose pimples relax and stand at ease. The sky is a magical shade of mauve and gray in thick clumps of swarming cloud — like lilac cauliflower. I look up to savor the Disney cloud display, the purple patches drifting so quickly, and I feel the refreshing plink and splash as cool droplets roll down my forehead and dapple my silk shirt.

Without warning, the conductor of the skies ups the tempo, and the initial light prelude suddenly gives way to a fast and furious downpour, each drop drumming its beat on the tarmac and splashing back up on my ankles.

"Don't just stand there." Will laughs. "Run!" He grabs my hand with his hot palm and pulls me into a confused canter. The rain speeds up in rhythm with our stride, — determined that we should not escape — and I leap over the puddles with abandon. Will steers me in the direction of the car. He opens my door and bundles me in out of the rain before running to the other side and diving into the warm, dry shelter.

We sit on either side of the car, breathing heavily. I can feel his hot eyes on me. I can feel the cold, wet strands of hair plastered to my scalp, the peppery residue of mascara on my cheeks, the rivulets of rainwater trickling down the hills and valleys of my skin, soaking into watery horseshoes through the fabric of my blouse and bra. My favorite pale, blue silk, made vivid with precipitation, clings to the curves of my chest as it rises and falls with each exhilarated breath. I'd forgotten what fun it was to run with the wind and the rain in your face.

I flick my wrists to shake off some of the excess water, but he catches my right hand and pulls it toward him. I follow his lead and lean over the hand brake, my lips finding his, clashing in a hot, wet union. His stubble drags across my skin, all gentle pretense dispensed with. He is rough and keen, grazing against me as if trying to erase my skin, to uncover my bones, to mine my marrow. I gasp as his stubble scratches a trail to my earlobe, and his teeth clamp down and sink into the soft, peach furred flesh.

"Ouch!" I cry, jerking backward into my seat. I press my lobe and feel the hot dome of blood rise to my touch, the vibrant red dying the whorls of my fingertips. "You bit me!" I say with disbelief.

"Sorry," he says, not sounding sorry in the slightest. "I was only playing. You just look fucking edible."

"No. You're not sorry, and you weren't playing. You wanted to hurt me. Well, you have, and now you can drive me to the theater please."

"Oh, Enna, don't be like that!" He reaches for my hand again, but I sit on it. "I don't know. Just pent up adrenaline…aggression or something. Come here." He paws me with his hands, raking the silk of my shirt.

I bat him away with a few lame shoves, but he grabs my wrists again. I flick and turn them, but he has me manacled. His grip gets tighter, and I flail hopelessly, frustrated by this inappropriate affection.

"We haven't got time for this. Let me go. I'm not joking. Just… let…me…go…" I struggle against him, twisting my wrists, writhing in my seat, and suddenly, he loosens his lock. My hand flies through the air and lands a crashing blow into his jaw. His face absorbs the energy of the blow, and like a crash test dummy, his skull smacks against the car window.

"Oh my God! Are you okay?" I shriek, as he reels with his head in his hands. "Will! Talk to me! Are you okay? Say something."

His hands cover his face. I can't see if he's bleeding.

"For God's sake, Will. Nod if you're okay."

He nods slowly, but he does not speak. I see him open his mouth, testing his jaw, clicking it into place as if he were one of those astonishing animals able to dislocate their own jaw.

I slip my arm around his shoulder, needing to touch him, to hold on to him. Quick tears prick my eyelids, and hasty words rush to my lips. "I'm sorry. I'm sorry. You scared me. I'm sorry. I didn't mean it. I promise I didn't mean it."

The aching minutes pass by, filled with my whispered apologies, as I wait for Will to recover. I feel every millisecond of every minute — an eternity of time — before he regains his voice.

"Wow, can you land a punch!"

I throw my arms around him and shower him with kisses.

"Ow! Ow! Watch it, Rambo."

"Are you really okay?"

"I'll be fine. I think I may have swallowed a filing, but I'll worry about that later."

"I feel terrible. What can I do?" I beg, the annoyance and earlobe throbbing I had felt just moments ago supplanted by consuming concern.

"Forget it."

"The day was going so well, and I—"

"It's forgotten already. We should be heading to the theater. Curtain's up in an hour. We should get back anyway."

Will turns the key in the ignition and flicks the windscreen wipers on, erasing any trace of those elemental spermy trails. I wish the atmosphere inside the car was as quickly wiped clean.

Silence.

I snatch a glance over in his direction. He is focused on the road ahead. The windscreen wipers squeak across the screen, relentlessly repelling the rain and casting it off dispassionately somewhere along the A3.

We exit at the roundabout and rocket along the back road, passing Chessington World of Adventures. The horse-chestnuts and sycamores loom large on either side of the carriageway. Without their leaves, they are an oddly imperfect sight, the asymmetrical branches and knobbly limbs dark against the changeable purple backdrop. Branches reach up like umbrella spines blown inside out. Though far from forlorn in their unabashed nakedness, they are defiant Goliaths, standing strong against the elements.

> *Deciduous trees,*
> *Without leaves,*
> *Are nature's naturalists.*

I silently rap in time to the squeak.

The rain slows, and the wipers start to squeak louder as the rubber scrapes against the glass. The lilac sky has faded, replaced with a murky, steel gray. The street lights have come on, illuminating the shiny, viscous pools puddling on the pavement.

He pulls up to the theater, the engine running, and jumps out, leaving me to shift over and park. He dodges through the theater-going throng, getting halfway up the steps before turning round, and in front of the attentive crowd, he darts back to the car. I wind down the window. Has he forgotten something? He leans in and kisses me tenderly, warmly on the mouth.

Chapter 19

"Thank God you are here!" Mum exclaims earnestly as I stagger into the box office booth for a minute of quiet sanctuary. "Long day? Well, don't worry, sweetheart. I've been talking to lots of people today, and they said that the review didn't affect them at all. They didn't pay any attention to it."

"That's good." I cast my eye over the reservations, the will-call tickets stacked in their respective envelopes, and the pink envelope… it's not there.

"Ma, where's the pink envelope?"

"The comps for *The Stage*? Yes, they were collected."

Oh God. This could be the death blow or the triumphant victory, and there's not a damn thing I can do about it.

Will lights up the stage, his expressive face luminous like alabaster under the spotlight. Even from the back of the house, I can see his eyes ablaze, twinkling nuggets of fiery, chocolate-flecked amber. His raps flow seamlessly as the characters morph before the audience's rapt attention. Whether spurred on by his critic resentment or simply on a high from the success of the radio vindication, his performance is electric, pneumatic, and utterly captivating. *He* is bewitching, consuming, intoxicating.

The curtain falls and the audience, usually in a hurry to beat the traffic clog, remains transfixed. The applause is slow to kick in, but then it breeds, filling up the high moulded ceilings of the auditorium and ringing around the atrium, right up to the gods. Appreciation of this bohemian rhapsody fills the air, and it seems almost tangible.

I see Colin poke his flustered red face out from the wings, looking feverishly up at the sound booth, his brows knitted in consternation. I see him mime—badly—hauling the pulley, presumably asking if he should close the curtains. I shrink in my seat. *Please don't let* The Stage *journo see. Pretty please.*

Glistening under the hot beam, Will basks in the applause, taking a third bow and a fourth. Applauding patrons rise to their feet and stand in admiration, holding out their clapping hands, abandoning their usual reserve and polite approval. Will disappears from my view, masked behind the navy suit rising in front of me. I stand and bob just in time to see Will smile at the crowd.

"Thank you!" he mouths exaggeratedly over the ringing applause. I think I can feel my heart melt into my bloodstream, bubbling slightly, like a Chinese rice cracker or tangy Skips crisp dissolving to nothingness on my tongue.

I cross my arms against the chill as the audience, eventually, filters out of the revolving doors into the cool night. Absentmindedly, my right hand drifts to my ear. *Oooh!* It feels slightly swollen and tender. My mind rewinds to the car tussle just hours before. I had rather forgotten it with all that followed, but now alone again, I think of him leaning in, licking my ear with the tip of his tongue, sucking my earlobe and then…bite!

Now that my ear doesn't pulse with pain, I really don't know how to feel about it. Was he trying to assert dominance or something, or was he just trying to be all fifty shades of kinky? He was probably just playing, and I should just tell him I'm not into that. The encouraging, sweet smack of his palm to my butt cheek as I straddle him over the office desk is one thing; giving ear teeth-piercings seems a smidgen overzealous. I'll tell him later and let him bask for now. Now, all I want to do is to curl up in his warm arms and sleep.

No one mentions the bad review. No one has to. The box office says it all, and *The Stage.* The five-star review blasts away all traces of *The Advertiser* muck. There are not just sell-out previews, but there are weeks of full houses; there are months.

I should be used to his face by now — the head of tousled curls rubbed dry from his post-show shower; the towel jettisoned somewhere along the corridor as he gallops up the steps to the office — but it still surprises me. The other face, the face I used to expect, is stored away.

"Come on, get your coat! Let's go for dinner! No work! We've made it through our first month, and I think we should celebrate."

I imagine the slice of quiche lorraine, its cold, graying pastry waiting for me in the fridge.

"Besides, Bella Donna is one of our program sponsors. We ought to support the place."

"All right then," I say, remembering that we can afford nice dinners out now.

"That's my girl," he replies.

That's my girl!

His hand gently kneads my shoulder — *oh, that feels good* — his fingertips fitting into the hollow of my clavicle, urging me forward.

He phones ahead and speaks in mixed tongues of quasi-Italian, "Eh! Eh! Eh!" Any minute, I expect an exaggerated shrug of the shoulders and a "Forget about it." It is nearly eleven p.m. after all. But Signor Vito, it seems, agrees to stay open for us.

"Do you always get what you want?" I ask, as Will snaps shut his mobile.

"Always," he replies with his incorrigible smile.

Bella Donna Italian Taverna, a taste of Tuscany in the heart of Ashtead! Seems unlikely, but at eleven p.m., I'm not there to question the geography. The closed sign hangs at a jaunty angle on the glass door, but Will releases me, throws it open, and ushers me in. It's a romantic little place. Candles drip their wax volcanically down the sides of their glass carafes and cast a cave-lit glow across each table. Violin music plays softly, disguising the lack of other diners in the room. The booth at the back of the dining room is already set up for two.

"Signor Guglielmo! I let zee Chianti breathe for you," Vito says, filling the empty space with his exaggerated Italianate enthusiasm.

Probably born in Basildon, I think.

Flamboyantly, he suspends the wine bottle in its white linen sling, pouring its ruby contents in two long tempered bursts and filling the glasses to their rims. "Is good, no?"

"Perfecto, Vito. Grazi."

"I put in an order of zee especial calamari for you, signor?"

"Grazi, Vito."

"When did I step out of the theater onto the set of *The Sopranos?*" I whisper across the table, clinking his glass and taking a sip. The wine tastes good. I hadn't realized until now, with the wine waking my taste buds, quite how hungry I am. I didn't think I even liked Chianti — Hannibal Lecter had rather killed the appeal, along with that of the harmless fava bean — and yet, the light and floral elixir dances its traditional Tuscan tarantella down my throat and draws out the poison of the day. It warms my veins.

Will wants to toast everything: the audience, the schools parties, the volunteers, the sound system, Shakespeare, my parents, me, my parents for making me…With every charged glass, we take a hearty gulp and drink the bottle dry with oblivious gusto.

Vito appears with the starter. If Vito were an insect, he would be a big, fat dung beetle — *Coleoptera Scarabaeidae.* The black iridescent sheen of his slicked-back hair, the generous thorax, and abdomen dressed in his dapper suit, fastened tightly around him like scarab wing cases, the plodding progress as he holds his hefty forearms aloft, pushing the loaded plate of calamari in front of us. He huffs and puffs diligently through the swing door of the kitchen, returning with more wine, with black pepper, with…

"H'enything aye-lse for zee b-yowtiful signora?" *A ball of dung perhaps?*

He fits the classification perfectly.

Will forks a ring of hot, sweet calamari and holds it out for me to try. Why do people always have this desire to feed me? Hungrily, I brandish my own fork and smile as I take the biggest O and fit the entire squidgy circle in my mouth. The light batter adds a satisfying crunch to the sweet, tender squid meat. It is delicious.

Vito sidles up to the table, his mandibles chewing on the hot air of anticipated praise. "You like? I add-a my especial touch…bene, bene." He beetles off once more.

We dip the warm bread in olive oil, and we laugh. We chew the sweet rings of squid, and we laugh. We drink more, and as he chivalrously offers the last crisp ring to me, I realize I have passed the point of no return. I am red-faced, giggly, and completely intoxicated.

Vito shuffles through the swing door, his back first, laden with our main courses: the chicken and asparagus risotto he lays before me, veal scaloppini before Will. We exchange glances over steaming dishes and bury the guilt of already sated appetites in the pattern of the table cloth. Vito stands on, expectantly. Will takes a bite of his veal. I follow his cue, forcing a few forkfuls of delicious, but unnecessary, risotto down.

"I feel sick," I confess in an altogether too loud stage whisper.

After much fork pushing and plowing through the landscape of rice, Vito finally takes the hint that he has us beaten and calls us a cab.

"Look at all this food! What an awful waste. Vito must think us so rude."

"Eh! Whaddya gonna do about it?" Mafiosi Will replies, taking out his wallet. A thumbed wad of notes make the leather bulge.

"A-ho ho!" I say, gauche with wine. "Wow! Have you been moonlighting?"

"What?"

"The wad of cash. And here I thought you were the struggling bohemian." As soon as I've said it, I can hear my mother reminding me how rude it is to comment about money. "I mean, you're packing quite a wad there, William." It truly is the wine talking!

"That's what they all say," he replies, gathering me in his arms and dropping a huge tip on the table. Who knew I was seeing such a high roller?

I recline in his arms in the back of the cab destined for my house, neither of us being at all capable of driving. He whispers songs into my hair, funny lines from musical comedy shows about me being so beautiful he'd like to buy me a kebab, and, clearly sponsored by Chianti, I say loudly, "I bloody love you!" before passing out.

It's not just the adult audiences who give Will standing ovations, but the schools are in raptures too. The more schools come, the more schools book, and the profits are reaching sums I don't know what to do with.

"Perhaps it's time we bring in an accountant?"

"Sure thing." Will twizzles in his desk chair. "I have a friend. Archie. Good bloke. He'd do it for you. He's a CPA and can do it in his sleep. He's given me great business advice, and he's never steered me wrong."

"Sure, sounds great. Why don't you give him a call, and we can set up a meeting. Figure how much is clear profit, how much we owe for the loan, that sort of thing."

"I'm on it. I was thinking though; maybe keeping the profit in the small business account is a bit of a mistake."

"How so?"

"Well, the interest we are generating isn't very much at all, and with that kind of sum, we could be making an income off the capital. If audiences keep up as they have been, we can look to bag somewhere near seventy-five thousand pounds per week. Now multiply that by eight weeks, and you've got one nice little earner."

"That's what? Eight times seventy-five is six hundred, right? Six hundred thousand?" I almost swallow my tongue. "You mean six hundred thousand pounds from just box office?"

Shit just got real. Pinch me!

He draws his lips across his face in a smug, thin-lipped smile.

"The interest on that could be thousands, tens of thousands. Will! That is genius! I could kiss you."

He smiles and twirls in his chair. "I'll call Arch."

I do a bit of online investigation, banks versus building societies, stocks and shares, PEPs, ISAs, bonds…It's all a bit foreign, but I'm not afraid of a bit of homework, and I'm grateful to be meeting with Archie in a week. I'm sure he can answer a lot of my questions. The sooner we squirrel away our earnings, the sooner the interest can start accruing, and that is a concept I like very much indeed.

The adaptation of *Pirates of Treasure Island* is coming slowly — not through any lack of imagination, just a lack of peace. The telephone rings constantly, and when it is silent, all I can hear is Will's voice lulling me over the PA system. What I need is a quiet retreat, somewhere inspiring so my brain can concentrate, somewhere I can switch off the noise.

Soon after I first started working at the theater, Mum brought me a biscuit tin to keep in the office. "For emergencies," she had said with a wink. I remember asking her what theatrical emergencies might require the swift aid of a chocolate bourbon or a Jammie Dodger, and that perhaps a first aid kit might have been a better idea. Not that I was ungrateful. Mum was always thinking of little things to help. "But, Enna," she had said, "you never have anything for guests should they drop by. Not everyone lives on a diet of caffeine and theater."

"But, Ma, you are the only person who drops by!"

"Well, exactly!"

Bored, restless and completely lacking inspiration, I decide to look for it in the biscuit tin. Garibaldi biscuits are, after all, far easier to attack than Long John Silver.

The phone rings, rescuing me from the shame of demolishing the entire packet.

"I'm calling from Munich," Lucy shouts down the line. "Are you busy?"

"Where?" I shout back.

"Munich, Germany."

"Oh. *Ja Gut!* Men in lederhosen!"

"Well, sorry to call you at work, but I am bored out of my enormous mind! I'm here all on my own."

"How long are you there for?"

"That's the problem. I'm here for two weeks. I'm doing a piece for *Foreigner's Friend's* European City Special, so it's a pretty important piece."

"Yikes."

"And there is this lovely rooftop pool which overlooks the onion domes and spires of the city center. And there are all these great restaurants and—did I mention—I'm *all on my own?*"

"Poor bunny. Sounds like hell." Oh, to be paid to lie in the lap of luxury for two weeks!

"So, how are things with Shakespeare?"

"Brilliant. Couldn't be better. The theater is making money hand over fist. It's a weight off, I can tell you."

"Okay, so that is the theater. Now tell me about you and him."

"Oh God, I don't know." Why do I feel nauseatingly coy? "He's… what is he? He makes me laugh. He makes me safe. He makes me smile, and I don't even realize I'm doing it! I spend half the time feeling utterly ridiculous. Giddy. Just looking at him makes me want to cry."

"Cry? Whatever for, you silly tit?"

"I really don't know. It's just this overwhelming feeling, an all-consuming thing that just *gets* me; it grips my stomach, twists and pulverizes me. I sound ridiculous, don't I? It's just…my intestines feel as if they are being passed through a meat mincer." There. That'll do. That just about covers it.

"Nice. So he gives you chronic indigestion?" She laughs loudly down the line before it goes quiet for a second or two. "You love him then?"

"Yeah, I think I do," I say without deliberation.

"Bugger."

"Why bugger?"

"Because, I wanted you to be desperately lonely and in search of a great German adventure. I had hoped you would fly out here on the next plane and join me for spa, sausage, sex, and sauerkraut."

"Oh, that's a new combo."

"Not as popular as 'sun, sand, and sea,' but less chance of getting a sunburn, sandy crotch, or eaten by a shark."

"Do they have sharks in Germany?"

She ignores the question and tries on her sulky, pouty voice. "Well, you could at least join me in this gorgeous hotel for an orgy of German chocolate."

"*Schokolade.* Now you're speaking my language."

"What?"

"*Schokolade*—chocolate in German. Don't you remember Frau Poole's riveting classes? *Schaschlik? Schwein? Weiner? Apfelstrudel?* And my personal favorite, *saure lunge?*" I list my bizarre menu of German with a progressively thick accent.

"See! That's why I need you. Seriously, there are a lot of scary, meaty things here. I'm not sure I could tell *schnitzel* from scrotum. I need you here to translate."

"I only really remember the odd foods that were in the German song we learned for that European evening."

"I don't care. I'll take what I can get. Last night I ordered soup, because I thought that would be fairly harmless. It was spelled a-a-l-s-u-p-p-e. Do you know what that is?"

"Sorry, no idea."

"Eel. Eel soup. And I ate it. I actually ate it because, until the English speaking waiter came over, I had no idea. I came back to the room and brushed my tongue for about ten minutes. Solidly. Enna, you have to save me before I really do end up eating liver or, worse yet, pig's testicles."

"I thought that a globe trotter type like you would be used to foreign foods by now."

"Paella I can cope with. Escargot, grenouille—I know what I'm getting, but these salted meats…who knows what comes from where? If you don't get your bony arse here soon, I'll die of starvation!"

I can hear a twang of desperation in her voice—she really isn't joking.

"*Leber*," I respond after a pause on the line. "You'd be eating *leber, mein liebling*."

"What my what?"

"Avoid *leber*. L-e-b-e-r. Luce, I'd love to, believe me, but I can't possibly leave the theater for a *fleisch*-fest with you. I have to write this *Treasure Island* adaptation."

"Can't you do that here?"

Her question takes a moment to register, and only when I am halfway through my automatic decline and regret speech, does her idea penetrate the auto-shield and actually impact. Retreat! This is it! My chance for peace and solitude, to actually finish this adaptation. But I couldn't leave Will here to perform and handle all the admin, could I? No, I couldn't.

"Oh, come on! You said it was going well. 'Hand over fist,' you said. Surely now you can wangle a week off? You're the artistic director for Christ's sake! Just let go for a week, five days, please?"

Chapter 20

I place the receiver back in its cradle. I shouldn't go. My hand creeps up the sagging plastic sleeve, inching toward another Garibaldi.

"I mean, I probably could go," I tell the poster of a golden-toothed Long John. And actually, with rehearsals for *Gaslight* and *The Pirates of Treasure Island* starting in three weeks, I really need to get this stage adaptation written, pronto. Time away would definitely help to do that. Then, with rehearsals, directing, publicizing, there'll be no time off for good behavior for the foreseeable future.

Maybe I could allow just a little trip? Between weekend shows?

It's seems so self-indulgent though. Who just books a ticket and flies off to a lovely hotel with a spa and chocolate and…onion domes? What the hell are onion domes? Are they like onion rings?

On the other hand—what an opportunity! I've never been to Germany, and the hotel would be paid for so—

"I can't. I shouldn't."

Poster Long John stares down at me, that evil glint in his tooth, his presence a constant reminder of what I haven't done and need to do, *schnell.* I run along the corridor to the balcony and am relieved to find the matinee of Will's diverting theatrics in full swing.

I stand at the back, high in the gods. Even from this perspective, he seems ten feet tall, his awesome shape-shifting transpiring magically in front of my eyes. Part actor, part illusionist. Not part manager. I can't throw that one at his feet. I simply can't go to Germany, and that is the end of it.

Will greets the cries from the besotted school girls with his usual charm and grace. After receiving his usual standing O, he jumps down from the stage and signs some autographs for the audience. He is great with this, the P.R., effortlessly connecting with each scrabbling teen thrusting their program in his direction. He takes the time to talk with everyone, to look each teen in the eye and make them feel like they have something interesting to say, and that they are special.

I make my way back out of the balcony and down the stairs, watching the trail of happy teens chatter excitedly as they get back on the buses. Through the main entrance of the auditorium, I can see he is still talking, a small crowd of teachers milling now. For a second, I wonder if there is something wrong, some controversy. I breathe deep, pull my shoulders back, and forge forward into the fray. The gaggle is locked in intense conversation.

"It's an original but a classic," Will says.

"We don't teach it, but if it gets the kids interested, we are all for that."

What? What'd I miss? Huh? Huh?

"And it means we can have a paid afternoon out of the classroom. I love field trips!"

"But, what we really want to achieve here is education, not teaching Shakespeare or Robert Louis Stevenson. We aren't trying to be *Cliffs Notes*, but I—" he sees me on the cusp of the crowd and pauses to give me a smile "—we want kids to have a taste of theater, to love it, and be encouraged to use their imaginations, to read, to dress up, to pretend."

"Well, I will definitely book for our juniors. There are more of them, so we might have to come on two consecutive days, but that will be okay, won't it? I'll phone you next week if that's all right."

"Me too."

"St. John's will want in too."

With the teachers palming literature and promising to return, they chatter as excitedly as the schoolgirls before them, and leave on the buses with grins lifting their faces.

I slip my arms around his waist and rest my head on his back, enjoying his silent moment of post-show satisfaction. His muscles expand under my cheeks as he stretches around, takes an arm, and circles me to his front. He's still slightly damp with sweat, and there are one hundred and one inappropriate things I would like to do with this man now. If I weren't such a professional…but it is an afternoon of duty and denial.

"That was impressive. How wonderful to line up those bookings already!"

"It was nothing. They are here, and they are excited. Might as well sign them up, right?"

"Spoken like a true Donald Trump."

"Watch it!" He kisses my nose.

How did I find such a capable man, this education and outreach liaison? He does everything so effortlessly. I peel his encircling arms from me and send him to the showers. I must get on and write this adaptation — especially as schools will be phoning to book.

Or that is my intention — honestly — but as I sit at my desk, I have a new barrage of emails. *I'll just check these first.* There is one from Lucy.

Subject: Rescue me!

I move the mouse to the top of the list and double click.

Dear Enna,

Didn't mean to sound like an ungrateful bitch. Just the salted meat here Is doing funny things to me. I know you are busy. It does feel like we haven't seen each other for ages though, doesn't it? I know that is my fault (as well as yours) with this traveling, but you did used to text or email every day. It just seems that Ashtead has completely overtaken your life. Do you ever actually go home? Lol. And now that you and Will are together, you are even more embroiled in "All things theater."

I sound jealous, don't I? Well, maybe I am, but tell me, when was the last time you had a normal conversation with someone outside the theater, that didn't have anything to do with the stage? If you start saying, "Oh, dahling," I'm divorcing you as my best friend!

I do want to tell you something though, and as best friend, I have the right to say what I think without you hating me forever — right? Well then, as a friend, I think you need to let go, give yourself a break. It's not just me. People have even been talking — no, don't roll your eyes — but you do look horribly thin at the moment, Enna. Gaunt and pale and, frankly, ill. (Don't hate me.) Now do yourself a favor and TAKE A BREAK.

Have attached BA flight itinerary below—look how unbelievably cheap!

Love you, you silly tart.

Love me. X

British Airways: Heathrow—Munich

Depart Mon 21st—09.40—arrive Munich 12.30 only 56 pounds

Depart Sun 26th—13.15—arrive Heathrow 14.20 only 56 pounds

Inclusive total ONLY 112 pounds.

(Also, may I remind you, you spent more on that pair of L.K. Bennett boots, and the heel broke within a month! Think of all the long-lived memories you could have with me, Fritz, and knuckle of roasted pig in Munich.)

I read the email a second and a third time, each re-read breaking my smile the same as the first. The screen blackens as the exhausted system falls asleep.

You do look horribly thin…pale and gaunt. Huh! I do not. I'm slender and ivory-toned! Some of us have to work all hours of the day and night in little black boxes, not exotic climes!

I fight the urge to shake the mouse from slumber and type away email protestations of great health and hardiness, to hold my head high and tell her everything is wonderful—everything is, isn't it?—but the impulse fades as quickly as the words on the computer screen. My attention falls instead on the outline that comes into focus, the familiar face that I sometimes find so hard to recognize.

I trace the lines of my cheeks reflected in the black screen. Seeing with the fingers of a blind man, they run down my neck, tripping up, squashing the crescent moons of bendy cartilage. I count four distinct ridges, such flimsy hardware to keep my trachea open.

My fingers can feel the slow thud of a pulse—intermingling platelets, red and white cells rafting through the plasma rapids. Finger meets thumb at the super sternal notch. Two thin sinews, like taut elastic bands, converge in a V. They feel so rigid and distinct; I can pluck them like a violin string. I depress the hollow between them, above where they meet bone, and feel my trachea close under my one-finger chokehold.

How has this place evolved so unprotected, with no bone, no cartilage, no shield or carapace—a little shadowed bull's-eye at the bottom of the neck? My fingertips glide back and forth across the deep V, along the defined collarbone—a skateboard of digits rolling up and down a half-pipe.

I'm just busy!

Christ, I can't take a bite of a stale Garibaldi biscuit without being interrupted! Matinees and evening shows are just not conducive to having normal eating times. It's not that I'm on some crusade to be the thinnest.

Busy, Enna, really? Or is it that, when life is circling and constantly surprising, being hard on yourself is one thing you can control?

"No!" I say out loud to the ghostly reflection. I am not a control freak. I don't *have* to keep to the rules. I can be *fun*. I can be spontaneous. I can give myself a break! And, as if to prove the point, to put myself to the test, I seize the mouse and navigate to the British Airways web site.

Chapter 21

"I think you should go," he encourages, chomping his way through his tuna salad baguette. A creamy blob of tuna escapes from the end of its doughy confines—a dolphin-friendly plunge for freedom, which lands—*splat*—on the flight times.

He takes another large mouthful and chomps on. "We've made enough money to get a temp in for a week to cover the phones. What you need to do is write the script! If you can do that in Germany, and you can see your friend at the same time, do it."

"But what if something went wrong?"

"Like what? What could go wrong? Really?"

My brain leaps to various scenes of worst-case scenario.

"Fire…flood…earthquake…volcano?"

He raises his left eyebrow. "In Ashtead?"

Okay, I know, I'm being over the top, but I suppose I had rather expected that he would say he could not do without me. I am a little dashed that he can do without me so easily.

"It will be absolutely fine. The show is effortless for me now. I could do it in my sleep. As long as the front of house voles show up, I'll be golden. Everything else will work itself out. If I have a question, I'll phone. I believe they do have phones in Germany."

"Promise you'll call me if you need *anything.*"

"I promise." He circles to my side of the desk and holds his hands around my shoulders.

I try not to think of potential tuna-mayo fingerprints on my blouse, but I can't help it. I stand to face him and shrug off his fingers to lessen the chances. "I'll have to rearrange my appointments with the set people, the interview with *The Chronicle* journalist—that was a tentative anyway—and can you reschedule your accountant friend?"

"No problem."

"Okay then. Right. Well. If you're absolutely sure?"

"I'm sure. But you know—" his fingers graze across the silk and trill down my sides, around my back "—a whole week without you. A bloke could get pretty lonely." And with a magician's sleight of hand, my skirt falls to the floor.

The plane touches down on the runway, right on time. Passengers race to get out of the stalls, release their lap belts with a satisfying clink of metal on metal, and charge down the aisle before their opposite number. I am buffeted along by the herd, my fuchsia pink wheelie case gliding along at my heels.

The tunnel from the plane leads into a bright, clean, glass terminal. It's like I am stepping onto the set of a futuristic sci-fi film. The endless interlinking glass passageways spur off to stairways and escalators that face their opposing direction. Faceless travelers wheeling their luggage capsules glance blankly at themselves in reverse, those going down passing those on the way up. It is difficult not to be impressed by this industrial chic: the clean lines, the un-smudged glass surfaces; it is so quiet, so uncrowded, so unsullied—the antithesis of Heathrow. Even the other Germanic looking travelers—businessmen commuting for meetings in London; women with sanguine expressions of nobility, wrapped in their pashminas, toting bags with the green and gold of Harrods' trademark; the smart, uniformed patrol officers, all with matching short back and sides—make me, in my Joseph beige bootleg trousers and cashmere blend turquoise jumper, feel grubby.

The customs officer smiles. "Hello."

"*Guten tag!*" I say with relish and hand him my passport.

He unleashes an incomprehensible spiel of fast-paced German. To my ears, it sounds like: "*Vish-leber-dish-nicht-heron-von-schlaslik?*"

"Umm?" My eyes widen improbably. I regress rapidly to Frau Poole's German room. Those classes spent listening to the conversation tapes, straining to interpret *Deutsch*, staring into the whiteboard and hoping that the traces of erased German sentences might appear to me, like invisible ink.

"Ich bin Auslander, und sprechen nicht gut Deutsch," I reply, delighted to remember the phrase: I'm a foreigner and don't speak good German. Frau Poole would be so proud!

"Ja. Sur gut. I said, 'Are you on holiday?'" he annunciates in perfect English. *"In der ferine?"*

"Oh! Yes. I mean, *ja." I'm on holiday. Crikey! I'm on holiday!* How delightful!

He waves me on my way, and I emerge, passing the luggage conveyor belts, into the long, glass arrivals hall, the taxi cabs lining the street outside.

"Enna!" A very English accent cuts through the sterile silence, and a blur of blue rushes at me, big open arms scissoring around my own. "Enna, thank God you are here!" She folds my arm around hers and takes me out to the awaiting car. "I've been here for ages waiting. And here you are! Love the jumper," she natters as we walk across the car park.

"Bloody hell!" I let my wheelie handle plummet to the smooth, black German tarmac. "A BMW?"

"Not bad, huh?"

"Not bad? It's beautiful," I say admiringly, feeling the heated leather seats warm me.

"When in Munich, do as the Munchens do! They have the BMW headquarters here. We'll pass the building. Head honcho executives and celebrity-types come here to road test the new, top-of-the-line BMW models. I thought it would be good research for my article. So, let's burn it up on the autobahn, baby!"

The black convertible purrs, enjoying the bursts of freedom permitted by the changeable and sometimes scarily limitless speed limit. Like the almost deserted airport, the autobahn is equally empty. The long stretches of road are ours for the taking, and the car is eating them up. In spite of the fact it's winter, I open the window and enjoy the fresh, invigorating Bavarian air as Lucy blasts the efficient in-car heating. I could almost be carefree Julie Andrews singing to the Alps were I not a few hours north, on an autobahn, in a car, but nevertheless! The hills are, indeed, alive with the sound of engines.

Lucy negotiates the exit off the autobahn and darts along the *strasse*, passing fountains, statues, and vast buildings, all beautifully uniform in style yet individual in design. My head swivels to take in the façades, the gargoyles, the intricate masonry—every building boasting features that give me a mild case of whiplash.

"You're going too fast. I'm missing things!" I shout through my meshed veil of knitted hair blowing out the window as I lean out for closer look.

"Don't worry. We'll see it all later. You can get yourself sorted out in the room, and then we'll have a little walking tour."

She swings the car around the U-bend of the *Promenadeplatz*, over the cobbled *strasse* and pulls up in front of the enormous façade of the Bayerischer Hof Hotel. Royal blue and white flags—some checkerboard, some striped, some solid blocks of color—wave to us from their first story golden hoists, heralding our arrival with nonchalant pageantry. The vast building has an imposing majesty: a grand seven story Renaissance structure, no gothic arches or pointed roofs, but altogether more square and Germanically efficient in design, its plainness balancing its size. It is a grand edifice.

"Leave your bag. The bell boy will get it."

"But it's only a carry-on. I can wheel it."

"Who do you think you're not? Victoria Beckham?" She laughs as she grabs the handle and wheels my case inside, muttering over her shoulder, "No sense of style."

Far from the stark elegance of the glass airport, the hotel is an opulent truffle-filled chocolate box of refinement. I trot behind Lucy, self-consciously hearing the loud clatter of my heels click-clacking on the polished floor, and as my eyes adjust from the brightness outside to that of the interior, I indulge in a moment to take it all in.

The foyer is a mutedly dazzling exhibit of soft light reflected off the shiny marble which covers the floor, the walls, and the large bank of the concierge and reception. Every surface seems to glow. The marble is quite exquisite. Swirls and veins of peach tones blend with ripples of ocher in which nestle nuggets of deeper, fiery tiger's eye; every slab is unique. The mellow yellow beams from elaborate sconces bathe the walls in pools of light like melted butter. Cream-colored sconced columns stand impressively before the mirrored elevators to the left.

At the center hangs an enormous chandelier, each intricately looped and scrolled golden limb festooned with a shower of crystal teardrops projecting iridescent rainbows in their prisms. The showpiece hangs just above head height, giving the open space a cozy but classy intimacy. A marble table glows beneath the twinkling antique, its top a pale amber lozenge supported by gilt lions' paws. As if an extra show of grandeur were needed, a golden urn sits proudly atop, the long gilt neck coiffed with a marvelous beehive of exotic off-white lilies — hundreds of them — a non-descript green ivy cascading from the rim to the tabletop.

Whilst Lucy consults with the valet, I tiptoe past the table, inhaling the rich, thick smell of the bouquet, and I peer into the next room. The light palette changes again from the soft butter yellows to fresh linen white. The space is so large it would be sure to induce panic in any agoraphobic. There are hundreds of tables laid with starched spotless tablecloths, studded with silver Villeroy Bosch cutlery and smudgeless glasses. An artificial blue tint flashes up from the silverware, not a tinny disco-lit blue, nor a smoky blue haze, but a clean blue. The sun shifts and the blue creeps like a stain over the tablecloth. I lift my gaze and see its source — the overhead atrium, a Goliath glass dome of blue and white crowning the room and flooding it with clear blue light. It is one of those almost religious moments, when you can hear a chord play in your head and you know that you are meant to be there, to be seeing these wondrous things, even if it's just the beauty of a clear, starch-white cloth, gleaming with silver and glass. All thoughts of Ashtead float out of my ears and up into the blue. I have arrived.

The end of the room exhibits a sweeping staircase — a Cinderella meets Prince Charming sort of staircase — that circles down from the balconied level to the chandelier-lit dance floor beneath.

I can just picture it, a *Pygmalion* scene: I appear at the top of the staircase, dressed in classic white couture, elbow length white gloves and dark hair swirled up, adorned with a genuine diamond tiara on loan from Such and Such of Mayfair. I glide down the stairs without tripping. I take a flute of champagne from the silver salver held by the liveried footman and sip delicately — my nose does not get in the way. I slice through the curious crowd to whispers of "Just who is she?" A tall gallant wearing a mask steps in front of me and asks for my hand in a Viennese waltz. I politely nod. *But I don't know how to dance the Viennese Waltz! It doesn't matter; he's a fabulous lead!* He is. I am in his arms — *where has my champagne gone* — spinning around and around. At the end of the music, he kisses my hand, and I reach for his mask, untying the ribbon at the back of his head. It drops into my hand and there is his face, that face, and I lose my breath in surprise —

"Oi!" Lucy says. "Country mouse! You're not supposed to be here. You'll break something or fall over. I know you."

—and he's gone. I try to conjure him back, but Lucy takes my arm in hers and shepherds me out into the lobby, keen to start our tour.

The bedroom is modern in style. There is carpet and non-marbled walls. The focal point is the large bed, a sea of burnt orange, burgundy and beige shiny satin. The head end spills over with shameless flounce: copious pillows, shams, bolsters, and cushions; the foot end is Spartan in comparison, with its tightly manicured edges. On the count of three, we throw ourselves through the air and land in the nest of German poofery.

"Here's to us and to *Foreigner's Friend Guide Inc.* For what you are about to pay for, we are truly grateful."

"Amen," I reply.

I had not realized Munich would be so…cobbled. The gray pedestrianized *strasse* is a sea of heel pinching, flip-flop stubbing, ballet pump tripping, cobbles. We stutteringly promenade arm in arm following the tram tracks leading to the main street. *Weinstrasse* opens out to a busy square with expensive looking shops on the right and a shortly cropped grass area in the center. The car-less street is filled with Germans walking with purpose and tourists ambling and halting annoyingly in front of them. Tanned Germans in cobble-sensible boots languish outside the pavement cafés, even in this weather, sipping espressos with poker faces.

I drag Lucy past the shop windows, gawping at the chic displays: a single pair of gloves and a hat, pyramids of cobble-defying shoes, spangle-trimmed boxes full of chocolates. Here we stop. The morsels are little works of art, very different from the pretty French or Swiss truffles or their English copies. We marvel at the square shaped truffles, each a different blend of dark, milk, and white chocolate mixed but separated within their own little square, like mini checkerboards of chocolate. Black slabs of bittersweet chocolate gleam in the display, stacked high on wrapped bars of unusual flavors: kiwi fruit chocolate, mango chocolate, chocolate covered marzipan, chili chocolate—

"Chili chocolate?" we exclaim in unison as we turn to each other, our horror reflected in the window glass. "Ew!"

Around the corner the view changes dramatically, boasting the same vast buildings. Here is even more grandeur; we have hit the epicenter. The *Marienplatz* opens out into another large cobbled area, dominated by the gothic Rathaus. It's an impressive structure.

"Look at the *glockenspiel!*" Lucy points to the colorful carillon towering above us. "It does go around. It shows a couple of knights jousting. The knight from Munich wins, of course."

"Of course," I say, unable to make out the distant figures.

"Seem tiny, don't they?"

I nod.

"Well, they are life size."

"How do you know that?"

"I earwigged on an American tour yesterday, and the woman was very informative. I'd recommend it."

"What? A tour?"

"No, earwigging. You never know when you might pick up a gem of an anecdote to thrill and amaze your publisher with. For instance, did you know that if a barnacle were a man, its penis would be the size of Nelson's Column?"

"You heard that on the tour?"

"No. But it makes you think, doesn't it?"

The Square is randomly uniform, with its grand gothic architecture abutting Italianate ornate baroque, Renaissance and classical romantic, but all have a height, a beauty, and give an impression of history—albeit rebuilt history—and national pride. Looking into the distance, I see a patchwork of steeples, spires, towers, slate tiles, and some domes that look faintly like onions. *Ah! Onion domes!*

There is not a 1960s post-war high rise or a ridiculous architectural atrocity, like London's glass paneled City Hall, in sight.

"That's your nickel tour for today. I'm starving. Let's eat!" Lucy frog-marches me through a series of charming cobbled alleyways, home to beautiful balconied baroque buildings, incongruously filled with football shirts, cuckoo clocks, steins and other cheap tourist tat. She halts as a throng of merry tourists spill out from the arches beneath an impressively vast establishment.

"There!" she says with game-show-host display. The light stone is bedecked with the blue and white colors of Bavaria, flags, a maypole, and insignias sporting the initials HB. "It's the famous Hofbrauhaus. Hitler drank here, gave speeches here. It's an important historic landmark. Important for article research."

The heavy door opens onto a scene far removed from the cheap inelegance of Saturday night at The Leg of Mutton — even after it went gastro. The Hofbrauhaus is a medieval banquet, an animated tableau brought to life.

The tidal wave of noise is overwhelming: hundreds of eager mouths working in unison between slurps of beer, speaking a disorientating whirl of languages; the tinny accompaniment of dropped cutlery; and the occasional cymbal crash, as a slippery plate eludes the waiter's grasp. Over this chaotic backing track, a four-man band in stylish lederhosen complete the cacophony, blowing their horns and pumping the accordion, valiantly competing for the attention of the chatty masses. The rush of sound hits me then rolls on, and with adjusting ears, I shuffle through it.

The narrow corridor between the columns of tables is filled with massing people, like insects, waggling their antennae in search of an available table. The end-to-end tables extend as far as I can see.

"Bloody hell! We'll never find anywhere to sit," I shout to Lucy with exaggerated mime. We thread through the crowd, treading air like water. Lucy spies a table at the side by the kitchen and makes a dive for it, wheedling her shoulders through the kaleidoscope shift of blouses and T-shirts. She is glowing with satisfaction when I eventually crawl through to her.

"You're too polite, you know," she yells in un-Lucy-like decibels. "You are never going to get what you want if you stand there on ceremony and wait to be asked. No asky, no getty."

"Thanks," I yell back, though the sarcasm is lost with volume. "I hadn't realized I hadn't been getting what I want."

"What?"

"What what?"

"What you want, what? Wait? Why?"

Oh, give me strength, I think, as I battle the still rising tide of noise, and skirt around the table to sit next to her.

"There, that's better. Can you hear me now?"

"You realize everyone will think we are lesbians?"

"We're in Germany," I say, shrugging, and somehow that wickedly satisfies both of us.

I can see for myself what a beautifully clean, efficient, proud city Munich is. The people seem happy and dapper, not the weirdos the late-night programs on Channel Four had led me to believe.

"That looks good." Lucy nudges my elbow, redirecting my attention to a hunk of meat being devoured at an adjacent table. "What is it?" she demands.

"It looks shanky."

"Skanky?"

"No, SHANKY! Pass over the menu, and I'll interpret."

One year of German classes have not exactly prepared me for this. The *speisenkarte* offers a feast of, well, unidentifiables.

"*Hallo!*"

I lift my head from the confusing puzzle of *Wirsing pflanzerl* to see the red-faced waiter contemplate me with a long-suffering half smile. He holds five full glass steins in each hand.

"*Guten tag.*" I smile, but his expression doesn't change; he just stands waiting, and I feel the weight of the amber trophies sinking in his grip.

"Coca Cola," Lucy chimes in, buying me some time. Ah, God bless the international language of brand name products.

"*Ja und ich mochte ein bier*. Die Hofbrau original. *Und einen grossen brez'n.*" I smile.

He doesn't look impressed by my efforts.

"What did you ask for?" Lucy huddles over the menu to see my choice.

"This isn't easy, you know. I need more time to read it. I got a beer and a large pretzel to share."

"Oh."

I can hear the disappointment and bury my head back in the stubbornly indecipherable words. Within a minute, our waiter swoops the two brimming drinks onto the table without spilling a drop and lays the enormous pretzel on its white serviette between us.

"What *is* that?"

"It's a pretzel. They're bready here, not the hard, snacky things. It is a Bavarian speciality."

She rips the sea-salt speckled golden crust open and exposes its white, doughy innards. She takes a chunk and places it in her hungry mouth. And I wait. Slowly, her jaw begins to chew, and automatically her hand reaches to tear away another bite-sized piece.

"Nice?" I peep over the menu.

"Delicious," she shouts through her mouthful of scrambled bread.

The band has stopped playing—when I don't know—but I am suddenly aware of comparative quiet of rolling waves of talk.

"That's better!" Lucy declares, as she licks her fingers for any stray crystal of salt. "Now I'm not so incredibly hungry. I can think properly. So tell me everything! Still deliriously serious with Shakespeare?"

A smile automatically spreads across my face. I know it. I can't help it. I'm a businesswoman, a professional, and yet a hopeless teenager.

"It's ridiculous, but I can't explain it. He is just…I can't put into words how he makes me feel; it's visceral."

"Yeah, you said on the phone. Puke!" She pulls her schoolgirl photo booth pose—the one where she looks two steps from the asylum. "I'm happy for you though. Does he think the same of you?"

"Yes. No. Well, he hasn't said it like that, but he loves me. He would do anything for me. I mean, with this trip, he was completely fine about it. Pleased for me even. It is such a relief to find someone I can rely on like I can on Will.

"And he's so clever!" I run on, after a slurp of the cold, fresh beer. "Really clever. We've some great plans for how to invest the profits, so our next productions will be fully funded with revolving sets, costumes and a professional cast, and I will be able to get back to my acting roots and perform. We have investors champing at the bit, ready to go and…it's just amazing how things have turned out."

Lucy finger-tiptoes across the table to my untouched half of pretzel.

"I can't wait to be on stage with him either."

"I'm happy for you, Enna."

I lift my stein with both hands and take a sip, enjoying a secret smile behind the rim of my glass.

Lucy raises hers too and hails, "Cheers! To England and St. George."

"*Prost!*"

In a joint effort of ill-pronounced but enthusiastic German from me and much pointing from Lucy, we finally order our main courses. I start with the roasted pork knuckle. It is succulent and tasty, complemented by sweet red cabbage, braised with apple, perfectly balancing the salty pork, and the potato dumpling provides a pleasing, stodgy texture.

With salt levels rising, we swap dishes halfway through, and I gain a plate of original *hofbrauhaus brotzeitteller*, which I learn translates into a platter of multi-hued sausages with bread and butter. Lucy has already picked over the ones she will and won't eat. She greeted the Bavarian specialty, white veal sausages, with a look of sheer horror and hurriedly pushed the unappealing offering to the outer rim of the plate.

"Thanks for coming out," she says as she smears the last forkful of pork in its remaining juices and plops it in her mouth. "Really, I would have starved without you. And," she says, swallowing, "you're quite good company, even if you are loved up and moony."

The waiter, with unimproved humor, cleans our plates away and leaves us with the bill. I count out my multi-lingual money—paying is far easier than ordering—and we stroll out into the night with content tummies and salt-swollen ankles.

Munich by night seems a different city again. The sharp military corners and vast façades are bathed in uplighters and moonlight, and the whole city seems softer and more magical. We meander through Munich, arm in arm, talking about everything and nothing, finally collapsing into bed and scoffing the chocolate mints left on our pillows.

We lie in the dark, as we did for sleepovers when we were young. I feel like a beached whale on the quilted satin shallows. My stomach groans with the weight of its intake, Bavarian fare sloshing horizontally along an intestine caught napping. Lucy laughs at my musical body.

"How can such a little stomach make so much noise?" she asks the darkness.

"It's busy doing its job. Leave it alone!"

"It's gross! Does it squelch like that when you're in bed with Will?"

"I don't know; we've always been too busy with other things to notice."

We laugh in the darkness.

"Cole used to say that my stomach was just like me—loud, active and wanting everyone to know just how hard it is working!" The words trail out of my mouth before I have time to think about them, and now that they have escaped, they hang in the air. A conjuror's trick, sleight of mouth, and *poof!* I've said it.

Lucy switches on the bedside lamp and turns her face on the pillow toward me.

"Do you think about him a lot, Enna?"

"No," I reply before I can think about it.

She looks doubtful.

"Yes. Okay, I suppose I do."

"And what do you feel?"

"Regret, I suppose, that I acted so rashly and my last memory is of him shouting at me. I wish if things had to end—which of course makes sense now—we had done it with some fucking decency, but at first there was so much hurt, so much anger. Now there's just this huge emptiness, this loss.

"There's overwhelming sadness sometimes too, when I catch sight of our photo together in the office, the photo-booth ones from his cousin's wedding that I've been unable to take off the fridge, when I hear a song I know he loves—anything by Muse, or The Who, or Kiss from his childhood—it squashes my heart all over again. It hurts that we don't get another chance, that we can't lead parallel lives."

"But what about Will?"

"Oh, Will's easy." And I am instantly smiling. "We have so much in common. He can literally do everything at the theater. I don't even need to ask."

"Isn't that kind of suffocating? Spending all that time together? Working all day, side-by-side, practically day and night?" She boosts herself up on her hip, folding her arm and resting her face in her palm. "This is what I see: I see you working like a dog, responding to my emails at all manner of ungodly hours, closeted away with this guy, playing pretend in this theater which owns you…it's almost like you're two addicts…"

Her speech is so surprising, so completely unsettling; the only response I can think to make is to laugh. That is ridiculous after all. "Lu! Is that what you really think? Will and I work together because we love the theater. We work hard because we want it to succeed. It takes a lot to make a theater run, to produce a show. Are we addicted? No, we're *committed.* I guess you could say that performing, applause, the creative process, the achievement is a bit of a drug, but you could find that in any job, couldn't you?" I'm exhausted and turn to get some shut-eye, hoping that is the finale of this conversation. I'm wrong.

"Do you think Will would pick you?"

"What?" I ask, turning back with a weary slump.

"I mean, if he had to choose between a touring life in theater or you, who do you think he'd choose?"

"Me, of course," I say, flushing, before remembering his reluctance to "hitch his wagon." But things have changed since then, haven't they? Our relationship has got closer, deeper, stronger.

"Really? Well, I can't wait to meet him." She stretches up and switches off the bedside lamp. "Most of the actors you introduced me to always seemed like pompous, self-centered pricks. That's what made Cole so different. He was the one bloke who seemed to put you first, Enna. He was the one who would do anything for you."

"But you don't know Will, Lucy. He would do anything for me. And, actually, it's not that I need him to do all these things for me—I'm not some incapable damsel in distress—but the fact he wants to help, the fact we are such a great team is…well, it's perfect. Now, please, let's end the Lucy Winfrey show and get some sleep."

I thud my head to the pillow again. I'm not going to think about it. I've made my choice, and this is the happiest I've been in ages. We all have regrets, but that's life. And Will would pick me. He did pick me. He had the decision of whether to stay or go. He could have married Melissa and toured across America, but he didn't. He picked me.

Chapter 22

I will start writing; I will. I have five days here. I can do it tomorrow. Today is for being with my oldest friend and taking in the sights of Germany! Besides, it is too nice to sit in the windowless business center and write about pirates.

We board the train bound for Lake Tegernsee, billed as "an oasis of tranquility nestling in the Alps." The concierge recommended this picturesque spot, notable for its deep crystal clear lake, its serene and majestic mountains, and the eerie existence of Hitler's Eagle's Nest. After studying Hitler's Germany in GCSE history, Lu and I are goggled-eyed to this important landmark, the infamous Berchesgarten. In the pursuit of insightful travel journalism and morbid curiosity, Lucy and I head south.

The view does not fail to impress, but the spectacle is due less to the scenic view and more the scale—how in tune, German nature and architecture! The steep mountains cradle the narrow lake so that, as the boat sails us across, it feels like we are winding our way through a ravine. The guide points out the rock formation and recites his folk tales of mountain peaks formed in a witch's profile, of peaks representing the king, his queen, and their children. Lucy makes notes wildly, but I lie back and let the gentle hum of the boat's engine and the lap of the small wash lull me into thoughtlessness.

The captain stops the engine in the center of the lake, and a fading fan of ripples bobs away. I dangle my fingers over the side and trace fleeting patterns in the surface: E looping into a P, W looping around an E, an E cradled within a C. The linked monograms cut through the clear water but disappear instantly, the ghost trail of one initial fading before I can lastingly join it to mine.

Lucy nudges her elbow between my ribs and gives me a disapproving teacher look, corralling my attention toward the captain. In his tourist-pleasing Captain Nemo uniform, he unhooks a brass instrument from its peg and is commanding the audience with stiff banter. I can't tune in to what he is saying. I watch as he raises the horn to his lips and blows a short phrase. He stops, moves the horn to his side, waiting. And then we hear it, seconds later: the same tune echoing off the sides of the mountains. Our boatload of tourists sing out appreciative *oohs* and *ahs*—surprise crossing all language barriers. Nature's architecture steals the scene from Munich's historical artifice.

After hiking the suggested scenic trails, we stop for a light lunch. Or, at least I hope it will be a light lunch. My body is already missing the color green, but a glance through the bilingual menu—I admit, I'm peeking at the English—suggests that the only form of apple is in the strudel.

We sit on the sun-drenched terrace of the beer garden, with the heat lamps roaring away to keep us warm. The Alps crest all around us. A stream trickles close by, its babbling accompanied by the occasional growl of a passing engine or the crunch of tires on the gravel.

Only a thousand miles away from Ashtead, and it's so calm, so peaceful. I couldn't feel further away. "It's beautiful," I say, feeling the fresh, clean air rush up my nostrils and inflate my lungs.

Lucy squints against the bright light. "Beautiful but boring. You couldn't live here. You'd go crazy." She takes another forkful of wiener schnitzel with cranberry jus and skewers it. "I mean, in the day you've been here, how many Germans have you seen with a laptop or a cell phone? Answer: none. You couldn't possibly survive without being plugged in."

"Luce—"

"No, seriously! I'm going to count the number of times I see you check your phone from now on."

"Let's not get back onto this, Lu! I get it. You don't approve of the theater. Can't we just enjoy our time here?"

"That depends. Are you going to let go for the week? Or are you going to be running to the business center to check your emails every morning, noon, and night, calling the box office temp and texting away like a hormonal teenager all week long?"

"I have to stay in touch. That's my job."

"I knew you couldn't do it."

I shake my head with incredulity. Thing is, she's right. I couldn't wait for the plane to touch down and the steward to give the all clear to switch on portable devices. Then, there was the flurry of phone calls I placed when she was showering, and the hour I spent in the business center this morning.

"So go on. What was so important that you had to rush off to use the computer during breakfast?"

"Nothing."

She looks unimpressed.

"Just trivial things, okay? Some financial meetings, that sort of thing. Will needed to know about some appointments we rescheduled due to the trip. He's taking care of it."

"Good. Then you won't have to check business again, will you?"

"But I enjoy it!"

"But you're on holiday and I invited you, and you're being no fun. I'm working too by the way. Difference is, I don't let it govern every waking minute. So switch off, unplug, and be goddamn present, please!"

"*Ja, mein Führer!*"

She takes a long sip of Coke. She doesn't say anything but replaces her glass on the table. She leans back in her chair and closes her eyes in the bright afternoon sunshine. Is she *really* upset with me, or just joking? I know my work schedule has alienated most school and university friends—I'd sent so many "with regrets" that the invitations had stopped arriving—but I thought Lu and I were beyond that.

I'm open-mouthed, gormlessly trying to work out how I should answer her rant, or mock-rant, or whatever, when she opens just one eye and says mischievously, "So, was it really business, or was it easing a guilty conscience after thinking about Cole last night?"

"Lu! You're incorrigible. It *was* business."

"No dirty emails or phone sex, then?" she says, unable to stop the smirk curling upward.

"No!"

"How disappointing."

The enormous slice of apple strudel arrives, the fresh cream pooling around it like a moat circling the pastry and softening its baked layers.

"Agh!" I groan. "Are you trying to make me the size of a zeppelin?"

"I told you, you are on holiday." She brandishes her weaponry and throws a spoon at me. "Dig in!"

We cut through the crisp ladder of pastry, through the hot apple, into the soft, soggy cream-soaked layers beneath. It is so good that, in spite of bloated Self, I spoon joust Lucy for the last bite before resettling to digest and take a quick nap.

The afternoon meanders away from us, creeping into its second hour, and we are in no hurry to relinquish our sun-trap. Lucy quietly dozes under the umbrella as my restless mind thinks of all the productions I will stage at Ashtead: *Gaslight, Pride and Prejudice, The Day After the Fair, Dangerous Liaisons, The Go-Between* — is there a stage version available? I must check this. I could play Marian, and Will could be Ted, and we'd have to cast a big name to play Hugh — I wonder if I could talk Alan Rickman into it? Then we will need a couple of comedies to throw into the mix, another murder mystery for around Halloween, and a musical for Christmas. I will absolutely refuse to do a panto, with all the cross-dressing, musical shenanigans and some C-list personality trying to revive his or her career.

I will organize a meeting as soon as I get back and review the programming schedule with Will. Yes, there is so much we can do now; it just makes my brain bubble with possibilities.

"Shit!" Lucy erupts. "The train!"

"Oh, balls!" I'd forgotten too. I check my watch, and my legs spring into action. She grabs her backpack crammed with spiral notepads, and we race — amazingly — in the direction of the S-Bahn. The thought of having to overnight here powers my legs to their unathletic maximum, and I run as fast as I can.

Having witnessed the German efficiency, I am doubtful of a delayed departure, and sure enough, the train is already at the platform in its shiny, ungraffitied livery. We sprint down the platform, paddling our arms through the air like oars, fighting to carve through space more quickly and make it to the automatic door in time. The train starts to move as I run alongside it. I slam my palm on the open button, and the doors retract. I check for Lucy. She's a stride behind me, red-faced and brow etched with determination. I leap into the carriage and whip around to extend both hands to Lucy. She clasps onto my wrists, her sweaty palms slipping on my skin.

"Hang on! Hang on!" I plead, but her hands lose their grip on my wrists, and her fingers slip down to the white-knuckled hold of my fingertips. I can feel her lose momentum and start traveling backward.

"Can you jump?" I shout over the locomotive hum. She looks at me as if I am completely insane, her face now the color of a ripe nectarine.

"Get…out of the way…you silly tit!"

"What?" I yell from the doorway, as she jumps across the crevasse of metal tracks and cannons into me. We land on the carriage floor, breathless and jubilant with relief.

The metal doors slam shut together, and the train chugs quietly, its schedule unimpeded—no thanks to those clownish Brits! The carriage full of honey colored Germanic faces with broad juggernaut jaws and high foreheads stare with disdain.

"Well, if they didn't think we were lesbians before, they certainly do now!" she pants, flopping into our horizontal hug.

Chapter 23

The next few days are a laughter-filled whirl of the sights, sounds, and tastes of Munich, with just a little writing sprinkled in to salve a guilty conscience. We visit the overwhelmingly gaudy Asamkirche, a bedazzling expression of Catholic opulence. The green and gold marble walls, spiral pillars, columns plastered with gilt effigies, ornate balconies festooned by a flock of gilt cherubs, an abundance of gilt frills, colorful murals covering the vast ceiling—all these tasteful works of art cumulatively reach an inspiring level of tastelessness.

We take a tour through the bustling market of *Viktualienmarkt*. Our eyes bulge with our bellies as we weave through displays of white asparagus—still no green!—rounds of raclette, brie, gruyere, *schnittkase* and *Obatztem*; small wooden kegs brimming with different types of olives, peppers, garlic, chiles, gherkins; ice-packed stalls offering fresh, prehistoric-looking fish with glassy eyes and dental problems; hot rotisserie stands offering bockwurst, bratwurst, weisswurst, leberkase, and frikadelle, offered between soft, pillowy buns and lavished with sweet, grainy mustard.

We stand mesmerized before the long stretch of butchers' windows lining the market, the wording above proclaiming *die Fleischerei*. Can a German word be onomatopoeic? *Fleischerei* sounds so perfect for bloodlust butchery! The window displays have the uniformity of everywhere else, but where before they exhibited the innocent rosy display of farm fresh eggs in hay, or the tempting pyramid of forbidden truffles, the window of *die Fleischerei* resembles the precise, sterile showcase of animal anatomy. In this white plastic tray: pigs' trotters—whole pig heads with ears; in this, great lengths of girthy meat, tongue, animal unknown. Some trays are empty, evaporating rings of brown blood staining the brilliant white like a muddy halo.

We rubberneck past each window with gruesome glee as we identify another foreign body part—an ordered, methodical car crash, body parts butterflied for our viewing ease.

We visit the Olympic village, a strange moon landing launch site. Buildings are covered by tarpaulins of steel-netting supported acrylic glass, creating a roofline of oriental hats.

I sit in the gardens of the sprawling yet stately *Schloss Nymphenburg* and try to write while Lucy takes the tour. The property semi-circles the river, the main building in the center and the other smaller buildings adjoined by arches and one story roofed apartments. It is hard to focus in such unusual surrounds, and my mind is easily diverted.

When will Lucy appear?

I must look out for her.

Oh! That's a strange insect!

I wonder what we will eat tonight?

What is Will doing right now?

On my fourth night, I wake up abruptly and try to catch the elusive end of a dream, but it vanishes from memory. The morning light is already creeping through the small cracks between the Roman blinds and the thick overhanging drapes, the motes of dawn dancing, twirling around and around in their natural spotlight. I open my sleep-encrusted eyes wider to not see Lucy beside me. Five minutes of the mote Viennese waltz, my eyelids flicker to be joined once more, but Lucy still has not returned. I bat away the almost overpowering force of the desire to sleep for another ten minutes; I struggle not to be sucked back under into that warm, comforting, dark haven. I roll over to re-examine the red digits silently shouting the time: five fifty-five a.m. I wait another minute before staggering from the cozy cocoon through the air-conditioned chill to the bathroom.

Light streams from under the bathroom door. I put my ear to the door but hear nothing. I knock quietly.

"Lu? Lucy are you okay?" I strain to hear a reply before knocking again, more loudly this time. "Luce? Open the door. Are you okay?"

I push the handle; it offers no resistance and swings in its arc to reveal Lucy lying on the cold marble tile, scrunched up in a ball, hugging her legs to her stomach.

"Luce! What's the matter?" I dive to her side, slipping slightly in the unseen puddle of vomit. Her eyelids open fractionally, the bathroom light too bright for tender eyes. Suddenly, she grabs my elbows, launches herself up, and lets fly with a gullet full of projectile vomit. The retching noise and the acrid smell fill the little room. Once the impressive stream is staunched, she collapses, exhausted, resuming her fetal position.

"I'm okay. I'm okay," she mumbles quietly as a tear rolls over the bridge of her nose and plink on the marble. She is clearly not okay.

"Take small sips," I instruct, holding a tumbler of water to her lips, remembering the directions as they were given to me on many a nauseous night in the Petersen household.

She does as I say, and I stroke the sweat-plastered strands of hair from her face.

"I don't feel well."

"I can see that, darling. Don't worry. I'm here. Just take small sips. It's okay."

She seems content, and her eyes close before she is suddenly gripped by another wave of nausea and hurls herself headfirst into the toilet bowl. She holds her head hovering above the seat, as if to make sure, but she launches again and her body jerks forward, like a learner driver stalling a car. I rub her back, swaying ineffectively from foot to foot.

She lifts her head from the bowl, eyes bloodshot and bloodhound droopy. "Enna," she whimpers. "Please stop rocking. You're making me feel seasick." She heaves again but only brings up bile. The stench is unbelievable, a pungent whiff of spiced sausage and sauerkraut. I try to be efficiently German and mop up the slowly expanding puddle by the foot of the toilet, but I give up with the too-absorbent toilet paper forming puke clots in my hand, and smother the patch with the fresh, white towel.

After half an hour, I hoist the dozing Lucy off the bathroom floor and guide her back to bed, placing the beautiful enamel wastepaper bin in the puke trajectory.

When the morning attains a more reasonable hour, I creep out of the bedroom and head to the breakfast bar on a quest for dry toast and a carafe of strong coffee.

"Luce, wake up. I brought you some toast. Not exciting, I know, but you probably need something to keep your energy up."

She winces and rolls away from me, onto her side.

"You still don't feel good?"

I hear a grunt in reply and leave the toast on the desk. I contemplate the mound under the eiderdown. *I should leave her to sleep,* I tell myself, quietly retrieving a spiral notepad and turning on my heel for the business center.

"Where are you going?" I hear her mew pathetically from the mound of duvet.

"Just slipping to the…pool to write," I lie.

"Nooooo! Stay here, Enna. I think I'm going to die." A limp forearm thuds from the covers.

"You're not going to die. But you do need to rehydrate and get some rest. Come on, just take it easy and get some sleep."

"I feel so weak. It even hurts when I —"

The shrill ring of the telephone cuts through, and she is too spent to battle it.

"Unplug it. Unplug it." She moans, flailing her limp wrist at the phone. "It'll be *Foreigner's* Fucking *Friend* giving a deadline update. Please just unplug it. My head is going to explode."

I scrabble to follow the neatly organized cables, over the desk, under the desk, neatly twisted around the leg of the desk, squeezing through the gap at the back. *What am I doing? Tunneling in bloody Colditz?* I give the cord a yank and it falls, inert and disarmed from its socket.

A feeble "thank you" mews pathetically from under the covers.

I kick off my shoes and recline on the sofa, attempting to write some more of the play. It is coming along nicely, and I can't wait to read it with Will. He will make a great Long John.

I write for several hours, accompanied by the whirring snore coming from the mound. She's sound asleep. I put the play aside and quietly locate the forbidden mobile phone. Perhaps I can sneak into the corridor and make some calls. That would be okay, wouldn't it? I mean, it's not like I'm deserting her. I can hear her if she calls, or pukes, or swallows her tongue.

I switch the phone on and watch as it flickers then flatlines. The little bar fades to non-existence, and the screen loses power. No charge? My mind races first to the last place seen and finds the charger exactly where I had left it, collecting dust under the desk in the office. Shit!

I hear the bed springs compress, and a befuddled head worms its way from beneath the covers. Her bloodhound eyes have recovered some of their elasticity, and her green pallor has faded. Alabaster white is probably better than *Exorcist* green.

"What's the time?" she asks groggily.

"Twenty past two."

"Urgh!" Her head falls back on the pillow. "I'm sorry to waste your last day."

"Don't you worry about me. It's you I'm concerned about. How are you feeling?"

"As if somebody carved a hole through my back, pulled my insides out, used my intestines as a scarf and my kidneys as earmuffs."

"Well, that is just a beautiful image. I take it you don't feel any better then?"

"I don't think I'll be sick, but I feel so weak. It hurts to move. I don't think I can get out of bed quite yet."

"You don't have to. I'll get everything you need."

"Thanks. You're a great friend." Her eyelids flutter closed once more.

"So are you, Lu. Don't worry. I'll be here. You go to sleep. I'll be here."

As afternoon fades to evening, and the stink of vomit slowly dissipates, she grows stronger and is at least able to raise a smile. She assures me she will be fine and insists that I travel back to Ashtead as planned. I wish I could stay, as I hate to leave her.

"Promise me you'll call."

"That's my line," she says.

"Yes, but *Foreigner's Friend* will pay for yours!"

"Cheeky sod. Safe flight. Give my love to Shakespeare."

"Will do," I say, giving her a final squeeze. "And you take care. See you back in Blighty soon." With my pink suitcase at my heels, I wheel my way down the corridor.

She stands at the door of our room, huddled in her robe and waving weakly.

"Miss Petersen! Miss Petersen!" the gawky, bespectacled concierge pecks her way around her marble perch and halts me by the chandelier.

"Yes? Ja?"

"Miss Petersen, I have an urgent message which arrived for you. You are leaving, yes?"

"Yes, I am. Miss Pearse will be remaining for a few days more."

"Ah. Just so. You will be needing the message. I will get it for you." She stalks her way back around the desk and produces a Bayerischer Hof headed notelet.

> For: Ms. Enna Petersen
>
> Room: 628
>
> From: Ms. Kay Petersen
>
> Have been trying to call, but no answer. Please phone home. Don't worry. Don't wish to alarm. All well, but do need to speak urgently.

"Thank you."

What could Mum want? I rifle through my handbag for the requisite Euros to feed the pay phones, a slight panic swirling in my stomach. At least, I hope it's panic and not the stirring of Lucy's vomitous erruptous.

"Ms. Petersen, the airport transit is leaving," the concierge pecks efficiently.

Shit. *Oh, well, I shall call her at the airport,* I think, re-packing my handbag and trotting out to the Germanically punctual minivan.

It is only a few minutes into the journey before my mind comes back to the oddly worded message. What could Mum want? Why, when she knows I am coming home today, would she go to the effort of placing an international call to tell me something that couldn't wait until my return?

Imagined scenarios escalate within seconds. The many headed Hydra of Perilous Possibility and Unknown Circumstance swirls in front of my eyes. What could have happened? And why is it that when people say, "Don't worry," it means you do the exact opposite?

I see my father in all manner of mechanical mishaps. Did he tackle that leaky roof on his own and fall from the ladder? Did he accidently drill a body part with his new Black and Decker? Did he re-wire something and not turn the power off? I battle with each ridiculous hypothetical, hacking away with reason, trying to cut off the swirling, evasive potential that Dad could be hurt or worse.

"All well," Mum had said. This doesn't really mean anything. "Well" is relative. It's not "all good." Someone could still fall from a ladder whilst trying to fix a leak in the roof and break one's legs, but "all well," because it could be worse.

Maybe it is Leo? His lead foot acceleration and brake slamming have slipped for once, and he has plowed the lovingly waxed Corrado into the back of a ten-ton truck; or the tires have blown out at high speed on the M25, and the vehicle has launched through the air, catapulted into the central reservation, and spun on its roof like a totaled dinky toy. Or he has accelerated to pass a vehicle on one of the country lanes near Mum and Dad's house and slammed headfirst into the path of a speeding articulated lorry! Gory visions of shattered glass, twisted metal and unidentifiable, disorganized British body parts strewn over the blood wet tarmac have me gripped. Gruesome thoughts of mangled man and machine fail to be beaten. But "don't worry. All is well."

The scenery passes in a blur of green and gray. So, if it *is* all well, what does that leave? Mum? She must be okay because she sent the message. So what else could there be that would warrant a phone message and request to phone home on the very day I am returning home anyway?

The minivan pulls up to the terminal entrance.

"British Airways. Anyone for British Airways?" the driver asks, eyeing us in the rearview mirror.

I raise my hand. I had not realized it was trembling.

With the wheelie case champing at my heels, I waste no time with niceties, and I make my way to the check-in desk, request my window seat, and sail through security.

I loiter around the departure gate, listlessly fingering the useless mobile phone lead-lining my pocket. I count the pitiful collection of unspent Euros in my hand. I have a one-Euro coin, and two two-Euros. Not enough to call home. I have Sterling, crisply folded British tender, but what use is that in a German payphone? I have my bank card. I pry the card out of its snug hub in my wallet and hold it in my hand. But I can't do it. I don't want to know. There is absolutely nothing I can do about it.

I will be in Heathrow in two hours. Then I'll brace myself for whatever news. For now, I'll just have to be in that purgatory where there is still hope that everyone and everything will be all right. That Dad is safe from fix-it disasters. That Leo is well and not speeding in his Corrado. That Mum is as strong as ever and just too busy with the theater to send proper communiqués.

Flight BA0951 leaves on time. I watch the progress of the little animated plane on the screen. Progress? Ha! Any slower and it might plummet out of the sky. *Can't this thing go any faster?* It is painful. My window seat is over the wing and I can see the top of the engine and its blades whirring. *Go faster, go faster!*

The large man beside me has wedged himself in his middle chair and is spilling over; his forearm, the size and color of a Christmas ham hock, has elbowed my wrist off my tray table-containing armrest and has bouldered it shut. It would not frustrate me as much if, a) the beefy German had not promptly fallen asleep on takeoff, thereby, b) preventing me from actually using the table, and c) forcing me to hold my drink, which led to, d) a jolt of turbulence slopping the hot beverage up the sides of the cup and sloshing the contents over my pale pink capris, which may have, e) slightly burned my pelvis and, f) daubed a stain not unlike the map of Australia right over my crotch. *Scheiße.*

I feel the impact of the landing gear thud and bounce, thud and bounce onto the runway tarmac—I want to burst into relieved tears. I'm home!

I slalom through the mass of bodies as we filter off the plane through baggage claim, then customs and arrivals, passing dawdling loiterers who lack any purpose, direction or sense of urgency—the flotsam of the traveling world. I look out over the sea of faces lining up behind the barrier to welcome family and friends home. I squint to focus, scanning the bobbing crowd for those broad shoulders, dark hair, chocolate brown Malteaser eyes and melting smile.

Another two flights are getting in from Europe, and the arrivals gate is a blur of tides rushing toward each other, a loud mix of colors, accents and languages. I stand still; no one rushes to meet me. He had taken the flight details. He had said that he'd be there, waiting. I knew I should have ducked to the business center to confirm the information with him.

I trundle to the phone booth and dial his number—hoorah for Sterling! It feels like weeks since I have seen him, months since I've heard his voice, bathed in the joy of his laugh. I can't wait to tell him my travel stories. Maybe he knows what Mum's message is all about.

The telephone rings, and I bounce from foot to foot, twisting the ridged metal cord between my fingers. I can't wait to hear his voice or feel the touch of his thumb sweep my cheek, the warmth of his great arms around me.

His voicemail service does not kick in. *Odd.* I replace the receiver in its vertical cradle and feed my fifty pence in again, dialing his number with slow, finger pad precision. Still no answer. His voicemail should record even if he's busy or the phone is off, surely?

I slot the fifty pence in again and this time dial home.

"Hello?"

"Mum, it's me. Is everything okay?"

"Where are you?"

"Heathrow. I just landed. Sorry I didn't call before. I was just leaving for the airport and—"

"I'll come and get you."

"It's okay, Ma. Will's coming. He's just a little held up, I think, and my bloody mobile has—"

"I'm coming. I'll meet you by the bus stops outside terminal one. Give me thirty minutes."

I duck through the reunited families, friends, and lovers, and take up sentry duty by the conveniently situated Starbucks. I nurse a latte, watching and waiting, taking long sips without removing my eyes from the ever-changing ethnic sea. I glimpse the back of a dark head, the right build, the right height, and I stand on my tiptoes to get a better look, readying to wave my arms like a desert island cast away. "SOS! SOS!" But the head swivels, and the eyes are not the ones I'm desperately searching for.

I resume my seat and stir my coffee with the wooden stirrer, marbling camel colored patterns through the white froth, until all the white is tinged with brown.

I drop the stirrer on the table, the light bulb suddenly sparking.

"It's Will!" I say out loud. "It's Will!" The emergency message was to tell me about Will; that's why he's not here. That's why he can't answer his phone. It's Will. He is injured or dying. "Oh my God!"

I grab the cup and the handle of my case and rush through the reunited, happy, carefree, free-spirit people. I need air. I wait by the terminal entrance in the hope that my presence there will somehow speed my mother's arrival. I stand practically in the road to see the oncoming cars, buses and motorbikes as they circle into view from the roundabout. Each silver-gray vehicle causes a mixture of panicked relief as I dart in and out of the road, my meerkat neck at hyper extension, trying to get in a better position to identify the car as Mum's.

At last, the correct make and model pulls up in front of me. The door swings open, and I chuck my case through the gap and into the back seat. I scurry inside, and Mum drives off before I even close the door properly.

Panic has numbed my tongue. It could be cut out and displayed for all to see in *der Fleischeri*. Mum is fixed on the road ahead, the steering wheel held tightly in her grip, a bloodless white spreading from her knuckles. She must feel my gaze, pleading for answers, for she lifts her hand and clutches my knee for a few seconds before regripping the wheel even tighter.

A single tear breaches and loosens my tongue. "Mum, I—" I want to say that I know. I've guessed.

But she cuts me short. "Enna, it's going—"

"But, I—"

"It's okay."

It's a duet of awkwardness, staccato offerings racing to the crescendo of the piece.

"You go."

"No, you first, darling."

Another tear rises and traces the well-run course down my cheek. "I know it's Will. Isn't it? Mum?"

Time stops, I can't breathe.

"Yes, darling," she says with military precision.

Chapter 24

The decapitated Hydra lies vanquished, heads scattered around me: my father is safe; my brother is whole; my mum is well beside me; my family home and all its occupants are still standing.

The air rushes from my lungs, as if each slain head were a balloon of unreality that I have been holding on to for the last four hours and can now, finally, exhale.

"Pull over. Please pull over."

She does so without question. She turns the key, unstraps her seat belt, and turns toward me.

"Is he going to die?" I ask, my face crumpling in on itself.

"No, darling!" She sounds surprised, her sympathetic voice almost breaking into a chuckle. Why would she laugh? But if he isn't going to die, then he is safe!

"Oh, thank God!" The dam of fear lifts, and relieved tears surge south. I hold on to her, as if the reality of being able to touch her will make everything else all right. Wasn't it Mum who always made things all right? I cling to her now, wiping the last of my tears away with the back of my hand, the small stock of tissues already well-used.

"Will you drive me to the hospital now?"

She straightens in her seat and pulls the seat belt over her.

"Why don't we go home first?"

"No, Mum. I need to see him. He'll be wanting to see me."

She starts the engine and rejoins the carriageway.

"Mum?"

She concentrates on the stream of traffic joining from the tributary. Is it me, or do her knuckles turn even whiter?

"Mum? I need to go to the hospital. Mum, I need to see him."

"Darling, I'm sorry if I've given you the wrong impression. I never meant to, but Will isn't, to my knowledge, in the hospital."

"No?" I can feel my brow pucker in perfect synchrony with the O forming on my lips.

"No." She turns her head from the windscreen, directing this unequivocal, solid rhinoceros of a "no" head-on.

My mind stumbles over this hurdle. I wait a minute, impassively watching the white van pass us, its crew of shirtless workers leering and jeering out of the window.

"But he is okay?" I ask numbly. "He is well?" The ambiguous word sticks in my throat.

"As far as I know."

"So, where is he?"

"I don't know, sweetheart. Nobody knows."

I don't go to the hospital. I don't go home. I insist Mum drop me off at the theater, which she reluctantly does.

"There is nothing you can do that can't wait until tomorrow," she pleads. But there is much I should be doing. I have to find Will. He could be hurt, or kidnapped, or robbed of the box office takings and left for dead in a ditch by the rail tracks. Didn't all murder mysteries, whether with *Frost,* or *Poirot, Morse,* or *Rebus* terminate at the railway station? Wasn't it the murderers' locale of choice? Where some poor victim would be found, unrecognizable, under the bridge by the abandoned railway siding.

He must be hurt, unable to answer his mobile — that would answer everything. I must help him.

This much Mum is able to divulge: after a sell-out Friday matinee, Will left to fulfill his usual Friday duties before the evening performance. Thursday's four-star review in *The Daily Mail* from the not easily pleased Quentin Letts had ensured a bumper audience.

But he never showed up. Mum and the temp girl, Lacey, manned the box office, Maureen and Sheila took the ticket stubs at the door, and at eight o'clock, the stalls were full and eager for the curtain to rise. At eight twenty p.m. it did, for Mum to walk on stage and tell the multitude that "Due to unforeseen circumstances…"

Refunds were issued, tickets were re-issued for a following performance, and refunds were promised after the box office ran dry. Mum had frantically tried to telephone Will that night, but the number she dialed rang and rang without answer.

I sit at my desk and try his number not once, but tens of times, again and again and again. Each time, the number of rings I listen to becomes shorter.

I call Ashtead Police and am told that, as an adult, he is not technically a missing person, and, "If he has only been gone for less than twenty-four hours, madam, it is not really of any concern. He's probably in the pub."

I try the hospitals. I give his name and description, but no unknown males or males of that name, height, and characteristics have been admitted.

"Are you a relative?"

"Well, no, actually I'm—"

"I'm sorry, but in that case we couldn't help you anyway."

I glance at the clock ticking away the moments that he could be lying unconscious without any of the emergency services giving a shit. It is five past six. If they won't do anything, I will. I hurriedly type a letter for the soon-to-be disappointed Saturday audience and tape it to the revolving door.

> Dear Theatre Patrons,
>
> Thank you so much for your kind support. Unfortunately, due to unforeseen circumstances, tonight's performance of *The Shakespearian Rap* will not run as planned. I am sorry for any inconvenience this has caused. If you would telephone the box office on Monday, we will do our very best to accommodate you at a future performance or refund any unused tickets. My deepest apologies again.
>
> Yours regretfully,
>
> Enna Petersen, Theater Director

I press my palm to the cool glass, about to push through to resurface into the cold, real world, but I can't resist giving it one last try. I race back to the office and dial his number. At twenty-four rings, I hang up.

"Why doesn't he answer?" I ask his neat, Germanically clean desk. The Formica faux wooden surface does not bear the same coffee-ringed Olympic pattern of my own. The papers are shuffled and stacked evenly, no random edges sticking out at acute angles. The pens are separated from the pencils in the pot. The drawing pins, staples and paper clips all have their individual housing sections. The only item at odds with this order is a torn cutting from the newspaper stuck to the corner of the computer screen surround. The black, gray, and white dots form a blurry likeness of the two of us, his arm around my waist as we smile our Chardonnay smiles for the camera.

I remember the photograph being taken after the performance following the victorious radio interview. We were in the bar, appeasing patrons, and every now and then, we'd catch each other's eyes across the room, bursting through the surface for a gulp of air before being pulled back down into the depths of theatrical conversation. We circled around the fishbowl, until finally, after what seemed like hours of treading water, he sailed across the room, caught hold of me, his arm hooking my waist and reeling me in.

The camera appeared from nowhere, and we were both so buoyant and elated that we didn't have time to think about feeling self-conscious.

And now I am alone. Now he needs me, and I don't know what I can do to help. All I know is that I must do something.

"I'm trying!" I tell the photo.

Within seconds, I peel off my stained pink capris and sweater and rummage through my case. Everything smells of sauerkraut and mustard—Eau de Biergarten. I don a pair of black trousers, and a polo neck and hurriedly leave the office.

The foyer display of moody black and white headshots catches my eye, and I unpin Will's headshot from the glass case. His eyes shine back at me with his mischievous twinkle. *I will not cry,* I school myself. *I have to be strong. I have to find him.*

With photo in hand, I take a deep breath and push through the revolving doors. It is a short walk to High Street. I pass my old school playing fields, the retirement home, the petrol station and the pub, which is starting to fill up with Saturday revelers.

The bank sits discreetly on the corner. That would have been Will's first Friday stoppage. The impenetrable oak door is firmly bolted. The reinforced glass windows are for giraffes only and emit light from seven feet or higher. I cannot see in. I cannot see Will tied to a desk chair, held hostage by a lunatic mental institute escapee, who just happened to launch his crazed attack as Will was casually depositing the takings. I listen at the door for signs of a struggle or duct-taped muffled cries, but all I hear is the hum from the pub juke box and the random cheers as the pub locals watch Chelsea versus Tottenham.

I pass Bella Donna, full of Saturday night glow and bustle. I stop at the window to scan the diner's heads for dark curls. Red-faced Vito is animated with his usual largesse. I see familiar faces, faces engaging in coffee and desserts, waiting for a bill before leaving for a fine evening of entertainment at the theater. Should I slip in, tell them not to hurry, to have another bottle of wine and the cheese platter? I should, but I slink away, breaking into a run.

I weave between oncoming traffic, running with the wind in my face, directionless, but looking. It feels good to run, converting the pent-up energy in my cells. I run up and down High Street, across to the rec, round the pond and—just as I think I can't run another step—I see the light from the little coffee shop where Will suggested we meet all those months ago, and I sprint toward it. It's been nine long hours since my airport latte, I calculate, and without any better ideas, I stop running and go in. It takes me a minute or two to catch my breath.

"One hot tea, grande and one—" I scan the chiller cabinet for inspiration. "One ultimate chocolate cheesecake. For here."

"I'll bring it over," the nonchalant barista replies.

I choose the corner where we had first sat together. I hold tightly to the sofa arm and am whisked back to the day Will held my hand and begged me to stay in Ashtead. I drum my fingertips over my lips to keep them shut, to distract Self from wanting to scream, "Where is he? Why won't somebody help me?" Am I shaking? Oh God, I'm shaking. I'm a bundle of nerves.

Nerves bundled…like frayed electrical cables ripped from their sockets and tied up in a pile. They splay and spasm as live impulses shuttle back and forth, sending out the distress message along the neurons. Mayday, Mayday! Will somebody help me? But frayed nerves can't reconnect. Brain and muscles can't help them. Their

SOS goes unheard. They are, after all, just a bundle of nerves. Alone, transmitting without effect. I drum my lip faster.

The lanky barista, with skin a cool blend of dark coffee and amaretto, bends to place the scalding tea on the low table. I release the headshot. It unrolls from my runner's grip, its edges softened from my clammy hand, and I take the plate and saucer from him. The photo flutters off my lap onto the floorboards. The barista bends low as I fumble to clutch it, and we both pull up short, an inch shy of clashing skulls — his wide forehead under a mushroom of tightly coiled afro waves, without doubt the contest favorite.

"Sorry." He smiles, tilting his head to get a better look as I recover the headshot.

"Oh man!" he says with surprise. "It's him. I'll miss him. He was about the only brother round here who would leave a tip. I mean —" he pauses contritely " — not that I expect a tip, but it's nice, you know?"

"Miss him? I'm sorry, I don't quite understand. You know this man?"

"Yeah, Mr. Breakfast Panini with a latte, extra shot of espresso, no syrups."

I look to the open-fronted refrigerator. I can feel its chill from here. "Do you have a minute to sit down and talk to me?"

A man sits at one of the round wooden tables, his nose buried in the paper. At another table, two pretty teenage girls chatter excitedly as they suck on their frappuccinos and play with their straws. The other tables stand patiently waiting for company.

"Hey, it's not like I'm rushed off my feet. I can give you a minute, but I'm flying solo, so if anyone comes in, I'll have to jet. No 'fense."

"None taken. Thanks."

He lands with a thump in the other corner of the sofa, crossing his long be-denimed legs in the shape of a Gallic number four. The hem of his jeans rises to reveal box-fresh, white Converse hightops. The shoes seem almost naked without their denim shroud, and their exposure steals my concentration.

"I know it's not busy, but I ain't got all day."

"Oh right, yes, sorry." I try to catch up, to look as if I know what comes next.

"Oh, wait a minute. Wait a minute, man. Are you his girlfriend? Did he stand you up, or something?"

"No. No. We are just work colleagues," I lie, swallowing hard. The connections behind my eyes suddenly click together like pieces of a train track. If Will has disappeared but is not hurt or held hostage, then I suppose I have been stood up. "But you see, I've been away and I missed saying goodbye."

"Yeah, don't think he'll be back neither. He just ordered his latte and asked for a double shot of espresso in it to keep him awake for his long journey. He told me to keep the change, 'cause I make it so good, and 'cause he likes my rapping style."

"Oh," I say, conjuring a Botox smile. "Did he say where he was going on this long journey?"

His large white teeth are eclipsed by his solid pout. "Man, are you sure you ain't his girl? I don't want to get in no trouble."

"No, no. Truly. But I do have some CDs he lent me, and he left so quickly I didn't get a chance to return them."

"That's too bad. Yeah, I don't know where he was heading, but he said he wanted to enjoy his last good coffee, 'cause he wasn't going see me again for a long, long time."

"And what time was this?"

"What does it matter what time?" He eyeballs me suspiciously, edging his back further into the corner of the settee.

A playful shriek comes from the two teens as they paw their straws and practice unsophisticated attempts at flirtation.

"I, well, it's silly really." Inspired, I look up girlishly through my long, tear-clumped eyelashes. "I've been away, but I landed last night" — the lie spills easily from my lips — "and if he left early, he could have stopped at my house and said goodbye and I wouldn't have been there, but he might have *tried* to say goodbye. Whereas, if he left late, I would have been at home, and I know he didn't come around, so I will know that he *didn't* try to say goodbye." I smile again, as if what I have just said makes perfect sense.

Now it's his turn to be dumbfounded. "Girl, I is going to give you some advice, and I don't want you to take this the wrong way, but you need to find yourself a man."

I almost laugh at the irony.

"I better go and clean the machines." He jumps to his feet, bringing the curtain down on his Converse peep show. "But, you cheer up," he says, towering above me. "He left here at about six. I was just due for my break. So maybe he stopped by and just missed you."

My head is abuzz, the random facts connected by a web of unknowns. Here at six p.m.? Going on a journey? So he had *no* intention of returning to the theater for the evening performance. Why would he go? Why would he leave?

Something must have happened. Some sudden, calamitous event. A death in the family. But why wouldn't he leave a note? A phone message? Why would that stop him answering now?

For the first time since I landed, I am half hoping that he *is* hurt and unable to answer the telephone, because the alternative—willfully abandoning the theater, willfully ignoring my calls, and willfully turning his back on me—is too painful to even contemplate.

I push the untouched slice of cheesecake across the table, repulsed by its silent complicity. The teaspoon resounds with a tinny rattle as it chinks on the tabletop. I seize the photo and leave quietly before the shameful tears can rise and crest.

The cool air feels good on my face, the breeze smacking my cheeks, demanding truth not drama. I walk unseeing, stalking the neighborhood for invisible shadows, searching for plausible excuses behind every corner, every bush, every defoliating tree, but his reason eludes me. The rain starts to fall, pattering in step with my wide strides. I can feel the drops prick my skin as they needle through my thin jumper, cold and numbing, and I want to be numb. I don't want to feel it. I want my bundle of nerves to stop transmitting. I spin across the pavement, arms stretched wide in some tribal rain dance. Bring on the rain.

Between the tornado of thoughts and the loud downpour, I don't hear "Carmina Burana" resounding from the crevice of my trouser pocket. It is the constant vibrating which finally breaks through the crust of my subconscious. The wet material clings to the mobile and resists my frantic attempts to retrieve it. As the music rises to a passionate crescendo, I seize the phone out just in time.

"Yes?"

Pause.

I neither move nor breathe, afraid either will unbalance or intercept the magical sound waves transported through space from his mouth to my ear. I take in a heart-squashing breath, my little pump peaking with systolic pressure.

There's a click — *no, don't hang up* — and suddenly the voice comes in loud and clear. "Why the bloody hell haven't you called?"

Lucy.

Diastole. Systole.

"Enna?"

"Sorry. Manic day," I say, pushing off into the building wind now whipping lashes of wet hair back into my face.

"Just wanted to know that you had landed safely, that's all." Pause. "What's that noise?"

"The wind and rain. I'm walking home, so it's not really a great time. Are you feeling better?"

"Yeah, yeah, I'm fine. I went to the Hofbrau Haus just to get another giant pretzel. I don't trust anything else right now."

I try to keep it back. I bite my lower lip. I press both unkissed halves, but a pained gasp makes it through.

"Enna? En? What was that?"

I want to reply. I want to tell her, but only guttural sounds come out. "Will's…" The intake of breath knocks back the flow of adult reasoned explanation. "He's…gone…and…I can't…find…him," I manage to stutter to the wind before its wailing overtakes my own.

"Enna, Will's gone? I can't hear. Bastard line. Bastard country. Look, don't panic. If something has happened, I am sure it will work itself out. Fuck! I can't hear. I'm phoning Kay. Get to a landline. Then text. I'll call you in that. Love you."

I lean into the wind and ride its back as it carries me home.

The house is dark and unwelcoming. The door fights my pushes, barricaded by the small pile of mail. I barge with my shoulder for a fourth time, and the pile landslides across the hall floor. Maybe he's written, left me a note. I fall to my knees and drip over the cache of free newspapers, Indian takeaway offers, pizza menus, and bills, scrabbling through the assorted, brightly colored printed trash for a glimpse of something handwritten or white and unofficial. There is nothing. I look around the lounge, helpless, for some sign of his presence.

Sergeant Bob Whipple looks on glibly, his tank lights casting a green glow across the dark room. The tank is empty but for him. Oh. Another sweet partner Bob has eaten. "I can't trust you with anything!" I shout petulantly at the nonchalant fish.

With heavy limbs and sodden shoes, I drag my sorry self upstairs and strip the black, wet layers, exposing white, numbed flesh pricked with goose pimples. I glance at the mirror in appraisal, ready to collapse in self-pity, but something holds me back. I look deeper into the mirror at the pale reflection. The flint gray eyes look disapproving. *You're stronger than that, Enna. Survival of the fittest.*

"What am I supposed to do?" I ask this woman in the mirror, but she just frowns.

After a round of worried phone calls from Mum, Lucy, Mum again, the phone is silent, the callers reassured. I lie on the sofa, wrapped in the warm arms of a fleecy bathrobe. Bob eyes me from his tank with disdain.

Sunday's break from the rain brings no change. The tornado whirl persists, spinning catastrophically through the gray whorls and nodules of memory. I replay conversations over and over, wrestling with dialogue for unseen, unanticipated clues of things to come.

In the raw, overcast gloom of day, what did I actually know about this man? I only knew what he had told me. Jesus, I didn't even know where he lived. *"Your house is cozy and much closer to the theater."*

I'd never thought to question it or ask, "In the event that you unfathomably up and leave, please be so kind as to disclose a contact address so I can hunt you down. There's a good chap."

He had said there was no point sending his wages in the post. "Save the stamp," he joked, as he took a freshly signed check from my hand and a plump kiss from my lips.

No. No. I wouldn't have, couldn't have been so blind. Everything about him — his enthusiasm, his hard work, all his many kindnesses — they *were* genuine. He *was* sincere. Why else would he go to all the effort of resurrecting the theater and making me fall in love with him if he intended to just up and leave without a word? Why would he do that?

I map our dialogues as if they were scripts: the introduction, a chance meeting at the embassy, not something that could be engineered…could it? No. He would have needed papers to have the medical, to be submitted to the embassy. He had all of that. But, what if…what if that's when he started to plan? After all my yapping away about the theater at the embassy, he found his mark. Could he have seized the opportunity, played me and waited patiently to cash out all this time? Had he waited for the pot to get sweet enough and for my back to be turned?

NO! He genuinely loved the theater. He didn't play me, he loved me. Loves me. He wouldn't, he couldn't, have faked that. Could he? I go round and round in circles, believing and disbelieving, unable to break through the repetitive loop.

On Monday, I have to get out of the house. The answering machine at the theater is full of messages. I listen to the annoyed tirades of Tales of a Wasted Saturday Night and Other Stories, hopeful that one will be from him. If he phoned, he did not leave a message. Mum arrives, bearing fresh éclairs to cheer me up. I can't even think about eating; my stomach is full of simmering acid.

I put Mum to work calling the schools, offering vague explanations and full refunds. The weight of responsibility carves into my shoulders. I will need money to pay back all the pre-sales. We had taken thousands of pounds in pre-ordered tickets, and now I would have to watch it disappear. The money from ticket sales of shows already performed would, thank God, at least cover the loan and the set and costumes for the next productions. I could start again.

I will advertise for a new lead male. We will produce *Gaslight* and *Pirates of Treasure Island,* and I can continue to build on *Shakespearian Rap's* success. This is a setback. The business I can manage.

But my heart…

I believe my own spin and almost feel positive as I push the heavy oak door and enter the bank.

The bank manager is loitering behind the chirpy cashiers, all three lined up in a row. I remember his rosy face from our first meeting and wave a greeting. He turns, looking behind to acknowledge the imaginary person I must be waving to, before rounding his bemused frown on me again. He opens the security door and approaches me, his gray suit slightly too shiny on the knees.

"It's Mrs. Petersen, isn't it?" A smile plays on his ruddy lips, pleased with himself for remembering.

"Miss, actually. Yes."

"I'm surprised to see you in here so soon," he remarks jovially, rubbing his pork sausage fingers together.

"I'm sorry?"

"After Friday. I said I didn't think we'd be seeing Ashtead funds for a while, but I'm glad to see things are going well for you. I thought that literature would change Mr. Angler's mind. I know the rates aren't as high as those risky accounts, but they are steady. You'd like to set up a new account then, I take it?"

"I'm sorry. I think we have our wires crossed, Mister…"

"Digby."

"Oh yes, Digby. What do you mean 'new' account? What is wrong with the old one? And why wouldn't you expect to see me?" I feel horizontal pleats of skin forced together by the question, a forehead kilted with confusion.

"Wha—" His round pig face passes through a color wheel of red hues before he stutters, "Perhaps, er, perhaps we can go in my office?"

Chapter 25

Reluctantly, I let him pull my sleeve—I am a waking somnambulist—and lead me through the security door into his faceless, faux hub. The laminate boards squeak as I pass over them and sit at the clean, faux wood desk in the faux leather chair, eyes fixed on the faux Monet above the desk.

"I must say, Miss Petersen," he says, rolling out his own leather throne and squelching into its cushy confines, "that I am more than a little confused."

"That makes two of us."

"Mr. Angler sat in that chair just three days ago and provided all the necessary paperwork to close the account, documents requesting the transaction with your signature, a letter of intent from you, all above board. He said that you were away in Germany but had authorized it."

I watch his rubbery lips pregnant with tidings and focus on the foamy spittle forming in the corner of his mouth, sud by blabbering, salivary sud. On the unfocused periphery, the magnolia walls around us seem to lean in, just as my ribcage constricts and squeezes my lungs just a little bit tighter.

"I'm sorry," I say, taking shorter breaths. "He closed the account?"

"Yes."

"So, there is no money left?" I ask with slow, controlled, unmis-interpretable diction. I can feel the quaver rising in my throat, but I clamp my jaw shut, waiting for the blow.

"None. Shut down entirely."

"And the balance that was in there was—"

"Around six hundred thousand, give or take."

"Ah." I snatch a breath. "And the money was transferred to an-other account or—"

"Well, actually, no. Usually we do an electronic transfer, but not in these circumstances. Mr. Angler did specify a number of days beforehand that the money would be needed in cash. Irregular, I know, but under the circumstances, with all the repairs on-going at the theater—I'm sure you don't need me to tell you..." He trails off, the embarrassed jovial note soured by my stony stare.

My tongue, pressed hard to my ridged palate, shrivels and dessi-cates, a frazzled rasher of meat shrinking pathetically. There is nothing left to say. Will did not deposit the box office takings; he took the lot. He planned this.

I slide back from the desk, the false leather unsticking from me, and give Mr. Digby's paw an angry squeeze. I make it through the heavy oak door before the acid bile can reach my tonsils. The wind is up again. It slaps my face, knocking back my internal revolt.

I am not sad. I am not disappointed. I was yesterday and the day before and the day before that, but that was when I had hope. Now, I am not hopeless; I am hope-empty. Now I am angry. I am furious at myself, at him. Oh God! The excuses I made! All the benefits of the doubt I gave him—I must have been thick. But I will not let him get away with it. I will hunt him down until I have every penny of my theater's money back. And after I've finished being angry, then I will let myself be sad.

I make these bargains with myself, wishing I had the blind faith to pledge these vows to God or the winds, fulfilling some kind of theatrical artistry, but I realize, as I stride into the wind, I can only have faith in myself.

It's a long shot, but I have to check. I call in to every one of the building societies along High Street. With much pleading and "I could lose my job for this" responses, I learn none have knowledge of large deposits made on Friday for the theater, for Enna Petersen, for Will Angler.

I am not surprised. It's just a matter of ticking off boxes. I knew as soon as the shiny, gray-suited, sausage-fingered Digby had stuttered that Will had asked for cash, that both Will and the money were as good as gone.

It could almost be funny if it was not so heartbreaking.

I recall our last exchange via email and rush back to the office to reread it.

"Ms. Petersen!" An unfamiliar voice stops me as I charge up the steps to the revolving doors, and I look up, almost clashing with the microphone rammed in my face. "Ms. Petersen, Candice Burke, *News Tonight.* After its miraculous resurgence, Ashtead Theater has been disappointing patrons by canceling its current hit show, *The Shakespearian Rap.* Would you tell us, Ms. Petersen, why you haven't opened your doors since Friday?"

I take in the hairs-prayed, lipsticked Candice, her rock solid backcombing immovable. The wind does not touch her, and yet it seems to punch me.

"Yes, Candice, you are right. Ashtead hasn't been able to open since the Friday matinee. I am extremely sorry about the inconvenience this has caused our loyal patrons and am particularly sorry for the schools which had organized trips to see the show. I know how much planning goes into these excursions."

"Yes, but why has this happened?"

"Why?" I see the halo of dark brown hair with just a hint of curl hedging around the camera lens, and my pulse quickens. Will I ever be able to scan a room and not look for dark curls?

"Yes, why?" The lipstick, teeth, and gums gleam.

Why indeed? Because I was an easy mark, a soft touch, a gullible fool so desperate to keep my theater and be loved at the same time that I gave it all away to the first charming bastard who could see the prize and didn't mind a little hard work, flirting and fucking in order to get it.

"There must be an explanation," Candice persists.

To tell or not to tell: that is the question. If Will were me, he'd probably whip up a media storm — interviews on the national news, cover stories for the broadsheets, midsheets and tabloids; he'd air the whole laundry basket.

But, I'm not him. I can't rip my heart into my mouth.

"I'll do my best to resolve the situation. I'll refund monies for tickets already paid for. Those who have ordered tickets will obviously not be charged. *The Shakespearian Rap* will not be performed at Ashtead again this season."

"Sources have said that you, Ms. Petersen, were having a tempestuous relationship with the performer, William Angler. Is this premature termination of his show the result of a lovers' tiff?"

The question trips so lightly off her slicked lips, sounding so sweet with her home counties accent, but it hits its target. A small gasp escapes from somewhere in my chest.

She waits, holding the microphone aloft, and I know I'm missing my cue, my chance to air bitter accusations. I stare into the miniature reflection trapped within the glinting circular camera lens. I pull her microphone close and grip it tightly so no one will see that I'm shaking.

I open my mouth and close it. A thin-lipped secret smile slices across my face. If he's watching this, I want him to know: I know. I remain resolute. I'll bide my time. I'll track him down. I will not waste my day in court by venting and prejudicing the jury—isn't that how these things happen?

"Good evening, Ms. Burke." I turn and stride up the steps with Oscar-winning confidence.

> Darling,
>
> Spoke to Arch today, and next week is tough for him—he's flying to Grand Cayman. He'd like to fit us in this week. I would be happy to show him the spreadsheets so we don't waste another week of investment income! What do you think? Shoot me an email and let me know if this is okay. It'll be great to get the wheels turning here.
>
> Hope you are having fun in Munich. I miss you!

I read it and reread it and re-reread it. I try not to focus on the "I miss you!" Really? Really! Son of a bitch.

Arch—yes, that's the important bit. Now what was his first name? Or was that his last name? I can't recall. Shit! I switch on Will's computer and click on his contacts, looking under A. No Archer, no Arch, no Accountant. I seize the *Yellow Pages* and thumb through the accountants in the area, searching for a list of CPAs. Nothing.

I click on the Internet and type variations of the name into the search engine: *Archer*

Archie

Archibald + accountant + Ashtead + Cayman

I try every different conceivable combination, but nothing.

What do I do now? Where do I start looking?

Ridiculously, Englishly, I make myself a cup of tea.

Caught in a moment of inactivity, it suddenly hits me, the enormity of what I am facing. There is a lag-time between the knowing and understanding; My brain needs a tea break to catch up. Like Cole's proposal which translated into "uproot your life," the translation of Will's betrayal also takes time to percolate through my senses.

I have no money.

I've never had a negative bank balance. I've used credit cards, but I've always paid them off. In full. Immediately. I'm the saver. The offspring Mum and Dad would come to and borrow a fiver. The one who scrimped and saved to get what she wanted. The one who understood work ethic and celebrated it, who sacrificed her social life but who was happy to do it for her theater. The one who signed her shared house as equity to secure the loan for the theater.

I have no money to repay patrons…I could be sued.

I have no money to repay the loan, and Leo's and my house will be repossessed.

I have no money to pay the bills that Will had said to "leave until next month."

I have no money to pay for the new shows, set, costume, publicity.

I have nothing.

But surely, that cannot be! It cannot be! I wipe away the tears of frustration. I'll phone Digby at the bank; Will couldn't have closed the account without paying the loan off first, could he? And what about fraud? Maybe the bank will be nice and accept they made a mistake in accepting only his signature. Isn't that the whole fucking point behind having a co-signatory, so everything is done and confirmed together?

I must fight. I must call the police. He has three days head start already. He could be anywhere — Brisbane, Bombay, Bognor. I admit it; I need help.

I dial the police line. "Hello. It's not an emergency, but it is very important I talk to a detective. I have been…" What, exactly? Played for a fool? "…robbed."

"Is the robbery still in progress, ma'am?" says the disconnected voice on the other end of the line.

"No. It's not that kind of robbery. I guess it is more fraud. My bank account has been cleared, and I need to speak with someone."

"All our detectives are out at the moment."

I'm sorry, what?

"We'll send someone as soon as they are available, but it's getting late. It might not be until tomorrow morning. What's the address?"

Perhaps I should try again?

Hello? Yes? My carotid artery has just been slit by masked murderers.

Yes! And I'm speaking! Amazing, huh?

Oh, your detectives are busy? That's a shame.

Well, pints of my blood are currently gushing out all over the handset, but no problem. I'll wait for the morning! I do hate to trouble you.

Absolutely fucking peachy!

Who can help me? I need to do something! I scroll through the list of names on the contact list and see Cole's. Cole, my go-to-guy for all things technical and slightly geeky. Maybe he can find Arch on the computer.

I click compose.

> Hi,
>
> Need to find someone. Urgent. His name is Archer (Arch) and he is an accountant working in or around Ashtead. Things have gone badly wrong on my end, and I really need to speak with him, but I can't find him. Do you have any suggestions of how I can go about this, given my limited info? He may have connections in the Grand Cayman?
>
> Sorry to bother you. Please and thank you.
>
> E

I press send and close my eyes. Please be there. Please be able to help. The computer whirs as it receives another flurry of irate emails filtering through cyberspace and into my inbox. People wanting answers I cannot provide. I glance over the subject lines peppered with the words "refund" and "disgrace."

I try to hide, to blank it out, and bury my eye sockets in the heels of my palms, but the endless circles of ramifications spiral in front of me, no matter how many layers of flesh and bone and blood and cartilage buffer my vision. The spirals coil on and on, some hallucinogenic helix that cannot be broken, because there is no solution. What can be salvaged? Nothing.

Without money, I can't operate the theater. Without the theater running, I can't make money. Without money to pay the loan, the house will be taken; my family will hate me for guaranteeing the house for the loan; I will be homeless; Leo will be one hundred thousand pounds less well-off; I will be sued by the schools for breach of contract; and I will be jobless, penniless, and there is nothing I can do.

My brain throbs. The weight of blood and water squeeze it as the mass fills with lies and questions. I look up at the clock. The numbers swim, black and white icebergs moving around the periphery. I blink, but they will not be displaced. They just progress to another corner, malingering, disappearing for a couple of seconds to reappear denser than before. These watery clouds seem to orbit, circling my pupils around my lens, and just as they are out of sight, around the back, they rain down needles into my optic nerve. Not little pin pricks but thick, solid hypodermic needles lancing through the tough membrane.

Is the thick black hand on the seven or the eight? That late? Has time overtaken me again?

I close my eyes and blindly feel through my handbag. My hand snatches at the bottle of strong migraine medication that I already know isn't there. Why had I not replaced the last bottle? *Oh, Enna!* My hand does clasp gratefully around a pot of paracetamol, which responds with a jostling jig, its eager volunteers calling out, ready for action. I greedily gulp down four. They're not strong enough to shift a migraine, but they are better than nothing.

The eye icebergs circle, and I know I haven't been fast enough to act. Next to go will be my speech. Then, I will vomit until I choke on my bile. I know the pattern of my body's rebellion. I must get home.

I clumsily fumble for my key, lock the door, and slip out of the stage door entrance with uncontrolled momentum. I shouldn't drive, I know, but the urgency of getting home overtakes me. The car awaits me in the car park, exactly where I left it, before Will drove me to the airport.

The clutch bites underfoot, and the engine revs as I drive off. The white lines shepherd me around the bends, along the straights, keeping me clear of hedges or sideswipes. I squint at the glowing brake lights of the car in front, the traffic light blinking at me, and I drive.

The smell of too-ripe banana wafts up my nasal passages as I open the front door, and I gag. I must find the Migraleve. I crawl up the stairs on all fours. My head feels less heavy closer to the ground. I ransack the medicine cabinet and pour the contents of the Tupperware box across the bathroom floor. The gray sleeve is open, and for a foggy, split-second, I wail at the thought of finding no packet inside, but there it is—a whole sheet of Barbie-pink pills. I wolf down two dry and lie back on the cold tiles, waiting for the pounding, the needling, the icebergs, the nausea to stop.

The ceramic cradle is hard, the flat, toothless tiles biting into the two rounded knobbly bones at the rear of my pelvis, cutting into the vertebrae of my upper back and grinding against my scapula. I shift awkwardly but am too heavy to crawl to the bedroom only feet away. The pain behind my eyes is excruciating, the constant stabbing buoying me up above the surface of sleep.

I try to let myself sink, to see the helix and icebergs. Icebergs and helix recede, falling back from them rather than traveling perilously into them, but this invisible torturer, with his set of sharpened implements, keeps me levitating and prods me ever forward, ever upward, ever wakeful, further into the vortex of the migraine.

I can reach the gray sleeve with the tips of my fingers. The packet slides across the tiles with ease, and the pink pills pop out of their foil seals with little pressure. Another two, and it will all disappear. I must sleep, but the needles and the spirals and the icebergs…the needles and the spirals and the icebergs…and no money and no theater… and no Will and no sleep. I must sleep. But it won't come. I nuzzle my bones deeper into the cold floor and try to sink into sleep, into the black, dark depths.

I don't know how much time passes as I writhe in wakefulness—five minutes, an hour, two, three? I hear "Carmina Burana" burst out from somewhere downstairs, the passionate melody pricking me further into painful consciousness.

"Sleep! Just sleep!" I slur to the bathroom ceiling.

Turning on my side, my thigh crushes one of the bottles from the medicine cabinet fallout. I pry a swollen eyelid open as I extract the plastic bottle: Unisom, non-addictive, non-prescription sleep aid. Sleep! My fingers work feverishly to pop the childproof lid and release the little, blue gel capsules which spill into my hand like jackpot money gushing from a slot machine. And I gulp them down my dry, sandpapered throat.

It is darker now. My eyelids play less static, and slowly, almost too slowly to be aware of the change, a gear is shifted. I am pulling back from the spirals, floating, and then softly, incrementally, I can feel the warm waters lap over my skin; the needles at my back, through my flesh and impaling my eyes, retract but slowly, ever so slowly. I am no longer pinned to the surface. I am free and can dive like a dolphin. Like an aquatic ape, I dive and drift and sink to the bottom, the warm crystal waters clinging to my hairless hydrodynamic flesh, insulated by mammalian blubber. I am warm. I am safe. I can sleep now.

I turn and tumble, weightless through the water, letting the current steer me whichever way it may. My lungs have evolved, have expanded and sustain me. I dive deep, blindly trusting that other creatures will make way for me, that I will sense the coral, the submerged rays, the spiky lobsters, before I collide with them.

The deeper I swim, the colder it gets. A darker shadow passes beneath, brushing my thigh, and I shudder with the shock of its electric touch. I can feel the creature there, circling, and I look through the dark water to see the glint of its eye. As it gets closer, I see it is one of those fish that look almost reptilian or Jurassic — the huge, elliptical head slit open with a psychotic grin full of sharp, triangular teeth arranged at strange, inward angles. But this fish is different from ones in my dinosaur picture books; this creature has inexplicable growths, like vestigial hypodermic needles, protruding between the small, glinting fish eyes. I should be scared, I suppose, but instead I find the creature fascinating. How could such a fish exist in the darkness down here? How could it find a mate, find food?

I feel it again, the sweep of its scales rasping around my legs. As I look down through the water, the creature swims deeper, and its needle glows — some benthic bioluminescence? The ugly fish angles the pretty glow stick toward me. The light helps me to see through the dark waters, and I do want to see what is down there. I follow the pretty light deeper and deeper.

We must be near the bottom now; the water is so much colder down here. Suddenly, my guide turns back, his lightning rod charging toward me and illuminating the darkness so I can see the whole of him now, his grotesque, ghoulish, craterous jaws opening wide and sucking me in, swallowing me whole. The jaws clamp tight. It is dark and it smells, and the water buffets me against the inward teeth, the pointed, razor-sharp blades stabbing me and ripping my skin to ribbons. The fishy cavern of his mouth is airless and rancid. I need to fill my lungs, and automatically, as if given a programmed cue, I claw the fleshy cheek tissue and anchor my nails in holdfasts. I bring my knees to my chest and kick as hard as I can.

My legs punch hard, and some teeth break off. I take my chance and writhe through the small, toothless gap. A desperate flapping of legs and feet into the midnight blue darkness, lightening to petrol blue, then turquoise—I can feel this sea devil behind me at every stroke—then azure, aqua, and as I break through the surface, white. The creature recoils, scorched by the sun, and slips away.

The salt stings as it fills my nose and mouth. I choke, trying to swallow and breathe at the same time, gasping for oxygen in a hungry gulp.

I can feel the warmth of the sun on my skin and the glow on my cold, white cheeks. I bob on the surface, catching my breath and recapturing my heartbeat. My eyes find their equilibrium and focus to see an island not far off. There is a beach of white and a figure waving. I know that figure.

The current sweeps me closer. I watch the figure curiously as he waves and calls something I can't understand. Is it Robinson Crusoe? No, I'm sure Robinson had a beard. This islander seems so small at first, a lone figure on a broad expanse of Tropicana, but as the waves surf my body toward the shore, I see he is a giant. A giant with arms stretched wide and a big smile set in a square jaw. He runs into the shallows toward me, but I don't feel scared or confused; it seems like the most natural thing in the world, being swept up into his arms, out of the unknown, frothy waters and out onto the sand. He lays me down gently without speaking, his hazel eyes filled with concern. Out of the water, I feel heavy again. My eyelids close just for a second. I'm sure it is just for a second, but as they raise the eyelash fringed curtain again, the friendly face is gone. All I can see is the white hot haze of the sun.

I lie dozing, the shells and tiny, calcareous limbs pricking my skin. Hermit crabs scuttle up and down my arm, a sideways pepper-potting as the curious creatures take a closer look. I listen to the waves lapping up the hot sand and those crashing further off. There is another sound—I can't place it. Oh! Oh! It's background music playing! I strain to make it out. It's a tune I don't know, a continuous techno track of beats and beeps playing far off—probably at some beach bar. I'd like to find it, but my stomach, still full of sea salt, churns noisily.

Unexpectedly, I feel the rush of fluid rising up my throat, burning past my tonsils and gushing from my nostrils and mouth. The flow is uncontrollable and passes almost mechanically out of me, water divined by some greater power. No mess, no fuss, a salt water purge. I'm not in pain, even though my throat is dry and sore, and my nostrils feel as if they are clogged open with sand. I will just lie on the beach and sleep for a while, then I'll get up and do something productive.

I squint into the round orb above, the fuzzy haze of light around the sun. My heavy lids flicker and squint again, but the sun is eclipsed by a shadow. My eyes re-adjust, pulling in their focus to recognize the big red face of the giant. He smiles, but I can see the dewy trails streaking his cheeks. Maybe he is the giant from a fairy story and is misunderstood. I lift my finger to touch his big, hairy hand. Maybe I can comfort him. He seems surprised but smiles more at this. He takes my limp fingers in his in palm, and I feel his hand squeeze mine. His lips move, but I can't understand what he is saying. The waves and the techno drown him out. Then he disappears, just as before. I don't want him to leave.

"How are you feeling?"

The bright, fluorescent light-strips blind my retinas with their industrial beam. The synthetic mint green draperies are no more welcoming. I swivel my head to take in the full mint immersion: the green floor linoleum, the walls, the curtains, the side tables, one blanket, one chair, one mother.

"Mum?"

She gets up slowly from the chair and hovers over me, resting her soft palm on my forehead.

"You're in the hospital, sweetheart. You're going to be okay. Don't you worry about a thing." Her red eyes glisten. An escapee tear makes a run for it over the top.

"What am I doing here? What happened?" I un-recall with sudden confusion. "I had a migraine…I left the theater…did I crash the car?"

"No, darling, no."

"What then? Do I have a brain tumor?"

"Look, darling, get some rest. Dad'll be along soon. He only nipped down the hall to get me a cup of tea. You just missed Leo. He popped in to sit with you, and Lucy flew back early yesterday so she could be here. Oh, here's your father!"

Dad appears, his eyelids fleshier than usual. Like Mum — who is now hovering and fussing with straws and water jugs — his bravado is synthetic, lacking the usual gung-ho gusto. "Chickadee!"

"Please just stop fussing and tell me what happened. I am not two years old, and I don't need a straw, Mum. What I'd like is to know why the hell I am lying here, hooked up to the machine that goes *ping?*"

They exchange sorrowful glances.

I am shocked — horrified — when they tell me.

"And you didn't even call us," she says.

My addled brain cannot quite process whether Mum's so upset at the thought of losing me, or that I didn't call or have the good grace to scribble a quick thank you and goodbye note — the Petersen standards. *"Going to accidentally off myself. Cheerio! Will be on the bathroom floor if you want me. Love me. X."*

"We knew you had been under a lot of stress," Dad says, holding onto Mum's shoulder, "but we had no idea how badly things had gone. You should have told us. That bloody Will's going to pay; you can mark my words. I've been in touch with the police, and we'll sort this out. And don't you worry about the theater. I'll see that everything is all right."

"Dad! I appreciate it, I do, but it is my problem, and I have to work it out. You don't have to wrap me in cotton wool. In fact, as stupid as it sounds, I feel stronger and more determined than ever."

Dad circles the bed and sits on the edge, slipping his big, weather-beaten hand under mine. "Enna, you don't have to keep this to yourself. We know about the house and the loans."

My spirits sink to the linoleum. I had forgotten that.

"It's okay," he whispers. "It is all okay."

I bite my lips together. I won't cry. "What can I do though? It's all such a mess. And the house! However am I going to pay Leo for the house? It'll be repossessed."

"Now, now, there. It's messy, all right, but nothing a bit of hard work, effort, and legal advice won't solve." He fixes a fugitive tangle of hair behind my ear. "We'll get you fixed up. The loan has been repaid already, so you don't have to worry about the house. You are surrounded by people who love you, you see, and who'd do anything for you. It'll be all right. The police have some enquiries going on in Grand Cayman and they'll catch that slimy bastard. It appears he wasn't quite as clever as he thought he was."

I take this information in. I picture him there in Grand Cayman, lying back in the sand, sipping a beer, his chocolate eyes melting on some bikini clad tourist, giving her the charm offensive. "What are you reading?" he'll ask her.

"Dad, wait! You repaid the loan money back?" His charity is suddenly more upsetting than the prospect of financial ruin. I know he can't afford to bail me out.

"Oh, chickadee, I would have loved to, but Christ, if I had that sum of money lying around, I would be cruising the Atlantic on a yacht."

"Then how? Did the bank admit culpability? Did they pay it back themselves?"

"Yes, that's right," Mum pipes up suddenly. "They probably didn't want the bad publicity."

"But I don't see—"

"Anyway, the doctor told us not to tire you out, so we ought to go. We'll be back tomorrow. We love you. And don't you dare think of doing anything like that again, or you'll have me to deal with."

I am told to rest and recuperate. Do doctors really understand quite how hard that is swaddled in starchy sheets that smell of disinfectant, on a thin, narrow mattress, lying in a cubicle next to some mad old crone who exhibits hourly performances of what can only be described as *Tourette's: the Musical*? And, it's not that I expect fine dining, but when I am—finally—allowed to eat, why is it that my flaccid ham sandwich smells of wee?

I am told not to think about the theater. What the bloody hell else am I supposed to think about? Daytime TV is enough to drive one to suicide, even without my problems.

The police arrive with my father. The uniformed WPC sits and opens her notebook. The plain-clothed detective paces around the bed. He is slightly daunting with his gruff, disapproving sideways glances. I explain the whole tangled story, from our first meeting at the embassy to our last emailed communiqué. I leave out the wild torrent of sex, the romantic dinners, the kind gestures.

Detective Shugard rolls his eyes; he's heard this all before. I am one of those poor, deluded women as seen on daytime TV. Maybe that's why watching *This Morning* makes me shudder; I've been just as gullible as those cretins. Shugard's cynicism makes me feel every inch a fool.

"He is an actor, detective, a very good one. I don't know how much of what he told me was true, or if anything he said or did was real. I'll probably never know if I was a target from the very beginning. That is something I'll have to live with. I'm not asking for your sympathy. I want to find this man and get the money he stole from the theater."

They won't let me leave until I agree to meet the hospital psychiatrist. She looks at me over the frame of her glasses. "It's natural to feel overwhelmed in situations. No one would blame you if you felt that you couldn't cope. Tell me again exactly, what you were feeling when you were lying on the bathroom floor? What was going through your head?"

"Pain."

"Yes, yes, pain. Yes, you were grieving and yearning and at a loss…" She tilts her head solicitously.

"No, my head hurt, and my eyes, my neck, my back. Basically, every nerve ending connecting my head and my spine. That tends to be how migraines affect me."

She forms a suspended O with her over-animated lips. "But, you've never overdosed with a migraine before. Maybe subconsciously, though you don't want to face it right now, the recent events had thrown you over the edge, so to speak?"

"No. My head hurt so I took the Migraleve, and I needed to sleep so I swallowed the Unisom."

She leans further in, her upper lip curved faintly upward, so at odds with her tilted head and sympathetic nods. She thinks she is getting somewhere. That she is going to expose a deep psychological disturbance.

"It was a mistake! I wasn't thinking straight. I didn't read the instructions. I could barely see…Look, I didn't load a revolver, hold it to my head, and pull the trigger, did I?"

"Have you thought about that?"

"Oh, dear God!"

"You seem angry. Are you angry?"

"Yes." I sit up straighter. "I *am* angry. Very bloody angry…with Will. With myself. I can't believe I was played. I was such an idiot."

"Do you mistrust your judgment?"

"Yes, I suppose I do," I say automatically, but as soon as I hear it out loud, I know it's not true anymore. "No, actually, I don't. Not now. I think I looked to others before for direction. Imagine that! A director needing direction! But I think I let others influence me. Other people determined my happiness, and that made me doubt me. Choosing Cole, the theater, Will.

"I wanted to please each of them so badly, to make them proud and to love me." I look into the cup of tea growing cool in front of me, and it strikes me, another clear-sighted revelation: "You know what? They didn't love me back, or not enough, to be honest with me! And who is here now when I really need someone? Not the theater, not Cole, and certainly not Will."

She just nods, and I find my tongue freed.

"Maybe Will was right; I don't owe anything to the theater. It's not my home. I don't have a home. All I have is my brain, my heart and my guts."

"So, what's your plan now?"

She waits patiently for my reluctant response. "I don't know. The doctor said I have to recuperate so I'll be staying with my mum and dad."

"And then?"

Pause.

I don't bloody know! "Maybe I'll run off to the circus or something."

Head tilt. "Do you always run away from your problems?"

"That was a joke."

"Not really," she says as she writes something down. "You're a runner."

I must have said something right, because after a five minute review with the nutritional counselor and the doctor, in which I promise both I will be more mindful of my hunger and eat regularly even if I am busy, the doctor signs me off, and I return to the wall-to-wall pink of my childhood bedroom.

"Tea, darling?" Mum offers again in her overly cheery tones. In the week that has passed since the "incident of which we will not speak," I have been parentally nurtured rather like a hothouse flower. I'm kept warm and frequently watered.

"Ma!" I exclaim. "Please don't fuss. My bladder can't take it!"

Her head disappears back around the kitchen door, but I know she is listening for me: alert to the clicks of childproof lids being twisted, the rattle of pills being palmed; the gush of bath water and length of my bathing; the squeak of the cork being eased from the bottle and the tinkling as the glass is filled again; the music I turn up to disguise the noise of me quietly dying.

Mum listens so intently because she feels blind. I have plenty of time to watch her home in on my sounds and plenty of time to analyze it. I listen for her too. I can hear the muted sniff as she stands by the kitchen sink. Possibly she's looking out of the window onto the back garden, not seeing, but instead overthinking, and I hear her quietly weep and blow her nose. It's not that she doesn't trust me, I know; it's that she didn't see this coming, so she thinks she failed her maternal duty to keep me safe.

"I love you, Mum." It's all I can offer her. So I sit in my chair, not watching TV or reading, but listening for the crack of the eggshells we are all treading. And I'm stewing with anger, because it's not just my life that Will has savaged. His fallout peters through every close relationship I have. Never will Mum and Dad look at me harmlessly swallowing an aspirin, parcetemol — shit — even a vitamin, without sucking their breath through their teeth and holding it, wondering if this is the spiral of dependency they've been anxiously waiting to diagnose and intercept.

I spend hours on Facebook. I seem to have regressed to a teenager, but it is wonderful to reestablish contact with all those close friends that work had distanced. I ask questions and enjoy reading their replies. It's funny how you don't really have to volunteer much about yourself or your own massive fuck up situation. People are quite happy to chat about themselves and their own fuck ups, a courtesy "So, what's happening in your neck of the woods?" tagged on the end — easily evaded by focusing on their news.

I search for him. I spend hours scrolling through online photos, scanning for those eyes, those lips, that face. I have become intimately acquainted with the photo albums of everyone on Facebook who ever attended Warwick University. But maybe that was a lie too. I scan reviews, bookings and theater listings of every touring house and studio in England. Nothing.

I press the standby button, and the familiar, sultry "Welcome" greets me. The screen refreshes and blinks. "You have a new message."

"Dad! Dad! You've got a new message."

My teenage communicatory yell goes unanswered. He is probably in his tool shed, hiding any implement that might do his chickadee harm, or maybe he is just sanding that panel and thinking he should. I wish they understood that I was — I am — okay. That I'm stronger, more determined than ever that Will will be found, and he will be sorry. I push back from the desk to and find Dad.

Maybe I should check the sender? After all, he is only going to ask who the message is from, then I'll have to come back in here and then go back out there…

I sit back in the chair, circle my finger to locate the cursor, and click on the message.

> Bob,
>
> Sorry it's taken a week to email. I am back, but the jetlag got me good. Thanks again to you and Kay for letting me stay. I know you can't have been in the mood to be troubled by a houseguest.
>
> How is she? I hope back to full strength.
>
> I've been making a whole heap of calls, and there is some poet guy doing this live entertainment at one of the big resorts on Grand Cayman.
>
> I've shared this with DC Shurgard, and he thinks it's going to be pretty simple to throw the book at Angler. His forensic team can prove the signatures on the bank documents were faked, and Kay's info has been helpful too. She was right. He did pay for Enna's spa gift voucher with a credit card, so they were able to trace that and freeze his account.
>
> As for my small part in this, I would rather you don't let her know — not because I want to be secretive, but I think it would complicate things. I just wish I'd got to her house sooner. Tell Leo I am sorry about the door too. I couldn't think of a better way to get in. Man, I can't tell you how scared I was seeing her on the floor like that.

Please don't worry about repaying the loan. If the police or bank can get it back, sure I'll call it in, but I won't accept your offer.

I can't help feeling partly to blame in all this. Maybe if I had fought for her rather than let my pig-headed pride get in the way, she would have been here, safe from that ass.

Anyway, that's all from PA. I'll let you know as soon as I hear from Shugard or my Cayman contacts.

Best,

Cole

My ears fill with the slow lub-dub sound of coagulated, red molasses pumping around my body. Cole? My bundle of nerves short-circuits, firing unanswerable questions of what, where, how and who across neurons. I…I don't understand.

Cole knows all about Will?

Cole was here?

Found me?

Has paid off the loan?

I feel I have missed the vital chapter. I feel confounded, battered, bruised, foolish, gullible, and yet, as I swallow these truths and my eyes grow wide with wonder, I feel thankful and protected, championed and — in spite of everything, in spite of leaving him, choosing work ahead of him — loved. Cole. Cole!

The immobile icon and untouched keyboard fade to the screensaver: a windswept island of white sand baking in the sun. I stare into the blue with disbelief. Sand…sea…the image triggers some memory, some déjà vu, some unremembered dream.

It creeps up on me like a cold wave that rushes in unexpectedly and licks the soles of my feet. The giant, his square jaw, the generous smile and the concerned, hazel eyes. He was calling me from the shore. He carried me in his arms. He leaned over me with tears in his eyes. It was Cole.

Chapter 26

I buy an open-ended ticket, traveling sans flaming-hoop-jumping fiancée status. The maximum three months for a normal English tourist should give us enough time to work things out. I promise DC Shurgard I will fly back to testify when the case goes to trial. Did Will's monumental arrogance really make him believe we were too dumb to work out the Cayman connection? I am rather looking forward to staring at him in the dock while I give my testimony.

I have only one question for him, one thing I really want to know, and that's if any of it was real, or was it all some grand theater trick?

The board agrees that I can come back as theater director, despite the Shakespearian debacle. But Ashtead needs someone new, someone less passionate, more management. And I need something new too, something to begin, to grow strong, to cultivate my own traditions, a theater school for children, perhaps. I hand-deliver my notice and revolve through the glass door for the last time. An enormous weight seems lifted, the pressure of old dreams crumbling, and new visions aspiring.

Mum is a stoic picture of glassy-eyed, stiff-lipped pride as she waves me off at the entrance to the long TSA line. Dad puts his arm around her and smiles with gusto. Finally, they are breathing normally, not holding on to the air, puffing themselves out, waiting for something to happen. They know I will be safe with Cole.

I shuffle up the line, turning repeatedly to check if they are still there, and they are, unfailingly, still the solid, smiling mass of parental unit. I wave frantically, and they wave back, our waggling limbs connected by invisible strings.

The TSA officer examines my boarding pass and my passport, thumbing the X'ed out visa page suspiciously.

"You're not going to be able to use this, you know."

"I know."

He squints and ushers me, not through the metal detector, but instead through the full body X-ray machine. I look at the travelers filtering through flight security before me, weighed down with laptops, iPods, bags that look far too big to fit in the overhead compartments, none looking at me, all focused on getting to the conveyor belt and unpacking quickly without holding up the line. I place my bare feet in the yellow, upside down bowling pins painted on the floor of the booth.

"Raise your arms, bend your elbows, and stay still."

I do just as the officer instructs. He steps away from the machine. In those five, maybe ten seconds, I look ahead. I look at the woman reflected back in the dark imaging screen, holding her head high. She wears a soft, wraparound dress with swirls of green and navy. Around her neck, on a lobster chain, she wears a brilliant emerald ring dangling next to her chest. There she is, arms aloft, assuming the "frisk me" position, oblivious to the light flash as the X-ray scans her body sans skimpies, and she's beaming for the camera. I recognize that woman, and my smile spreads, lifting my cheeks sky high.

The seven-hour flight seems interminable. I open my book, but the middle-aged couple to my left won't stop kissing and giggling, and it's really most off-putting. I can't concentrate on the words. What *are* they doing under that British Airways blanket? Will Cole and I be like that in twenty years, oblivious to all around us and unable to keep our hands off each other?

How will he react when he sees me? Will he throw his arms around me? Will he burst into tears? Will he be speechless? I enjoy rehearsing the possibilities in my head. Unlike his proposal so many months ago, now I am prepared. I have all the words to tell him how I really feel, and yet the imagined scenario I like best is when he opens the door and I don't have to say a thing. He just looks at me and loves me and then wraps his big arms around me.

The attendant wheels the drink carts alongside my row, leans over the amorous couple, and asks for my order. I am tempted to go with the soporific properties of the mini bottle of wine, but I am starting anew, afresh. It'll be water all the way.

The tiny microwave meal of hugely calorific proportions congeals in its toy town miniature plastic container. The canoodlers stop swapping spit for long enough to gorge their faces and then they fall asleep.

The images on the screen flicker. Mindlessly, I attempt the in-flight magazine crossword, hiding my entries so no one can see how badly I'm doing. Slowly, the minutes crawl by.

The plane icon, plotting our route and progress on the screen, passes Labrador, and I have to pee. The couple snooze on, their tray tables still down, their legs still entangled, blocking any escape route. I look around for the attendant, hoping that he can do something, but the crew has vanished like that of the *Marie Celeste*. I throw pleading looks to fellow travelers behind me, hoping someone will notice, but no one appreciates the art of mime.

My bladder will not—cannot—make it to Philadelphia. I look around the cabin again in a last desperate plea for rescue, but my silent SOS is unheard, unseen, or ignored. The gentleman in the center seat in the row behind me creases his paper, stows it in the seat back, and unimpeded, he staggers up the aisle to stretch his legs.

Now is my chance. I stand on my chair and lunge over the gap in the backrest to the bank of seats behind. Holding aerial arabesque, the surprised, but rather entertained fellow in the aisle seat, stands to give me a hand to dismount. Several amused travelers applaud lightly. My cheeks burn—a mixture of embarrassment and, by now, toxic shock—and I re-adjust my dress and my pride, and take a bow. I suppose theatrics will follow me wherever I go.

The remaining hour of the journey passes uneventfully. I brush my teeth, complete the green immigration slip, and try to stop myself from checking my watch every minute.

After processing through the long line at immigration and fielding the complicated explanations I knew would be asked for, I snaffle my bag at baggage claim and brave the biting wind to queue up for the Martz bus that will take me to him.

"One way or round trip?"

Crikey, it's cold here.

"I said, one way or round trip, lady?"

"Oh, err. One way. I think. I mean, can I get a round trip for three months' time?"

"Lady, are you crazy?"

"Ah. Right. One way, then."

The bus makes several stops, each bringing me a few miles nearer. When the bus finally rumbles down and up potholed Lackawanna Avenue and makes the sweeping turn into the Scranton bus terminal parking lot, the sharks swimming in my stomach really start gnawing at my spine. My calm, my predestined, peace is peppered with nervous excitement. In thirty minutes, I will be there.

I haul my bag into the waiting taxi as the nonchalant driver watches me struggle and finishes his cigarette. He tosses the butt, slams the trunk shut, and returns to the warmth of his cab. I give him the address and turn my head to the window. I am revived by these familiar sights and the weary hours of traveling shrugged away. I see the Krispy Kreme doughnut shop, where Cole took me late one night for fresh glazed doughnuts, and La Trattoria, where we had enjoyed a romantic Italian meal and laughed at the waitress who didn't understand a word I said.

"I'd like a water, please."

"A wha?"

"A water, please."

"A wha?"

"A wha-tter."

"Oh. Wha-tter! Why didn't youse say?"

The billboards advertising places we had been, places we had planned to go, flash past as the driver speeds south. He crosses the steel bridge, and I can hear my heartbeat in my throat. He turns into the tree-lined avenue and slows where I tell him to, opposite Cole's house. He leaves the engine running and the car door open as he retrieves my luggage, quickly pocketing the cash. It's too frigid to stand out in the cold.

The house is just as it was: the white siding with the hunter green shutters, candle shaped bulbs lighting up each window sill, the Stars and Stripes waving proudly from the porch — the picture book, manicured American home. I wheel my suitcases behind me, heaving them up the three wooden steps to the door. My finger hovers over the doorbell as I take one calming, hopeful breath.

This is the entrance from the wings that really matters. My mind blanks of all the lines I had rehearsed on the plane, yet I don't care. It doesn't matter. I'm here and he's here. I press the doorbell anyway.

The security light is thrown on, blinding me for a moment while the door swings open. Blinking through the light, I smile at the dark shadow. He steps out onto the porch, his giant's face blank of expression. Surprise!

"Enna? Enna, what are you *doing* here?"

This is my cue. This is my chance to tell him.

"I know," I swoop to say quickly, before he can stop me. "I know what you did for me. I know everything. Dad didn't tell me. I found out, it…doesn't matter how. But I'm glad I know, because it cemented what I thought I already knew: that you are decent and generous and loving and kind. What I didn't know was my place in the world, where I should be, who I should be with. It's hard, you know, having to choose between everything you know and have dreamed of doing, and giving it all up for an unknown. It's a gamble. And when I found out about the not being able to work here, I got frightened. I needed to work; I needed that so that I wouldn't miss Ashtead. I couldn't have stayed here and been content to darn your socks while Ashtead went under.

"And I thought that to be happy, you had to be successful, and I didn't see how I could do that when I couldn't get that job here. And I was so angry at you for making me believe that job was mine, but I understand it now. Sometimes, we'll say anything to keep our loved ones close to us. I know you were doing it because you loved me too much.

"I don't need the theater to prove that I can be a success. I don't need a whopping great emerald ring, I don't need a five star review; what I need is to know my own mind and to be happy with my decisions, to focus on what I want and never quit. And you're the one I want to be with. Because you are decent and generous and loving and kind, and I love you."

I can hear the piped laughter from the television in the background as seconds skip by.

"I love you," I echo again, stepping forward to take his hands.

He folds his arms. "Rather by default, though."

I look from his face to his folded arms, looking for the answer. "No. No, not default." I look up into his sorrowful hazel eyes. "I can explain. It wasn't like that. I didn't come here because I had run out of options. I came here because I realized that you had been there for me all along, even when I didn't deserve it, and I wanted to say thank you."

"Enna, if Will hadn't left, you'd be happy enough living with him in your cozy little theater."

"No, I wouldn't, because he wasn't what you are." I gulp for air. *How do I explain?* "I've been so lost. And I was swept along by something that wasn't real. It was all pretend. It's such a joke! I was played by an actor! I wanted to believe him. God, I wanted so much to save the theater and to have someone love me. I must have been thick. But now I know where I am. I know where I am going. I'm not lost anymore. I am not swept away by your heroic gesture. I just finally realize what I really want, what really makes me happy, where my place in this world is. And that's with you."

I can see the plume of breath as he exhales.

He's not listening. Oh God, he's not listening.

"No, Cole, really! I *was* lost and…and I was drowning. Literally, without you I was drowning, sinking into the depths. And I thought I had this dream that you ran into the waves and carried me to safety, and I was so pleased to see your face! But it wasn't a dream. You were there! You found me and rescued me. It was your face I saw. I didn't know it then, but I know it now. I didn't even remember it until I read your email and Dad's screensaver came on. But—oh, this is so stupid and not at all how I planned this—but I've come to say that you are my hero. And I love you. And I'm sorry. And I never, ever meant to hurt you. And I want to come home."

He stands silently rigid, my flurry of words hanging expectantly in the cold air between us.

He exhales another blast of hot breath to the night and runs his hand across his face, shaking his head, "Yeah, well, I guess even heroes need to be rescued sometimes."

I lift a cold hand up to his face, trying to touch him, but he shifts, moving out of my reach.

"Honey? Honey? Who is it? You're letting all the cold air in."

"Who's that?" I numbly whisper with childlike confusion, pulling my hand away as if I have been burned.

He turns to the house. "I'll be right in, sweetie. Give me a moment." He shuts the door quietly. "Look, Enna, I don't know what to say—"

"Who's that?" my lips mouth, my brain reverberating with "sweeties."

"That's Patricia."

"Oh."

"Look, do you have somewhere to stay? I—"

"Yes. I'm fine. Fine. I have a hotel booked and, really, I must get there and check-in soon or they'll think I'm not coming." I stutter over the lie, my blue lips trembling but braving a thin smile.

"Oh, okay. Can I drive you there?"

"Where?"

"Your hotel?"

"Oh…no need. I'm disturbing." *Yes, very fucking disturbing, coming here unannounced, declaring my love with airplane hair and snot freezing at the tip of my nose.* "I'm fine." I nod repeatedly. "You go in. You're letting the heat out."

"Okay. As long as you're all right."

"Oh, yes. I'm fine." *I'm fine.*

He slips back indoors and closes the door gently.

I turn to the unforgiving Pennsylvania night. A tear rolls down my cheek. He loves me; I know he does. And when he realizes that, then he'll change his mind.

I hoist the suitcases down the steps and wheel them along the street. The heavy green gem bounces against my chest with every step. I can hear the staccato plucking of my heartstrings fill my ears, the soundtrack to my disappointment. Music swells inside my head as my tears run tracks down my cheeks. I hear Coldplay's "In my Place" like a soundtrack. I have, surely, been put me in mine. I search the street for a cab and whisper the words, releasing my human exhaust into the night.

I see an illuminated taxi speeding toward me, and I step out from the dark sidewalk, waving my hands. *Stop! Please stop!* The car plows toward me. *He doesn't see me, does he?* I drop the suitcases and wave both hands. *Oh my.* He swerves, and I close my eyes, hearing only the screech of brakes.

"Jesus, lady!" he shouts, retracting the window. "I almost hit ya! Walking around this time of night like a ghost. Where d'ya need to go?"

"I…don't know. Scranton…downtown, I suppose."

With much pissed off muttering, he hoists my suitcases in the trunk, and I get into the back seat.

We drive away, but the traffic light at the end of the street turns red and holds me captive a moment longer. I look back at the white house with the candle bulbs in the windows lighting the darkness. I suck in the tears and wipe their trails with my freezing fingers. The security light beams on again, and the front door swings open.

Bolting from the front door and down the steps is a tall, slender blonde. She fumbles in her pockets as she walks toward a car parked on the street. The headlights flash as she unlocks it. She climbs in, slams the door, and heads the other way down the street.

The tears start rolling again, but this time accompanied with a little, hopeful smile. I'm not lost. I have a brain, a heart, and courage; I have a home.

The traffic light blinks to emerald green.

Continue reading for a preview of the upcoming sequel:
Jazz Hands

Preview of Jazz Hands

I had lied about the hotel, of course. That was pride rearing its rejected head. I wasn't going to actually admit I had traveled three thousand miles across the Atlantic without stopping to consider that he might not want me after all.

Right now, in practically all of my in-flight scenarios, we were supposed to be deliciously wrapped around each other's' naked limbs, promising — between the unstaunchable flow of kisses — that neither would ever let go, ever again.

But instead, here I am. Ta da! In a town called Rejection, Population 1 — or Scranton, Pennsylvania, to be more geographically precise. Stranded in Scranton without my unfiancé, hotel-less, in a city lacking a functioning passenger railway service, sans buses at one a.m., I think I just paid off the only taxi in the city, and the wind chill factor feels more like wind kill factor.

I vacillate between feeling hopeful and empowered to frightened and lost. Where in Hades do I go now? I realize how ridiculous this is. *Enna, you are ridiculous!*

I puff out loudly to the sleeping city, "RIDICULOUS!"

No one hears. Or no one is listening. Either way, if I don't get out of the cold soon, I'll be deadiculous. Already, my fingers are bone white and slow to bend. I head for the lights of the old railway station, now a grand hotel, sitting majestically elevated at the edge of downtown.

The deserted lobby echoes with the sound of my four wheels. I meet no one. Not a soul as I wheel my way across the marble, turning in to a little bar. I remember this! We had downed late night drinks there and called it "The Affair Bar," the perfect spot for an illicit rendezvous. Unpeopled, it feels like a deserted set, a sepia-tinted still, just a row of empty leather-topped stools, the wisp of old cigar smoke, hanging like a sleeping spirit. *It's the people who make a place.*

I wheel through to the larger bar—the one with the enormous chandelier that must weigh as much as a baby elephant. What had we said about that?

Yes! Cole slid his palm to the small of my back and breathed hotly in my ear—is it any wonder I can't remember quite what he said—something about the chandelier being a gift to the Scranton family from a Russian princess.

I cried, "Bullssshhhhit," overly wined and overly loudly, and the whole bar silenced.

We turned to each other and erupted into childish giggles.

Oh, my heart. We had fun here. We were a team here.

Will everywhere I go in this town be preceded with echoes of us, ghosts of happy memories I seem to have murdered?

A woman looks up and stops wiping down the granite counter top.

"I'll have a cup of tea. Hot tea, please."

The bar tender lifts a questioning eyebrow.

"If you're still serving."

She looks at the empty stools to the left and the right of me and seems to consider her reply. Maybe the thought of staying open merely to serve some strange foreigner with two huge wheely cases, and clearly a head full of baggage, is not appealing. "Sure. But I gotta close at two."

"I also need a room. Is it too late to check in?"

"It's never too late. I'll buzz the front desk and let them know. Just pick up the key and sign your paperwork when you leave here. Reception is just through that door. You Australian?" she asks without looking, tossing the rag into the sink and reaching for the pyramid of mugs stacked on the end of the counter.

"British."

"Ah."

"Close."

"Huh?"

"We sent our convicts there, transported to Australia or Tasmania, so it's a similar root of the language," I spiel with surprising alacrity.

It's 1:25 a.m. I have no plan, no reunited fiancé, no transport, no hotel room. I am, in fact, for all intents and purposes, stranded, or to use the proper Anglo-Saxon, fucked. Yet, here I sit, the cases that contain the remainder of my transatlantically-uprooted life sitting up at attention around my ankles like loyal Springer Spaniels. I'm drinking tea with my impossibly stiff upper lip, exchanging niceties with the sole employee — her name badge says "Larissa" — at an old railway station bar, faded and jaded but stoically ignoring and carrying on. It's all very British. Someday I will find this ironic. Someday.

"My family was from Ireland. Way back. Don't see too many Brits here in Scranton. What brings you here?"

Ah! The million dollar question. The man who was my fiancé. The man who I left. The man who flew to England to find me lifeless on the bathroom floor. The man who got me to the hospital just in time. The man who saved me. The man who, two hours ago was blissfully — what? — snuggled up on his black leather sofa with the leggy blonde in his arms. The man who let me spill my heart at his door, a messy fountain of feeling, and still closed the door and let me wheel myself away.

"Work," I reply, burning the roof of my palate with the scalding water. "I'm here looking for work." It just seems easier.

"Pickle."

It was the nickname that melted my marrow, the syllables that he could utter from the other side of a crowded room, and I would feel on my neck as if he had whispered them directly to that silky spot beneath my earlobe. He could, in fact, deliver any kind of poison, but served with that particular condiment, it would always taste sweet to me.

I place the mug back down on the granite counter top. Cups, theaters, hearts all plummet to ruin held in my hands. Vertebrae fuses together, unbendable, as the mere sound of his voice — the single word he has uttered — has dissolved my bones, some oral alchemy that changes calcium to chromium and marrow to oil. Paralyzed, I'm unable to turn around. I want so desperately to believe it is him yet don't trust my eyes to prove my ears.

Larissa starts to say something about being closed but stops before a grammatical sentence is complete.

"That was very romantic." His voice sounds different, lubricated. "You should have called first."

I finally locate my tongue stuck firm to the roof of my throbbing palate, like a fleshy mussel obstinate in its hardened black shell, but say nothing.

"She's gone. She really means nothing, you know."

I look up from my tea, the bagged leaves still infusing their ruddy stain through the water, and I raise my eyes to the mirror behind the counter. It is him. He's lost weight. He's grayer around the temples. He's wearing the Ralph Lauren hunter green sweater I bought him on that shopping trip to New York when he spent oodles on me, when he wrapped the most scintillating sapphire around my neck, and all I could afford to buy him was an inadequate jumper. He's Cole, with those hazel eyes and that strong, square jaw that I just want to hold in my hands. I take the inventory of him that my tongue and my ego and verbal bulldozing did not make time for an hour before.

There is so much I want to tell him still. So many directions this could play out right now. I roll clips from different scenarios in my brain. This is a real-life improvisation.

You're an actress. You're a director, Enna! Think! Being witty, being sharp, being accusatory — all knee-jerk reactions that will make him defensive. Tell him what you really want. Be open! Be honest! You've thrown your heart over the line once today; why stop short of the line now?

The muscles in my tongue lunge into action. "How did you find me?"

Enna! I inwardly scold myself the second the words are through my lips. *What does it matter? Who cares if he's the fifth member of the* A-Team *trained to track you down. Focus!*

"It wasn't hard. There are only a few cab companies, and a British accent is kind of distinctive. Besides, I know you have a thing for beautiful old buildings. I didn't think you would resist staying here."

"Well, seeing as I have no career left and will almost certainly be in debt soon, I thought, why not do it in style?" I mean it to sound fun and flippant. It trails in the air between us, sad and inappropriate. I look at him and pull a small, uncertain smile tightly across my teeth.

He looks at me and turns away to the bar. "I'll have a Jim Beam. Double. Light on the ice."

Larissa takes a tumbler, swirls ice cubes around it, throws the ice away, places three cubes in, cracks the metal tags as she unleashes a fresh bottle, and pours a hefty glug of amber. The liquid fractures the ice, and the rich, syrupy color highlights the little cracks on the surface. We watch this seamless production. I'm aware of every little detail, suddenly hypersensitive to this intermission, both keen and reluctant to get to the conclusion.

Cole swirls the tumbler—it looks tiny in his hand—and then pours practically the entire glass down his gullet.

Wow.

He shakes his head and sucks the air through his teeth.

That's a new…what? Thing? Habit?

Enna, stop thinking! Start doing!

"I don't care about her. The other woman." *Other woman? Shit, I'm a walking, talking cliché.* "If you say she's nothing—she's no one—I'm relieved." And I really don't care about her. Truly. It wasn't as if I was the Virgin Mary during this…hiatus, but Will? He can rot for all I care now. It is all about Cole. It's amazing how one can switch off or on like a tap when betrayed or loved unconditionally. And Cole does love me. He flew to England and found me when I needed him most. "I just want you to give us another chance. I want to find a way to brush this whole thing under the carpet and start again."

"Ha!" He chuckles. *Chuckles?* "You know that one of the strange laws in Pennsylvania is that it's illegal to sweep things under the rug?"

"What?"

"It's true. It's a law."

Oh. "I mean, figuratively. I mean, let's just start over again. Can't we?"

"You make it all seem so easy." He sits on the stool next to me.

Larissa looks sheepishly through her fringe. She seems unsure of what to do or where to put herself, whether to get him another drink or skulk back in the kitchen. After a sway of hesitation, she tops up his glass and silently vanishes through the swing door.

"You can make it complicated if you choose. But it *is* easy when you know what you want."

He says nothing.

Despite the exhaustion, the starvation, and the sheer delirium of the past few weeks, or maybe because of that, I continue, blinkers on, a body of jolted nerves and adrenaline firing the same frantic, futile impulse throughout my body: *I must — I have to — make him see.* It all seems so obvious to me now.

"I know what I want Cole. Take a moment. Please, just take a moment. Think of how special it was. When we would sit, as we are now, but interlaced, knees locked together, talking, listening, eating, drinking, doing everything together, not being aware of anything or anyone else but the other."

He looks away from me again toward the large, distressed mirror on the other side of the bar.

"Remember that time we went up to your friend's cabin out by Montrose? Remember when we took the quad into the woods for you to show me the hunting trails? You cut the engine, swiveled around in your seat, and we kissed, and we touched, and as you breathed on my neck and I looked up to the trees standing sentinel around us, I thought I could never love anyone as much as I love you. Cole, it doesn't have to be complicated. I know I hurt you, but if you love me — if you ever loved me — give me a second chance."

His eyes remain fixed away from me. *Did he hear? Did he get it? Did he remember that magnetism?* It was chemical, biological. It certainly got very animal.

"Please?" Oh God. Do I sound like I'm begging? I sound like I am begging. Mum would walk away. She'd hold her head high.

I sit waiting for his response for what must be over a minute. He is resolutely silent.

I pull out a five dollar bill and leave it on the bar. I stand.

Oh, stop me!

Stop me!

Stop me!

I turn the bags around. *He's not going to stop me. Again.* I start to wheel. *Motherfucker.*

"Enna."

I stop walking immediately, of course. Mum wouldn't like it, but I want to leave no shadow of a doubt that I am committed.

"Enna, I can't forget. You left *me*. After everything, after looking me in the eyes and telling me what you told me, you left. I'm loyal. I'm committed. I spent over fifteen thousand dollars in applications and legal advice to get you here — that should tell you something — then you waste that money, waste that visa, leave for your theater and some actor. That…that *killed* me, Enna. It makes me sick, physically sick, to think how quickly that all happened. You seamlessly jumped from my bed to his, didn't you? And then — what an ass — I still come when you call and find you practically dead on your bathroom floor. So don't tell me that I'm a bad guy and that I don't care. I have a hard time believing you right now. And I don't honestly know if I can ever forgive you. The trust is gone."

It's a verbal bullet, and it strikes me in the stomach.

He raises his glance and catches my desperate, disbelieving stare. He doesn't trust me? But he's the person I would trust with my life. How could things have become so skewed? So screwed. I look around, taking in once again the cold marble and granite, this empty, unused chamber, and I realize that there is nothing left to say. I have served my heart on a plate, and he has sent it back, untouched. I can't *make* him trust me. The more I say that he can believe me, the less he will — isn't that how it goes?

What if I were to just fling my arms around him and squeeze out all of his doubts? What if I suggested he come up to my hotel room? Could I wrap my legs around him and slowly, tantrically, remind him of all that was good and true and full of wonder?

I nod, mentally balling up these inadequate suggestions and tossing them away, and instead I take a step toward his stool, kiss his cheek, take one last deep inhale of the scent of him — oh God, how can I not be with this man whose mere smell triggers something unholy in me — and I whisper in his ear. I kiss him a second time because, well, his cheek is there — and fuck it, I want to — and I awkwardly wheel myself and my large cases through the bar.

It's not a graceful exit. I am trying for dignity, and pride, and getting out of the room before my face trembles and gushes a flash flood of tears, but one of the unwieldy cases catches on a chair leg. As I tug it to heel, it knocks the chair to the ground with an almighty clout.

I should stride on, leaving a trail of downed chairs in my wake, and I try; I roll the cases one table further before I have to turn around and, ridiculously, bob and excuse the clumsy scene, like some chastened maid from *Downton Abbey* or something. Oh God, rejection and humiliation, complete! I pick up the fallen furniture. Both cases then clatter to the floor from their upright position, and as I swoop to grab their handles and leave the room, I look back at the man who I thought would be watching, to see that he's not. He is facing the bar, his head in his hands, his stained glass beside him, drained empty.

Acknowledgments

The amount of gratitude I have borders on the completely uncool. I have so many people I want to hug and pet and squeeze and call them George. Omnific Publishing has been fabulous, in particular, Enn Bocci, Colleen Wagner, Joannie Smith, Kimberly Blythe and Elizabeth Harper. I appreciate you championing my little novel. It means so much to me.

There have been so many spirit-soaring people who have cheered me on and offered advice, Kleenex, coffee, hummus and wine — not necessarily in that order. Those lovelies are Hildy Morgan, Michaela Moore, Corine Coniglio, Indra Lahiri, Ronni Deisler, Lucy Stewart, Tara Gadomski, Andrea Talarico-McGuigan, Matt (Mung Bean!) Mang, Oliver Gwyn-Jones, Jerry Kaufman and, of course, my darling Ma and Pa, Bridget and Garry Gwyn-Jones.

Oh, Michaela, the chocolate almonds were also very important and should not be forgotten. Nor should the Katy Perry impressions.

Don Lafferty is a social media guru par excellence; not only that, but a true friend. I am so lucky to have virtually met you, then actually met you. Who would have thought at that first Kings of Leon concert that you would become one of my most trusted and beloved confidantes?

Thanks to Baba Brinkman, whose hip hop take on Chaucer, evolution and sexual selection really got my cogs turning. I have such appreciation too of Elmo J. Rinaldi for finding the wine and words to spur me on.

ROAR to my Lionhearts! I could not have afforded to be a writer had it not been for my Mary Kay business giving me the flexibility, fun, friendships and finances to be a "stay-at-home-writey." I so appreciate the Wonder Women on my team and the fabulous customer-friends we serve. #Supportlocal #IlovemyMaryKay

Much love to Frinton Summer Theatre, the repertory that opened my eyes to theatre. Whilst I am getting nostalgic, I want to send thanks into the ether for the men who were always giants in my eyes: Wing Commander Evan Gwyn-Jones and Prof Herbert Dartnall. I wish they had seen me published. I hope I did them proud.

And lastly, thanks to my rock, my superhero, Joe Mik, who taught me that there is more to life than work, who rescued me from the soul-destruction of touring theatre, who allowed be to silly and belch spectacularly, and who I forgot to appreciate as much as I should have. Mink, this is all for you. Many thanks for everything you have done for me. Truly, I still adore you.

About the Author

Eleanor Gwyn-Jones lives in Scranton, Pennsylvania, but originally hails from Surrey, England. Huzzah! She studied biology at Southampton University before taking to the stage as an actress, agent and administrator of a touring theatre company. She performed in theatres, studios, schools and festivals across the British Isles before moving to the States. It was whilst visa-dangling and unable to take on acting work that she started to write and decided she far preferred it to anything else in the world! In 2008, Eleanor started her own "at home" business to afford her more time to be with her "book babies." Now she spends her time writing by day and teaching ladies to look fabulous at night. She is a travel junkie — it's research, darling, research! — a gourmand, a yogi, a sometime blogger and she adores her family and friends beyond all measure. She is currently putting the finishing key strokes to the sequel to *Theatricks*, due for release in 2014.

If she weren't writing, she'd like to think you'd find her in Downton, The Paradise, or having a goblet of wine with Tyrion in King's Landing.

›————→Young Adult‹————›

The Ember Series: *Ember* & *Iridescent* by Carol Oates
Breaking Point by Jess Bowen
Life, Liberty, and Pursuit by Susan Kaye Quinn
The Embrace Series: *Embrace* & *Hold Tight* by Cherie Colyer
Destiny's Fire by Trisha Wolfe
Reaping Me Softly & *UnReap My Heart* by Kate Evangelista

›————→Erotic Romance‹————›

The Keyhole Series: *Becoming sage (book one)* by Kasi Alexander
The Keyhole Series: *Saving sunni (book two)* by Kasi & Reggie Alexander
The Winemaker's Dinner: *Appetizers* & *Entrée* by Dr. Ivan Rusilko &
Everly Drummond
The Winemaker's Dinner: *Dessert* by Dr. Ivan Rusilko

›————→Paranormal Romance‹————›

The Light Series: *Seers of Light, Whisper of Light,* & *Circle of Light*
by Jennifer DeLucy
The Hanaford Park Series: *Eve of Samhain* & *Pleasures Untold* by Lisa Sanchez
Immortal Awakening by KC Randall
Crushed Seraphim & *Bittersweet Seraphim* by Debra Anastasia
The Guardian's Wild Child by Feather Stone
Grave Refrain by Sarah M. Glover
Divinity by Patricia Leever
Blood Vine & *Blood Entangled* by Amber Belldene
Divine Temptation by Nicki Elson
Love in the Time of the Dead by Tera Shanley

›————→Historical Romance‹————›

Cat O' Nine Tails by Patricia Leever
Burning Embers by Hannah Fielding
Good Ground by Tracy Winegar

www.ingramcontent.com/pod-product-compliance
Lightning Source LLC
Chambersburg PA
CBHW020356120726
47904CB00002B/582